ARRAN'S OBSESSION

BODY COUNT - BOOK 1

Jolie Vines

DIVINE DIVIDE

WWW.JOLIEVINES.COM

Editing by Emmy Ellis at Studio ENP.

Proofreading by Lori Parks and Patricia Brown.

Cover design - Natasha Snow https://natashasnow.com/

Alternate skull cover design: Qamber Designs Media.

Cover photography by Wander Aguair.

Cover model: Beau P.

Formatting by Cleo Moran / Devoted Pages Designs.

Gangs and skeleton masks?
sighs, chin on hands, hearts in eyes
Guess you and I are morally grey all the way, little
maniac.

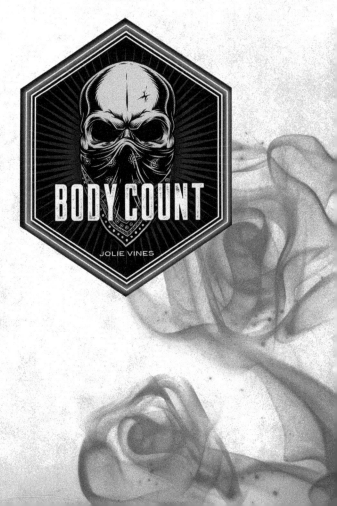

READER NOTE

Dear reader,

Buckle in, because Arran is about to take you on a wild ride with murder, mystery, and a twisted dark romance.

The list of potential triggers is long, but one thing I get asked most is does the hero hurt the heroine? Nope. Arran is a man obsessed, a gang leader, and a spicy club owner, but an abuser of women he is not. None of my men are. They push boundaries, sure, but that's all part of the fun.

The full list of warnings is on the next page.

Enjoy audio? The audiobook is multicast and incredible, with Shane East and Allie Rose reading Arran and Genevieve, and Ella Lynch and Theodore Zephyr reading further characters. There are sound effects! Listen along as you read - it's hot AF.

I also want to point out that the city of Deadwater on the border of Scotland and England is my invention. It does not exist. Therefore I get to do anything I like there. Cue devilish smirk.

Think you've met Arran before? You smart cookie. He was first seen in my Dark Island Scots series. You can read that here: https://mybook.to/DarkIslandScotsSeries

Now, take my hand and let's skip into the darkness together.

Love, Jolie

TRIGGER WARNINGS
(may contain spoilers):

Masks
Gangs
Sexual assault
Sex work
Murder and death (adults only)
Torture (hero to bad guys)
Dubcon
Gratifying punishment
Edging
Orgasm denial
Voyeurism
Somnophilia
Spanking
Use of objects as intimate toys
Candle wax
Knife play
Dangerous games
Violent sexual assault
Prostitution
Car accident
Blood
Sexually explicit scenes
All the nudity
Fear of the dark
Nightmares
Bondage
Group sex

BLURB

I never planned to fall for my skeleton-masked captor, but now there's no turning back.

I hated the gangs that ruled my city.

After my friend was killed and my father vanished, I had no choice but to infiltrate one to figure out why. Entering their infamous club quickly showed me I was in over my head.

Then the most feared gang leader took an interest in me. Arran was corrupt, deadly, and his searing gaze both terrified and tempted me.

In my search for answers, I stumbled into his dark and dangerous game. The result? I belonged to him, with no chance of escape.

In a heartbeat, I became Arran's obsession. And in a terrible twist, I think he's becoming mine.

***

Arran's Obsession is the first book in an interconnected dark romance trilogy featuring a murder mystery, a dark city, an adult entertainment club, and a crew of men who are possessive over what's theirs.

PLAYLIST

Girls Like You by The Naked and Famous
Cola by Camelphat and Elderbrook
Midnight City by M83
Judith by A Perfect Circle

Closer by Nine Inch Nails
i like the way you kiss me by Artemas
I Can Fix Him (No Really I Can) by Taylor Swift
Come Through by Rui + Voluptuöus

On Your Knees by Ex-Habit
Rush by Dutch Melrose & benny mayne
Take Me Back to Eden by Sleep Token
The Death of Peace of Mind by Bad Omens

Songlist curated by Jolie Vines Reader Group on
Facebook. You deliciously sultry people.

1

Genevieve

From the shadowed cemetery across the road from my flat, I concealed myself behind an old stone wall and watched the two men at my door. Sweat trickled down my back, from fear, but also the hot August night, a heatwave blanketing the city.

"Sweets, this is my spot. Move your ass on," a voice ordered from behind me.

I jumped and spun around.

On the steps of the church, a woman fixed the hem of her ultra-short dress. Her gaze narrowed on me, then she huffed, her pink bobbed hair swinging. "Oh, it's you. What the fuck are you doing out here dressed like that? Thought you were turning tricks."

I returned my gaze to the Victorian crescent of flats that curved inwards around the hill, pretty from the outside with neat stonework and windows that overlooked the centre of town below, but that reeked of mould and with walls that shook.

The flat I shared with my dad and brother was halfway along, at the top of the building. The whole place should've been condemned fifty years ago. Maybe that's what the strangers were here to do.

"I went for a run." I explained my sports bra and shorty shorts. The half-drunk bottle of iced coffee in my hand. "Cherry, did you see those men arrive?"

The sex worker neared, the fruity scent of her e-cigarette preceding her. Together, we watched the upstairs hall window, my flat entrance visible beyond.

They were thugs, definitely. Thick-necked and dressed in black. Probably not burglars considering they were knocking and not booting in the door. No one was home, so they were shit out of luck if they were after money.

"Sketchy as," Cherry decided. "Don't go up there. Your dad home?"

I shook my head, and strands of my blonde ponytail caught on my sweaty neck. "I haven't seen him in a week."

One of the men thumped on the door again, the sound ricocheting in the heavy night air and across the rows of houses that descended the hill.

Cherry shifted beside me. She'd owned this patch for as long as I'd lived here, though caught shade from more than one of my neighbours for her work. After one particularly shitty comment from Mrs B in the flat below ours, I'd made a point of asking Cherry her name then chatted with her whenever I passed. I didn't envy what she did for a living but bet your ass she outearned my food courier job.

A job I'd be late for if the men didn't leave soon.

"They were outside half an hour ago. I don't usually miss a thing but I had a client. One of your neighbours must've let them in the street door. Probably that daft cow with the little dogs and the stick up her ass."

The second of the goons stooped and collected a piece of paper from a briefcase. He pinned it to my door.

Cherry hissed and jabbed her vape towards the street. "Bailiffs. See the red writing? That's an eviction notice. I should know, I've seen my share. Your old man's been stiffing the rent."

My stomach twisted with anxiety. Every month, Riordan and I paid Dad enough money to cover the bills. The government did, too, with disability benefits. Keeping a roof over our heads was vital—we'd been homeless once.

"He can't have. He's..."

"Run off with the cash. You said yourself he's MIA. Come on."

I swore, earning a throaty chuckle from the woman at my side. Surely Dad hadn't done that. He went on benders with some frequency but he always came back.

My phone chimed in the pocket of my tight shorts where it was wedged uncomfortably with my keys. I pulled it out and sat cross-legged behind a tombstone beside the graveyard's mossy path, hiding the light in case the men somehow spotted me, then silenced the chime—my work alarm. I'd already done a six-hour shift over lunchtime and was due to head back out for the late-evening slot. If I couldn't get into the flat, I'd be doing it without a shower and in my skimpy running clothes.

Not ideal for a job that took me in and out of busy restaurants then to customer's homes. I was asking for trouble.

Paging over to my phone app, I called Dad. No answer, just like every other time I'd rung him in the past week. Then I tried Riordan. My brother's phone rang out, no answerphone. Jerk. I tapped out a message to him.

> **Genevieve:** Some men have stuck an eviction notice on our door. Have you seen Dad?

No reply came.

"For fuck's sake," Cherry cursed. She swiped at a line of liquid running down her inside thigh then flicked it into the bushes. "Last guy came like an elephant."

Gross. I gave her a sympathetic grimace, my stomach curdling. "Make sure you don't get knocked up with a baby elephant. I hear pregnancy's a bitch."

She snickered. "Don't sweat it. Even if I did, elephant guy's a city councillor. He can afford the bill." Her amusement dimmed, something darker tugging her lips down. "He'll be back on the weekend, recharged. Said he'd bring a friend. Not so keen on that one."

My sweat cooled on my skin. "Do you ever get scared of your clients?"

"Cute that you're worried. It's almost always lonely old boys. They all want the same thing, and it isn't my blood. It's better for me this way. I won't belong to one of the gangs."

Fuck the gangs.

The sounds of the city seemed to get louder, the overtone ramping up my fear of the bailiffs and of losing our flat. From the city centre below our hill, horns blared from the cars that flowed with red taillights like blood through arterial streets. Shouts came from rowdy folk on a course for the nightclubs and bars.

The aura of the bad men who ran the place permeated everything, their threat to slice into an urban vein ever present.

I loved the city but despised the gangs with my whole heart. They'd cost me too much for the blind eye they expected from everyone else.

Twisting off my bottle cap, I chugged the last of my coffee, warm now, but still a dose of caffeine. The bailiffs were leaning back on the wall, chatting and definitely not budging, and I couldn't turn up late to my job, which meant I needed to move it or lose it.

As I stood, I touched my gaze on the line of cars parked outside. My brother's old Rover was wedged into a spot, which meant Riordan was out on his motorbike tonight.

There was something draped over his seat. His leather jacket?

If it was here, that meant he was out biking in the city in his shirtsleeves, the idiot. But it also gave me an opportunity. I took a breath and fished out my keys. I didn't have a licence, but my brother had given me a few lessons. He could damn well loan me his jacket until the early hours.

"Cherry," I whispered. "Could you do me a favour? See that dark-blue car? It's my brother's."

"That boy's hot as fuck."

I shuddered, ignoring that. "I need his jacket to wear to work, and it's on the car seat, but I'm worried those men might somehow know who I am if they look down."

She brightened and stood taller, a hint of pride in her smile as if no one ever asked her for a favour that wasn't at the cost of her body. "I'll fetch it. Which window should I break?"

I burst out with a laugh and held up the keys. "Use these?"

She sauntered to the graveyard's exit and over the road. In a minute, my pink-haired friend had the coat and was back, handing it over with my keys. "Here you go."

"God. You're a lifesaver. I owe you."

"You don't, sweets. It's just nice to have someone smile when they pass me and not turn up their nose. You're kinder to me than most. Means a lot."

Drawing on the leathers, I tucked my fair hair underneath and checked the time again then swore. "Got to go. Stay safe."

"Always do."

Cherry blew me a kiss, and I hustled down the road, heading for the busy street at the end. It led down the hill and into town, and just a couple of minutes' walk away, had the side street lock-up where I'd collect a scooter and helmet for work.

I'd get into my shift then try calling my brother again so he could help me find Dad. Eviction would be a nightmare for both of us. The thought sickened me.

At the end of the street, next to the old church, I peered back, catching movement in the graveyard amid its stones which poked up like broken teeth. Cherry with a man. One of her old boys by his grey cap of hair. She took his hand and guided him away, maybe to blow him on her church steps. Or fuck him.

Wrinkling my nose, I looked away and stuck in my in-ear headphones, a song playing to start my night. 'Girls Like You' by The Naked and Famous.

Weird choice, phone.

I stepped onto the main road, lines of shops either side

but most closed for the night, still with neon lights in the window. Despite the music, the need to hurry to work, my mind was still in the graveyard. Any one of those assholes could end Cherry's life with a snap of her neck or his hands around her throat. Any one of them could—

Brakes squealed. Bright lights bore down on me.

Solid, hot metal smacked into me and sent me skidding across the tarmac road. Coasting on the leather jacket's ribbed shoulder, I slithered to a stop against the kerb, my headphones popping out in the crash.

Holy shit.

Dazed and in shock, I sat up, one hand to my thigh which had caught the road. It came away sticky with my blood.

A car door opened. "Fucking hell," a low voice bit out.

I raised my gaze to the driver climbing from his huge black vehicle, one hand to his upper arm, and his dark-blond hair falling in his eyes.

Steam rose from the grille.

Oh God. I'd walked straight out in front of a car. An expensive one. Perhaps even injured the driver from the way he held himself. I had to find my feet and fucking run.

But the moment I was lifting, he was on me in long strides, and I was going nowhere.

2

Genevieve

"Did you hit your head?" the stranger asked.

"N-no."

"Get up." He offered a hand, taking my elbow when I ignored it. With minimal effort, he righted me, a deal taller than me and much broader, biceps stretching his black t-shirt.

"What the hell happened?"

I opened and closed my mouth, no answer forming.

The man exhaled annoyance. "That scratch on your leg needs looking at. Come with me."

"It's fine." I should apologise but I just couldn't.

He didn't listen either, propelling me along with a grip around my arm so I had no choice but to go with him. He'd stopped his huge black car on the side of the road, parking it outside a pawnshop so the traffic could pass.

Sliding open the back door, he made as if to put me inside.

"I won't get in your car," I managed.

"I'm just going to sit you on the back seat so I can clean

up that injury."

I snorted, still reeling from the shock. "And get kidnapped? No, thanks."

The man's features twisted into incredulity. He was pretty. Grey or green eyes under the shop's neon sign and that blond hair darker at the roots. At a guess, I'd put him at mid to late twenties, so a few years older than me, but pretty people had even less reason to be trusted than anyone else.

He planted his hand on his hips, then he reached to extract his wallet from his back pocket. He handed it over. "Hold on to that, if you need reassurance. I'm not in the habit of abducting women who throw themselves under my wheels. Now sit on the fucking seat while I find my first-aid kit."

Stunned, I turned the wallet over in my hands. Brown leather. Cards or something inside by the ridges. Mr First Aid and Fancy Car pointed at the seat. Like an idiot, I perched on it, and he circled to the boot.

My thigh pulsed with a deep ache, bright-red scratches across my pale skin and road dirt studding it in dark patches under the streetlamp. I winced, suddenly feeling the hit of the accident. My arm hurt, too, my awareness of my body returning.

I'd never once in my life done anything that foolish before. Let my distraction lead me to walking straight into the path of a car. I puzzled at my actions.

The driver returned with a small, green, zipped bag with a white cross on it, plus a bottle of water.

"Hold on to those, too." He handed over my headphones.

I hadn't even noticed him pick them up.

In efficient moves, he took a packet from the kit and

opened the bottle, tipping the powder inside and shaking it to mix it.

"This is to cleanse that wound and get the grit out. After, I'll spray antiseptic over it and tape on a bandage."

"You a doctor?" I asked.

Without looking at my face, he curled his lip and gave a short laugh like I'd said something funny. "No. Take a breath. This will sting."

He tipped the liquid over my graze. Pink water trickled down to my knee, and I winced then tried to angle so it pooled on the road, not the expensive car's interior. The man didn't seem to care, instead opening packets of sterile wipes. He linked his gaze to mine for permission, then took hold of my thigh.

My world melted.

His fingertips indenting my skin knocked me off my axis. A rush of good feeling, addictive and sweet, woke an inactive part of my brain. I was hot and sweaty, barely dressed under the leathers, and my body warmed all the more.

What the heck was that?

As if he'd felt it, too, the man paused, his focus still on my thigh. Then he shook his head and scrubbed at the wound.

I yelped, the sting he'd promised delivered.

"It needs cleaning or you'll get an infection. The streets are fucking grimy," he muttered.

Giving a sharp nod, I closed my eyes and let him do his thing, concentrating on breathing, and only peeking again when he taped down a white bandage.

"Where else did you hurt yourself?" he asked.

"Nowhere. I'm fine." I shuffled to the seat's edge, embarrassment mixing in with the pain, the odd attraction, and every other emotion from the night. I'd delayed here too long and needed to move.

But he caught my wrist.

"Your arm's dripping blood."

It was the one I'd slid on, that Riordan's jacket hadn't fully protected. Sitting back down, I unzipped the leathers and pulled my arm from the sleeve so it was half off me. An inch-long cut slashed my upper arm, something presumably having pierced the coat.

Maroon ran in a line down to my fingers.

"It's not that bad," I mumbled.

But the stranger was staring at me, and consciousness dawned. I was in his car dressed in a skimpy sports bra and shorts. He blocked my way out. All he had to do was push me fully in and I'd be trapped.

Considering how young he was and how expensive his ride, and the fact he did first aid for fun, what kind of man could he be? Oh God.

I was face-on with a gang member.

Breathless, I stared back, my heart rate soaring. I'd lost my ever-loving mind.

He had a hand to his shoulder like he was hurting, too, but his gaze slid over my body and back to my face. Judgement was right there in his eyes. "You a prostitute?"

My jaw dropped.

Of all the things he could've said. My temper rose in a rush as fast as the hot attraction had struck.

"Are you kidding? You think I'm a whore working the streets?" I spat out, venom on my tongue.

"It's just a question."

"Fuck you for asking. I'm not one of them."

Sending a silent apology to Cherry in her church steps domain, I leapt from the car, forcing him back a step. I didn't judge women who worked the streets, even if I found their job distasteful. What right would I have? But my anger didn't stop.

Headlights flooded us. Another car pulled up, a big silver grille at the front and the outline of two men in the window. My accuser didn't react to the incomers.

His men, had to be.

Shit. I'd fucked up so badly here. I looked between the stranger and his newly arrived gangster friends.

Then I took a breath, threw his wallet in his face, and ran like the devil was chasing me.

Three hours later.

*L*eaving the city centre on my scooter, I zipped into an urban suburb and along the dark street of Paignton Place. Riordan's girlfriend lived here, and my brother still wasn't answering his phone, so I was doing a drive-by while on the way to collect my next delivery.

I had to find Dad and talk to him. I needed Riordan to answer my goddamned calls. As neither were forthcoming,

I'd moved on to plan B.

Even if this was the last place I wanted to be.

Work had been stacked all evening. At a little past midnight, the queue of jobs was still deep and more adding, though the food choices changed from fancy restaurants to late-night take aways and cheaper options. The city was full of university students as well as young professionals who lived in expensive waterside apartments and enjoyed the nightlife. Then there was the underbelly of the gangs and their hangers-on. It made for a rich after-dark industry. On my two wheels, I cruised past it all, headphones in, and only the stabbing pain from my injuries distracting me.

Outside Moniqua's block of flats, I parked my scooter, hoping it would still be here in a few minutes, and jogged up the steps, stretching to tap on the buzzer. I didn't have any contact details for Moniqua so couldn't warn her in advance, but I'd texted Riordan. Not that my brother had read his messages.

The box on the wall clicked, but nobody spoke.

I pressed the intercom again. "It's Genevieve, Riordan's sister. Can I come up?"

A pause followed, then the door popped open.

The sharp stench of piss welcomed me inside, and the sole hallway light flickered, giving the long row of entrances beyond it an ominous feel. Only once had I visited here in the past, when Riordan and I had dropped off groceries.

I'd never warmed to Moniqua but I was glad Rio was a good boyfriend to her dumb ass.

Five minutes, in and out. I could do this.

Up the stairs, I skipped to the third floor, not lingering

in the corridors. Music pounded from somewhere, and a mixture of odours beat out the urine, the acridity of crack overlaid with the sweeter notes of a joint.

At my knock, a man opened the door. "Well, well. See what we've got here."

I recoiled. If I disliked Moniqua, I was scared of Don, her cousin. He was a gang member through and through, from the tattoo of a spiderweb on his face to the violence built into his every move.

In his casual grip, he held a knife.

"Only to see Riordan, if he's here," I whispered.

Don drew his gaze down me, lingering on my bare legs. Then he jerked his head for me to go inside. My brain rebelled, my limbs wanting anything other than to squeeze past him into the flat, but this was necessary. The door opened straight into a wide living room, a collection of worn chairs and sofas at one end and the kitchenette at the other.

Don paced over and dropped his blade so it embedded in the carpet, right beside Moniqua who leaned on a sofa, a woman at her back wrapping her thick hair around a curling tong. She scowled at her cousin who snarled back.

"Clean it, and take that fucking look off your face."

Don strode away, and I exhaled fear.

I scooted over to Moniqua. "Is my brother here?"

"Can you see him?" She picked up the knife, her pouty lips curling in disgust.

"No, and he isn't answering his phone. I need to talk to him."

"What about?"

I hesitated. "Family matters."

"I'm his woman. I know everything about him."

I doubted that, but I wasn't about to say as much to the person cleaning a questionable brown stain from her cousin's weapon.

Moniqua pursed her lips. "He's busy out in the city tonight, you know, boys doing business. If I call him, he'll answer, but ask your little question of me first so I can see if it's worth his time."

Fucking hell. I forced calm, ignoring the implied message that Riordan was out doing gang work, because that was a lie. "Okay. It's actually our dad I need to find. He hasn't been home in a week."

"So? Why does that matter? He does this all the time."

I waited her out. She had a point—Dad was about as reliable as the weather for the majority of the year— but this time felt different. He usually announced his departures, and I'd get the occasional badly typed reply to my messages.

Moniqua hissed then slapped out at the woman doing her hair. "You burned my fucking ear. Be careful." Her gaze came back to me. "I saw your dad a few days ago. He's with Sydney."

"Who's that?" I'd never heard the name before.

"A stripper." She smiled, clearly loving this.

I gritted my teeth more. "Do you have a number for Sydney?"

"What am I, dial-a-stripper?"

"Any idea where she works?"

Moniqua rolled her eyes. "There's only one strip club in Deadwater, and she's probably there tonight, but good luck getting in looking like that. What did you do to your leg anyway?"

She pressed a finger to the white bandage, and I cringed at the pain, backing away.

"Thanks for the help," I grouched then let myself out.

Down the corridor, I escaped, my mind sprinting over what my father was up to. Since Mum died, and he'd been forced to take me and Rio in, he'd had a series of girlfriends, none lasting long, so this new woman wasn't much of a surprise. But—

A hand grabbed mine from behind.

A body slammed mine into the wall.

My breath left me in a rush, and I stared up at the empty voids of Don's eyes. He was high on something. The smell of it tickled my nose. But dread beat back every other thought.

"Where are you going in such a hurry?" He lowered to run the tip of his nose up my jaw.

"Let me go," I begged.

"Nah, don't think I will. Sounds to me that you're not safe at home with your dad gone."

I trembled, my mouth drying.

"Are you scared? I'll take care of you. No one will touch you if you're my girl." His hot breath crawled over my throat, his body pressing mine into the concrete brick wall. Then he gripped my breast through the leather jacket. Hard. "If you were mine, I could find anyone you like."

Struggling, I couldn't move him an inch. I had no power over the creep. No way to get him off me.

"I'll be in trouble with work if I don't get back," I managed.

A moment passed. Another.

Don reared back. "You'd take that shitty little job over me? What-the-fuck-ever, bitch."

He pushed off me then spat at my feet and returned to the flat. Alone in the darkness, I sagged, my fear bright and real. But screw standing around waiting for him to change his mind. The city at night had any number of dangers, but I'd learned fast to navigate them. This was just another of those crappy realities, and at least I had a lead on finding my dad.

Lucky for me, outside, my scooter was where I left it, though my app listing my next job flashed red with a late penalty.

It was another hour before I could cruise down the river to the huge red-brick warehouse that held the epicentre of the city's clubs.

Thudding bass rocked the industrial street made of old dockyard buildings. Throngs of people ambled along a wide, harbourside boulevard.

From across the road, I watched the entrance of the huge, eight-storey building containing the clubs.

There were two lines, one where men streamed into a doorway, a curtain concealing the interior and a bouncer giving each a cursory check but moving them quickly inside. The hot-pink sign over the door read DIVINE. That was the strip club side. The other line was busier, with people held in a queue for the nightclub, that side named DIVIDE. I'd never been inside either, so sussed it out.

A pair of bouncers turned away a couple, the dude yelling that he only had fucking trainers so what was he supposed to do. I still had on my running shoes and shorts under a now very distressed leather jacket that was several sizes too big. There was no way I was walking into the nightclub, and not a single woman was entering the strip club side.

Still, I had to try. Straightening my shoulders, I crossed the road and marched up to the bouncers like I belonged there.

The first eyed me. "You lost, miss?"

"No. Can...can I come in?"

"For what purpose?"

I opened and closed my mouth, momentarily stuck on an explanation. Damn, but I couldn't think of a single reason other than to snoop.

"The only women wanting in here are hen parties, girls dragged in by boyfriends, or the staff." He folded his arms. "You aren't any of those, sweetheart."

"No, but—"

His gaze left me and went to a group of men advancing down the path. "Do yourself a favour and get out of here."

My breath left me in a rush of disappointment, and I retreated to my position as watcher behind the line of cars. I needed a better plan if I was going to find my father and his stripper girlfriend.

A taxi halted across from me, and two ladies climbed out, both beautiful and sleek, with their hair glossy and makeup on point. They strolled arm in arm up to the entrance, and the bouncer waved them in without an ID check or a single word. Staff, had to be.

Just like that, an idea came to me.

Tomorrow, if Dad hadn't appeared, I'd be back, and this time with a way to get inside.

3

Genevieve

Friday evening rolled in. I'd worked a ten-hour day, clocking in ahead of the lunchtime rush then quitting at eight, despite requests from my boss to do overtime.

At home, I arrived with the small hope that one of my family members would've appeared, but no one was here, same as when I'd got back in the early hours. I'd taken down the eviction notice and studied the small print. Cherry was bang on the money—Dad owed thousands in back rent. We had thirty days until the heavies threw us out.

Terror held me in its grip.

Finding Dad was all the more vital.

At least my brother had texted back. It was a short '*I'll call you*' message, but proof of life when I needed it.

I took a hasty shower, the power use burning through the money I'd put on the electric meter, shaved everything, and took off the bandage the stranger had taped on for me last night. My road rash was bruising with shades of purple and red, but it wasn't bleeding anymore. Neither was the cut to my arm. I needed to cover both if I was going to look the part tonight.

Pulling on a dressing gown, I dried my hair in my tiny bedroom and moisturised my skin until it gleamed. Then I entered the living room, hunting down my makeup bag.

From the window, I caught sight of a figure outside.

I did a double-take then stared, my heart thumping. It was him, the man who'd mowed me down. He stood alone under a streetlight, the yellow glow falling over him and softening his handsome features. Like yesterday, it was a roasting evening, the heatwave unending, and my mystery man wore a close-fitting t-shirt and jeans.

I hadn't forgotten my reaction to him. How his touch did something weird to my brain.

If he was here for me, that was...interesting. Perhaps I'd had the same effect on him.

Or maybe he was like Don and just another gangbanger wanting a woman to mess with.

Adrenaline rose in me. I had a half-drunk iced coffee from the convenience store beading condensation on our dining table, my caffeine addiction my only real vice, so my heart was already racing. That was my only excuse for the action I took.

Cranking open the sash window, I leaned out. "Hey."

The man sought out my voice. He tilted his head in recognition then crossed the street.

"Why are you lurking outside my house?" I demanded.

Stupid, stupid girl. Now he knew where I lived. What the hell was wrong with me? One face-off with a pretty guy and I'd lost all sense.

"Hunting you down, little maniac. My best guess was

the same place at the same time as yesterday," he called up.

I perused him. "In case I leapt in front of your car again?"

His lips formed a smile. "Something like that."

My stomach flipped. Smiles like that ought to be illegal.

At my lack of a reply, he continued. "I was concerned. Your injuries looked bad but you ran away."

My mind supplied what it was that bothered me. The mistake he'd made when he'd asked if I sold sex for a living. I wanted to correct it. For some reason, it burned as a tight knot inside me.

Now he was here and I had a chance to set the record straight.

"You alone?" I asked.

He spread out his arms. "As you see."

"Wait there," I ordered and slammed the window closed.

In my bedroom, I dressed quickly in shorts and a spaghetti strap top, then tugged on ballet flats. Grabbing my keys, I left the flat and jogged downstairs.

Outside, a series of wide steps led to the paved street. The guy waited at the bottom.

In my light summer clothes, my injuries were fully on display, but his gaze stuck on my face. Heat crept through me, that weird attraction blooming low in my belly. I closed the door, still warm in the dusk, and leaned back on it.

For a moment, neither of us spoke.

Then he cleared his throat. "My name's Arran. I wanted to see you—"

"Because you hit me with your car and wanted to be sure I didn't sue or die on you? I got that."

His mouth curved in amusement. "I don't give a fuck about being sued. That hit was hard. I smacked the steering wheel with my shoulder and bruised from it. You came off a lot worse. I needed to see you were still walking."

I eyed his shoulder, picturing him bare-chested. He had a nice shape to him, as well as an edge of danger. A fighter, maybe, like my brother sometimes was, though Arran's knuckles weren't busted and his nose was straight. "It was my fault. I deserved whatever I got."

His gaze slid down to my thigh. "Does it hurt?"

Somehow he made that so distinctly sexual.

"Do you want it to?" I found myself saying.

Where the hell did that come from?

His eyebrows merged. "Probably not, but I'm open to being convinced."

A dark-green car eased down the street, slowing as it neared. I squinted at it, then my blood ran cold. Don was in the driver's seat, Moniqua's violent cousin. He stared at me and at the man I was talking to.

God. Don was the type to pack heat. I'd never seen him with a gun, but he was easy with the knives and that was threat enough. If he was here for me, I needed either to run or put him off.

I tore my gaze back to Arran. "Come inside. I want to take a look at your shoulder."

He didn't move. "You're worried about me?"

I was, but not for the reason he thought. Still, he wasn't budging.

"Give me your wallet again for safekeeping, and I'll trust you. Just keep your hands to yourself."

This had him climbing the steps, hands shoved in his pockets. "Course I will."

Upstairs, I let him into Dad's flat, suddenly seeing it through the stranger's eyes. I hadn't grown up here, and none of the furniture was mine. Black mould stained the corners of the living room, the wallpaper peeling where I'd scrubbed it too many times. It was tidy, at least, no piles of beer cans littering the surface from where Dad would spend days on the sofa. No long-legged Riordan taking up space.

Just me and the big man. In my home.

The moment he closed the door behind us, fresh wariness settled over me. Arran held something out, and I fixed my skittish gaze onto it. His wallet, his driving licence on top.

"Take it. Send a picture to a friend or a neighbour if you want."

I accepted it, scanning the details automatically.

Arran Daniels, twenty-eight, the picture of him wildly handsome in a way that wasn't fair on government ID. At least he'd been honest about his name.

He crossed the living room to the window I'd hailed him from and watched the street. "Who was in the car?"

I breathed out. "How did you see that? You had your back to the road."

"I have ears, and I was looking right at you."

Which meant he could read reactions. I shivered, wrapping my arms around myself. "Bad news. Hopefully he's gone now."

For a moment, Arran kept his gaze on the dark road then stalked to the dining table, claimed a chair, then took it right back to the window where he could be seen from outside. "I have to get to work soon but I'll wait to be sure you're safe."

"You don't have to do that."

"I know. It'll serve double duty if you show me that scratch of yours."

I lifted my chin, not budging from my spot by the door. "You show me yours first."

A pause, and a smirk replaced his neutral expression. Then the guy leaned forward and plucked his t-shirt right over his head, revealing his naked upper body. He rolled his shoulders. "I'm giving the bad-news brother a show from the window. Don't be alarmed."

Alarmed? I was anything but. My imagination had done a poor job of filling in the blanks of his shape. He was toned, but ruggedly male, too, with powerful muscles. Lines marked him, scars perhaps, and tattoos in black ink decorated his side. A black circle with an image in it. A skull. Goddamned mouthwatering.

Then I caught the shadow of a bruise at his shoulder. It had my feet moving until I was right in front of him.

"You hit the steering wheel when you braked for me." My hand came up. I withdrew it. Touching him would be insane.

"It's nothing."

"Are you kidding? That's a huge mark. I'm going to get something for it."

"Not necessary," he called after me.

"You're not the only one with a first-aid kit," I hollered back. In a few moments, I returned with cotton wool and a bottle of arnica. I soaked a handful of the wool in the medication then set the bottle onto the windowsill. "Want to do this or shall I?"

"What the hell is it?"

"Arnica? It brings out a bruise. Gets it healing faster."

Arran wrinkled his nose, obviously dubious, but turned his head to indicate for me to proceed.

Leaning into his space, I extended my hand, trying to ignore the rush and rise of tension from how close we were. I dabbed his skin, the sharp tang of the arnica eclipsed by his much more pleasant scent. Something dark and masculine. It had me inching closer still.

The solution darkened the bruise, some small balance restoring after I'd hurt us both.

More, my body was having a field day at being next to a warm-blooded, attractive man. My last boyfriend had been over a year ago, and I didn't do the casual thing.

Need built in a steady, insistent coil. It was boosted again by Arran's short intake of breath as I moved between his spread knees. His fists bunched.

"Do you often walk into traffic like that?" he said, low and gruff.

"No. I'm normally better at self-preservation. I was distracted."

"By what?"

I shrugged and changed the subject, trying to keep my brain in order as attraction continued its climb. He didn't need to know my personal life. "You said you've got work. What kind of job starts at night?"

"Management."

"Of what?"

I pressed his collarbone, where the bruise stained darkest, and Arran winced. Abruptly, he stood, taking me by the hips to reverse our positions. "Your turn in the chair."

Carefully, I sat, wide-eyed at the switch. "I'm okay."

Arran knelt and peered at my cut-up thigh, not touching me but close enough that the man-effect was doubling. "You haven't even told me your name."

"Genevieve," I breathed.

His lips curved. "Pretty."

The atmosphere shifted. Tightened. My body became molten.

His question to me returned, and I laughed under my breath, a nervous sound, betraying everything inside. "Still not a prostitute."

He blinked. "I know. Wouldn't matter if you were. There's nothing wrong with that."

I eyed him. If I leaned from the window, I could probably see Cherry on the church steps, getting abused for cash by some grimy piece-of-shit guy. No one could think that a great career choice, regardless of the right for women to choose. What I didn't get was why this man was protesting.

"Yes, there is. It's a shitty job, if you can even call it that."

Arran sat back, the haziness in his eyes clearing. The air between us cooled, and he stood from his crouch and shrugged his shirt back on. All business again. "You share this place, right?"

I nodded once.

"Good. Then you won't be alone long."

He leaned over me, and I froze, but he only plucked

his wallet from the windowsill, slotting his card back in place. On his way to the door, he spied my iced coffee, the ice cubes nearly all melted. "This yours?"

Another nod, and he picked it up and took a goddamned sip from my straw.

"Not as sweet as I expected."

I gaped at him.

Then the confusing-as-hell stranger disappeared out of my door.

I lurched for my precious coffee and opened the window again, gazing down at him walking away as I drained the cup. Sirens wailed somewhere nearby, life as normal in the city.

But just like when I'd run from Arran yesterday, he didn't look back.

4

Arran

*F*ists clenched, I strode through the club's busy corridors, managing an acknowledgement for the people who greeted me.

In my office, Shade already waited, reclining against the red-brick wall. My friend frowned at his phone, his fingers curled around the tattoos that crawled up his throat. On the back of his hand was the lower half of a skull. The other had a Scottish flag, a homage to his heritage.

"Problem?" I dropped into my leather chair, the manager's seat for both Divine and Divide.

He lifted his gaze to me. "Intense police activity in North Town. A murder, rumour has it. Naw us, for once."

I stiffened. North Town was the part of the city I'd visited earlier this evening. The place Genevieve lived. It wasn't all that nice but it was outside of the gang territories and above the worst of the city's dangers.

Yet someone had driven by her house and scared her. Targeted her, perhaps. The memory chilled me.

"Anything known about the dead person?"

Shade gave a single headshake *no*. "Hit up your contact?"

I grunted and texted a query out into the ether, a bad feeling taking host in my gut. There was no way it could be her. I'd been at her flat just an hour ago. Then again, only the night before that, the woman had nearly killed herself by walking out in front of my car.

The reply took fucking forever.

DetD: A hooker. Not one of yours.

DetD was Detective Dickhead, the name I'd once heard for my police contact and which had stuck in my head. He was Chief Constable Kenney to everyone else and a callous bastard. I didn't share his disregard for the dead woman.

Disgust warred with my instant regret for the loss of life.

Arran: Description?

DetD: Pink hair, roll of condoms, a lot of blood on her naked body. You getting off on this?

Shade listened as I relayed the details, his gaze distancing for a beat. I knew his mind had gone to another place, of dark streets, the competition and the chase, of red blood spilled in our shared pastime of cleaning up after shite like this.

"We need to find out who did it," he snapped.

"Agreed. How the fuck did that woman skip our radar?"

Shade's expression shifted, his focus returning from the pull of the night to settle on me. "No fucking clue. We'll work this out, aye? We'll work out who, and he'll pay."

We would, but it was too late for the deceased.

"Ye can't save everyone," my friend added.

I didn't accept that.

As a minimum, I could try. Tonight, I'd failed.

I also couldn't leave the office right now, as much as I wanted to. The clubs were busy, a line outside of both. The women working the tables, poles, and beds would be happy. I would have to make do with the fact the cops would be all over North Town for at least a day, therefore keeping the residents safer than average in a city of sin.

Didn't stop me from wanting to drive back over. Nor could I explain the urge to stop in on the maniac jaywalker again. At least she still had her life intact.

My brain abruptly took me back to her flat. To the shape of her thigh when I'd knelt to check her over. The dip and curve of her waist. When she'd touched me, it sent shockwaves.

The fuck was up with that?

"What's on my table tonight?" I grouched.

Shade pocketed his phone. "An employee wants to see ye then we've got an applicant for the game."

"Late notice." The game was tomorrow night, and every other player had been booked in for weeks.

"We had a dropout. She's next in line."

A knock rattled the door, and Shade answered it. He

jerked his head for the person to enter. Dixie, one of the strippers, sauntered past him. She was in her club uniform of sky-high heels and a see-through underwear set with her tits pushed high and forwards. Normally if one of the women needed to talk to me, they threw on a robe first.

I gestured to the vacant seat on the other side of my dark-wood desk. "How can I help?"

Dixie slanted a disdainful look at the chair, then rounded the desk to perch on the corner nearest me. She posed, like she would onstage, tipping her body forward, presenting her big tits and narrow waist at the best angle. Then she threw a less indulgent glance at Shade. "Could we have a little privacy?"

Shade tilted his head in bemusement, and I hid a groan.

Every now and again, one of the workers got the wrong idea about me. A seduction routine would play out, and I'd be in the middle of it.

"Shade stays."

Dixie arched her laminated eyebrows then gave an easy shrug. "If that's what you guys are into. I'm down for anything. In fact, I've been thinking how lonely it must be for you alone in here, Mr Daniels. All that responsibility and no one to share it with." She inched forwards. "I know you have your crew, but that's not the same as someone taking care of you. Someone here for your every need."

My brain shifted gear and left the woman in the middle of her seduction and jumped right back to Genevieve. Who'd let me in. Who'd tended to my bruise like an injury to my flesh mattered.

I'd sat there while she'd done it, my dick hard and

every fucking sense gone.

Abruptly, Dixie dropped her bony ass into my lap, curling her arm around my neck. "I've been watching you. You're lonely, I can tell. It takes a woman to know, and obviously none of the other chicks in this henhouse are doing it for you. Let me show you how different I am. Let me be the one to make you feel good."

Across the room, Shade pressed his hand to his mouth, stifling a laugh.

Dixie unclipped her bra. With impressive speed, she swivelled to straddle me, grinding down on my very uninterested dick. I didn't budge, making no attempt to steady her or cup her ass. This happened with a regularity like clockwork. One of the newer women would see the opportunity of being my girl and make every move to chase it.

Rolling her hips, Dixie gave up a moan of pleasure, making sure her tits grazed my chest, pushing them to my face. But sweat beaded at her brow. This wasn't working for her, and she was realising it.

"Fucking hell." Shade gave up and belly laughed.

Dixie's gaze flew to him, her lips pouting. Then her chin lifted in triumph as if she'd had a brilliant idea. "Hey, laughing boy, come and join in? Kiss me while I fuck the boss? You can both have me. I'll unzip you, and you can fuck my mouth right next to him. We can share. Or you can both fuck me at the same time. I've been training."

Shade sighed and tapped on his phone. "I'll get Alisha."

Dixie's eyes brightened. "Yes! Girl on girl. We'll do whatever you want. I'll lie on your desk, and she can eat me out right where you can see us."

Then she made a mistake. Her red-tipped nails dug

into my shoulder, straight into the bruise that Genevieve had treated. It wasn't the pain, but something else that had me shooting to my feet.

Dixie dropped from my lap to the floor.

I stepped back, arms folded, and Shade beside me. At the same second, Alisha swept in, long platinum curls draping elegantly over her purple robe. The older woman raised her eyebrows expectantly at us then spotted her employee on the floor.

Her mouth twisted in frustration. "Not another one. I'm so sorry, Arran. Honey, get the fuck up."

She advanced on Dixie who was climbing to her heels, shock turning to red-faced humiliation.

"What kind of sex club owner doesn't like sex?" Dixie whined. "Doesn't your dick work? Is there something wrong with it?"

If she thought to embarrass me, she was failing. My tolerance was pretty much all out, though.

I gestured to Alisha, my operations manager, though she hated the title and wouldn't use it. "Get her out of here. But come back after, I need you for something else."

Dixie shrugged Alisha off, struggling to clip her bra back in place over her rigid fake tits. "Is he yours, then? Why didn't you say?"

"Yes, he's mine, and I'm an evil fucking bitch when anyone touches my man." Alisha gave me a quick wink behind Dixie's back.

"I didn't know! I thought he was available. Please don't fire me."

On the other side of the door, a guard took hold of Dixie's arm, bending to hear Alisha's order, possibly to see the woman off the premises or maybe to give her another chance if she promised to only chase the dick she was paid to. That wasn't my territory.

I closed the door on them.

"There's nothing wrong with my dick," I said into the quiet of the office.

Shade burst out laughing. "I didn't say anything."

"You were thinking it. Get your mind out of my jeans."

"Sure thing, brother." He went to a cabinet, sliding open the top metal drawer. From inside, he took two bandannas. Skeleton masks, the pattern a lower half of a skull like the tattoo on his hand. The mark of my crew.

Tossing one to me, he pulled on the other so it covered him nose to jaw, leaving only his piercing blue eyes under a thatch of dark hair. Automatically, I did the same. For anyone who already worked for us, we didn't bother masking up, but the next on the list was a newcomer.

Outsiders needed to fear us.

At my father's knee, I'd learned that terrorising the people around you guaranteed results. I hated everything he'd taught me, but that tactic had proved useful when it came to the world I lived in. The one I'd carved out for myself and bled for.

Alisha returned and took a seat at the side of the room, not bothering with a bandanna. The door opened again, and Convict entered, another member of my crew. He took a position behind me, face already covered.

Shade opened the door to admit a slender blonde woman.

For a split second, I froze up.

The applicant for the game appeared so much like Genevieve it gave me pause, but it was only the dim room.

The shade of her hair. Another second and she was in the light, and the similarity was gone.

I was fucked up if I was seeing my little maniac in others.

Not-Genevieve peeked at each of us, gripping the back of the guest chair with obvious nerves.

"Sit," I ordered.

Quickly, she dropped into the seat, then took a breath, regaining her composure.

Shade stepped forward and addressed her. "Natasha Reid, twenty-four, a New York debutante then a socialite. What's a woman like ye doing entering our game?"

My mask hid my smile. Most of the women who entered were like her.

Natasha swallowed. "I... I want to be claimed."

He gave a dark laugh. "Interesting choice of word, but accurate. Your paperwork is good, and you've signed the disclaimer and said ye understand, but are ye really prepared for what goes down there? Twenty men, five lasses. You'll be chased, stripped, pinned down, fought over, then fucked. Ye don't get to choose. Ye don't get to say no once you're in. There will be blood. Whichever man wins takes ye home, and you'll have no say over that. From the second ye walk through that door, and the lock turns at your back, until the time is up, you'll belong to him. Your owner. Is that clear?"

The woman's chest rose and fell, her pulse at her throat thrumming. Natasha was picking up what Shade was laying down. It was the reason the game worked. The compelling nature of the contest.

It got the blood rushing like nothing else. It did exactly what the contestants wanted it to do. Or so I was told.

She gave a swift nod.

Alisha took over. "You understand the commitments the men make as well?"

Natasha jerked her head more readily now. "It's what I want. A woman from my sorority was in it a year ago, and she's so...satisfied. I want everything she's got. I'm ready."

"You understand the time constraint, too?" Alisha added.

"Yes. I don't work and I've just finished my degree. It's all in the forms I filled out. Please?"

Alisha clucked her tongue then took the waiting contract from my desk along with a pen. She tapped the pen, drawing out the moment, then passed it to Natasha who scribbled a signature with obvious relief.

Another one bit the dust. I wondered if she'd be so sunny when smashed to the cold stone floor by a pack of hungry men tomorrow night.

The new applicant was shown out.

"Alisha," I said, a warning in my tone.

She'd forgotten something.

Alisha hurried after Natasha, picking up the photo of a child from the shelf on the way. Down the corridor, she raised it and asked my question. Natasha squinted.

Like every time, I held my breath.

As always happened, the newcomer shrugged and my disappointment cut deep.

I sank in my chair, letting the wave of frustration pass over me.

"One day, someone will say yes," Shade offered. He'd shifted back to his usual position at the back.

I didn't answer. That child would be eleven or twelve

years old now. A decade older than the sole picture I had. With every year that passed, my hope grew slimmer.

"She was a fucking knockout," Convict commented from my other side. "The fights she's going to cause. Someone's going to split her in two."

I rolled an unimpressed but tolerant look his way. "That isn't what it's about."

Even though my thoughts had gone the same way.

"I know, but it'll be a fucking riot to watch."

My crew were never, ever allowed to participate, but we always had watchers. They acted as judges, and couldn't help if they got off on what they saw. They were needed as arbitrators after, too, should the need arise. I rarely monitored the game myself. Other matters occupied my time.

Alisha returned. "We've got two walk-ins. Both showed up in the last few minutes."

"What's the ask?" I queried.

"The first wants in on the game as well. The second said she wants a job. As anything."

I didn't like that *anything* comment. It smacked of desperation. The women, and fewer men, who worked here generally came in knowing exactly what their limits were. Some only wanted to strip. Others never danced and worked the level above, earning their living on their backs. Or fronts. Or knees. Upside down. Whatever the cash they took demanded.

I sighed, and Alisha opened the door. The applicant stepped inside with a confidence the last woman had been lacking. Curvy as hell, and in a sparkling silver dress that wouldn't be out of place at an award ceremony, she touched her gaze on each of us masked men in turn, not in fear, like the person before her, but as if seeking out something.

"I'm here for the game," she announced.

"No," an answer came from behind.

Shade had spoken, low, dark, and deadly certain. It wasn't usual for him to offer a judgement like that. We all had our roles, and I led the way, but if he was cutting her off, I'd back him.

I cleared my throat. "Not this time. We're booked up."

The woman swept her long, brunette hair over her shoulder. "From what I heard, you're always needing women. There are more than enough men. You can take me as well. I filled out all your forms."

Shade made a sound almost like a growl.

"Sorry, but the answer is no," I stated, completely flat.

"Then I'll come back next time."

The woman pursed her lips in annoyance, but Alisha took her arms and towed her away.

"Stamp your little foot and run back to daddy," Shade groused under his breath.

She was shown out, Alisha taking a moment to show the picture, and my disappointment inevitably following.

"Last one, then we can get out of here," Convict announced. "Shade, did you know that girl?"

Shade didn't reply, slinking back into the shadows of the office. He clearly had, but he was entitled to his secrets.

Alisha beckoned in the last person of the evening.

I adjusted my skeleton mask, ready to leave. Sitting behind a desk wasn't my style. I was down to patrol the building, watching for trouble with the punters. Hit up the police for more details on the murdered woman.

After that, Shade and I were free to take on the city and let loose the darkness inside us. Start a hunt of our own.

But my thoughts ground to a halt.

Under the bright spotlight we shone on visitors, Genevieve walked into my space.

5

Genevieve

My plan was working. I'd got past the bouncer by saying I was applying for a job, falling into a short line of people waiting to be admitted to an office. But now, it was my turn, and I was facing off with a room of men in goddamned skeleton masks.

I hated masks.

It scared me that I couldn't see their expressions. Or recognise them again if we ever met. Anyone could be behind them.

Across the ultra-masculine dark-wood desk, the men watched me silently. The office was wide with an industrial feel, the walls of the red-brick warehouse left uncovered. Nothing soft. No pictures, no couch.

Not much light either. The men were half in darkness while I was bathed in a spotlight. My skin prickled in awareness, and my stomach tightened in trepidation.

Then a woman to the side asked a question. I'd barely noticed her, so freaked out was I by the masked men.

"You're looking for work. What exactly do you want to

do?" she said.

I swallowed. "I'm open to anything. I need the money and I work hard."

"Go to the bar next door. They have vacancies," she commented.

"What about the strip show?"

The four of them stared. Only a few hours ago, I'd snapped at Arran, the stranger in my home who I'd somehow seen half-naked, about women who took their clothes off for money. I wasn't a prostitute, and I wasn't a stripper either. I didn't have the skills.

All I needed was to walk through the building and find the woman my dad was hanging out with.

He might even be here, somewhere, though I didn't think that likely. It was over a week since he'd last been home, and the money would've run out, surely.

The man at the desk leaned back, one of the others stooping for a short exchange of conversation I couldn't hear. He was the boss, I took it, the one in the chair. Big, and muscular. All of them were, the two supporting guys heavily tattooed as well.

The one he'd spoken to lifted his chin to me. "Ever stripped before?" he said in a Scottish accent

I winced. "No. At least not for money."

None of them laughed.

The boss man steepled his hands. "Yet here you are in a strip club. What makes you think you'd be any good?"

His voice was familiar, but I couldn't place it. I didn't have an answer for him. I could hardly say I'd only come here to find someone. They'd throw me out faster than if I'd yelled cop. "Surely there's a place I could start out."

The one who'd addressed me first replied. "Perhaps. Everyone who works this side of the warehouse has to audition. Are ye prepared for that?"

Audition? Shit.

My mouth dried. Thinking fast, I scrabbled for a way out of this that didn't involve taking off my little black dress. "Would it be okay if I had a quick tour of the place? I know I can be what you need, but I'm new to this. Just give me a chance to orientate myself."

They'd say no. I could already tell. I had a backup plan of hanging around outside and asking people as they came out if they knew Sydney, but that was weak. I really wanted to get one of the women alone.

To my utter surprise, the boss man tilted his head in agreement. He gestured to the woman who came to him and listened to his quiet instruction.

She smiled and pointed a beautifully manicured finger my way. "I'll take you. It'll be short, then we'll return here. Don't waste my time, Jenny."

I jumped up, ready to go, not even caring that she'd mangled my name. I was Gen to my family but only them. Genevieve to everyone else. Jenny was leftfield completely, but I'd wear the name if it helped me find my dad.

Outside the office, I breathed a sigh of relief from being away from the skeleton scrutiny but waited to speak until we'd passed the bouncer and had moved deeper into the club. "That was intense."

"Working here's no walk in the park."

"What's your name?" I asked.

She slid me a look. "Alisha."

"Have you been an employee long?" I really wanted to find someone who knew all the women.

Alisha didn't reply. She tapped on a keypad then pushed open a door that gave way to a dark hallway, the walls decorated with thick pink fabric that continued underfoot. It muted the pulse of music that came from the other end. Either side of the hall were closed doors.

"Private rooms for dances." She indicated left and right.

At the end of the space, the door opened, lights whirling and bodies in view through the narrow slice. A stripper in only a tiny pair of knickers led a much older man whose gaze was fixed to her chest. The old dog was practically drooling and barely noticed us as the woman directed him into a room, shutting the door.

"Do you offer..." I picked over my words. "More than the dancing?"

"Do you work for the police in any capacity, whether employed or contracted?" Alisha stopped dead.

I opened my mouth. "No. I deliver food."

She appraised me. Compared to her, and the woman I'd just seen with a client, I was severely under-styled, despite the fact I'd curled my blonde hair and dabbed on smoky eye makeup. Alisha's appearance was exaggerated but seriously impressive. Red lips, heavy fake eyelashes, hair extensions to her ass, all impactful.

She tapped her fingers on her thigh as if making a decision then indicated for me to follow her. At the room the stripper had entered, Alisha flicked back the cover to an eyehole.

"See for yourself what the expectation is."

I peered in. Sprawled on the couch, the old goat client gazed up at the dancer, his knees wide and his hands gripping the couch cushion. In front of him, and with her back to me, the woman wound her hips in a tight circle, timing her moves to the beat of the music. Her hands were at her breasts, her feet bare on the carpet, and her straight black hair tumbling down her naked back, following the path of a line of Chinese symbols down her spine.

As the beat changed, she said something to her client, and he shifted so both arms were on the back of the plush sofa, then the dancer leaned in to brace herself over him, her tits in his face, millimetres away from touching him. She undulated to and fro, so close to him. His hand came up, but she arched away, waggling a finger. His chest rose and fell. Mine did the same, my breathing coming harder.

This was seduction in action. A woman earning her cash. It was hot as fuck, and she'd barely begun.

The man dropped his hand to his very obvious erection that strained at his pale chinos. He stroked himself, his features twisted in a need I'd never seen on the two boyfriends I'd slept with.

The stripper eased her fingers into her thong. Stripped it.

"Have you ever fucked anyone for money?" Alisha whispered in my ear.

I jumped and broke my gaze on the act. "No."

"Ever put on a show for a boyfriend?"

My cheeks warmed all the more. "Not really."

"Huh. You don't say."

"Everyone's got to start somewhere," I babbled, my mind still half on the hypnotic scene in the room. I couldn't do that. I wasn't sexy enough. "You must've trained people before?"

Alisha walked away down the hall, calling back quietly, "Yes, we can train people, but usually if someone's here, it's because they started this line of work themselves, or were made to do it, if you catch my meaning."

She opened the big doors to reveal the wide room of the strip club, floor lights marking the edges and spotlights on stages. Tables and booths were packed with groups of men, and a line of occupied chairs mirrored the shape of the main stage.

I scanned for Dad among the punters. No luck.

Onstage, a woman peeled off her micro dress, revealing neon underwear. Then she dropped backwards, belly pointed to the ceiling and the apex of her thighs to the audience. In a move worthy of a gymnast, she put her full weight onto her hands, arching back so her legs were over her and open in the splits with only the barest scrap of her pink thong covering her core.

The men roared and whooped.

My host tapped my jaw closed. "Have you even been in a strip club?"

I shook my head, and she gave a more sympathetic smile.

"How old are you?"

"Twenty-two."

"Clean little thing, aren't you? It's odd for me to meet someone from the other side of the tracks. My whole world is this place."

I didn't know exactly what my side of the tracks looked like to her, and I didn't get a chance to ask as a man in a suit hustled over and spoke in her ear, urgency and apology in his expression.

Alisha listened then rolled her eyes. "I need to go fix a backstage disaster. I'll be right back. Someone will take care of you."

She left me in the middle of the club. The perfect opportunity.

I snagged a passing waitress in a cute, skimpy serving uniform and with a tray of empty glasses on her hand. "Hey, is Sydney here?"

"Sorry, hun, I only just started so I don't know everyone yet. Ask Clem at the bar?"

She wheeled away, and I trotted after, her steps leading me to a brightly lit bar.

An older woman with deep ebony skin pulled pints in plastic cups, her sizeable chest stretching an identical uniform to the waitress. She noticed me and smiled. "We do table service here, darling. Go sit down and someone will be with you."

"I'm not a customer. I'm trying to find Sydney. Is she around?"

The barwoman frowned. "Not familiar with that name. Is she staff or does she dance?"

Moniqua had said stripper, I was sure. "She's a stripper. A dancer, I mean."

"I know all the girls on my floor, and she ain't one of them. Not here, not upstairs."

A strange warning swept through me with a shiver of cold. "How do I get upstairs?"

"If you don't know that, I'm not telling." She placed the pint of amber beer on a waiting tray and narrowed her gaze. "Who are you here with?"

Someone tapped my shoulder. I turned to find a woman about my age waiting, her outfit the same black and pink as the other staff. There was a logo on her waistcoat. A black-and-white skull, just like the men in the office had worn.

"You Jenny? I'm Lara. Alisha asked me to show you back to the offices. Follow me."

Damn. This was all going wrong.

Lara took me back through a different route than the one I'd come, along another hall. Her short brown hair flashed in the light, pretty pink metallic strands woven into it.

The shade reminded me of Cherry's pink. I hadn't seen her earlier this evening, but I'd make a point of checking on her once I got home.

Around the corner, we passed a stairwell behind glass. From the lower flight, a man strode up the steps, taking on the next set purposefully to jog out of sight upwards. He wore a suit but had the same expression of need as the private room client I'd watched earlier. What was down there? I tried to picture the exterior of the warehouse. We were right on the river, so it could have another entrance, a lower one around the back, more private for those who didn't want to enter the public way.

As they might if they weren't here for the dancing side of the club but something else. An even more taboo offer.

My pulse skipped.

"Lara, can you show me upstairs?" I asked.

"Um, no? Sorry. Alisha just said to take you back."

"I'm trying to find someone called Sydney. I think she's up there."

"If she is, she's busy." My escort linked her arm through mine, making it clear I wasn't going off alone. "It'll be even busier here tomorrow."

"Saturday night," I mused.

We neared a door off the main floor marked *Private*. A

bouncer held it open for us. Ahead, two women entered what appeared to be a changing room. A clipboard hung outside. A rota? My pulse picked up even more. I needed to see it.

"That, sure, but they're running the game. It gets a lot of attention, and men flock in. Some women, too," my escort continued. "Even if they restrict entrance."

She talked on, but I stopped listening, slowing to scan the list of names with urgency. Bonnie, Maeve, Dixie, eight more. Damn. No Sydney. Not that I could see.

Then we were back at the office again, and dejection filled me.

Alisha caught us up. "See all you needed to?"

I sighed because no, I really hadn't. Not much more than a paying customer. Inside the big room, the three men in skeleton masks waited. I wished it was brighter in there, but the room was set up to intimidate people on the wrong side of the desk, judging by the lamp shining in my eyes.

"It's an amazing setup here," I lied. "I'll do it. I'll strip. I can learn."

I needed that second opportunity to come back.

The boss angled his head, drawing his focus up and down me. Something in his eyes caught my attention.

"So you think you understand what it takes to work here now. One walk around and it's all clear."

He was going to refuse me. I took a guess. A wild burst. "If it works out, I want to move to the floor upstairs. To sell my body."

All four people in the room sharpened their attention on me. But it was the man in the middle who kept the floor.

"To fuck for money?"

"Y-yes."

He flexed his hand, his short nails on the desk surface. "What makes you think that happens here?"

"It does, right? And I want to work doing that."

His intense stare didn't let up, a hunter toying with his prey. "If such a job existed, there would be rules for new staff."

"Of course. I'll obey them."

"They'd have to fuck me. To be available when and where I need them. They can't say no if they want to work here."

Horror sank through me.

One of his men laughed.

My jaw trembled. "I can do that."

"You're giving me permission?"

Recklessly, I nodded. If I couldn't find Dad, I couldn't sort out the rent, and we'd lose our home. Besides, if I was called in to sleep with the boss, I'd quit and run. He wouldn't make me straight away.

"You've agreed to fuck me, but what about anyone else I order?" he asked. "Like right now. Get on the floor. Take off that dress."

"W-what?"

But as I stuttered, an awful, icy recognition suddenly hit me.

That voice. The shape of him. I'd touched that rounded shoulder. Heard him say nicer words in a gentler tone. He'd tended to my injuries and returned to check I was okay.

I stood on shaky limbs. Crept forward to the desk so I could see beyond the blinding light and confirm my suspicion. The soulless grey eyes over the mask held mine.

Arran.

The man I'd spent two nights thinking about. He'd told me he worked in management. Liar. He led a fucking gang.

Outrage had my mouth dropping open, anger bubbling up. Reality quickly followed, my skin crawling from the hostility of the room and the wall of gang members.

Arran kept that steady gaze fixed on me. "You heard me. Prove yourself if you want me to believe a word you fucking say. You want to spread your legs for money? Get ready to be fucked."

A wave of overwhelm eclipsed every other emotion.

Again, I fled the man and didn't look back.

6

Arran

*C*onvict gave a low whistle. "Damn, that was rough."

I glowered at him, unspeaking.

"What? You did the right thing in scaring the pretty little rabbit off. She didn't belong here. She's probably wearing a wire or some shit anyway. You were smart with your words."

He left the office, Shade giving me a quirked eyebrow then following him. Leaving me with Alisha and her judging stare.

"That was cruel," she said.

"Convict's correct. She's wrong for this place."

"Even so, you don't talk to the girls like that." Her tone held a question as much as an admonition.

Fifteen years ago, Alisha had been one of my father's pets, experienced and skilled though barely older than my twelve years. She'd been allocated to see me into manhood. To take my virginity and start me on the path my father wanted me to follow.

She and I had spent most of our time in my room in his

mansion playing videogames.

"Who is she? You knew her, didn't you?" Alisha persisted.

I chewed over that, working back through the woman appearing in front of my car. Her calling to me from her window. Why the fuck I'd gone back to look for her?

"She's sweet, a complete innocent," Alisha continued. "She watched a private show and blushed so red she practically glowed in the dark. Then when Lara brought her back here and talked about the game, she shut down and didn't make a peep. Lara told me outside the door. What's the deal with her? There's a reason you gave her that leeway. A freaking tour."

"It was necessary."

She paused, her gaze pensive and something else there I didn't recognise. "I've never seen you like that. I don't trust her."

"She's no one, drop it," I snapped, ending the conversation.

Because she wasn't. Not to me, not now. I was almost certain that Genevieve had targeted me for some reason I could only guess at. Maybe she worked for a rival gang or some other agency who wanted a piece of what I'd made. I had more enemies than I could count. A selection of whom would do anything to take me down.

My life was a balance of staying alive and running the business, and no pretty face was going to compromise either.

If I saw her here again, she'd take what was coming.

Even with my thoughts twisting into darkness, I still tapped out a message to one of the crew, ordering him to follow Genevieve home. Just to make sure she got there.

The cops on her street would keep her safe after.

Alisha made a sound, bringing my focus back to her from my phone.

"I apologise again for Dixie. I'll make it clear to all the new girls that you're out of bounds. I was joking when I said it to her, but it worked. If it's okay with you, I'll tell them you're mine."

That odd expression intensified.

"Do what you need to," I replied, but it was hard to even care.

7

Genevieve

"Of course, she had it coming, the dirty slut," Mrs B mouthed the last word to another of our neighbours, her yappy white dogs waiting at her feet. "Doing that kind of thing right out in the open where anyone could pass by. Children live here! It's disgusting."

I stopped still on the path. Across the road, in the churchyard, a white tent closed off any view of the steps. A guy in a forensics suit exited, snapping off a pair of disposable gloves. They had blood on them.

My friend was dead.

She'd been killed there last night.

In the time it had taken for me to go to the club then return, Cherry had been murdered. The beat cop who stood at the church gates wouldn't say for certain who the victim was, but no one else hung out there after dark, aside from the occasional group of teenagers smoking weed, and if it had been someone's kid, there would be news crews. An outcry.

Not the quiet of the police processing the murder

scene.

My heart hurt. Cherry had been kind. Funny. She deserved so much better.

"Nice of you to speak ill of the dead," I bit out to my crazy old bat of a neighbour. "What did she ever do to you?"

Mrs B's beady gaze shot to me. "Good families live around here, though obviously not yours if you think this is anything but a good thing. What that woman was doing was disgusting. A stain on the street."

The only stain was her judgement and Cherry's red blood, but anger and upset held my tongue, and I couldn't get out another word.

Mrs B drew a look up and down me, her thin lips forming a sneer. "I heard you won't be here much longer anyway. Good riddance in both cases. It's nice when the trash takes itself out."

She turned back to the woman she'd been talking to, and I stomped past, heat painting my cheeks. The other residents of the Crescent might be celebrating, but a good woman had died.

In my flat, I rinsed off the grime of my full shift, dressed, then perched in the window, alone, sad, *horrified*. The sun set, and cooler night slunk over the city, and I traced over the silhouette of the city buildings, the dark curve of the river, the red-brick warehouse to the right. All the while keeping an eye on the police presence at the church, the uniformed officer on guard, and white-and-blue incident tape across the gates.

Cherry's wry and kind face appeared in my mind. Alive one minute and gone the next. One of her clients was probably the culprit, and I worked over what she'd told me a couple of nights back. Not much. Damn. She'd been so vibrant. Sharp, too. My eyes welled again, and I dashed away tears.

When we'd first started talking, we had a conversation that stuck in my mind. Cherry asked if I had a boyfriend. I'd said no and told her about my last who had been less than enthusiastic in all things, most of all in bed. She'd asked if he'd still paid good, and I'd laughed.

"Not that kind of boyfriend."

"He didn't pay at all? You were ripped off, sweets. All sex is transactional, whether you admit it or not."

Another time, she'd commented on my coffee and said she liked the super sweet and hot kind, leading to more man jokes. Next time I saw her, I'd brought her a pumpkin spiced latte. In return, she'd made hearts with her hands whenever I passed.

I'd find a way to commemorate Cherry. She deserved nothing less.

Just as I needed solutions to my own problems. I was in the mood for something fucking drastic.

Today, between jobs, I'd taken time to call everyone who might have seen my dad. I'd stopped in at bars and doss houses. Finally spoke to my brother. Riordan knew nothing and had sounded so stressed I'd pulled the punch and told him I'd handle it.

I wanted to talk to him about Cherry but had kept that in, too.

No, tonight was all me, the drive in me to resolve the problems in my life and the small yet burning hurt at what had happened with the gang leader. He'd shown his true colours, and it cut deep.

How the heck did I give him that power? That smallest

start of a crush had died a death now.

I took a shaky breath then swallowed back the last of the heavily caffeinated mango energy drink I'd snagged from the fridge. What Arran hadn't realised in his attempt to make me run was my stubbornness. I was going back to that club, and this time, I was going to explore the other floors. I knew the layout better. I had energy to burn from my pain over Cherry and an axe to bury in the god-awful gangs.

On the horizon, purple night claimed the sky.

It was time.

Thirty minutes later, I hopped from my cab two streets over from the warehouse then slunk down the river to the back of Divine and Divide. A car park spread out, well-lit and packed with vehicles but with enough patches of darkness for me to make it close to the building.

A doorman waited by a much less fancy entrance.

That was it. The way into the staircase that led to where I needed to go. As I watched, a group of men approached and spoke to the doorman. He admitted them with a few words. Damn, that was easy. Just had to fake the same confidence.

Another group approached and were shown in without a problem.

The words of the woman who'd led me back to the office returned. She said there was a game running tonight and an expectation that they'd be busy. I'd been so occupied trying to read the rota that I hadn't paid attention beyond that. Maybe it was a sport of some kind they could watch while the women entertained them in other ways.

There was nothing left to do but find out.

Like last night, I was dressed for the occasion in my

same little black dress, but I'd gone heavier in my makeup. Prettier in my lingerie, just in case.

With my shoulders back, I crossed the distance and presented myself to the man. "I'm here for the game."

The huge man with a thick neck that bulged over his collar raised his eyebrows then he checked something on his phone. It looked like a photo. "You Natasha?"

I was whoever I needed to be. Faking brightness, I smiled. "That's me. Natasha. Nice to meet you."

He huffed in apparent relief and hauled on the door, the effect causing his suit jacket to open. It revealed a leather holster. For a knife? A gun? The movement was too fast for me to be sure, and I snapped my gaze away.

The doorman propelled me inside. "You're late. You've got a few minutes to prepare, that's it."

"Traffic was bad," I lied.

He directed me past the stairs I'd wanted to climb and to another door, plain and sturdy, no window to see in or out. He tapped in a code, and it popped open. "Hurry."

Inside, another corridor fell away, grey and unadorned. But it was a route in. I'd take it. "Thanks," I breathed.

"Good luck. You're the last to arrive. Door's locking now."

He closed me in with a thud and a click of metal. Something about his words felt final, and a slither of unease curled around my determination. Yesterday, I'd been able to walk in and walk out unbothered. Even on the floor of the club, I hadn't felt in any kind of danger despite the clientele the women were there to serve.

Getting locked in the basement felt very different. I turned and stared at the door. No handle. Not even a keyhole. Above, a camera trained on me. I hadn't noticed them elsewhere in the club but I hadn't been checking either.

The urge filled me to thump on the door and call the man back, but I'd come too far for retreating. Stifling the panic, I forced myself down the hall, grateful for my dose of caffeine that kept me going.

Around the corner, the corridor opened to a vast expanse. A concrete floor stretched the width of the huge building, pillars supporting a gantry to an upper level, and huge warehouse doors along one of the walls. The kind that lorries could pass in and out to offload goods, or whatever used to happen a century or two ago when this place was built.

Cameras overlooked the space in its shades of grey and industrial white, and bright lights left nothing hidden.

From behind me, a figure skittered out across the floor, a woman in a bandage dress, her feet bare. Carefully, she climbed the metal steps to the gantry then entered a room, not sparing a glance at me.

"Are you the last?" another voice followed, an American, from her accent.

I turned. A woman my age exited a room behind, my glimpse into the space showing sinks and lockers. A bench with towels on.

"I think so," I answered. My voice came out weak, so I cleared my throat and tried again. "The doorman said he was locking the door. Why would he do that?"

She was already moving away, her brown hair swinging in a high ponytail and her dress tight, like the other woman's had been. "Didn't you read the rules? We're here until it's over. They won't open the doors until all of us have been claimed."

"Wait," I begged. From my pocket, I pulled out my phone.

The woman's brown eyes widened, and she hurried back over, her hands out. "What the hell are you doing? You can't bring a phone in here. Put it in the lockers before someone sees."

She snatched my wrist and tugged me into the changing room. Opening a locker, she took my phone and placed it inside. "Put your bag in as well. And take that necklace off if you don't want it broken."

I obeyed automatically, undoing the simple pendant that once belonged to my mother, the urgency infectious.

"You're lucky the cameras aren't on yet. It's cardinal sin one-oh-one to bring a phone in here." She stepped back and peered over her shoulder. Like the other woman, she was barefoot.

My sense of unease exploded into a full-on panic, my energy drink rush fuelling a paranoia I was beginning to think real. For some reason, I fixated on that last detail among all the wealth of information. "Where are your shoes?"

The American grinned and hopped on the spot. "Believe me, it's better to be barefoot. You can run faster. Make it a better game. Really make them chase you down."

"What am I running from?"

"Oh, that's good. They are going to eat that sweet and innocent attitude right up. Listen, we've got a minute or two before the siren. I need to hide. No point in making this easy. You should do the same."

"Hide?" I breathed.

"There's twenty of them to our five. If you make it easy,

that's a fucking waste. Aim for the captain's office if you're stuck for a starting place. See you on the other side."

With a final grin, she was gone.

I'd fucked up.

Certainty rushed with my blood in my veins. Taking a fast breath, I kicked off my shoes and sprinted back down the corridor, thumping on the door. "Let me out," I yelled. "It's a mistake. I'm not meant to be here."

No answer came. No sound but the thrum of my pulse in my ears.

I tried again, yelling at the top of my voice. Still nothing.

A siren pierced the air. My heart all but leapt into my mouth. The time was up. I couldn't get out. My only chance was to hide.

8

Arran

*W*ater rushed, the river in full flow beneath us and our man of the moment.

Shade pulled a needle from the neck of the rapist piece of shit we'd picked up this evening, who dangled from his chained hands over the drop in the floor. He'd just injected an antidote to his sedative that would wake him in five, four, three—

His eyes sprang open.

Shade's demented grin broadened, clear to me despite the fact we both wore masks.

"I'm going to rip the tape from your mouth, then ye have one chance to redeem yourself. Scream, and I'll gut ye and tease out every entrail until it drops into the river."

I smirked at the favourite game my friend was playing. He toyed with his prey. Made them think there was hope for the situation they'd found themselves in.

There wasn't.

Fact: We didn't make mistakes.

If someone found themselves in our hands, it was game

over. Shade and I had been practising our art of cleansing the community for years now, and we didn't miss.

Also a fact: Deadwater River had one of the highest tidal ranges in the world. It filled and emptied on a schedule, the drag of water to the estuary and out to sea perfect for disposing of bodies with little effort. With the way we handled them, they didn't rise for weeks, or even months. One or two had never floated to the surface. If they did, they were unrecognisable from the effects of their sea journey.

Personally, I liked this disposal method, as did the local cops because it took the worst offenders off Deadwater's streets, and the corpses' appearances were always in someone else's jurisdiction. Our city bordered Scotland and England, and the river that split the metropolis formed the boundary. Neither police force wanted to take ownership of dead men floating. Sometimes they even ignored them.

Shade didn't feel the same. It was too clean for him. But if my friend had his way, he'd have a trophy room in the warehouse of dead eyes and femurs or some such shite, and that just begged for trouble.

With a purity of focus, he tore the tape from the man's mouth.

"I didn't do it," the fucker blabbed, struggling against the restraints, the rope tying his hands together strung up to a chain over the boathouse's overhead beam. His toes touched the walkway below then dangled over the gap between. "She's a lying fucking cunt."

"That a fact?" Shade asked. "Huh. My bad. Hold up and I'll untie ye."

Without warning, he snapped back and threw a fist at the arsehole's face. Bone crunched, and the man moaned, blood ebbing from his shattered nose.

Behind my mask, I grinned.

"You said you'd let me down," Bradley said between shuddering breaths.

"Eh, changed my mind. Pity, because ye were this close to freedom." Shade pinched his fingers a centimetre apart.

He never spoke this much unless dealing with business.

"This is about the girl, right? She fucking flaunted herself in the window," our prey blurted in desperation. His gaze darted between us in our skeleton masks, the terror in his eyes a delight. "Brushing her hair. Dancing around in little shorts. All of it was a message for me. Every night, when I climbed up to the roof to see her."

Through his eyes, I saw the innocent girl in her bedroom, unaware a predator had her in his sights. In his, she'd become a tease, a target.

Also, not the one we'd taken him in for.

"That's why you followed her," I pressed.

"I didn't follow her. She opened the door. Don't you see? She wanted it."

"What was her name?" Shade asked.

"I... I called her my little girl."

Shade and I swapped a glance. This happened too often as well. Our mark would give up another crime to the ones we already knew about, sometimes as a bargaining chip. This piece of shit had been released from jail a few weeks ago after serving ten years for rape. He'd been on our radar and down to be watched. But we didn't have eyes everywhere. I hated that we'd had a blind spot for Bradley's fresh reign of terror.

He'd followed a fourteen-year-old girl into a park and

dragged her into the bushes. Forced himself on her. She survived his attack, and her description to the police gave us everything we needed.

Three fucking weeks, he'd been free. Two girls hurt.

It killed me inside, pain I couldn't handle.

"What about the woman in the churchyard?" I pressed. I had no reason to suspect him for the murder on Genevieve's road, but it was worth asking the question while I had a captive audience.

"Not interested in women," Bradley admitted. "Don't pin that on me."

Shade turned his back to the rapist and cocked his head at me. "I'm done. Let's get on with the fun stuff." He lifted his bruised fist. "Rock, paper, scissors, shoot."

I copied his action, blunting his scissors with my rock.

Shade's expression dropped. "Fuck. At least use my blade?"

I accepted his hunting knife and let my grin spread, my need for revenge on men like this waking every part of me. It got me out of bed in the morning. Had my blood flowing like nothing else.

Well, like almost nothing else.

It had flowed straight to my dick in Genevieve's flat.

I centred myself on Bradley then flicked the knife's holster open, the action well practiced. A slice opened his shirt, revealing a sagging belly. I cut the rest of his clothes away until he dangled naked.

Then I held his gaze. "This is for the girls you raped and terrorised."

With a flick of my wrist, I sliced at the stem of his dick.

His shrivelled member fell into the river below, a

stream of piss and blood following. The screams echoed into the night. With a sigh, Shade slapped on more tape to save our ears.

"Teeth, remember," he warned.

Right. Bradley's stained set had to go, for the practical reason of making identification more difficult. No problem, because I had all the time in the world to eviscerate him.

Come to think of it, I hadn't done a workout today.

Balancing on the balls of my feet, I shot out a quick one-two into his gut, punching holes with the blade as I went. Images of my father hitting me in the same way returned, minus the stabbing. If only Bradley was him.

"Tenderising him. Nice," Shade commended.

Bradley moaned behind his gag, blood trickling. Every girl he'd touched deserved this revenge, even if they'd never find out. Every finger he laid on them would be fish food. Piece by piece, we'd help him regret his choices. Removing his head from his body was the least we could do.

Shade frowned and reached for his pocket, extracting his buzzing phone. "What the fuck? Thought I'd turned it off. It's jailbird C. He knows what we're doing tonight."

Like with us wearing masks, Shade wouldn't give up Convict's crew name. Hanging-man-Bradley was as good as dead, but we didn't take unnecessary risks.

I didn't like the sound of that phone call. Convict was holding the fort back at the warehouse and wasn't the type to interrupt us without reason.

A warning played on my senses. "Answer it."

He did, listening. The frown spread. "This could've waited until we were back. Aye, we'll be a while." Shade hung up. "That murder up in North Town. The identity of the woman is now known. Her name was Chelsea Gains, known as Cherry. He said her throat was slit and she was handcuffed and gagged."

My stomach dropped. The warning grew louder until it blared in my ears and the image of a murdered sex worker danced before my eyes. Not Cherry, but someone more closely connected to me.

History repeating in exact details.

It didn't feel like a coincidence that I'd been right there on that street, and the way Cherry had been killed brought back memories I didn't want to heed.

My mind ran over the events, pulling facts together to make a picture that could be wildly wrong or right on the dirty money. I'd gone to see Genevieve, then a murder had happened on her doorstep. Had someone followed me? Killed a woman in a very specific way to give me a message? It felt unlikely, yet I couldn't deny the connection to my past.

With a tight gut, I moved away from sobbing Bradley, the jerks of his body clattering the chain above him.

My brain offered an alternative. On that night, Genevieve had seen someone in a car and hustled me to get inside. She knew who that person was. I'd bet any money her mystery man was Cherry's murderer. Relief washed through me. Yes, that was the more likely explanation.

I needed to find Genevieve and get information from her.

I held up my fist to Shade once more. "Rock, paper, scissors."

"Shoot," he said. This time, he won, wrapping his tattooed hand around my fist, though the Scottish flag was blacked out.

I jerked my chin at the rapist. "Finish him."

Shade blinked, need clear in his eyes. He took back his weapon. "Are ye sure? You're the best." Then his eyebrows beetled, his enthusiasm dimming for a moment. "I'll make it quick. Wait up and I'll go with ye to handle whatever just fucked with your head."

"Don't worry. Enjoy yourself and make this good."

Outside the boathouse, the muffled, high groans from our captive indicated that Shade was settling in for some fun. In my car, I switched my phone back on, my thoughts still dwelling on the horror.

My thumb hovered over a name, the one person who knew me better than anyone. And my twisted past. *Jamieson.*

But before I could dial, it rang in my hand, my head of security calling.

At my answer, the man spoke in a worried tone. "Sorry to disturb you, boss. The game's underway and everything's good, but there's a woman at the back door who's claiming she should be in there. Natasha Reid, the last applicant. But all five women and twenty men were checked in."

"Probably trying her luck." I pressed the engine button, my lights illuminating the deserted plot.

Excitement was high when the game was running. People lied and begged for a place. It was one of the reasons we kept it so locked down.

Though not the main one.

"That's the thing," he continued. "I don't think she's lying. She has ID."

What the fuck?

"I'm on my way," I said, then hung up.

I was only fifteen minutes from the warehouse which sat at the west side of the centre of town, everything beyond giving way to an industrial zone along the river, including the location of the boathouse.

But instead of putting my foot down, I took a second to pull up the camera feed for the basement. Select few had access to this. The paying guests in the suites above, some in a room with drinks on tables, others locked up with one of the working women, getting off on the scene.

The violence. The blood.

My access allowed me to see everything, including the exterior shots of the applicants arriving. The camera gave me a clear view of a slim, blonde woman, faking confidence as she stepped up to Geoff, one of the newer doormen.

I froze with recognition, suddenly sickened.

A lucky lookalike, not Natasha Reid at all.

Whatever she said worked for him as the fucking moron had let her in. Locked her in with twenty men who'd do anything they could to be the first to fuck her. They wouldn't stop. No one would listen. The rules were clear, and they'd kill each other to get inside her pussy.

And to own her for weeks after.

Genevieve had walked into the path of my car and now into my game. If I couldn't reach her, she was lost to me.

At last, my muscles unlocked, and I stamped on the accelerator, speeding to intercept as fast as I fucking could.

9

Genevieve

My breathing came in quick pants, my hand crammed to my mouth so I didn't scream out and give myself away. For twenty minutes, I'd hidden high above the warehouse floor, making it to the gantry then scrambling up a frame to lie flat on the roof of the captain's office the American woman had told me about.

I'd been seconds ahead of the men. So many of them, each in a skeleton mask and bare-chested. Some with black warpaint daubed on their flesh and across their eyes. All with hard muscles and savage yells when the siren indicated their release from pens either side of the open space. They'd fought each other even before they'd located any of the women.

The first girl had been caught right below my hiding place.

A redhead with pale skin and freckles on her shoulders. She'd screamed out a mix of fear and lust, her dress ripped from her and her limbs held down by two different men, then three. Another pitched into the fight and instantly reigned dominant. Huge, with dark skin and rippling muscles, he'd clashed with her attackers, blood flying from hits and two contestants knocked unconscious so their bodies landed prone next to hers.

At the far end of the space, another woman had made a break for it, and some of the pack had taken off in furious pursuit. The ones left around the redhead weren't ready to give up.

They brawled for her, but the huge man stood over her body, keeping them at bay and dealing out lethal hits. Black tattoos down his arms moved with his swings. He'd bared his teeth in clear warning. Finally, he'd caused enough damage to the others that it gave him the space he needed to open his jeans.

He'd freed his dick and knelt, tearing away the last of her clothing to expose her naked form. Then, so strangely, he'd ducked to make eye contact and laid a tender kiss on her lips. The woman sobbed and threw her arms around him as if the act of hurting the other men around her had been a gift.

He whispered something then fucked straight into her where she lay, his dick penetrating her until their bodies were flush together. Both breathed hard. Blood decorated her skin, red specks alongside her freckles. Then the two of them writhed in it, their desperation-edged moans adding to the yells of the sport others were having elsewhere.

Only at their moment of sexual connection had the losers left them alone.

At that whole scene, I'd been able to peek.

I didn't dare now.

Metal creaked. A footstep?

My very soul cringed in on me. The past few days had

been filled with shitty situations. A threat of homelessness, the hit by a car, Cherry's murder. Now I was moments away from a pack savaging me.

There wasn't a single thing I could do to stop them. It was more than apparent that none would listen to me even if I begged. From what the American had said and the redhead's reaction, the women were willing prey. They *wanted* this.

I absolutely did not, but my body was betraying me. My skin so sensitive and my flesh dying to be touched. I was excited, thrilled in a way I hadn't been ever. Not that I desired being hurt, but the animalistic sex had done the unthinkable and turned me on. I didn't want it in the same way the other women did with their eyes shining bright, but I did want *something*.

My imagination had made it Arran. His gorgeous face behind a skeleton mask. Him bruising and breaking bones then forcing me down and fucking me in front of the other contestants.

Claiming me. Obsessing over me.

I could cry for how messed up that idea was, but keeping him in my head was helping me get through the terror.

Another crack of the metal gantry below. Someone was nearby. Above me, a red light blinked on a camera. I shot my gaze to it, unable to move for fear of being seen but focusing on the glass like the watchers would help.

Then I clocked the reflection.

I could see him. The approaching male. Not Arran as my errant heart hoped, but still familiar. One of his gang members, I was almost certain. I'd leaned across the desk and got a good look at the three of them, focusing on the other identifying details since their faces were hidden. The one to his right had had a snake tattooed around his arm, and he held his head at an angle, as if finding everything funny. Just like the approaching man did now, though warpaint had been daubed over his tattoos.

"It's no good," the incomer called out. "We're everywhere. You can't escape us. Run, little rabbit. I want to fucking bring you down."

From further away, someone jeered.

I shuddered. There had been yells from his fellow contestants but nothing of this taunting. The other men were far gone on bloodlust.

A scream tore through the air to my left, furious shouts following.

The man nearer me gave a dark laugh. "Girl three has been found and is about to get fucked by her owner. You want that, too. Isn't that why you're here? Come out, come out."

The very last thing I wanted was to be found. In my heart, I knew that desire was futile. One of them would get me if it wasn't this one. It could be better to submit and just let him take me. Bring it to an end.

I wished I could go down fighting. Hurt him like he would hurt me. But I was scared in a way I'd never been afraid in my life. It felt like everything was falling apart again, like it had when Mum died, but I wasn't fifteen now. I was grown and I'd brought this on myself.

Tap, tap, tap.

More footsteps, closer still.

A wave of terror built inside me.

Abruptly, a howl of triumph came from closer by.

"Got you," a man yelled, his accent thick where the others were a mix of nationalities.

The fourth woman had been caught. She mumbled something that let me pick up her accent—it was the American who'd given me my hiding place. Who'd helped me survive this long.

She moaned and choked out a protest, or perhaps encouragement, a struggle playing out that I could only imagine. Her high ponytail being used to control her. Her tight dress ripped and shredded, no concern in her attacker of the pain it might cause her.

Another man howled like a damn dog, the smack of flesh a fight. Something wet splatted. Blood.

Then the unmistakable punch and grunt of sex.

I brought to mind her face and twisted it from distress to rapture. She'd signed up for this. As terrifying as it was for me, I couldn't get over the fact that she and the other three women welcomed the savage attack.

The sound of her having sex with her winner grew louder, her moans and his pleasure echoing in the space. Slaps of skin hitting. Muttered encouragement from whoever was watching but no longer touching. It built into a crescendo, their orgasms loud and giving me a burst of unwanted need so strong my breathing stuttered and my core clenched.

"Four taken now," my tormentor called. "Sixteen men left with one objective."

The gantry creaked.

"Number five, where the fuck are you?" he shouted abruptly.

Another voice answered, the American woman, breathless in her aid. "Try the roof of that hut. I want this over so we can leave."

Oh God, no.

In the reflection, the man closest to me lurched, scrambling for the same route up I'd taken. I yelped in terror, rolling up to scurry to the edge. I stared down. Below me, two couples were having sex on the floor, nothing hidden from the group of men around them.

But they all saw me.

"There!" one yelled.

My breath caught. Behind me, at the other side of the roof, the snake-tattooed man appeared. His eyes sparkled his victory. His route the only one up.

Unless I jumped.

Panicked, I peered down again. From here, it was a drop to the metal walkway, but others were already running to reach it. I had no hope. Still, I couldn't stay.

Flipping my legs over, I lowered myself to my fingertips then let go, my knees catching on the stubbled exterior of the captain's hut before I landed hard on the metal walkway. The pain barely registered. Had to move.

I took off down and away, a thud behind me telling me the man was close behind. Ahead, two approached from the other end of the suspended floor, both huge, one so bear-like I felt like I was in a twisted fairy tale. Between us, another set of steps descended. I made a break for it, descending with a squeak of fear right as one made a grab for me.

There were too many of them. This was too much. My heart couldn't take it.

I hit the concrete floor of the warehouse and sprinted.

Five metres, ten.

A body slammed into mine. I fell hard, the man landing over me with a grunt of victory.

The arm with the snake tattoo braced me, the man's body pressing mine down to the rough surface. His cock pushed against my ass.

Down here, the smell of sweat and sex dominated. The floor was cold in the hot night. He was going to take me right here, just like the others were having sex not twenty feet away, still joined.

"No, don't, please," I gritted out.

"Fucking hell, baby. I love the way you beg," Snake-Tattoo answered, his mouth above my ear.

I shuddered in revulsion and bucked him. It did nothing, the control he had over me complete. His hand twisted into the straps of my dress then ripped, tearing the material at the seams.

"Why bother with the underwear?" he grunted.

"I'm not supposed to be—" I started.

At the same moment, my attacker surged, swiping a fist at another man whose naked, hairy feet came into view. I jolted with their fight, a puppet on a string, then the man lifted from me to defend his prize just like the first guy had done. Seizing the opportunity, I scuttled back, my dress falling away as scraps.

In only my underwear, I shot my gaze to Snake-Tattoo brawling with two men. Down the warehouse, the pack reformed. They'd seen us. Regrouped. Started our way.

My heart sank, all hope evaporating. I was going to be torn in two.

"No!" a furious shout came.

I spun around on my knees, the rough concrete cutting

into my skin.

A man with dark-blond hair burst from the corridor I'd used. The one with the exit that was supposedly locked until this was all over. He put his head down and drove his limbs hard, every muscle taut, fury in his eyes and his skeleton mask doing nothing to hide pure anger.

The fight at my back paused.

The bigger of the men swore. "What the hell?"

He groaned as Snake-Tattoo threw another fist at his ugly face, and I readied to run. But that tattooed arm was around my throat and I was hauled up, my back to his bare chest.

With a wrench, my bra was ripped down me and torn away so my breasts were exposed. The bear man shot out a punch, and Snake-Guy stumbled, but he didn't lose his grip on me.

Instead, he grappled with his jeans, opening them, his knuckles grazing the small of my back. His dick prodded me. A fast wrench shredded my underwear.

"No," I screamed.

Another body slammed into his, taking us both out. I dropped to my hands and knees, naked, and agog at the fighter carving through the mob, the blond man who'd appeared from nowhere. He smacked a punch into the bear's gut, doubling him over, then wheeled around, a wild man defending me. An animal but cold and exacting.

Snake-Guy stumbled and backed away. I expected him to square up, but he went still, his muscle tension dropping. As if fear had claimed him, as if facing off with a bigger predator than he could handle.

Abruptly, he turned and ran.

The peace didn't last. Another man rushed in with a

scream of fury but couldn't dodge a stunning series of hits. He dropped with a low groan and didn't get up. A third went down the same way.

Around me, bodies slumped.

Then *he* was in front of me, that blond hair in his eyes and blood smeared and spattered on his skin, over the bruise at his shoulder. His fervent gaze took me in, and my recognition was complete.

Arran. Here. The lying gang leader saving me against the odds.

I breathed for what felt like the first time in an hour.

The respite couldn't last. The rest of the contestants fast approached, their shouts and footfalls blending back into my consciousness.

Arran noticed, too.

Without pause, he grabbed me by the waist. Manhandled me onto my back once again. He forced his body between my thighs, spreading my legs wide around him.

His gaze returned to mine. Held it. He got himself into position and wrestled his jeans, then for some unknown reason, paused to tug down his mask so I could see his treacherous mouth.

What the—?

One thrust of his hips, and he fucked straight into me.

His dick speared my flesh, my body doing the unthinkable, so wet and ready to accept his that an uncontrolled moan slipped from my lips.

I pulsed around his thick intrusion.

Like that, the game was up.

10

Genevieve

Still inside me, Arran lifted and carried me, his arms supporting me entirely else I'd have fallen. Down the corridor, the door opened and voices followed. Cheers of congratulations raised as we passed, and I sensed the weight and crawl of their gazes on my naked skin.

Unbearable.

I dropped my head to his shoulder and closed my eyes, my humiliation absolute.

Then we were outside in the cooler night air. I peeked at Arran's car, driver's-side door open and the engine on.

He rounded it to pop the passenger door then placed me down on the seat. For a moment, he stood over me, jaw tight. His dick pulsed, and he swore then jerked back his hips to slide out.

I gasped, my pinnacle of upset and ecstasy so strange that I couldn't get control of my mind. Then I snapped my knees closed and cringed into the seat, too aware of the faces looking on.

A car next to ours had the rear doors open and a

uniformed driver waiting alongside. Another cheer went up as the huge man carried the red-haired woman from the basement entrance. Naked, she sobbed in his arms, holding on to him like he was her saviour.

He carried her straight to the car, his driver shutting them in. I caught her smile up at her man right as the door slid closed, her expression one of rapture and need. His whispered words that appeared like absolute admiration, pride in his eyes.

They appeared so happy together. The fit so perfect.

Material hit me. I blinked my attention from the other car and found a t-shirt on my chest.

Arran slammed my door then got in the other side, revving the engine to send the crowd in the car park running from our path. "Put that on before I lose my fucking mind."

In shock, I fumbled to tug the oversized t-shirt over my head, concealing my naked body. Automatically, I clipped in my seat belt.

"Are you taking me home?"

He laughed in disbelief and drove out, barely pausing at the exit to check for traffic. Unlike me, he was bare-chested still, though luckily his jeans were done up once more. "No, I'm not. You know that isn't possible."

"I don't know anything."

"We need to leave the city. It's a rule for the first week."

"A rule? Of what?"

Arran breathed through his nose and gripped the steering wheel as if it were a throat in need of strangling. "Drop the act, for fuck's sake. Don't tell me you didn't plan this all out. You knew exactly what you were doing."

Outrage cost me some of my mind. "Are you kidding? You think I'd voluntarily put myself into that... That..."

He worked his jaw. "That's exactly what I'm saying because it's a fact."

Breathless, I stared. It took a long moment until I could speak. "It isn't. I didn't."

"You walk out in front of my car, come to my club to sell your body after you gave me your judgement on sex workers, implying you'd do anything but their job, then the very next night, you waltz straight into my event."

"I didn't know your sexual assault night was happening!"

"Fucking liar. If you didn't know the details from elsewhere, you were told about it on your tour."

Silence played out. Terrible, fractured, empty space. The car punched into the dark night, the route he'd set taking us over the bridge to the north and out of town. Scottish territory.

When I found my words, my voice shook. "You really believe I wanted to get attacked?"

"Everyone who signs up knows the deal."

"I didn't sign anything."

"No, because you purposefully snuck in and pretended to be someone else."

I shrank down, my world still spinning. The one thing I had to do was get him to believe me. After all that had gone down, my fear, the hot sex, and the chilling violence, I needed him to accept my version of events. "Yes, I snuck in, but I only wanted to be in the club, not to take part in that."

"What possible reason could you have for sneaking

around my club?" He swore again and made a fist on top of the steering wheel. "Actually, don't answer that. I don't care. I only have one question for you."

I waited, twisted horror still infecting me.

"Were you a virgin until I fucked you?"

"No," I breathed.

His lip curled in strong emotion. "I was."

*S*everal hours later, I jerked awake from a fitful sleep, the car slowing, the change in the engine sound bringing me to consciousness.

After Arran's ridiculous claim, I'd shut down. Turned away from him and watched the night. We'd crossed the Queensferry Bridge after circling Edinburgh, and bright city streets had changed to dark countryside. Then I'd passed out and lost track of where we'd ended up.

A long driveway led to a huge mansion, lights outside showing the extent of the palatial building.

"What is this place?" I asked.

Arran didn't answer, driving on to park the car beside a wide garage. He climbed out then came to my door. "Get out."

I shivered and wrapped my arms around myself, stepping out to the cool of the predawn, the gravel smooth under my soles. "Are you going to leave me here? Whose place is it?"

"Who the fuck goes there?" A figure stepped out of the shadows of the house. He crossed the gravel but stopped dead. "Arran?"

Then he was running, slamming into the man who'd brought me here with a sound of happiness. He spun him around, peering at Arran's face. "The fuck? Ye don't call, ye don't write. Now ye show up in the middle of the night barefoot, bloodied, and half-naked. With a woman? Ho-lee-shite. The lasses are going to lose their minds."

Arran's feet were bare like mine. He'd driven like that for hours.

Arran hugged him then backed off. "We needed a place to go for a few days. Is it okay to crash here?"

"Do ye even need to ask? Those rooms are yours for good—no one else has used them since we last saw your face, except maybe the kids. What's going on? Are ye in trouble?"

Arran's gaze slid to me, and his friend's followed. I cringed under the scrutiny, too aware of the oddness of the situation and how I was only wearing a t-shirt, though fortunately one that covered my ass.

"We just needed somewhere to go," Arran muttered.

The second man rubbed his hand over his dark hair. He looked about Arran's age, late twenties, and had a happy, chilled-out expression that made him feel infinitely less dangerous than the crew at Arran's club.

In his hand, something sparked. A lighter? My opinion revised fast.

"Let's get inside. You've been driving a while, aye? Probably need a drink." The man changed tack.

He started walking, and I trailed after. I had no choice. A quick glance around showed only pitch-black countryside beyond the expanse of lawn, no other houses to be seen. Wherever this was, it was intensely private. Plus neither man was trying to force me, for a nice change.

"I'm Jamieson, as my boy's too rude to introduce me. Welcome to the Great House. This is my home. Well, mine and my family's. You're very welcome..."

"Genevieve," Arran said for me.

Jamieson laughed and shook his head, climbing the mansion's shallow steps. "Like I said, the lasses are going to lose their minds over ye."

We entered a huge hall with a marble floor and a staircase that swept up to the next floor. A woman held the banister, peering down, her long blonde hair in a thick ponytail and her pyjamas with little hearts on.

"Who is it?" she asked, her accent English. Then her eyes widened. "Arran? God, are you okay? Where's your shirt?"

"He brought a girl, similarly underdressed," Jamieson quipped.

The woman gawked. Apparently I was the star of the show.

"Give me a minute and I'll explain," Arran said.

Without a word, he took my upper arm and towed me along with him, down the unlit hall to the right. We turned a corner, and I wrenched from his grip.

"I can walk by myself."

"But can I trust you not to run or go where you aren't supposed to? This is my friends' home. There are children."

"What am I, a monster as well as a sneak?"

We reached a room, and he propelled me inside the dark space.

"That remains to be seen. For now, I'm playing captor just the same as you trapped me. The windows are burglar-proof so don't try breaking out, it'll piss me off if I have to replace one. You're perfectly safe here, so don't fucking scream."

I didn't have a second to react. The door was closed, and a click indicated he'd locked me in.

11

Arran

Jamieson and his brother, Camden, waited in the entry hall.

"Christ, man. Long time no see." Camden dealt out the same hard hug his brother had, the low light not concealing the deep scar that scored one side of his face.

In most ways, the brothers were very similar, black hair, blue eyes, and all brought up on the streets of Scotland. Their home gave zero clue to them as people. None of them had grown up here.

That violence in them? Exactly what I needed right now, alongside sanctuary.

I rubbed the back of my neck. "I shouldn't have stayed away so long."

"Aye, that's a fact," Jamieson griped. "It's been...what, two years? If we didnae drive south, your face would be a fucking mystery."

Other than Shade, Alisha, and Convict, I trusted and cared about few. This family of four brothers, their lasses, and their increasing number of kids was my exception.

We'd lived through a nightmare situation together, and it'd forged a bond that could never be broken, even if I kept my distance at times.

The fact was, after the shitshow of our past, they'd got on with rebuilding their lives and making a future. Babies, marriage, jobs. It was all working out. My pain was unending. It would never be over. I wouldn't fall in love and settle down. As much as they were my family, coming here hurt as much as it healed. I was better off staying away.

Footsteps came from the stairs, and Summer carefully descended, a child now on her hip and items clutched in her other hand. Jamieson jogged up to meet her, taking the baby, their youngest.

Summer came to me and gave me a quick hug, handing me the bundle. "I fetched you some clothes, and this one woke up. Here, take this. Also, you're an asshole for staying away."

Muttering an apology, I took the plain t-shirt, socks, and trainers. Once, years ago, she and I had been roles reversed, and I'd helped her flee.

A lump lodged in my throat. I ducked to dress, hiding my face. Only this evening, when I'd heard the update on the murdered woman, I'd thought about coming here. They'd know why it mattered to me. They'd help work out if I was imagining ghosts or if my concerns were real.

Then the situation with Genevieve had taken over, and that was a clusterfuck on top of everything else. Another piece of advice required.

Over all of it, I just wanted a family.

Jamieson curled an arm around my shoulders. "Something tells me we're going to need a drink. Into the bar with ye."

Summer took the fussing baby back, and Jamieson kissed her, murmuring a quiet word, then the woman headed back upstairs. With the two brothers, I moved through a big pair of double doors and into the great hall. A decade ago, this had been a broken, part-burned wreck. Jamieson's work, the pyromaniac. They'd rebuilt and made it into a family space with groups of sofas and chairs, a kids' soft play area, and a bar in one corner. A chill-out zone with high stained-glass windows that was perfect for indoor hanging out when the Scottish weather came in. Which was often.

At the bar, Jamieson poured us all two fingers of brandy and brought the drinks to our table.

I downed mine then pressed the glass to my forehead. "I might need the bottle."

"That bad, aye?" Camden leapt up and claimed the brandy, giving me a refill. "Talk to us. If we need it, I can get Sin and Struan back by morning."

The two older brothers were off site, then.

"A woman was killed a couple of days ago, and I think it was a message to me. I also might be going insane. Help me judge."

"Walk us through it," Camden requested.

I shared the details. Visiting Genevieve, the sex worker murdered on her road not long after I left, the particulars of the killing. A haunted expression came over both of them.

I knew all of us were picturing the first dead body we'd seen that fitted that description. That look shifted to sympathy, and I hated it.

"Ye think it's to do with your ma," Jamieson breathed.

I downed the second glass. "Tell me it isn't."

"Yeah, I don't believe in coincidences," he went on. "That's a loud and clear pattern. The woman they chose, the method, the fact you'd been right fucking there. When was the last sex worker killed in your town? When has one ever had her throat cut and her body stripped? Handcuffs, a gag. Fucking hell."

Camden rested his forearms on his knees, his forehead lined in thought. "How many people know about Audrey?"

I pictured blood. A body on the floor that was Audrey, my mother. A showdown with the man who'd tried to break me over and over and who'd finally succeeded. "Everyone in that damn room ten years ago."

"Us, our fathers, a lawyer. Outside of that, no one else knows what she was to ye," Camden said.

"I screamed out that she was my mother. It's on a recording. I've never told anyone since, but that's—" My throat choked, and I tried again. "I've never mentioned her name to a single person, but the cops know. My father's long list of convictions included her murder. Over the course of a decade, that won't have been kept quiet."

Camden heaved a heavy breath. "Then we'll assume anyone in the police knows, or could've passed that information along, which means it could be widespread. Even playing devil's advocate and thinking this new murder might be some random act of terror, it'll pay to work this through. Who would target ye like that? Has anything else happened to make ye think you're drawing heat?"

Slumping back in the seat, I rubbed the space between my eyes and let exhaustion settle. "Nothing specific. There are a dozen men who'd kill me given half the chance, maybe twice that for cash. Some women, too.

Considering what I do, and the role I carved out in the city, I'm valuable dead and out of their way. I haven't had a second to even think through the rest of it, That's why I'm here. I just needed..."

"A sense check?" Camden suggested.

"That. And a place to take Genevieve."

The brothers eyed me, curiosity obvious. But they waited.

"She might have answers. When I went to her place, she saw someone she was afraid of. This was right before the murder. She lives opposite where it happened."

"Ye kidnapped her to question her on it?" Camden's eyes bugged out.

"That, and the fact I claimed her this evening. She was in the game."

And in every second since, I'd wanted her with a desperation that was only growing stronger.

The brothers took one look at each other, and Camden opened his mouth to voice the first question of what I knew would be many.

I beat him to the punch. "I fucked her. Which means I broke my vow. I need your help in paying penance." No need to admit it was a single thrust. That alone went against all I'd promised and at the same time was nowhere near enough.

Camden swore, and Jamieson flexed a fist as if anticipating what I needed from him. He'd do as I asked. The youngest and wildest of the family had taught me how to fight, taking time to make sure I wasn't going to die from the company I was keeping after my world had fallen apart.

"We going now?" he asked.

Adrenaline soaked me. I stood, and he did, too, gaze lowered and his mouth curved in the delight of sparring.

Unlike when we'd been younger, I wasn't going to fight back. I wanted the pain. The bruises on my skin to show Audrey I repented. To show Genevieve what she'd done.

It still wouldn't be enough.

No amount of hits would undo the wrong.

I paced a few feet away, Jamieson following, then rounded on him. "Don't go easy—"

He slammed a punch into my jaw. I rocked back on my heels but absorbed it, the explosion of pain exactly what I'd asked for. Behind me, Camden swore, never a fighter unless he had to be, but my focus stayed on his brother.

"Again," I yelled.

If he could take me down, I'd be fucking thankful of the darkness.

12

Genevieve

When I was little, I used to force myself to endure the dark. I'd suffer nightmares and would wake with a racing heart, pure terror gripping me, but I'd never go to my mother because she worked so hard and was always exhausted. Instead, I'd play games to get my brain to settle from the panic.

An alphabet game was my favourite. I'd pick a topic, like animals or food, then go from A to Z, naming one for each letter.

I still did it now, my unfortunate caffeine addiction messing with my sleep. But tonight, my mind wouldn't supply. I'd get six letters in then would find myself back in the basement of the warehouse, poised to be attacked by one of the violent strangers. Or with Cherry on the steps of the church, a blade flashing towards her.

I'd had a terrifying evening, but it could've been so much worse.

Even with the comparison, I was stuck here with no phone, clothes, or anything, with just the will of Arran to decide what was to happen to me. Damn me for not listening to his staff member as she'd walked me back to the office. I might've had a clue what was going to happen next with his game and the rules.

Silence played out through the rooms. I'd taken a shower, lights off, and climbed into bed naked, not wanting to put back on the t-shirt that was dirty with dried blood. Nor had I wanted to snoop in drawers. My fingers had been well and truly burned.

In the room beyond the bedroom, the door clicked.

"It's me," Arran said into the dark.

It had been a couple of hours since he'd locked me in. He appeared in the doorway. "Awake?"

"Yep," I squeaked.

"Why are the lights off?"

Because fear kept me alive. Because it meant I wasn't sitting here in a spotlight where anyone could see me. I didn't answer, and he tried again.

"Hungry?"

I shook my head, then said my answer out loud. "No."

"Is there anything you need? If not, I'll take a shower."

I repeated my *no*, and he disappeared into the bathroom. I gave it a few seconds then leapt from the bed and darted out of the room to the exit. The handle moved, but the door stayed locked. My heart sank. I returned to bed.

Water ran in the room next door, and I tried hard not to picture Arran's naked body. But now I'd seen almost all of it, since he'd been inside me, it was a losing battle.

Eventually, the water stopped, and he emerged back into the bedroom, naked and with the faint dawn light outlining him in silver. He scrubbed himself down with a towel, draped it over a chair, then climbed into bed next to me.

I tugged the sheets to my throat. "What are you doing?"

Arran thumped a pillow into shape then dropped down heavily. "Since you're playing ignorant about the rules, I'll remind you of the most relevant. We're stuck together. For the first week, we barely leave each other's side. We sleep together and eat together."

"You'll sleep in my bed?"

"It's my bed, and aye, I will." He waited a beat, then his tone darkened. "And we fuck, daily."

My heart thumped. "You'd force yourself on me again?"

A rush of bedclothes and he was over me, his forehead to mine, that frustration back in spades. Sweet brandy laced his breath, but it wasn't that which stole my focus.

Even in the dark, bruises shone on his face, his eye swelling shut and his lip cut and thick.

"Force you? When did I do that the first time? You forced me by the shit you pulled. And don't forget, in my fucking office, you gave me consent. You agreed to fuck me whenever I wanted, then you put yourself into a position where I had to oblige. So do me the courtesy of dropping the fake shock."

Against my body, he was hard, his dick pinned between us.

Desire rushed and pooled at my core.

"Are you going to do it now?" I whispered.

Arran inched back. Swallowed, his Adam's apple bobbing, just visible in the dark. Propped on his elbow, he watched me, some of the desperation in him easing. "We already did tonight, so you're safe. Or maybe that's me."

Cautiously, I rolled to face him, less afraid than I had the right to be. "What happened to your face?"

"Irrelevant. A woman was killed on your street the night I visited your flat."

I recoiled, ice cold suddenly despite the warm room. A thought rose, something I hadn't considered. Arran had been there the night Cherry died. Cherry was a sex worker, though she wasn't employed by him. Was her murder revenge for working outside of his cartel? God, was I here because I was a potential witness and he needed to stop me from talking?

The shock of the events of the past few days twisted into a terrible conclusion. "Was it you?"

"Was what me?"

"Did you kill her?"

Anger flashed over his features, swift and cold. Something else, too. It looked like hurt. "No, I didn't. I don't hurt women."

My mouth fell open. I was playing with fire again, but I couldn't stop. "Your whole life is set up around hurting women. Are you joking?"

Through gritted teeth, he made his answer. "I'm tired, and likely to act irrationally, so I'm going the fuck to sleep. Tomorrow, I'll ask you again, and you'll answer me. Don't bother trying to leave. I locked the door."

He turned his back. In a minute, he was out cold, and I stared into the dark room, my spiralling thoughts settling into better logic.

If he had been the murderer, he would hardly confess it to me. But a feeling in my gut told me I was way off the mark, even considering his lifestyle and the part of his empire that I'd seen.

Yet someone had murdered her. The same evening Arran was talking about, I'd seen Don drive by. I'd assumed he was there for me, and perhaps he had been, but he could've moved on to taking out his anger on the next warm body. Also, Cherry had mentioned some clients she was expecting to see. That was a starting place to rack my brain over. And to bury the oddest sense of guilt from accusing the gang leader at my side.

Eventually, sleep claimed me as well.

I woke to Arran's heavy arm curling over me. He grumbled and tugged me closer, burying his face in my hair, though his breathing stayed slow and deep, the undoubted pain from his injuries not waking him. I could've extracted myself, but I needed a hug. Even if it was from him.

When I woke the next time, daylight was fading around the shutters, night returning once again. I'd slept the day away. The bed beside me was empty, but noise and light from the other room told me my kidnapper wasn't far away.

He appeared in the doorway, thankfully dressed, and snapped on a lamp, a tray in his hand. His bruises had worsened, dark and shiny. "You slept hard."

"You slept mostly on me," I retorted and sat up, keeping the sheet tightly wrapped around my naked body.

He snorted, then brought the tray over. The scent of bacon reached me, and my stomach rumbled. The meal he offered was a bacon sandwich, a mug of coffee alongside.

"Sorry about what I said last night," I mumbled. Better to keep him sweet than make even more of an enemy.

Arran's expression remained neutral, but he nodded

once. "Thank you. Now eat."

Hunger took control of me, and I accepted the tray, chugging the hot coffee first before tearing into the sandwich. If he was poisoning me, I'd take the risk.

The gangster rumbled a laugh and settled in an armchair by the bed. "Couldn't make it iced coffee for you, but I figured that would be good enough."

I sent him an appreciative half-smile around the last mouthful, sitting back to sip the coffee in dizzying delight. He'd even added some kind of syrup, just a smidge, as I liked.

"You take good care of your prisoners."

He lowered his gaze. "You're the one who tied herself to me, so you need to be wherever I am, and vice versa. Also I can't trust you not to roam my friends' house unguarded. That's why I locked the door."

"Screw your rules." I wrinkled my nose. "What if I don't follow them?"

"I intend to, so you can either make it really easy, or very hard."

His gaze held mine. Heat zapped through me. There was something magnetic about this man. A draw towards him that wouldn't break. If I'd caught a tiny crush from him coming to my flat, his actions on the floor of the warehouse had boosted that to the stratosphere.

I hated him, but my craven, traitorous body didn't get the memo.

I swallowed. "Talk me through them. The rules, I mean."

"The game is a love match. The people who enter it are looking for something different to normal dating."

"Wow," I drawled. "Romantic."

"It is. Intensely so. Love like no other, for those involved. Once the lucky ones are paired up, they live together for four weeks. Share their lives completely. In the first week, they can't be apart for more than two hours. That eases as time goes on."

I widened my eyes. "I'm your prisoner for a month?"

My missing father, the eviction notice, the fact I couldn't text my brother to let him know where I was. It all crammed forward in my mind.

Arran continued, ignorant of my turmoil. "The couple eats together, sleeps together, and fucks every day. It's encouraged to go at it multiple times, but the commitment is once. Still pretending you don't know any of this?"

Hot emotion brewed in me. Jamming my fingers into my hair, I unsettled the tray still on my lap so the plate clattered. "I told you I didn't. I wasn't there to trap you, you thug. Why would I want to be hunted like that?"

Arran reached out a long arm and claimed the tray, setting it on a side table, the disbelief in his expression switching to something new. "Thug?"

"Gangster, liar, whatever you want to call yourself."

"I'm none of those things, but that's nice judgement from a sneak thief like you. Need I remind you that you stole that place in the game from a real contestant? Something my team is going to have to play down, though I have no fucking clue how we're going to explain my presence there."

Some of the fire went out of me. I didn't want to believe anything he said, but he had been so consistent it felt genuine.

"I assumed taking part was a perk of the job," I said

with a sniff.

"That's where you're wrong—I'm not interested in love. We run it for contestants only, and the people who pay to watch."

Watch? The camera above me. The crowd of people cheering outside, celebrating. Something inside me curled up and died. "People saw me?"

Arran nodded. "It's live streamed to screens in the club. A limited number of vetted people get to observe."

God, the humiliation. I set down my precious coffee and turned away from him, curling up under the sheet. I'd known there would be someone behind the camera, but I figured it would be a security team, perhaps. Not paying customers.

"Please can you get rid of the footage?" I begged, not looking his way. "If my family ever saw that, I'd never be able to face them again."

"Your family will never see it. It isn't recorded, and we take all electronics from the watchers. That voyeur side of it is a pure moneymaker for the club as well as for the thrill of the people taking part. It validates what they've done and the choice they made to have it witnessed."

I hugged my knees. The other women who'd taken part were enthusiastic beyond measure. They would have known all of this in advance. Voluntarily put themselves forward for it. I didn't want to admit it, but imagining those final scenes with Arran fighting off the men who hurt me then entered me on the floor sent waves of fresh and insistent desire through my nervous system.

My body cried out for him. Wet pooled at my core, and I ached to be filled again.

He was everything I should loathe, and in the same

heartbeat, I'd never wanted anyone more.

"Why do people do it?" I whispered.

"Like I said, they want to fall in love through a different means than polite dating. Both parties make promises including to uphold the agreement of staying together. The men promise financial support, and we tie them to that. Outside of that, the claiming is...binding. The savagery of it creates a bond like nothing else."

"What do the women promise?"

"Other than to be healthy and willing, they're the prize. They get to be adored and respected. They also promise faithfulness. Love. Children, if both want them. The woman can work or make a home, the choice is hers. This is modern dual-ownership. However their relationship operates after the four weeks is up is up to them, but out of the six times I've run this, no couple ever broke apart."

Six times five equalled maybe thirty couples forged by this brutal method. I'd taken that from Natasha, the woman whose place I'd stolen. For the first time, a sense of disquiet slunk over me. I didn't like it. Nothing about this had been planned. Nor did I want the terms his game offered.

"I wish you'd just let me go."

"And I wish you'd never got us into this situation, but it is what it is."

I twisted to face him. "You're the one making this decision. You can just say no. Fuck your damn rules. I have people who are going to miss me. They'll report me gone. What will you do then?"

"My reputation is built on my word, so no, I can't fuck my rules. There are a lot of people who work for me, a lot of eyes and ears watching us who'll spot a lie a mile off. If

I failed to uphold my own fucking decree, we'll both be back in that space. Understand?"

"Back inside that basement? You wouldn't dare."

"Entering the game is a commitment. Winning a privilege. If those winners disrespect it, they'll be dragged back in by the people who watched and celebrated them. That's the consequence. Regarding your family," he checked his phone, "your father, Adam Walker, and your brother, Riordan Jones, tell them where you are. I'm not stopping you."

I made a sound of disbelief. Not only was this getting worse by the second, but he'd done a background check on me. The nerve. "I don't have my phone. Or my bag or keys. Not even a single scrap to wear. Everything got left in a locker in the warehouse or torn off me."

Arran's gaze dropped from my face to my body. In my haste to yell at him, I'd let the sheet slip. Bared my breasts.

For a moment, neither of us moved. His chest rose and fell, and that insane claim he'd made of being a virgin until yesterday slammed into my head.

Another piece of information I refused to believe.

With obvious difficulty, he tore his focus away. Produced his phone from his pocket and tossed it to the mattress. "I'll get your possessions retrieved and delivered here. In the meantime, call your family. Just be aware that all communications are monitored, so I'll know if you attempt to give up your location or sell me out."

More slowly, I covered myself, the weirdest urge in me to do the opposite and throw back the sheet. "I can wait."

There was so much left to say, and so many questions I had, but everything faded behind the rising wall of lust. Every part of me was infected by it, the very air in the room heavy with need. I didn't know where it was coming from, but it was getting harder to ignore. Maybe he had drugged me after all.

"How do we handle the once-a-day thing?" I found myself saying. "Please don't tell me we have to film it as proof for your sick audience."

The gang leader rolled his bulky shoulders, his muscles flexing under his tight black t-shirt. "No. It'll be taken at our word, but once we go back, anyone who's interested will be able to look at us and know. Considering the idea of sex is so repulsive, we can resort to what I did in the club last night."

He'd entered me but that was all. No completion.

The strangest sense of disappointment sank through me. I wanted him to knock me onto my back, force my legs open, and fill the gap with his big body. Line up, fuck into me, make me scream. I wanted his face between my thighs. His mouth on mine after so I could taste us. It was a fast and shocking fantasy I'd never confess. I wasn't his to claim.

"What if we don't?" I asked.

Arran's gaze burned into me. "I break my word to my club and to all those who trust me. I'd lose my reputation. An unacceptable price. To safeguard that, I'm prepared to barter for your willingness."

He could lie about it, but my brain got stuck on a word. Barter? Like I was a sex worker to be managed.

A flash of anger consumed me again, riding the wave of my lust. I should challenge him more but I *wanted* this. With no sense in my head, I threw back the sheet and bared myself to him. "The first one's on me. Do what you need to do."

Arran stilled. A snake about to strike. Then he stood, and my gaze sank to where his dick tented his grey sweatpants. Either he'd been hard this whole time or he held the record for the world's fastest erection.

But oh God, the need in his eyes drove mine all the higher.

He closed in. I expected him to kneel on the bed, but something battled in his expression, and the gangster encircled my wrist with his hand and pulled me to my feet. Turning me, he shoved me against the wall so I had to press my face to the cool plaster. A rush of material and he was right there, his dick spreading my wet heat without warning but not going inside. My eyes closed by themselves, my nipples hardening, and my toes pressing up automatically as if to get into a better position for him.

Holding my hip, Arran crowded me from behind, his body hot and so much bigger than mine, and his other arm coming around to clamp me to him.

With one jerk of his hips, he filled me.

I cried out, instant ecstasy claiming my senses. My world shrank to the intrusion. Never had sex felt like this. The very first thrust having me almost on the edge of an orgasm.

I shuddered. There was nothing I wanted more than for him to finish what he'd started. What I'd started. Whatever. I needed him to make me feel good after a weekend of everything being messed up.

Around his rigid shaft, I throbbed, earning an answering pulse that thickened him all the more. Arran ducked his mouth to my neck. He kissed my skin. An open-mouthed, hot suck of my flesh. Then he stopped. Breathed. A predator over my shoulder.

"What do you want from me?" he asked.

I couldn't answer. Words were too hard to form.

The base of his dick stretched me so well.

"Why did you target me? Who paid you, or were you threatened into doing it?"

"None of that," I finally breathed.

He set both hands flat to the wall either side of my head, took another heavy breath, and abruptly pushed away, withdrawing with a grunt that sounded like pain.

Bereft, I peered around, tracking his exit from the room. He yanked the inner doors closed behind him.

Then I staggered back to bed, put my hand to the place we'd been joined, and sank two fingers inside me, unwilling to give up the feeling of everything he'd done, and refused, to my body.

13

Genevieve

It was an hour before Arran returned, his previous calm restored. "Get dressed. I'll take you to meet my family."

I curled my knees underneath me. "Suddenly you trust me?"

"Not for a second, but something happened that forced my hand." He crossed to a chair and collected a pile of clothes from the seat.

I blinked at it. "That was there all along? Why didn't you tell me?"

"Perhaps I prefer you sitting around naked."

He left me to get dressed, and I pulled on the shorts that must've come from one of the women who lived here and a t-shirt that was a little too big and needed tying into a knot at my waist. I took a minute in the bathroom to comb out my hair and brush my teeth using supplies from a visitor's pack. There was no kind of hair product or tie, which was a pity because my shower yesterday had left my hair an unfortunate frizzy mess. Not the best first impression, then again I'd showed up last night in just a man's t-shirt and spattered with blood.

It spoke volumes that his friends hadn't been fazed.

Outside the bedroom, Arran waited in the living room. The house was clearly centuries old, but the furniture more modern, like someone had redecorated recently and gone with what they preferred over the style of the house. I liked it. I also liked the image of the powerful man on a cream couch, taking up all the space.

His gaze settled on me. Desire curled in my belly once again. My need for him was getting stronger, no matter my intention to deny it.

Out in the wide hallway, with a marble floor and oil paintings here and there, we walked together. Last night, I'd barely noticed the detail. Now, I soaked it all in.

"What do you mean that something forced your hand?" I asked.

"You'll see."

Infuriating man. "How do you know the people who live here?" I tried. "Last night you called them your friends. Then earlier you said family."

"Found family, not blood. I don't have any family by DNA left."

"What happened to your parents?"

He shot me a look. "What happened to your mother?"

I shut my mouth. Point taken—we weren't friends. I didn't need to know his emotional baggage, and there was no reason to trust him with mine. Even if his check on me was tantamount to snooping.

Changing the subject, I moved on to the next question on my list. "One thing I don't get about last night and the game. How did you know I was in there?"

We took a corner, the echoing entranceway ahead. Thankfully empty. For some reason, nerves flew as butterflies in my belly.

"The real Natasha showed up, and the doorman called me. I was offsite, but I checked the cameras and saw you."

I pieced over that. He hadn't been watching, then. "Why did you come for me? Why not just leave me to the fight?"

"I was already planning to find you. There was something I needed you for."

"Beyond warming your bed?"

He gave a short laugh. "Is that what you're doing?"

If he'd wanted me for something, it had to be regarding Cherry, then. I joined the dots, some strange disappointment forming that it wasn't because he'd liked me and knew I shouldn't have been in there.

But the version of Arran I'd crushed on for a whole minute had nothing in common with the reality of him.

The doors to the entranceway ahead opened with a crash, and a petite woman appeared. She swung her gaze around and sighted us. "Holy shite, Arran. Summer said ye were back."

She sprinted and leapt for him, enclosing him in a full-body hug, her hair a wealth of wild black curls, and her features exquisite with her perfect little upturned nose and pouty red lips. I'd never seen anyone so beautiful. Young, too. She couldn't have been more than nineteen.

Arran absorbed the hit with a smile. He banded his arms around her. "Hey, Cass."

They fitted together so easily.

Pure and uncomfortable envy made its presence

known in my heart.

Beaming, the woman hopped down, turning her attention to me. "Oh my God. Not only is Arran home but he brings a girl. That boy is an ignorant pig man for staying away for so long." She swept a look up and down me with unhidden interest, her rolling Scottish accent so pretty. "Whereas ye, my new friend, are a sight for sore eyes. Welcome to our home."

The way she spoke to him was the same as I did to Riordan. My jealousy simmered.

"Did ye do that to his face?" She jacked a thumb at Arran.

He chuffed a laugh. "She wishes. It's courtesy of your brother."

"Did your dumb arse just stand there, close your eyes, and let Jamieson hit ye?"

He shrugged. "Pretty much. Also entertaining that you knew it was him and not Camden."

She laughed then grinned at me, her curls bouncing with her movement. "Aren't men idiots? What's your name?"

"Genevieve."

"I'm Cassiopeia. Cassie for short. We both got hit with the fancy name stick."

"Your mother was a wild child, too, then?"

Her smile dimmed. "I wouldn't know."

A buzz sounded. Arran collected his phone from his pocket and scowled at the screen. "It's Shade. Cassie, can you take Genevieve to introduce her to the family? I need to talk to my crew. Explain what happened. None of them know where I am."

I chewed my lip. They would've seen him arrive at the warehouse, fast, judging on his parking when we'd come outside, then raid his game and speed off with one of the contestants. "Did I cause trouble?"

"In all areas of my life? Yes."

Cassie looked between us then slowly backed away. "I'll just grab my bag from the car. Be right back."

Alone with Arran, I folded my arms. "Can't you just say you decided to enter because you felt the animalistic need to claim me?"

"You forget, nobody from my team, including myself, can be involved. I'm going to badge it as a misunderstanding. The woman I'd been seeing accidentally put herself into the competition assuming I'd be participating. Spotting you on the cameras, I realised what happened and had to save you, losing my head once I was in there. With any luck, outsiders will accept the sentiment. It goes with the vibe. The possessive need. My crew is another matter."

I twisted a toe on the marble, an unpleasant memory rising. "What about your gang buddy who was in there?"

"No one from my crew enters the basement while the game is in play. Aside from me this time."

"That isn't true. One of the men from your office was hunting me. I recognised him."

"You're mistaken."

"I'm not. He wore a mask like everyone else and had black face paint across his eyes, but he'd also tried to paint out a tattoo on his wrist. It was a snake wrapped around his arm. The paint must've got smudged because the snake's head was there as clear as day, right above his wrist. I also recognised the way he held his head at an angle. He was taunting me, calling me 'little rabbit', and trying to get me to run."

Arran's focus hardened, no hint of humour to him now. "You're certain of what you saw," he stated more than asked.

"Entirely. I've no reason to make it up."

"I believe you." He yelled to the front door, "Cassie?"

I'd known him a matter of days but I was starting to pick up telltale signs of the man. He was stubborn, yet I'd just provided the evidence to counter a fact he believed, and he accepted me. Simple as that.

I tucked that information away for later use. He hadn't believed my side of events on why I was in the basement, but taking emotion out of it, I'd make another attempt.

Cassie skipped back inside, clutching a small suitcase. Arran went to her and murmured in her ear.

Then he looked at me. "I'll see you soon."

"Two hours or under," I remarked.

He strode away, not smiling at my quip.

I watched him go then turned to his friend. "Did he tell you not to trust me?"

She had no reason to answer, but her face lit. "Something like that. Don't leave her alone," she put on a deeper voice and an English accent, then linked her arm through mine and directed me up the stairs.

"Arran's keeping me prisoner here," I blurted.

"Ooh, what did ye do?"

"Nothing!"

"Feels unlikely, but go with that if it's working for ye. Or maybe it's him. All the men around here are a bit cray-cray. Jamieson chases Summer through the woods sometimes."

"That's awful." I kept pace with her on the stairs.

"Uh, no. It's a mutual thing. Not every couple is polite conversation and a sensible car. In case it needs stating, don't try to make a run for it. I might be small but I can crack a skull without breaking a nail." She waggled her head. "We have sensors and cameras around the grounds, too. You won't get far. Now come meet everyone."

Getting her alongside as an ally was a losing battle. This woman was as nuts as Arran. "How many of you live here?"

We reached the upstairs landing. Family pictures lined the walls, the frames not matching and the spacing unequal, but it added to the effect of the place being a home and not a museum.

Cassie drew my attention to a huge picture with a group of people in it. Rapid-fire, she pointed at faces and gave a name to each. "A whole load, but half of us aren't here. This is my oldest brother, Struan, and his wife, Thea, with their two kids. Thea's a social worker. She got pregnant while doing her degree, so Struan did a lot of the childcare, mostly which involved being outdoors. Their son, Wulf, is just like him. A wild boy. They have a daughter, too, named Selene. That's her at the front. She's a perfect angel. Next to them are Sin and Lottie. I call them my parents, though Sin's also my brother. All four of the men are."

A surprised laugh flew from my lips. "I have one brother. He's a pain in the ass. I can't imagine having four."

Cassie blew out a breath. "Ye get me then. The overprotective gene is no joke. Now, Lottie's birthed four babies, so far. I don't think she's done. Conall is the oldest of all the tribe. He's ten and ridiculously tall for his age. Then there's Llyr and Daphne, their girls, and Magnus was last. Lottie took a baby break to study for a couple of years, but she's just finished, and I bet there will be a new bairn soon."

My mind spun with all the names.

My tiny replacement captor wasn't done. "Everyone I've mentioned so far is away. Struan's mother got married this summer, and we all went to the wedding, then half of us stayed on and half returned. I jumped in my car the minute I heard Arran was here." She made jazz hands. "No kids, much more agile."

The rest she named quickly. The other two brothers were Camden and Jamieson. Camden's wife was Breeze, and they had a girl called Wren and a younger boy called Raven. Jamieson's wife was Summer, and they had Ember, Blaze, and Seraphina.

At the last grouping, Cassie grinned. "The youngest of my brothers has a not-so minor obsession with fire, hence the names of his children. He burned half of this place down, once."

"He did what?"

"Oh, it was needed. Our father, who luckily for everyone is dead now, did terrible things in this house. Fire is cleansing, no?"

She continued along the brightly lit hall, the sounds of family life filtering from further down the corridor. Overwhelmed, I followed more slowly and trailed my gaze over the rest of the pictures. Arran was in one, a much younger version with his arm slung around one of Cassie's brothers. His hair was shorter, almost military-level neat. He had it longer now, the strands in his eyes when he wore his mask.

The photograph below his caught my attention.

A toddler posed in rainbow dungarees, with scruffy fair hair and the biggest smile stretching chubby cheeks.

"Who's this?" I asked.

The answer was at the edge of my mind, but I couldn't quite reach it. I recognised the youngster, but from where?

Cassie trotted back. "Interesting that you picked that. That's someone Arran's trying to find. I've always called him the lost boy, though we don't actually know if it's a boy or a girl, and it's the only picture he's ever seen. He's been hunting for that child for ten years, hence the duplicate picture in his office that he shows everyone. Arran's mother..." She stopped her mouth. "I need to shut the hell up. Arran can tell you his story himself."

"How does he know the missing child?" I asked.

She wrinkled her nose, clearly not about to talk. "Ask him."

I hurried on. "I'm sure he won't mind you telling me."

Her perfect, arched eyebrows shot up. "Thought ye were a prisoner? Doesn't sound like he's ready to trust ye."

I sighed, losing the will to fight for this. I didn't care if he was looking for that child. They were undoubtedly better off without him. "Whatever. I'm not his girlfriend. I don't trust him either."

"Why not? He's the best."

I stared at her. "He runs a strip club and a brothel. He earns his money by hurting women."

Cassie's cheeks reddened. "How can you say that? Do you even know him at all?"

"Not really, and neither do his friends by the sounds of it." I wasn't going to lie to protect him.

"Wrong. We know everything about what he does and

why. We've even helped. All the shite you're assuming is wrong," she retorted.

My blood heated. "Is it? How? Arran runs women. He deals them out by the hour and lives off the profits of them opening their legs for any paying customer. It's not him on his back doing the work. He's exploiting vulnerable humans for money. In my world, that makes him a pimp. Not even in a good suit."

Down the hall, a door opened, and the woman who'd been on the steps last night popped her head out. "Thought I heard voices. Are you coming in?"

Cassie held up a pausing finger to her then turned back, those pretty features twisted in hurt. "In my world, it makes him their protector, and ye have no idea how important he is." She took a step, pint-sized but menacing. "You're wrong that he owns them. They own themselves. You're wrong that he lives off their income. Any cut he takes is only to pay for the warehouse where they work in safety. It also pays for housing, therapy, outreach, and the bribe he pays the police. And that judgement you're laying at the women's doors can fuck right off, too. My mother was a sex worker. Same for my brothers'. How's the view from that high horse now?"

I breathed through my nose, unwilling to believe her but at the same time seeing no reason for her to lie.

"Yeah, right. He's so noble. You're delusional," I finished. But it was weak.

"And you're not good enough for him, so I'm glad you're not dating. I'll have Summer take ye back to your room." Cassie shot me one final look of disgust then strode away, her heels stabbing the floor in hard clicks.

Good enough for him? I didn't even want him. And he definitely didn't want me. Except for the fact of the chemistry between us, I could almost have believed myself.

14

Arran

On the other end of the line, Shade gave me a rundown of the shitshow I'd left behind at the warehouse. The fallout of what Genevieve had done.

"Sixteen of the men didn't get a fair chance at the fifth woman, and so far, half have complained and are demanding to talk to you. My guess is that number will rise as the news filters out that you were in there. Want me to talk to them all?"

"No. I'll tackle it."

"It's cool if ye just want to disappear for a week. Convict's dying to help out more."

Convict, my third-in-command, was a problem. He'd been a friend since we'd met in a fight club many years ago, but he had the bad habit of getting caught by the police for easy-to-avoid shit and landing a prison sentence every year or two. He'd recently been freed again and had come straight to me, fighting to prove himself useful. He was relentless when given a goal. He didn't feel pain either so had never lost a fight. That was my reason for keeping him close: He scared the fuck out of others, and I didn't want him as my enemy.

I liked him, too. Recognised the unsettled nature of his soul.

Yet he'd disobeyed a direct order the minute he was sure Shade and I were out of the warehouse. He'd called Shade with news that could've been sent as a text. A calculation I'd dwelt on. Inside the basement, my bloodlust had blinded me to the identity of who I was laying my fists into, at least by the tattoo that had come uncovered, but somehow, I believed Genevieve as much as I trusted him.

I considered my words. "Convict is an issue. He needs to be found a task."

"Is that code for offing him?" Shade deadpanned.

I could've laughed, but all humour had left me. "No. Just kept away from the warehouse for a week or two."

"Consider it done." Shade scraped something metallic. A knife, knowing him. "By the way, Alisha is majorly pissed off with ye."

I entered the front door of the mansion, leaving the cool night behind. I'd gone out for air but needed a run. Anything to take the edge off the constant yearning I had for Genevieve.

He continued. "She told the girls that your arse was hers. Then ye went and pulled that stunt. Ye basically cheated on her then married yourself off in one go."

I hid a sigh. Alisha would get over it, and I had bigger fish to fry. "Thanks for the warning."

"I'll get on with gathering up your shite, then I'll hit the road and drive up there. See ye later."

Jogging upstairs, I made my way to the family room and stuck my head in. Cassie was alone in an armchair, a book open in front of her.

Her eyes narrowed, a squint of annoyance. "If you're after Little Miss Prissy, we locked her in your room."

For fuck's sake. "What happened?"

"She pissed me off. Why has she got such a low opinion of ye? What have ye told her?"

"Nothing."

"Ugh, that's the problem, then. Men are ridiculous." Cassie returned her focus to her book. "Probably should remedy that before she slurs your name to the whole world."

I heaved a sigh and went to go, but she called me back.

"When do I get to dance at your club?"

"How about never."

"Why not? It'd be fun."

"Fuck around and find out what happens, Cass."

She poked her tongue out, so I turned on my heel and headed back down a floor and around to the wing that contained my rooms. The key was in the door, and I unlocked it and entered.

Like last night, Genevieve had the lights out.

"Asleep?" I called out.

"Nope," came her voice from the bedroom.

Strolling in and snapping on switches as I went, I found her sitting up cross-legged. The lamp behind backlit her hair so it glowed gold. For a moment, it was all I could do just to stare. If some divine being had downloaded my every desire, whether known or hidden, it couldn't have produced a better fit than this woman.

Everything from her poise to the shape of her throat and the expression in her blue eyes sank arrows into me. If I let myself even think about her tits, I was hard. Being in the same room with her on a bed, I was hard.

Cassie's criticism that I hadn't told her enough about myself to stop her hating me hit home. For the next month, I would be tied to Genevieve Jones. Having her not hate me would probably help with that.

I leaned on the doorframe. "Do you have an allergy to light bulbs?"

"Actually, it's the other way around. The dark freaks me out, so I make myself endure it."

"You're scared of the dark?"

I snapped on another lamp.

She raised a shoulder, her expression uncertain. "Everyone's scared of something."

The retort was ready on my tongue, the reply that *I wasn't*. But it would be a lie. I knew my greatest fear, and I'd taken pains to never let it happen again.

Genevieve took a breath. "Cassie told me a few things about your business which make no sense to me. She implied that you run the warehouse as some sort of place of safety for the women who work there. She said you don't take money from them for yourself. Is that true?"

"Cassie has a big mouth."

"Is it, though?"

"I've never taken one single penny from the women. Everything they earn goes back to them or to the running of the club and other concerns."

"What other concerns?"

"We fund a nursery. Housing. Education. Many of the women are studying, some to pick up basic qualifications they missed, a couple are doing degrees. We even have a lawyer to help out when needed. Thea, one of the women who lives here, is a social worker. She spends a lot of her time helping out."

"Then why do they need you and your skeleton gang?"

"Protection. If I didn't provide it, do you think the warehouse would exist untouched?"

That steady gaze of hers burned with a mixture of curiosity and reluctant belief. I didn't have to prove myself to her, but I wanted to. I needed her to understand everything I'd built and the empire I'd die to defend.

My phone buzzed, and I read the screen, glad for the excuse to stop our stare off. "Shade has your things from the basement. He asked if you want anything from your flat brought. He can go there with Alisha, and she can pick up some clothes if no one's home to help."

"How long will I be here?"

"A few days more. Then we'll go back to the warehouse."

"Days? How's that going to work when I have a ten-hour shift coming up on Tuesday?"

"It won't."

She dug her fingers into her hair. "I'm going to lose my job. I had Sunday and Monday off but I can't take more."

"When you get your phone back in a few hours, call your boss and tell him you've been arrested or have jury service. Whatever floats your boat. Lying comes easily to you. Make something up."

She shot me a dirty look. "That's only part of it. I'll be losing money."

"You're forgetting I'm duty bound to provide for you. While you're under my roof, metaphorically speaking, I'll support you."

"Paying me? Doesn't that make me a sex worker?"

"We'd have to have actual sex for that."

Genevieve's eyes flared. A shockwave of lust rushed through me, so strong I nearly staggered under the weight of it, my dick so hard I could drive nails into the plasterwork.

I swore and balled my fists. "I need to go for a run. Want to come or stay here?"

She slid from the bed. "I'll come. Tell your friend no thanks for going to my place. Summer had a bag of clothes ready when she brought me back here. Even running shoes and a sports bra."

"God, woman. Don't talk to me about your underwear unless you want me to tear it off you."

This earned me a smirk, then she flapped for me to leave the room so she could get changed.

I texted Shade who gave me a thumbs-up which I figured meant he was on his way.

When Genevieve was ready, we set off through a side door of the mansion and into the night.

"Does the dark scare you outdoors?" I asked.

Genevieve stretched to warm up, her cropped t-shirt lifting at the sides to expose her skin. My mouth dried.

"Now you mention it, not really. Probably because if I'm outdoors in the dark, I'm moving. I work at night a lot, but it's in the city where it's brightly lit and I'm on my scooter with a headlight."

We started running, and gravel crunched under our shoes. The mansion sat in acres of parkland which gave way to forests and wild moors, the Cairngorm mountains surrounding. There were paths here and there including a circular one which would take us on a decent running route.

A heavy yellow moon hung overhead, low, ripe, and nearly full. It lit our route well, and for several minutes, we ran with no arguments, just peace.

I wanted to get back to my questions about the murdered woman, but I held off, enjoying the tranquillity.

Likewise, Genevieve didn't rush to fill the space. The only sound was the thuds of our footfalls, a rhythmic beat in the night air.

At first, we ran apace, neither of us leading or trailing much behind. If the path narrowed, I'd let her go ahead, enjoying the sight of her backside in her tight shorts. When we ran through a short area of pitch-black woodland, she kept closer.

For some reason, that act of trust did something to my brain.

I was ultra aware of her, my skin fucking prickling. The exit to the woodland appeared ahead, and we flew out of it into a meadow. In daylight, this would be full of flowers. Now, it was ghostly strands of long pale grass that moved in a barely there breeze.

Genevieve scanned our surroundings. I was about to speak when she stumbled. I caught her, but her foot came between mine, tripping me. I rolled backwards into the long grass, and she fell, too, with a gasp of breath, landing astride me on the ground.

Right on my lap and directly over my dick.

The woman shot her shocked gaze down my body. "You're hard."

"Seems to always be the case when I'm around you."

"That can't be comfortable to run with."

I breathed a laugh, my hands at her hips. "I've known worse."

For a moment, she didn't move. The rigid length of me was right at the apex of her legs, only the thin material of our shorts separating us. She was mine. My claim. The need surged in me to roll her underneath me and take her.

It hit the brick wall of the fact I'd never touch an unwilling woman. Even a matter of days ago, I hadn't intended to touch any woman at all, but she'd strode straight through that boundary and smashed it to pieces.

I'd broken my vow for her. It pissed me off.

Ducking her head, Genevieve climbed off me. "Sorry for tripping you."

We set off again, my dick even more uncomfortable. I didn't fucking care.

We'd circled the mansion, and the path turned us back towards it.

Genevieve spoke fast. "I know you probably won't believe me, but it's important to me that you hear my side of things when it comes to how I got into the basement."

I shrugged, keeping my pace steady and matching hers. "That's fair. I've asked you to believe the apparently unbelievable. It'll make things easier if there's some understanding between us."

She shot me a dubious look. "I last saw my father nearly two weeks ago. He's been missing and won't answer my messages. The night I ran in front of your car, two men had been around to our flat and posted an eviction notice on the door."

"That's why you were distracted?"

"It was part of it. After the accident, I went to find my brother. His girlfriend said that Dad has been hanging out with a woman who's a stripper. The reason I came to your club was to trace her, and therefore my father."

I frowned, and she continued speed talking as if needing the words out.

"I asked a few of the people who worked there and peeked at the rota outside the dressing room. No luck."

"So you came back and lied to get inside for a second go?"

"Exactly. I needed to reach the other floor." She bounced as she ran, her eyes bright. "Nothing to do with you or your game. I didn't know anything about it. So you believe me then? I just wanted to find my father. Without him, I can't negotiate with the landlord about the money he owes. And I don't even know what he's done with the rent money because Riordan and I paid it to him."

"What's her name?"

"The stripper? Sydney."

My stomach tightened. I stopped on the path.

Genevieve halted, too. "You know her?"

"She used to work for me, right up until about a month ago when she joined another gang."

Sydney had stolen the other women's cash tips and run for it. I'd had confirmation of where she'd gone from a snide message from Red, the leader of the Four Milers, a rival gang. He'd once vowed to take every one of my women.

Then Genevieve showed up.

Fuck.

Every tiny speck of warmth I'd started to feel for the beautiful, treacherous woman who'd landed in my lap iced over so thickly it made my teeth clench. I'd been such a fool. I still wanted her like nothing else, but I couldn't believe she was anything but a horrible liar.

A plant, probably, assuming Red or another gang leader wanted something from me they couldn't get by sending someone into the club.

Her shoulders slumped. "Dad's never had anything to do with the gangs. None of us ever would."

More lies, and this one was on the nose because it paired with another fact I knew. I'd asked Shade to do some digging on her background, and he'd discovered that her brother was screwing a gang hanger-on. A woman named Moniqua whose brother was in the Four Milers, known for their gang tattoos of a spiderweb. I'd chosen to put that to one side as the guy held down a job and wasn't on our radar as a problem.

I'd been a fucking idiot.

Everything I'd considered twisted into something different.

Genevieve drove her toe into the ground, kicking up dust. "You know the gangs. Can you help me find him?"

"No, I fucking can't."

She recoiled. "Why not? I just told you that I'm going to be made homeless. Not only that but I'm worried about my father, too. He's not responded to me in all that time. What if they've caught him?"

"Gangs don't hold prisoners for no reason. If they've had him for all this time, he'll be dead."

"Don't say that!" Her eyes crinkled at the edges.

"Why not? It's either that or he's working for them."

"It's neither. Please, help me find him."

"I said no. Stop asking."

I started running again, anything not to look at her face. At the body I was rapidly growing obsessed with. I was furious at myself for hearing out her lies.

She dropped a few feet back. "Fine," she muttered.

But it wasn't. Life was anything but fine, and breaking my rules for a woman only proved that.

*S*hade arrived a few hours later. I locked the gang spy in my rooms and went out to meet him. It was after two AM now, but I'd slept all day, as was typical for one who worked at night.

He rested against his car's bonnet, hands in his pockets, his gaze on me worried. "Ye okay?"

Not at all. Not the tiniest bit.

"Perfect. Did you bring what I asked?" I snarled.

"Drop the shite, man. It's me."

I took a breath, dropping my head back for a moment. My pulse still sped along, but he was right. He deserved my truths, plus I had something to ask him.

"I'm anything but okay. You know what I did."

"Wish I knew why."

"I needed the woman, and I knew the second I saw her in there that it was by mistake. She didn't sign up for it. Plus if I lost her to some other guy, I'd lose the ability to question her on something important."

He tilted his head, waiting.

"I was wrong about the mistake part," I exhaled. "She's

not what she says she is. I was taken in."

Briefly, I explained her further link to the Four Milers. Our rivals who would do anything to see me rot. "I just have to wait out my time with her."

"I don't think that'll be easy," Shade said. "Ye claimed her in front of all the others. By your own words, ye started an unstoppable bond. Are ye keeping to the rules?"

I nodded a short, unhappy agreement.

The game did this. Forged couples in the most unbreakable way. I delivered that promise to the people who signed up and paid a bundle for the privilege. Sometimes, I'd felt envy for their easy lives and how they could follow the draw.

I couldn't. No matter what my body felt, I'd never love her.

"But you're resisting," Shade decided.

"It won't happen to me. Neither of us wanted this, even if she conned me to get it."

"You broke every rule in your book for her."

"Don't you think I know that?" I snapped. "It isn't for romance and fucking roses that I followed her into the basement. The woman who was killed, she knew her."

Shade rolled his hands. "And that's important because...?"

"I'm almost certain the murderer did it as a sign to me."

"So what information has your woman provided?"

"I'll get back to you on that."

He swore, disbelief in his eyes. "You tied yourself to her for no information. That's why I asked if you're sure. You're in for a world of pain if you're right and the same if you're wrong, because mistrust and lies are the thing that will destroy the relationship."

"If I wanted your opinion, I'd ask for it."

"What-the-fuck-ever."

I summoned my strength, because he wasn't wrong. It already hurt just to be close to Genevieve. Quitting her was going to kill. "Seriously, if you ever catch me slipping for a woman again, fucking stab me. Now, I have a job for you. Find out where her father is. Don't confront him, just locate the man. When I'm ready, I'll deal with him myself."

"On it. Convict can help. Ye also need to know that your pet detective came by the club earlier. He didn't say what he wanted."

Fucking hell. I ticked over what Detective Dickhead might want. "Shade, how did you dispose of Bradley?"

"Fuck ye for asking. I did everything I should've."

If he wasn't after me for that, then what? In time, I'd have to find out.

15

Genevieve

*V*oices filtered in from the living room to the bedroom—Arran on a video call with a client, his third. He'd been working since his friend brought our possessions, and it was nearly dawn.

I'd got my phone back, along with a warning that all communications were monitored here, and had tried Dad with no reply. Nor had he messaged. On the other hand, my brother had tried to call me a couple of times over the weekend then sent a single text saying he'd gone home but where the fuck was I?

Good question, brother.

I rang him. This time, he answered.

"At last," I said.

"It's four in the fucking morning. Where are you?" Riordan asked.

"Staying at a friend's. Sorry if I woke you. Any sign of Dad?"

"Had to get up for work soon anyway. Nothing from Dad. I drove around all his usual haunts and asked after him. Nothing."

"I did that, too. He should've shown up by now."

My brother cracked a bottle and took a swig. He had a thing for freezing cold water. Room temperature made him grumpy like it was a personal affront. "He's done three weeks in the past. Remember when he got a windfall and went on a bender with friends? I picked him up from hospital."

I sank against the pillows. "He doesn't have any money this time. At least not that I know of, and he's rubbish at keeping secrets. Where could he be? I've racked my brains and have no idea."

"Same. I tried the police and the hospitals, too. Nothing, and no unidentified bodies. Thank fuck."

My heart ached. "I didn't even let myself go there. I'm worried."

As flaky as Dad could be, he loved us. He'd loved Mum, too. He often said.

My brother went quiet. "I saw the eviction notice. What the fuck has he been doing with our rent?"

"I don't know. I don't have the faintest idea how we're going to pay that amount."

"I'm paying Moniqua's rent. I can't swing much more our way than I already am."

I clamped my jaw to stop my retort about his freeloading girlfriend because that wasn't the point. Paying the missing rent wasn't on him. "I have my savings—"

"No. Don't you dare. I'll come up with something."

My brother was the only person who really supported my dream to follow in Mum's footsteps and go into nursing. He'd tried to give me money from overtime in his construction job, but I'd never accepted. He found other ways, though. Buying our food and paying bills without me knowing. It meant I could save most of my hourly wage. I had it all hidden away. If we had no other choice, I'd use it.

"Who's the friend?" he said suddenly.

"What?"

"You said you're staying with someone. Far as I know, you don't have any friends."

"Mind your own business."

"If it's a guy, I need a name."

Cassie's comment about overprotective brothers came back to me. "Why?"

"So I can make sure he isn't a scumbag. I know people in the city, most I wouldn't want anywhere near you."

Presumably from hanging around with Moniqua. "Still not telling you."

"Just tell me it isn't Don. I don't pay much mind to that fucktard, but Moniqua said he made a remark about you. I haven't seen him around but I'll break his fucking face if he tries anything. He's seriously bad news."

So was the gang leader keeping me prisoner. I shuddered at a strange thought—if Don was looking for me still, somehow, I was far safer here than at home.

"It isn't him."

"Good. By the way, what the fuck happened to my leather jacket?"

Making excuses, I got off the call. I could've asked him for help, but Riordan would hate Arran on sight. The picture that painted in my mind was red with a bloodbath.

For his part, Arran thought I was affiliated with a rival

gang. I'd watched his face fall then his attitude change, and I didn't have the faintest clue of how to fix this.

Worse—I wanted to. Badly. His lack of faith made me inexplicably sad. It made no sense considering trust between us had never risen beyond a base level, but it was there and insistent. Just as much as the desire that haunted me.

I tried to ignore him by losing myself in my phone.

Mum's death and us moving to Dad's city lost me my friendship group, so I was lacking a bestie to chat with, but I was in a group with people starting the college course I was desperate to attend. Even their conversation couldn't stop me from noticing Arran and getting stuck on watching him.

Between calls, he'd pace the suite, visible through a gap in the double doors. Every time, I'd stare at his shape. Imagine him inside me. Frustration filled every inch of my needy body.

"I don't accept that," the man on the other end of the video call was saying. His voice had got louder throughout the call. "If this woman really was yours and she went into the game in error, why does nobody seem to know about her? Your team should never have let her pass. It doesn't add up."

"What I'm telling you is the truth," Arran stated.

"Where is she, then? This female you're so obsessed with. Something fishy's going on, and I call bullshit, Mr Daniels."

Arran's sigh came so heavily.

Jumping up, I marched to the doors, and pushed them fully open. At a desk beside the shuttered window and wearing his skeleton bandanna around his neck, Arran reclined in a chair, the client peering at him from a screen.

Arran's gaze linked to mine. His eyes darkened, and desire shot through me in a lightning bolt. I didn't wait for permission, continuing until I was right in front of him. He adjusted his position, and I sat on his knee and smiled for the watcher.

"Hello, Mr...?"

The man scrutinised me, his smart suit cluing me in to him being the business type. Nothing like Arran's rough-and-ready style. I didn't recognise him at all, but that didn't mean much. My memories were selective.

"William Hang. I remember you, Miss."

"I'm sure you do. It was a shocking night."

Arran's arm eased around me, and he gripped my waist. A full-body shiver came over me, and I peeked back to find his expression casual.

"You hid for most of it," Mr Hang continued.

"I wasn't meant to be there. The doorman got me confused with a woman who looks very much like me. It was terrifying."

"How is it you didn't know? How did you never hear what your boyfriend gets up to in his spare time?" There was disbelief in his tone, but his expression was more pondering.

"It was only the second time I've ever visited the club. Arran always came to me."

Arran's hand moved to my bare knee. I parted my legs and smiled at his intake of air.

Mr Hang considered that. "Tell me, is he treating you right? Upholding every part of what he's supposed to? I wondered because the terms of the game bind him, even if neither of you intended to be in there. It would be an outrage if he failed."

Jeez, they all took it so seriously. Realisation followed quickly. I had the chance to destroy his reputation in one sentence, except I was enjoying being close to him.

Lightly, I ground on Arran, riding his thigh, increasingly mindless for the chance of relief by his body. Arran's hand on my knee drifted upwards, grazing my sensitive skin.

Just a few more inches until he reached where I needed him to be. If he tugged my clothes aside and made a few passes over my slick centre, I'd tumble into utter pleasure.

My heart thundered. Even if this was just an act, one I'd initiated, I needed nothing more than him.

Arran squeezed my thigh, and I stifled a moan. Then I remembered I'd been asked a question.

"He's giving me everything I deserve."

Mr Hang took a deep breath, and his lips curved. "I can see that from just one glimpse at the pair of you. In no time, you'll be fully bonded and at that final stage. I wish you both the best, even if I confess my absolute envy. Well, Mr Daniels, I trust that errant doorman has been taken care of?"

"Of course."

"Then I accept your offer and extend my congratulations to you and your claimed woman. Until next time."

He disconnected, and the screen went to a holding platform, quiet falling across the room.

Neither of us moved.

"You lie well," Arran said.

"I didn't lie at all. What happened to the doorman?"

He made no reply, his hands on my body but still.

"What did you offer your client?" I tried instead. Maybe he'd give me to Mr Hang once he was through.

"To run the game again sooner than I'd planned. He'll get a second chance for free."

"What did he mean by the final stage to us being fully bonded? I thought the restrictions between us only lifted."

He rose from the seat, standing me with him, then moved several deliberate feet away. "We won't be doing it so you don't need to know."

"Can you tell me anyway?"

"No." He folded his arms.

I glowered, not at all put off. "Fine. I'll find out another way."

"Don't bother, you won't like it. But if you're so keen to get involved in my business, you can help with the next call."

He wanted my help. A small flame of hope kindled inside me. "Who are we talking to?"

"Natasha Reid, the woman you impersonated." There was a challenge in his eyes.

I wrinkled my nose but summoned my strength. "This one should be mine anyway. I owe her an apology."

"You're astonishing, Genevieve."

An answer stuck in my throat. He didn't mean it in a good way, but I wished he did.

Retaking our seats, he clicked into a contact list, and the video call blipped with a dial tone. A woman answered, her fair hair and heart-shaped face so like mine I stared.

Likewise, she blinked at me. "You're the woman who took my place."

I shrugged. "In the flesh. I can see now how the mistake

was made."

Her gaze travelled over the screen like she was taking me in. "That's what the other man said when I called. He told me you were mistakenly shown into the claiming ground in my place."

"True. I had no idea what was going on."

Her eyes crinkled at the edges. "I'd like to believe you, but I wonder if you have another agenda."

For a moment, I lost my train of thought. Nobody had asked me if I was okay. Arran assumed I'd been there on purpose. I'd upset Cassie and Summer, so neither had been forthcoming. Now this woman automatically assumed there was a further purpose.

"I don't, but thank you for hearing my explanation. I apologise for taking your place."

Her expression didn't change, but her focus shifted to Arran at my back. "Your colleague said that you'd made a claim. I'm devastated at missing out. You and I would have been good together. If I'd known you were in there, I would've fought tooth and claw for you. I'd never have dared be fashionably late."

My jaw dropped, and outrage swept through me. "Watch your mouth. You're talking to a taken man. He claimed me, and that makes him mine."

If she wanted teeth and claws, I had them in spades.

Natasha's cheeks pinkened. "I deserved that. I accept the offer of being in the next game. Got to go."

She disconnected, and I exhaled annoyance. The cheek of her.

Then I became aware of Arran's hands at my waist. They eased around the front of my jean shorts and popped the button.

"Hang reminded me of another obligation we haven't discussed. Do you know your bank account details?"

"Yes, why?" I had the same account that Mum had opened for me when I was eleven.

"Tell me."

He lowered my zip.

Half mindless, I recited my account number and sort code. Arran paused to make a note.

"Lift your ass," he ordered in a low and delicious tone.

I obeyed, and he stripped my shorts from me, keeping me facing away, perched on his knee. Desire heated my blood, my clit throbbing, the anticipation an overload of sinful need.

I peered back to see him free his rock-hard erection, though he made no attempt to stroke it. We were due our daily sex act, and maybe this time would be different. If I was riding him, I'd be the one in control.

But the expression in his eyes gave me pause.

Arran stood and crowded me to the wall like he'd done yesterday, forcing me to face away.

"Who was in the car the night I came to your flat?" he asked in my ear. "You were scared."

"Don, he's a relative of my brother's girlfriend," I replied instantly.

"Did you know the woman who was murdered on your street?"

Distress chased my good feelings. My fingers shook. "Cherry is her name. Was, I mean. I spoke to her the night before she died."

His dick slid between my legs. "What did she say?"

"She mentioned a client who was a city councillor and

a friend of his she didn't like. They were both due to see her the night she died."

"Get any names?"

"No. What are you going to do about it? I want to be part of—"

With a punch of his hips, he entered me, no warning, no easy slide. A hit of violence my body readily absorbed despite his thick size.

Just as happened last time, I didn't hide a moan, my pussy squeezing him tight.

If only he'd drive me into the wall with a few more hard thrusts, the pleasure would crest and break. The tension holding me taut would be over.

Arran exhaled, his breath ghosting over my shoulders.

Precious seconds passed, the tension almost hurting. Pressure pinning me down just as much as he was spearing me in two. My toes curled in the rug, and I flexed to press up on the balls of my feet, the slight movement so good.

Then the bastard pulled out and walked away, leaving me utterly desperate in every way.

I crept back to bed with heavy emotions boiling in my blood. My body needed to get off, but I couldn't with him right there, decidedly not participating. I'd tried yesterday and failed.

My phone chimed with a notification. My bank. Money added.

I opened the app and stared at the screen. All those numbers. He'd deposited twenty grand. Anger rushed. "What the hell is this?" I yelled.

From the other room, he spoke calmly. "As my woman, you're due a stipend."

"I get twenty grand for the pleasure of you imprisoning me?"

"Every week."

My words dried up entirely. That kind of money was life-changing. I could pay the missing rent. Get my own place to live where I wasn't dependant on Dad. Help Riordan so he didn't need to work so many hours.

Yet in no universe was I taking Arran's blood money.

With a stab of my finger and an ache in my gut, I reversed the payment.

The same happened the next day.

We slept the daylight away, he worked, we ran, he sent me money which I refunded, then he fucked me with that solitary, vow-keeping thrust. Nothing more, no matter what I needed.

And the day after. A pattern formed.

I didn't ask to see anyone, knowing Cassie would've poisoned the rest of the household against me. I messed around on my phone, idling over stories from students who'd done my nursing degree.

Arran noticed. "You want to be a nurse?"

I put my phone face down on the sofa. "Hard to do that from prison."

His lips twitched. "Seriously. Are you meant to be studying?"

"No," I reluctantly replied. "Eventually I will, but I haven't signed up yet."

He took his seat at the desk. "One of our most interesting couples to come out of the game included a surgeon. She was thirty-five and in a killer career. She didn't want kids but badly wanted to be owned and possessed."

I leaned in, intrigued. "Did she come to your office and tell you that?"

"Video call, but yes. She was time poor but had an opportunity in her career ladder to take a month out."

"Who caught her?"

"An MMA fighter. Savage asshole with a big personality and a liking for violence. On paper, they couldn't be more different."

I tried and failed to gel the two in my head. "But they worked out?"

"She and her claimer are deeply in love and happy. Look them up, if you want."

He provided a name. I tapped it into my phone, bringing back results for the surgeon. Her medical brilliance was side by side with results for her fiancé's social media photos and videos. She was pretty, with long auburn hair, and most of her pictures of her in scrubs or suits. He was tattooed and half naked in all his.

In the pictures of them together, there was a strange kind of middle ground. A shirt on him. A spiked necklace on her. The top result was their engagement announcement which he'd made at the end of a fight, bloodied, sweaty, and strangely compelling.

"They're engaged?" I said slowly, then raised my head. "When did you run their game?"

"November."

I reread the article with their announcement. It came in December, which meant they'd reached the one-month mark and put a ring on it.

The final stage was a ring offered on bended knee, then. At least that wouldn't happen to me.

I closed the search down and picked a book from the shelves in the living room instead. But I couldn't ease my Arran-shaped distraction. He filled my senses and dominated every thought.

The only time I got anything from him was when he was inside me. Held me for that moment. Laid a kiss on my throat or asked a question.

My desperation grew to dizzying proportions until there was only one option for me to break the deadlock.

Unseeing, I stared at the pages, a plan forming.

I just had to find a way to offer.

16

Arran

The end of the mandatory week of being tied to Genevieve was nearing, and tomorrow night, Friday, we'd return together to the city.

I had a task before we left. I needed to present myself to the woman I should've visited as soon as we'd gotten here.

The woman I'd vowed myself to and broken faith with.

It was for her that I'd promised never to touch anyone else. It was because of her that vow had been easy to keep.

I'd beg her forgiveness, but I wouldn't get it.

Running calmly beside me, Genevieve was ignorant of how she'd shattered my personal rules.

Every night, when I touched her, it fucking hurt. I was mindless for wanting her. Urgency dominating more and more. Back at the warehouse, it would be easier, and there would be distractions. Right now, I was going out of my mind with need, not just to fuck her, but to own her.

To brand her, to make her scream my name.

Her footsteps on the gravel track slowed, woodland surrounding us. "Arran? I need to ask you something."

"What?" I snapped.

My temper was ever frayed for her.

"Actually, it's less of a question and more of an offer."

"Spit it out."

We both stopped, about a quarter of the journey left to run back to the mansion. I waited, not all that patiently.

"Those phone calls we made the other night, making good the problems caused by me being in the game. I explained myself to the man in the first call then apologised to Natasha in the second one."

Planting my hands on my hips, I dug my fingers into my flesh. "Still not hearing a point."

I was trying to bait her, but her expression remained serious.

She considered me. "I never apologised to you. At first because I didn't accept the fault. I do, now. I can see the problems I caused. I don't like feeling this way. Which brings me to the offer."

For no clear reason, I held my breath.

"Free use," she uttered.

A storm of need built inside me. "Be more specific."

"You told me you were a virgin. I didn't believe you, because what man in your position with that damn face and a working dick wouldn't be screwing around?"

"I wasn't lying," I said. "I made a promise a long time ago."

"I know. I realised it must be something like that. I also realise that when you're inside me, you want more. You're fulfilling the rules of your game but holding back from anything further, probably because it complicates things between us. So I offer you my body. Free use to do whatever you want to me. You don't have to ask, or explain, and I won't say a word during. I'm yours to do with as you choose. It means nothing more than one time."

Pink-cheeked, she brushed her hands over her breasts, cupping them then going lower to her belly, a finger twisting in her waistband.

Desire held me in its grip. Genevieve suffered the same. It poured off her. The bond between us heightened every sense. I needed to touch her, taste her, to have her under me. To enter and to own.

I prowled a step closer. "What makes you think I want you?"

Her lower lip trembled, but she raised her chin in defiance. "I made you break your promise. I'm offering you the chance to break me in return. Whether you want me or not, it evens us out."

The last thread of control broke in my brain. I had the chance to dominate her without consequence.

There was no choice but to take the offer.

Reaching for my back pocket, I pulled free the skeleton mask bandanna I always carried and tugged it over my face. "Get on your knees."

Genevieve sank to the path without hesitation, kneeling in the gravel. "You don't need the mask."

She couldn't see my expression. I wouldn't allow it.

"No kissing besides my dick. Wrap your lips around me and stop talking."

She obeyed, freeing my dick from my running shorts, her touch making me throb for her. Lowering her head, she flattened her tongue and licked the pre-cum from the tip, a soft moan following. Dark need rose in me along with a rush from being touched. A fucking thrill.

Genevieve slid her tongue down my length then came back up, enclosing the end of my dick with a light suck.

I pressed my lips together, unwilling to make a single sound. But my nostrils flared under the mask. My chest rose and fell hard.

This was why she couldn't see me. I couldn't hide the want.

Or the guilt. I shouldn't do this. I had absolutely no choice anymore.

She fisted the base of me and took more of me in her mouth, stretching her lips around my girth, the heat of her driving me insane as she worked out how to blow me. My thick inches disappeared. I dug my fingers into her pretty hair, as much for fucking balance as the need to control her.

It felt too good.

I wanted to tell her but kept my damn thoughts to myself.

This wasn't the first time I'd had my dick sucked, but I'd resisted getting a repeat for years. All until she'd come along and destroyed my control.

To dislodge the sharp rise of emotion, I jacked my hips to fill her mouth, the head of my dick bumping into the back of her throat. Genevieve choked but didn't stop, another moan springing forth.

Her free hand came to my hip, but I batted it away, so she took it down her body. Palmed herself between her legs, over her shorts. All the while, hollowing her cheeks to take me deeper into her mouth.

She needed to come, too? Desire surged.

"Hands behind your back," I ordered.

She wasn't supposed to enjoy this. If she'd genuinely offered herself as recompense then it wasn't meant to be pleasurable to her. It defeated the purpose.

No matter what my deepest thoughts demanded, or how much of a thrill I got at the thought of her getting off.

Linking both hands at her spine, she sucked me, accepting my strokes in and out of her luscious mouth. I dug my fingers into her hair and tugged on the roots, working myself in a series of thrusts, pushing forward until I stood over her and tipping her off balance. Her eyes flew open but she moaned in pleasure. She was at my mercy, my hold on her head the only thing keeping her upright.

The position sent a fresh wave through me that was a mix of pleasure and success. She was at my command, only able to take my dick.

My balls tightened.

I hadn't come in forever. Every fucking night, when I did duty to my rules, I observed my vow. Breaking it while heeding it as best I could. Every moment, my body demanded I fuck her hard until I came deep inside her cunt.

Over and over, filling her.

At last, I could. This was only the start. I'd come all over her before the night was out. That last thought triggered a tsunami of lust. I was more animal than man, using her like she'd used me.

Inside my body, heat snaked from the base of my spine to my balls. I forced myself in deeper, her throat narrowing. She gave up another goddamned hot moan.

Abruptly, I withdrew from her lips and gripped my dick.

"Open your mouth for me, tongue flat," I ordered.

Panting in oxygen, she obeyed, still keeping her hands behind her. The blue of her eyes shone bright with desire.

Fuck, that did it. Pulled the trigger. Brought the flood. I came with a stunning smack of power, the effect devastating. Ropes of my cum landed on Genevieve's tongue. She accepted every drop. Held still to keep it exactly there in a pool in her mouth.

Fucking hell. Broken, I dropped to my knees.

Then I tipped back her chin, swiping up a stray droplet that tried to escape. "Swallow. Take me inside you for good."

Every drop disappeared down her throat.

Satisfaction rebounded, but I was far, far from satiated. This had been a fucking spectacular start, but the guilt only got stronger. Along with memories I couldn't contain.

17

Genevieve

With his hand gripping the back of my neck, Arran marched me to the mansion. I practically vibrated with need. Panted with it. A taste of him, and I was lost. His groan of pleasure had me almost coming myself, though I couldn't touch my body where I needed it most.

I wished I'd been able to see his face, but the expression in his eyes over the mask had been enough. How his gaze had fixed on me. How it'd shuttered closed right before he fell.

From the way he manhandled me now, certainty in every stride and his grip on me tight, his free use of me wasn't done yet. That had just been a starter. A taster for me. Literally. The masculine flavour of him was on my tongue. My lips, too, every time I licked them.

My desperation hadn't eased any, but some small satisfaction had joined it. He wanted me. Maybe just as much as I wanted him.

I had the rest of the night to find out exactly how much.

At the back door to the huge house, he shoved it open and guided me through to the end of the hall. He locked it behind us then stopped me with a small shake of the scruff of my neck.

"Strip."

I threw an anxious glance down the brightly lit corridor, and at the staircase that ran upward. No other voices could be heard, and all the kids would be long in bed, but any one of the adults could walk by. The question *Here?* was on the tip of my tongue, but I kept it in. He wanted my silence and obedience. I'd give him that.

Slowly, and with my gaze on him, I peeled the cropped shirt I'd been running in off my sweaty body, then unhooked my sports bra. My exposed breasts tingled, my nipples hardening even more than when I'd been blowing him.

Arran's gaze flew to them, his shorts already tented again, but he didn't move.

Next, I hooked my fingers into my running shorts and tugged them down my legs, leaving my body completely naked. Without much else to do in the past couple of days, I'd taken care of myself, using up the little tube of moisturiser that had been in my bag and shaving where needed using the razor I presumed to be his.

Armour against his steely focus.

"Kneel on the stairs," he continued, his voice cold and infuriatingly calm.

Shivering, I crept to the base of the staircase, climbing up a few to drop to my knees on the chilly stone.

Arran swivelled a finger, indicating I turn to face away. "Now on all fours with your hands a few steps higher and your head down."

Breathing out, I placed my palms onto the stair beside my head, my body on display and nothing hidden from his scrutiny. I pictured what I looked like to him, giving him an eyeful of my pussy.

Or anyone else who walked by.

"Ass out. Widen your knees," was his next command.

My pulse skittered, the insistent thump of need only getting stronger. Now there was absolutely nothing concealed of my wet core. It could've been humiliating, but I'd do it if it meant him joining me, crowding me from behind. Fucking into me right here.

Again, my pussy pulsed, desperately needing to be filled. Cool air touched the damp at my thighs. I'd dripped for him when his dick had been in my mouth. My arousal had only gotten worse since.

A door creaked somewhere nearby, a person moving.

I jumped and peered around. Arran had tugged down his bandanna so his face was no longer hidden.

"Did I tell you to move?" he said.

The footsteps came closer. Anxiety took hold of me, and I swung my head back around and gripped the edge of the step, listening hard for clues to how close the person was getting. I didn't want to be seen like this. His family might hate me, but I didn't want them to think any worse of me.

Or see me in such an intimate, exposed position.

"Thought I heard noises," a man called out from down the hall.

The stairwell in this corner of the house was tucked back. He wasn't close enough to see me. Yet.

"We went for a run," Arran replied.

Sweat pricked my brow.

The other man laughed. "You've been doing a lot of

that. Ye really shouldn't have the energy. I hear you're leaving tomorrow. Say goodbye before ye go this time?"

"I'll make sure of it," Arran replied.

We were going? I didn't think our week was up, but a quick calculation made it day six. For some reason, I didn't like the idea of returning to the city. I'd gotten used to being here. Swimming in his chemistry. Doing nothing but watching him. Waiting for something else to happen, some new feeling or a rush of our strange connection.

We'd made progress, and it was all going to come to a stop.

Then again, didn't I want that? I furrowed my brow, confused, turned on, and totally lost.

Arran was the very last man I should want, but still, here I was, revealing myself for his pleasure and obeying his every command.

He'd taken hold of my sexuality and switched it solely to him.

"You'd better not disappear," his friend said, the footsteps moving away. Then abruptly, they got louder again. He was coming back. "I meant to ask about your woman. Will ye take her out to the ruins? Have ye told her about—"

"My woman, as you call her, is naked six feet in front of me on the stairs. Come a step closer, and I'll have to burn your fucking eyes out," Arran snapped.

Silence, then a rolling laugh. "Holy fucking shite. Threatened with my own weapon of choice. What a way to go."

"Jamieson, I'm deadly serious."

"Aye, man. Walking away, walking away."

His footsteps faded into the depths of the house.

I sagged in relief. I hated that he'd told on me just as much as I was relieved I hadn't been seen.

Arran clucked his tongue. "Pick up your things. Get back to the room. Now."

Like a scared little animal, I scurried off the stairs and grabbed my clothing. Ahead of Arran, I bolted down the hallway and threw myself into our rooms.

Inside, I swung my gaze around, trying to decide where he'd want me. On my back on the bed or the sofa felt weak. I was overthinking it. All I needed was for the violent gang leader to fuck me hard and good.

I took too long deciding, because he was there, locking the door, then looming over me. Slowly, he pulled the bandanna wrap up off his head, then tugged it down over mine, unfolding it so the whole of my face was covered. He'd blindfolded me with his mark of the skeleton crew.

Parting my lips, I adjusted it, but he grabbed my wrist.

"Hands out in front of you, fingers interlaced."

Outside, his instructions had been icy cold. Now, they were heavy with desire.

I listened out for what he was doing, jumping when he took hold of my joined hands. Arran twisted rope around them. The curtain tie? It was some kind of silky weave. He tightened it, and I subtly flexed my hands to check the binding.

Arran tugged it, jerking me forwards. He was leading me like a dog on a leash.

Unable to see, I cautiously stepped, one foot after the other, following where he led. Other sounds came, material rustling, which I pictured to be him stripping. Something like a piece of furniture moving.

My foot touched something, and I stopped.

"That's the sofa. Lean forward over it. Hands extended out."

Slowly, I edged to the sofa back, ready to drape over it. But then a hand landed between my shoulder blades and pushed me down so I dropped onto the cushions, my toes momentarily leaving the floor until I regained my footing. Arran kicked my feet apart, his bare legs touching the insides of mine.

That was all the warning I had. Just like he did with his daily rule-following, he thrust hard inside my pussy.

I keened soundlessly, restraining the cry that needed out. Like every other time, it felt incredible. He was so big, but my body welcomed the burn. I could've used another moment to adjust. I'd become used to him just holding still.

But Arran didn't wait. He withdrew his hips then punched forwards again.

He gave a broken groan of need that destroyed half of my brain cells. We'd never done this. He'd always abandoned the act.

But the stops were off.

Again, he surged and filled me, bottoming out so our bodies were flush together. He rolled his hips, stretching me all the more, making me so full it almost hurt. Then he broke into an assault, taking his emotions out on my flesh with driving in and in and in.

Through the tight hold of lust and the cushions against my face, I took it, but I could hardly breathe.

Panic stole over me. I had my head down and my legs wide. My blood rushed to my head, every feeling all the more intense for not being able to see or move my hands.

My hearing muffled, too.

All of a sudden, it pulled in around me, overwhelming and crushing.

I'd so badly wanted this, but in my head, he'd been delivering pleasure. We'd both been involved. This felt more like a punishment. Like I was being used as a place to stick his dick. Nothing further than that. Of no more value. But wasn't that precisely what I'd offered?

I hadn't fully understood that consequence, and he was taking me at my word.

Arran kept going, lengthening his strokes but keeping the pace even. His fingers spread my ass cheeks, and he ducked to bite my flesh. Then he changed the angle, and the pressure shifted inside me to bright, sparkling pleasure. I clamped my lips closed, not willing to give up a single sound for fear of him stopping.

Yet over and over again, he hit that vital place. It eclipsed the bad and made it so, so good. A building, winding heat that had me forget my need for oxygen. Every part of me readied to let the wave of it take me under. I'd been dying for this. For him to deliver on everything the draw between us promised. I needed to come and to have him follow me down.

Whether he liked it or not.

I might've kept in my sounds, but my body betrayed me instead. My pussy pulsed around his dick, the very start of my orgasm catching alight. It was going to destroy me, I sensed the strength, how the slow build was about to inflict a brutal force.

I bit my lip, but Arran stopped like he'd been stung.

He pulled out of me altogether, leaving me empty and halting my pleasure in its tracks so I cried out silently in frustration. Noises came like he was jacking himself with his fist, then he grunted, and hot cum spurted over my core and ass.

A moan flew from my lips even though I was nowhere near the finishing post. Then tears quickly followed, dampening the bandanna. I'd wanted it so much, and he'd taken it from me.

Perhaps that's how he'd felt when he accused me of stealing his virginity. A sense of loss. Of wanting something you couldn't have. It swallowed me whole, and I sobbed once, gritting my teeth so it didn't happen again.

Something swiped between my thighs, Arran cleaning me up. Then he righted me and undid my wrists, sliding the mask free as his last act. I kept my gaze down, focusing on his hand at his naked thigh. His fist was bunched around the damp cloth, his knuckles standing proud. Surely having two orgasms to my none, the man should feel relaxed.

Resentful, I kept my head low, too aware of his scrutiny.

Finally, his instruction followed. "Go to bed, Genevieve."

I crept away from him, curled up under the sheets, and let my ridiculous tears flow.

18

Arran

On a work call, I tried to focus on business, but the sound of the shower kept interrupting my focus along with the thought of Genevieve rinsing me from her body. Her fingers on her soft skin. If I hadn't needed to talk to someone in a different time zone, I'd be in her again.

I'd barely fucking started getting my fill.

The client droned on, pissed off and needing me to hear it. The shower stopped, a hairdryer whirred, then silence from next door. Finally, the client accepted my offer to be in the next game, and I got off the call. My pulse sped, my dick hard instantly.

In the bedroom, Genevieve sprawled on her back on the white sheets, her golden hair fanned out, and the shutters closed against the daylight so the room was pitch black. She'd fallen asleep with the lamps off again. I didn't get why she did that. She was afraid of the dark. Why torment herself?

I left the door to the living room open so a slice of light fell over the bed, giving me plenty to see by, and knelt on the mattress. For a long moment, I just watched the woman who'd gifted herself to me. Her chest rising and falling, and the outline of her tits under a strappy top. The mound of her pussy in her tiny shorts, and the sheet only partially draped over her.

In my jeans, my dick pulsed.

Fuck, did I want her.

A loud buzz cut through the silence of the room. My goddamned phone. I snapped to shut it off and tossed it to an armchair, twisting back to Genevieve with my heart racing.

Thank Christ, it hadn't woken her. I'd exhausted the woman, and she was out cold, not even a flicker of awareness at the sound.

It gave me an opportunity, alongside dark thoughts that pierced me in shots of adrenaline and lust.

Placing my fingertips on the mattress, I leaned forward and peeled the sheet off her, slowly and carefully. My breathing caught. In the slice of light, her limbs gleamed, her curves sending me insane. She was more beautiful than she had a right to be. Hardwired to bring me to my knees.

I'd been around naked women my entire life. First with the ladies my father would buy in and abuse. After, the people I protected. I saw them fuck daily, all kinds of bodies doing all kinds of things.

It became commonplace. Banal.

Never once had anything come close to the erotic sight of Genevieve asleep and mine to touch.

I wanted to own every part of her. To do whatever I wanted whenever I wanted it. Right now, with her unconscious, she had no choice either. I didn't need to run the gauntlet of forcing myself not to make it good for her while punishing her at the same time.

She deserved my hate yet owned my lust.

It was going to be fun seeing how far I could take this before I woke her.

Ducking down, I pressed a kiss beside her injured flesh, the graze she'd sustained from my car. Then around to her soft inner thigh. Another higher.

Not a flicker. She didn't make a sound.

Higher still, I drew my mouth until I was over her pussy, and I took a deep inhale through my nose, drawing the scent of her inside me. Fucking delectable. Addictive. I put my tongue to the material right over her clit and traced the outline of her shape. Then I nestled in and bit lightly through her thin shorts.

Pulling back, I watched the damp patch appearing lower down. She was getting wet for me, even if she didn't know.

I needed a taste.

As lightly as I could manage, I hooked both sides of her shorts and drew them down her legs. Genevieve still didn't budge, letting me arrange her legs wide open, and giving me plenty of room to toy with her.

Wet gleamed at her core. I touched a finger to the centre of her, following a line of liquid down to the sheet. Then I replaced my finger with my tongue.

Heat sank through me at her flavour. I'd loved the scent of her, but her taste woke my senses like nothing else. Wild for her, I licked her from her entrance up to her clit, then kissed her pussy like I'd refused to do to her mouth.

But the angle was tight. I needed better access. To see everything. A pillow from the top of the bed would work. With the same measured care, I lifted her ass and set the pillow underneath and back so it wasn't in my way. It left her totally exposed to me, nothing hidden, her thighs wide. I could see everything from her clit to her pussy entrance and down to her puckered rear hole.

I gave her a second to settle, making sure she didn't regain consciousness. I needed this time alone with her body. No judgement. Just using her. Learning from her.

When I was sure she wasn't going to wake, I returned my mouth to the centre of her, swiping her clit with the tip of my tongue until more wetness pooled. I slid my tongue inside her channel, dying at the tight fit, and resisting an urge to get rough with her. My body didn't care about taking this slow.

My dick leaked, desperate to get in on the action.

Genevieve took a little breath, and I retreated to watch her face. Her eyes were still closed, and her head tipped back. Her nipples had hardened, the outline prominent under her top. I'd get to those later. It was a fucking trip— my actions on her unconscious body were turning her on more and more.

Keeping my touch featherlight, I drew a finger down her core then inside, centimetres at a time, keeping a close eye on her breathing. Her pulse beat at her throat. She was so wet, her juices leaked out on my palm, so I soaked my hand with them and stuck it into my jeans, painting my dick with her arousal.

God-fucking-damn.

She was such a good girl, letting me mess with her and sleeping so deep. Maybe I could even fuck her like this. I was so turned on, my dick so sensitive from fucking her earlier, but I didn't want to stop playing.

More than anything else, I wanted to continue pushing her body.

Above even that, I hated myself for all I couldn't stop doing.

Sitting up, I scanned the room. On a dressing table was my knife in its holster. Soundlessly, I crossed the floor to claim it, then returned to my position at the cradle of her body. I spat on my hand and used it to wipe down the handle, though it was clean. I'd used Shade's at our last job.

It wasn't as thick as my dick, but before using it, I had another idea. Keeping it holstered, I tapped the flat back against my hand. At the club, we had whole rooms dedicated to spanking ass, but I was all about the pussy tonight.

Taking a breath, I tapped her clit with the wide, flat leather.

Genevieve moaned, an arm rising and dropping heavily to the bed. Her toes curled into the sheet. Holy fuck, that was hot. It had made her wetter still, her core gleaming. I drove two fingers inside her, keeping still for a long moment before I hit her pussy again. She squeezed my hand tight with her inner walls, and I groaned silently. My dick throbbed for wanting her, the need to add my cum to the mess of her slick arousal growing.

I took the knife from the holder. Held it by the blade. Then I speared her open with my fingers and pressed the handle inside her. She spasmed again, her lips parting and her breathing coming harder.

Fucking hell. My knife bobbed with her clench, the blade flashing in the slice of light.

I'd never seen anything hotter.

The most difficult part of my game with her was holding off after any reaction. She needed to stay asleep. I needed to see the impact of my playing. It was a fine line, but I could be a patient man.

For several minutes, I just held the knife in her pussy, my two fingers alongside it, wet all over my hand and coating her thighs. With the fingers that weren't inside her, I felt down to her rear hole, and then pushed the tip of one finger inside. Her ass tightened around me, her pussy pulsing in response.

God, what it would be to fuck her ass. I ducked to lick her, then lightly bit her clit, holding it between my teeth and careful to avoid slicing myself. She was swollen and ripe from everything I was doing. If I let her finish, that would be one knockout orgasm for her. She was primed for it, so ready to take me in deep, choke my dick with her tight pussy.

But I had no intention of letting her get there. Awake or asleep.

Moving my hand slowly, I trailed my tongue around her clit. Sucked. When she moaned or pulsed, I stopped. When her breathing calmed, I started again. Endlessly, I kept it up, getting her so close then breaking off, denying her every time.

My heart beat faster at her frustrated whine, my breathing coming in a rough pull. I was dying for her, but also not wanting this to end.

I wanted her dreaming about me, even if I knew she wouldn't. Genevieve wanted nothing more than to reach her goal with me, whatever it was, and then to leave. She didn't want the bond between us. Didn't want me, except to keep me sweet.

If I featured in her dream, I hoped it would be a nightmare.

One where she was fucked with a knife, perhaps.

Genevieve moaned again, pressing her shoulders down into the mattress. Then she uttered a single, breathless word. "Arran."

I stared at her. Her eyes were still closed and her beautiful lips parted. Not awake. No return to consciousness.

How the fuck was my name on her lips? Rising, I withdrew my hand from her and the weapon with it, discarding the impromptu sex toy to the other side of the bed. On automatic pilot, goddamn hypnotised, I opened my jeans then stripped them and my shirt, kneeling back in place between her spread legs and her cunt raised on the cushion.

One word, and my entire reason had been lost. She wanted me. Holy fuck, she could have me.

I notched my dick to her entrance and slowly eased inside, one inch at a time, a devotee to the woman and her incredible body.

Inside her, I stilled, holding off on fucking the hell out of her. Somehow, over the course of several days of doing this, it had become a place of happiness. Safety. Huge frustration. That last part was over, at least in this moment.

There was something I hadn't done, though. Angling over her, I pressed my hands either side of her head, supporting my body above hers, my dick buried deep.

Then I pressed my mouth to hers.

Her soft lips yielded to mine.

My heart skipped a beat, and my stomach twisted. Kissing was so far off the table, I had no fucking clue what I was doing. I hadn't intended this, but I needed to know the shape and the feel. For there to be no act missed.

I opened her lips with mine, tracing them with my tongue. I was unpractised at this but I knew how well we fit together. She was perfect in every physical way. Her personality, too. There was nothing I didn't like except for her lies.

Suddenly, Genevieve's lips moved, and she returned my kiss. I broke away. But it was too late, her eyes were open and focusing on me. I jerked my hips to fuck into her, and she moaned, a hand coming up to touch my face.

The moment was broken. I couldn't give her what she wanted or succumb to the urge to make her scream my name rather than just whisper it.

Not now. All I could give her was more of the same. I jacked my hips, my pace picking up. She moaned, her fingers going to her clit. Her eyes closing again as if not accepting this was real. It wasn't. Not the way she wanted.

I slapped her hand away, and she whimpered.

Her pussy tightened around me, and it was all the warning I needed. I snapped back my hips and grabbed my dick in my fist, then three pumps and my orgasm struck. I came all over the outside of her pussy.

Genevieve sighed, her body going from rigid to slumping, sleep claiming her once again. Sitting back, I just stared at what I'd done to her. It wasn't over yet. I had so much more I wanted to do.

*A*n hour's sleep was all I needed to recharge, or all my body would let me have. I was too aware of the time limit, though not stated, of her free use.

She'd barely moved again since waking to me fucking her. Nor had I cleaned her up, only slinging the pillow and pulling the sheet over her.

I tugged the covers away again. My cum glistened on her skin, still damp at her pussy when I traced through it. I took my finger to her mouth and spread our combined arousal over her lips and onto her tongue. Her jaw flexed a tiny degree, but her eyes remained closed. Her breathing steady.

If she still dreamt of me, I had no idea. But I'd been dreaming about another part of her. I recognised what I was doing. It was a teenaged frenzy a decade and a half too late, and a wild rush of hormones and lust I'd never indulged in before.

Worse, I fucking loved it.

Sitting back, I trailed my gaze down to her breasts. Her spaghetti strap top which hid her from me was tight. If I tried to take it off her, she'd wake for certain.

Luckily, I was resourceful, and my boundaries were gone.

Again, I took up my knife, enjoying the play of life and death. Over her, I twisted one of the straps in my fingers then sliced through it. It jogged her full breasts. I repeated the act on the other side then hooked under the hem right at her navel. I touched the back of the blade to her belly, then sliced upwards, splitting her top in two.

Then I held the knife in my teeth and peeled the two sides of the material off her, baring her round tits for my viewing pleasure. Under my ministrations, she was completely naked. I could do anything to her. She was letting me, as well. She'd woken once and been aware of my night's work.

The things I wanted to do to her were neither sane nor safe. Perhaps I was the monster my father always intended me to be. The devil I promised my mother I'd never become. The thought only made me angrier. Taking my knife in my hand again, I put the dull side to her skin and drew it across her flesh, outlining one breast then the other.

She shivered, a ripple going across her.

Her nipples stood hard, begging for my attention. With my hand still holding the weapon, I touched one, then squeezed it between my finger and the blade. A thrill of need rushed through me.

I needed to feel what this was doing to her and if it was turning her on.

My dick was as hard as ever, and I took a second to fit to her entrance and enter her again. This wasn't for me, all I wanted was to know when her body liked something. She was just as wet, and so tight I needed to breathe through my urge to fuck.

When I had control of myself, I gave my attention to my blade. Starting at her nipples, and always with the blunt side, I traced lines across her ribs, belly, and down to her cunt where it welcomed me.

I drew the tip lightly across her clit. Then I flipped the weapon to push the handle down beside my dick. Over every wet and slippery part of us.

If my shaking arm gave out, I'd fall on the sharp edge and cut myself. Bleed on her.

Our conversation from a few days returned to me.

She'd wanted to know what the contestant from the game meant when he'd talked about a final act of bonding. She'd never agree to sharing blood with me, so there was no point in discussing it. I had the worst feeling that the same didn't apply in reverse.

I wasn't about to test that now. Drawing the knife back up her, I flipped it again then pinched her nipple, my finger and the metal squeezing her. Her pussy echoed the sentiment, pulsing around my dick. I repeated it on the other side, getting the same effect until her nipples were pebbled hard and begging for more.

I tossed the knife and stooped to take one in my mouth. Instantly, my eyes closed, and I sucked on her, enclosing her tight in my lips. With my free hand, I reached for her other breast, indenting her flesh, massaging her. Then I took that hand down to where we were joined and soaked my fingers in the wetness we'd both produced. Using that moisture, I teased her nipple as I sucked on the first. My heart thundered, but my body slowed.

This was strange. I'd stared at her tits for days and now had a chance to do whatever I wanted to them, except it felt like time had stopped. Like I was content at her breast. As long as I kept up the slow pulls, curling my tongue around her, everything else was okay.

Another entirely unexpected reaction, but not one I was willing to give up. I stayed like that, buried inside her and coated in my cum and hers, and with her nipple in my mouth. My free hand cupping her. Kneading her.

The teenage version of me that wanted to fuck her tits, or press the end of my dick to her nipples, or to come all over them, had quietened.

Whoever I was now had been lulled. Eventually, my sucking stopped, but staying just like that, deeply connected, I fell asleep on her.

19

Genevieve

*C*onsciousness came with a flex of my limbs then bringing them around the man on me. *In* me. Arran slept, but his dick was still buried in my pussy, and still semi hard. I'd woken once already to find him fucking me, or playing with me in some way, but I'd been so tired I'd just let him continue without participating.

If he'd needed me awake, he would've made me so.

I didn't hate it either. It felt like the beginnings of an addiction. The rush of desire and lust and need so incredible all I wanted was more.

It was new, the position we were in, both naked, hugging, connected. Throughout the past week, I'd often woken to him holding me, but he'd jump away the moment he realised. Now, he only hugged me closer.

Inside me, he pulsed, and I drove my knees into the bed and shifted on top of him. Riding him. Arran blinked his eyes open, his hands going to my hips. Then one came up to feel my heavy breast. I rolled my hips, working him in and out of me. This felt so good. All sweaty and sticky. Covered in him. I could taste him in my mouth. I didn't care. Only needed more.

I'd also never done this before, but with everything between us hostile, if he blamed me for my technique, or the lack of it, I could happily tell him where to go. Instead, Arran thrust into me, his eyes darkening with pleasure that jolted through me in a lightning strike.

Then he opened his damn mouth. "Don't come."

Oh, fuck him.

"Fine," I gritted out.

When everything was over between us, I was buying a vibrator and spending a week in my bed.

I kept working his dick, changing the pace so it didn't chase my pleasure. It was hard, though. My body was so ready for this. Need infected every cell. My skin tingled. Parts of me I'd never felt in my life bloomed with pleasure.

Deep inside, I spasmed.

Abruptly, Arran flipped me onto my back and withdrew from me. Kneeling over me, he jacked his fist then came over my chest with a groan of pleasure.

When his breathing regulated, a grin spread, satisfaction clear. "One of the only things I didn't do to you in the night."

Then he drove his fingers into the mess and spread it all over my chest, coating my nipples and covering my skin.

I grumbled and climbed from the bed, cum dripping down me. "Good for you, big man."

He came after me, slapped my ass, then passed to enter the bathroom first. The shower went on, and he extracted a fresh set of towels from the cupboard. "Get cleaned up then dress. We're leaving in a couple of hours."

My amusement fled. "Back to the city."

"Back to reality." He paused at the door, the thundering of the shower filling the space between us. "It changes things."

"I know. We no longer have to lock ourselves away. We can be apart for more than two hours."

Arran lifted his chin. If he had anything else to say, he didn't bother, leaving me alone to get ready to leave.

At dusk, we left his rooms. Arran had said goodbye to his friends already, but one of them, Jamieson, walked with us.

On the steps outside the house, I paused.

All week, the picture Cassie had shown me upstairs had played on my mind. The identity of the child had flickered at the very edge of my consciousness until a memory joined it. I stopped dead.

"I'm just going to say goodbye to Cassie," I told the men.

She'd watched from the top of the stairs but hadn't come down.

Arran let me go, Jamieson talking to him low about something.

Across the entrance hall, I quickly climbed the flight but found the hall empty. Good. Scanning the pictures, I found the one I wanted. The sweet toddler in the rainbow dungarees grinned back at me. Holy hell. I really did know them. I even remembered those dungarees in real life.

My mind raced over the connection. Who were they to Arran? At the point I'd met the child, their mother as I believed her to be, had been twenty-two, and dating my father. But she definitely wasn't Arran's mother. She wasn't old enough. Maybe the child was a niece or nephew?

That didn't explain why he kept a picture in his office, or why he'd been searching like Cassie had said.

"Thought you'd gone," a voice startled me.

Cassie approached from down the corridor. She was in a black playsuit, her hands in her pockets and her wild hair up in a chunky ponytail. She looked her age, almost, but the edge the woman carried added years in other ways.

I backed away from the picture. "I'm glad I saw you. I wanted to apologise."

She stopped a few feet away, one of her bare feet pointed. "Did Arran tell ye to come up?"

"Nope. I didn't tell him I upset you. I'm sorry I did."

"I wasn't so shy about pronouncing ye a grade A bitch for your view of him. I told him to be more open with ye. It's not surprising ye had that opinion if ye didn't know better. I also told him he was the worst."

I gave a surprised laugh, because he'd told me hardly anything. "All men are."

She grinned, her hostility shifting a tiny degree. "Right? I've been told I have emotional difficulties." She put the words in exaggerated air quotes. "Which I take to mean I can jump to conclusions. Maybe next time we meet I won't have reason to tear into ye."

"I'm not sure there'll be a next time."

"Oh, there will. I've been wanting to try out dancing at Arran's club for a while. See ye on the main stage, aye?"

Producing a half-smile, because I was a little scared of the fierce woman, I backed away, turned, then left.

Jamieson's car was already heading off, but Arran waited to help me in my door. When he climbed in the other side, I answered his quizzical glance.

"I just needed to apologise to her. She and your other friends were generous with clothes and things. I'll probably never see her again but I didn't want to leave a bad impression."

He tapped the steering wheel but didn't answer.

Exasperating man.

Staring into the dark countryside as it flew past the windows, I mused on the picture, considering how to bring it up. Then Arran spoke and set my teeth right back on edge.

"Cassie's a good judge of character."

I slanted a look at him. "Suggesting if she didn't like me, that's valid?"

He shrugged, but amusement played on his lips.

I changed the subject. The events of the previous night and day had left my body taut. "Is there something specific in your rules about not letting your claimed woman orgasm?"

A smile flirted with Arran's lips, but he concealed it. "The rules only state sex, not orgasms. I'm told not all women can come through sex, so it isn't so hard and fast."

I wished for other things that were hard and fast. In the shower, I'd tried and failed to make myself come. Which was insane because all he had to do was touch me and I was on the edge. If he'd broken my pussy, I'd kill him.

"Tell me all the things you did to me in my sleep," I demanded.

His hands gripped the steering wheel hard, though his gaze remained on the road ahead. "I stripped you, put my fingers, tongue, and dick inside you. Toyed with your ass."

My mouth dropped open. I breathed, but there wasn't enough air. "You cut my top off me, too."

"With my knife. I spanked your clit with my holster, fucked you with the handle of it, drew lines in your skin, and used the cold blade on your nipples."

Holy shit. My pussy clenched. "Wish I'd seen that. Maybe next time."

Arran gritted his teeth. Amused that somehow I'd got the upper hand, I faced away so he couldn't see my red cheeks.

The thought of him doing those things to me turned me on even more. Damn him to hell.

After a while, we left the brightly lit main road that took us south through the Cairngorms and plunged into dark countryside.

I squinted, confused. "I thought we were going back to the city?"

"We are. This won't take long. There's someone I need to see."

"Another woman to screw over?"

"Something like that."

A short while on, and we came to a pair of gateposts. I could just make out the house name engraved on the stone. *Kendrick Manor.*

I'd never heard the name, but something crawled over my skin, and I cringed in the seat. "What is this place?"

Again, no answer came my way, and we entered an avenue of trees, emerging into a park like the one in the house we'd just come from. Except for one huge difference. There was no house at the end of the road, only shadowy rubble and stones. It spread over a huge site, and it was clear that whatever property had been here before had been sprawling. And recently destroyed.

Arran parked up and climbed from the car. I followed suit, gazing in wonder at the ruin. Now we were right in front of it, I made out the shapes of rooms. Maybe towers from the circular bases. It had to have been a stately home, some place really grand. Huge blocks had fallen and tumbled, the grey stone an unkind shade but scorch marks cluing me in to what happened.

It felt like a place of darkness. Even weeds didn't grow in it. Nearby trees had been burned to blackened stumps.

Fire had consumed it all.

What had Cassie told me about her brother? That he'd burned down their home? I'd seen him casually spark a lighter, too. Was this his work or was that Arran's claim?

For a minute, my captor stared straight ahead, something shifting in his posture. He stood taller, shoulders back and chest out, something so lost in his expression that a pang of emotion broke free inside me. Stepping carefully, I made my way to him. Then like a damn fool, I took his hand and held it in mine.

Arran sucked in a breath. He broke his stare off with the ruin and switched his gaze to me.

"Why is this place important?" I asked. "What happened here?"

Instead of answering, because nothing could ever be that simple, he grasped my cheek and fitted his mouth to mine. He kissed me, with no second of warning or to give me space to process it. He'd said no kissing. We'd had a limit on the free use.

I didn't give a damn.

Hunger roared, and I kissed him back, just as hard,

even more urgent, our mouths clashing in perfectly imperfect presses.

Then a sound pierced my consciousness. A rumble of tyres behind us had him spinning around. Another car was coming down the avenue.

A pale-coloured saloon car with an unlit siren on top.

From the irritation in Arran's expression, the incomer was bad news. Taking me with him, he jogged to the left side of the destroyed house where woodland started. At the edge of the trees, he pushed me to continue. "Follow the line of trees in this direction. Don't use your torch and don't stop until you come to a small fenced-off area."

The engine sound grew louder, the headlights sweeping around the curve.

I shot my attention back to Arran, suddenly afraid. "Who is it? Why do I have to run?"

"Someone I don't want to see you. Now go."

He walked away and stabbed at his phone, lifting it to speak, hostility infecting him. I set my head down and entered the forest.

Trying to keep in a straight line was almost impossible.

I jumped at the flight of a small creature, then a twig snapped under my foot, jolting fear through my heart. Clamping my hand over my mouth, I kept moving, focusing on the line of trees so I didn't lose my path.

Darkness swallowed me. My pulse raced.

Any manner of things could happen. The unwanted visitor could hurt Arran. They could hunt me after and I wouldn't have a clue what happened to him. I could get lost in the woods and never find my way back to him. On the drive out here, there had been no other houses. Not a speck of light for miles.

I stepped on, dodging ghostly limbs and stumbling on the uneven ground. In my head, I started my alphabet game, picking countries as my topic. *A is for Angola, B for Botswana, C is Canada.*

A crunch sounded nearby.

I stopped dead.

My heart beat loud in my ears. That had been a footstep, I was certain. Not a scurrying rodent or a bird, but a heavy foot coming down. I'd been followed. Surely there was no one else out here in the trees. If it were Arran, he'd call out.

Terror gripped me. To my right was a large oak tree. Holding my breath, I crept around it, trying desperately not to make a sound. At the far side, I sank down with my back to the trunk. Night stared back at me from the forest.

I strained to listen. My imagination in the dark had always been a terrible thing, and I'd been wrong when I'd told Arran that I didn't mind it so much outdoors. That was limited to the city where streetlights or my scooter's headlamp chased away shadows. There was nothing out here. Not even the moon penetrated the thick cover of leaves overhead.

It was just shades of black and grey, and the cushion of forest floor underneath. Tree trunks were spectres. Falling leaves were evil things.

For a minute, nothing happened. No more footsteps. Nothing beyond the sound of my breathing and my pulse.

So badly, I wanted to activate my phone's torch, but I wasn't sure how far I'd come into the woods and whether Arran's visitor would be able to see me. More, it would make me a sitting duck, highlighted for anyone out there.

A twig cracked the other side of my tree.

Oh God. My fright crested, and I shook, my teeth chattering. I wrapped my arm around my legs to make myself as small as possible, my other hand still covering my mouth so I didn't scream.

Another crunch, closer again.

He'd found me, whoever the stranger was. He'd killed Arran and followed me. My brain offered up the only logical solution. And...it infuriated me. How dare he?

My shaking fingers were at my throat, and I found myself holding Mum's necklace which Arran had retrieved for me. If she was watching over me, I hoped she wasn't about to witness my end.

A short sound of breath came from my right, and I lifted my terrified gaze right as a body came into sight.

A pale face.

Dark eyes.

A deer trotted past on the forest floor.

A deer? I collapsed down, taking deep pulls of the air I'd starved myself of, my heart nearly giving out. Fucking hell on a handcart. Christ above. That had been the worst few minutes of my life.

I stood, and the creature spotted me and took off silently into the trees. Bloody thing. It managed to move quietly enough that second time. I scowled after it and returned to the other side of the oak, setting out once more. Grumbling to myself about animals and stupid, scary woods, I plodded on.

It was a false reprieve, though. Soon enough, the sounds of the woods got to me again. Sweat pricked my brow, though it was cooler here. My senses were mixed up. I'd been wandering a while and hadn't come across the fence Arran directed me to find.

I was very possibly lost.

For a moment, I stopped. Then I risked taking my phone from my shorts pocket and activating the map. It didn't load, not enough signal for what I needed. I tried the compass next then realised I neither knew how to use one nor which direction I wanted to go in.

This was ridiculous. I could've hidden in the car or concealed myself in the rubble and acted as backup.

If he was dead when I got back, I'd kill him.

A sound of frustration burst from my lips. What should I do, just stand here waiting?

A crash sounded. Another. Regular footsteps, undoubtedly.

My breath caught, and I whirled around, right as a man emerged from the murkiest part of the trees.

Jamieson, Arran's friend, stormed up and took my lit phone from my hands. "Put that down or you'll give yourself away," he commanded in a whisper.

"I'm lost," I squeaked.

"Are ye now?"

Towing me by the elbow, he marched us through the next line of trees, and there on the other side was a small fence, encircling a patch of clearer ground with an oblong of rocks in it. Leading me over, Jamieson held up a finger. "Wait here. I'll be back."

As fast as he'd appeared, he was gone.

I stepped over the fence and dropped to sit on a rock the other side, my legs giving out. He was who Arran had been calling then. He'd been out in his car and presumably nearby.

God, I'd been so afraid.

It felt like forever until he came back, and my mind had sunk to misery.

Jamieson stepped over the fence and took a seat next to me. "Arran's still occupied. I'm sure he willnae enjoy being apart from ye."

I sniffed. "Really? I can't imagine he'd care that much."

The man stared at me then gave a low laugh. "Yet he sent ye to his mother's grave and called out his best friend to come protect ye. Keep telling yourself that, sweetheart."

20

Arran

"What the fuck are you doing here?" Upon the flat stone that had been the front step of my house, I waited, staring down the approaching man.

Detective Dickhead, now Chief Constable Kenney, used to work for my father when he'd been chief of police. Kenney also used to run a sideline in private security, translation: hurting people for cash and body disposal. As far as I knew, the huge man had stopped all extracurricular activities in recent years, barely escaping prosecution after my father went down.

Still, I wouldn't put it past him to have fingers in many shit pies.

"You've been out of the city, I needed to talk to you," Kenney said.

He'd been to the club. Shade had told me.

"And you found me. Got a tracker on my car?"

He shrugged. "Lucky guess. I assumed you'd gone to McInver's boys but stopped here first."

"Don't call them after their father, none took his name.

Besides, you'll be shot on sight if you go there." Jamieson had once set fire to Kenney's prize BMW. He wouldn't think twice about doing it again.

Kenney tutted. "Making threats against the police?"

I held his gaze, because yes, I fucking was.

"It's been ten years," he finally groused.

"You're insane if you think any of us will forget, Detective."

"It's Chief Constable to you."

I inhaled, my nostrils flared. "Then you'll address me as Lord Kendrick."

His eyebrows went up. "Last I checked, your old man was still alive. Rotting in his jail cell but still breathing."

Dad's heart still beat only because I enjoyed knowing he suffered. He would meet his end at my hands when I was ready.

I lowered my gaze. "As fun as this is, going to tell me why you came to find me?"

"Your little psychopath has been stalking some of the councillors in Deadwater."

I held still, giving nothing away. Following Genevieve's information, Shade was acting on my orders, carrying out investigations into known users of sex workers in Deadwater's political ranks. Cherry had been expecting a visit from one along with his friend. We were looking into who buddied up to who. Which of their vices we knew about.

"Got proof of that?" I asked.

"He was seen."

"By...?"

"That's irrelevant, but I took a call from the goddamned

mayor about it. Now listen here, I give you and your whores a lot of leeway in my city. You'll call your dog to heel—"

I rushed him, snatched his arms behind his back, and smacked him onto the bonnet of his unmarked police car. Once, I'd feared him. He was bigger than me and acted like the cock of the fucking walk. But at twenty years older, he couldn't match my strength.

"Say that word again."

"What word?" he choked.

"Whores. When any one of those hard-working women is worth ten of you."

He shoved me off and whirled around. "Whatever. You can't fuck with the politicians. Even with the arrangements we have, I'm duty bound to protect them, no matter what."

Our arrangements served me well and kept my life and the lives of the women who worked with me sweet. But I also had a deal with the mayor, the top politician in Deadwater, something Kenney knew nothing about.

It was a secret only me and Shade shared.

A dark thought swept over me. If Shade's investigations pointed to the mayor, we had issues. Mayor Makepeace used sex workers, but discreetly. A very limited group of the women attended his office on the regular. It made him a suspect.

As Chief Constable, Kenney was around the politicians a lot, too. Giving updates on crime in the city and providing statistics at council meetings and events. He was the face of the police, and his job was in their hands—they had the power to order him sacked and a new Chief Constable brought in.

I came back to the friend Cherry had mentioned. That

could be a councillor, who Shade was watching, Mayor Makepeace, or even Kenney.

Coming to warn me off made sense in all cases.

I curled my lip. "What have they got on you to make you come all the way out here? Or is it more personal?"

Kenney huffed and opened his car door. "None of the above. They're asking for my help, and it's message delivered as far as I'm concerned. Keep the fuck in your lane."

"Before you run," I said. "The woman who was murdered in North Town, I want her autopsy report."

"Why? She wasn't one of yours."

"Just do it."

Without a goodbye, he slammed himself in and drove away.

I breathed out, my mental list of murder suspects growing. The urge came over me to tell Genevieve what I'd found, after all, it had been her conversation that clued me in.

A thumbs-up from Jamieson on my phone told me he'd found her in the woods. It also gave me a moment to gather my thoughts. The memories Kenney brought forward had the power to trip me up.

I stepped over a pile of broken stone and glass and entered the ruins of Kendrick Manor.

The dark sky held over my path through the house. Down what had been a corridor, passing on the right a huge entertaining room that my father used to fill with women he'd bus in from all over the country and beyond, many of them trafficked or bought at auction. From the youngest age, I'd witnessed the acts he made them put on. Live sex shows. Women fucking each other. Performing for him.

He didn't usually let me see him fuck, but exposing me to every other part of it was a feature of making me a man.

I stepped deeper into the bowels of the building. Further along, the footprint of the corridor turned, leading into what had been the staff quarters. I used to hang out there more than anywhere else, learning to read with the help of one of Dad's women after the tutor he paid to teach me spent more of his time getting his dick sucked.

I'd never gone to school. Or had friends of any kind.

At ten years old, I'd started to become aware that life didn't look like this for everyone. In the books I read and the stories I heard, women did more than stand around in revealing clothes waiting to be fucked. Still, I assumed my home was normal. The reign of terror my father dealt out on everyone around me, including my young self, typical for other people.

His beatings, screaming, and acts of humiliation were a daily occurrence.

In the rubble under my feet, I trod over a piece of carved stone. Part of the old staircase. Memories rushed. If I answered my father back, I'd be tied to the stairs and left. It was always cold in the manor, and my punishment meant I'd be there for hours, or even days. When I couldn't control my body anymore, I'd piss myself on the steps.

I'd positioned Genevieve on the stairs in a position of humiliation, just like I was forced to. Either I'd been confronting it, or maybe trying to replace the memory with something better.

For a long moment, I stared at the broken stone, lost in the sense of being trapped. Tied up and in horrible discomfort. No one was allowed to help me for fear of retribution, but they did.

Audrey did. My mother.

I'd had no idea who she was until it was too late. My recollections of her were just as twisted as anything else from my childhood. She'd been a broken woman, conditioned to serve and obedient to a fault. Until she wasn't. She'd stood up to Dad and lost her life because of it. Not once had she ever told me who she was.

My stomach curdled, and I strode out of the ruin and into the woods I could navigate blindfolded.

Near Audrey's grave and on silent feet, I stopped, concealing myself in darkness. Then I sent the short message I'd recorded for Jamieson, asking him to bring Genevieve back to the car.

In a minute, they appeared in the darkness, on track to pass me.

"You're wrong about him," Genevieve was saying. "He thinks I'm a gang member."

"Are ye?" Jamieson asked.

"No! I hate the gangs with everything in me."

"Why?"

They were right next to me now, passing only a couple of metres away. So close, I couldn't miss the genuine, unhidden hurt in Genevieve's features.

"They killed my mother."

Then they were gone, and I slunk to my mother's grave.

As I always did, I hopped the fence and laid out on the stone, staring at the starry Scottish sky. I spoke to her in my head, never out loud.

Hey, Audrey. Thank you for looking after Genevieve while

I was busy. I wonder if you would've liked her. Jury's still out as far as I'm concerned.

Just so you know, Dad's still in jail. One day, I'll kill him, and I'll do it in your name. Sorry you can't be around to see it.

I wish I could say I loved you, but fuck you for what you did to me. Fuck you for fucking me up just as badly as he ever did.

21

Genevieve

In silence, Arran drove us away from Kendrick Manor. I couldn't hold my tongue. "That used to be your home back there."

He kept his gaze forward but awarded me a tiny inclination of his head.

"You destroyed it," I pressed.

A slight tweak of his lips told me I was on the money. "Burned it down. Jamieson helped."

For a moment, I held my breath. "Why?"

"My father killed my mother there, but then you knew that."

Hurt bubbled up in me. "I didn't even know your name until ten days ago. Would you stop with the crap that I'm some gangster's mole trying to infiltrate you?"

"Gangster's mole?" He uttered an infuriating laugh.

"I believe you about your business setup, can't you return the favour and accept I am who I say I am?" I snapped, yelling at him for no other reason than I had no idea how to treat him now. His mother had *died*. Like mine. Except his father had murdered her rather than mourned her. God.

He worked his jaw. "Tell me everything you know about the gangs in Deadwater."

"I know about yours."

"I don't run a gang." At my astonished stare, he explained. "I call my team of people a crew. We act like a gang in that we defend our territory by any means, including by violence, but I don't share any other gang aspirations."

I pulled my lip between my teeth, chewing it. "Because you formed around running the club and protecting women."

"Exactly. Now back to you."

"I didn't grow up in Deadwater," I said slowly. "Though I was born here. My parents were a couple for the few years it took to have me and my brother, then they split. Mum raised us, then when I was ten and Riordan thirteen, our father wanted access to us again. We came back to Deadwater, where he'd stayed, and visited with him for weekends. Neither of us wanted to be there. He'd never paid maintenance, and we'd watched Mum struggle to make ends meet as a single parent. She did her best and even managed to complete a degree in nursing in that time. Her mother took care of us but died unexpectedly. Then when I was fifteen, Mum's life was ended."

"How?"

I gripped the sides of my seat, suddenly hot. "She helped a woman who was knocked up by a member of a gang, I think raped, but Mum didn't specifically say, probably because I was so young. The pregnant lady wanted to give birth in secret because she was scared of the baby's father and knew he'd never let them go, so Mum faked paperwork to say she'd lost the pregnancy. The woman moved far away and had the baby without the father knowing."

"But he found out," Arran said quietly.

"He suspected something after she vanished. He'd escorted her to appointments so knew where to go to find Mum. He intimidated her and made threats."

My beautiful, confident mother had been afraid. She'd tried to change her working location. Anything to escape him.

"Did he kill her?"

"No," I spluttered. "Not directly. Mum died in a car crash. She left work in a rainstorm and drove home too fast, ending up skidding onto the wrong side of the road and in front of a lorry. She was forty-three. Healthy despite her hard life. The stress and fear caused her panic, I'm certain."

"So there was no consequence for him."

I leaned my too-warm forehead against the glass. "No. Nothing happened to him at all. There wasn't even any proof he was there. My world disintegrated, and that bastard walked away without a care."

Lost in my own thoughts, I barely noticed that Arran had asked a question.

"His name, Genevieve," he repeated.

My mouth rejected the words, but I spat them out. "Jordan Peters. We lived in—"

"Newcastle. I know. Before that, London, and Manchester for a while. Then you moved in with your dad. Did you ever see Peters yourself?"

"Never, though Mum described him."

"Tell me what she said."

I cast my mind back. I'd told the police this but with precisely zero effect. "He was thin and wiry. Not tall but bigger than her and obviously strong. He had a bird tattoo by his eye and dots around it. Why?"

He didn't reply. I returned to thoughts of my mother. Then Arran's mother. I wondered if he'd ever want to talk about her.

"There are three main gangs in Deadwater and other nearby cities," he said abruptly. "The Four Milers, which your brother and father are linked to."

"They're absolutely not." I sniffed.

Arran shot me a look. "The Zombies are the second, my crew is the final one, if you insist on including us in the lineup. The Four Milers run drugs, the Zombies handle weapons. Our territory is sex work. Outside of that, there are small gangs that appear and disappear. I don't give a fuck about the others or what they do unless they encroach on my turf."

"So if any try to run sex workers?"

"I eliminate them. Used to be that women were trafficked here, but we shut down the routes. All those who wanted to come work in the warehouse did. Others we extended help and protection to while they got their lives back."

"If you're not a gang, why the masks? Why the big reputation?" As I said the words, I worked it through. "Because you're showing them what you want them to see, so no one tries to, what was the word you used, encroach?"

Arran nodded, his smile fleeting but almost pleased, or

approving. A little piece of happiness chased away some of my blues.

Jesus. What the hell was that? I locked down the emotion.

I was not going to fall for my skeleton-masked captor. Not even the tiniest bit.

"Tell me how your setup works, then," I asked. "And no, I'm not asking so I can feed this back to someone else."

His lips curved again. "What do you want to know?"

"I'm going to need to interact with your people. If we're selling the line that we're a couple, they're going to expect me to know this."

"I'm the leader for all intents and purposes. Shade and Convict are my right-hand men."

"Do they have real names?"

"Yes, but it's up to them if they want to share."

"Which of them came into the game and hunted me?"

"Convict. You won't see him tonight."

I'd barely thought of his crew member in days. Perhaps he'd just been after what Arran had claimed in me. From the big deal everyone was making about it, I'd started to understand it more.

Arran continued his explanation. "Alisha's my operations manager, though she objects to the title. She runs the women and is good at her job."

"Why doesn't she wear a mask? When I came in the first time, the three of you had masks on but she didn't."

"That's up to her. She once said that men only see the character she's wearing that day. Her wig, makeup, and clothes. Outside of the warehouse, she looks nothing like that and has never been recognised. She isn't trying to intimidate anyone either. That's all on me and the rest of the crew. All the men who work at the warehouse are ostensibly gang members. If they are working the club, on the door, or as security for the women, they're paid from Alisha's budget. If they're doing business on my behalf, I pay them."

"What does business on your behalf entail? Actually, I don't think I want to know."

He didn't answer either, driving us on, our journey a reverse of the one that had taken me to his friends' home. Soon enough, we crossed the Queensferry Bridge and passed Edinburgh, heading for the borders.

For a while, both of us were quiet, lost in our thoughts. When we got closer to Deadwater, Arran spoke again.

"I'm going to have to behave differently around you in the club."

I twisted in my seat, giving him my attention.

"People need to see that I'm enamoured. I asked Shade to keep the news of our bonding under close wraps until today. Obviously the watchers knew, alongside some of the staff, but it hasn't been made common knowledge. That changes tonight."

"Do I need to pretend I'm in love, too?"

"Do whatever you feel. Just know that if you run, I'll catch you."

I blinked at him. "I'm not going to run. I don't need to. You said yourself that now the first week is up, we're not chained together anymore."

"I only said a time limit of two hours lifted. We can now spend up to four hours apart, and that's the case for the next three weeks. You're still eating meals with me and sleeping in my bed. And fucking me. Did you think you'd escaped me? Guess again."

All my plans broke into pieces. Yet in the same breath, I was hit with a bolt of relief. I didn't even attempt to analyse that odd emotion, stacking it with all the rest that came with this maddening man. "I have things to do. I need to get back to work."

"Take the damn money you're owed from me and quit that delivery shit."

I stuck my nose in the air. "Nope. You have your standards, and I have mine."

He sighed but didn't argue any more.

Then we were there, crossing the bridge from Scotland to England and entering the centre of Deadwater.

At the warehouse, a huge queue lined up for Divide's nightclub, with an equal number of people streaming into Divine's strip bar. It was midnight on Friday, so no surprise. We drove around the back, Arran easing the car into the last remaining space. It had the letters AD printed in white paint on the floor. *Arran Daniels.*

Because all of this was his.

"Don't get out," Arran instructed me. He exited the car, then rounded to my side, opening my door with his hand out like a gentleman.

"So precious," an awed voice came, echoed with a smattering of applause.

Accepting Arran's help, I peered wide-eyed at the warehouse. There was no bouncer on the back door this time, but a group of people stood at the corner, clubgoers by their smart or skimpy outfits.

"Congratulations," another called.

"Beautiful," said a woman.

Arran produced a smile so natural it gave me shivers.

"Thank you," he called back.

We neared the group. A woman reached out and touched my shoulder. "I saw everything. Honey, that was so wonderful. You held out for him. My heart!"

I produced my own slightly stunned grin but kept on going.

We rounded to the front of the building, and Arran interlaced our fingers, lifting our joined hands as people in the queue shouted out for us.

"Oh my God," I muttered. "How do they know my name?"

He leaned in. "Told you. Shade made us public. We're a hot topic. Don't worry. The fuss will die down."

Except we were very much in that moment, just as he was very clearly leading me in the front entrance. Everybody was staring. I tugged at the hem of my short shorts then brushed back stray hair that had escaped my messy bun.

"I wish you could've warned me. I'd have put makeup on. I don't look like I belong here."

"Part of the attraction. You're beautiful."

That offhand compliment had no business making my heart swell. He only meant it as an outsider's observation, not from his heart.

Inside, Arran received slaps on the back from his team and strangers, people smiling at me, too. Making introductions, he gave me names I tried to store away.

"I need to spend some time with my team, then I'll give you a proper tour."

A kiss pressed to my temple earned sighs from the

spectators. Then we were in the management suite, and I could finally relax. He didn't let go of my hand, though, and in his private office, where a selection of his crew waited, he directed me with him around his desk, sitting me on his knee while he reclined. I went to stand, but he towed me down on his lap, banding an arm around me in a possessive hold.

I gave up the struggle and relaxed, enjoying the almost immediate prod of his dick against my ass.

Subtly, I scanned the room for the picture that Cassie told me was here. I spotted it on a shelf by the door. That same child, the one I knew and had played with. Another memory rose—Dad had a printed photo of us somewhere. He had a wall of pictures, sentimental over his family, friends, and ex-girlfriends. I was reasonably sure I'd seen it there. When I had time alone with Arran, I'd tell him.

At last, I regarded his crew. What a change from last time I'd been here. No masks, only interested expressions. Except one woman, whose jaw was clamped shut. Alisha, though in a red wig this time rather than blonde. She'd shown me around and called me a clean little thing. I wondered what her problem was now.

Arran extended a hand, gesturing to each in turn. "Shade, Alisha, Manny who's head of security, and Lara."

The younger woman peered at me with unabashed interest. I recognised her. She'd brought me back to the office. I raised an awkward hand. "Hi, everyone."

Both men dipped their heads. Lara waved gleefully.

Alisha stepped forward, her sky-high heels making her legs appear endless under her dressing gown, the outline of lacy lingerie clear. Arran had described her outward appearance as a disguise. To me, it gave her armour I wished I could have. I pined for ten minutes with my hairbrush and the makeup in my bag.

"Congratulations, Arran," Alisha forced out, though her expression didn't match her words. "A lot has happened since you disappeared."

Arran drifted his thumb up and down my waist. "I didn't disappear. I was very enjoyably present."

"Not where you were needed," she said.

"You're wrong. I was exactly where I was needed." He switched his gaze to Shade. "Anything happen that you couldn't handle?"

"Nothing big. We were all just happy for ye to honeymoon in peace."

Honeymoon. Like we were married.

Alisha's focus shot to him. "We had the cops come in. A dealer on the floor. There was a fight right in the middle of Divide."

Arran gave a short laugh, but his soft touch on me had stilled. I knew him well enough now to recognise annoyance. "A normal week. Do we have a problem?"

Alisha's gaze flashed with some emotion I didn't recognise. "Can we talk in private?"

Under me, his muscles tightened. "No, we can't."

Tension rose. Across the room, Lara sent me a wide-eyed look.

I exchanged it, then hopped up, turning back to Arran. "Actually, I wanted to talk to Lara about something. Do you mind if I step away for a minute?"

He watched me for a beat then reached up and cupped the back of my neck. And pulled me in for a very hot, and very public kiss.

My body melted for him. We weren't meant to do this,

yet he'd broken that rule twice already today. All I wanted now was to crawl back onto his lap but naked.

"Goddamn you," I said against his lips.

"Don't be long," was his low reply. To Lara, he snapped a different order. "Don't leave her alone. Manny, you're Genevieve's security when she's not at my side."

With my personal crew of two, I exited the office, exhaling in relief from being out of the loaded air.

"Holy crap, that was intense. I've never seen Alisha go up against the boss like that," Lara quipped. "What do you wanna do?"

Behind her, Manny stood like a sentinel, arms folded, glaring over our heads at people further down the corridor.

I uttered a small embarrassed laugh. "It's not a big deal, and only if you can spare the time. I realised when we arrived that I'm severely underdressed. I've got makeup in my bag, if you could just direct me to somewhere I could freshen myself up."

In her revealing but cute black-and-pink uniform, Lara clasped her hands together, her grin instant and big. "I've been assigned to you, so of course I have the time. We have a huge dressing room and a wardrobe of clothing. Down for a makeover?"

"Are you serious? I'd love that."

Lara linked her arm through mine. "You bet. The things I could do to your hair. Follow me."

Together, we traversed the corridors to the place I'd been desperate to access last weekend. This time, I had a new hidden agenda. People I wanted to talk to out of earshot of Arran.

Information to gather, and exactly the right group of

women to give it to me.

22

Genevieve

At the dressing room, Lara led me inside. Women, a few men, and a couple of perhaps gender-neutral folk, sat at stations with bright lights around mirrors, racks of clothes everywhere. Music pulsed, coming from an exit at the far end with a sign above it that read *Stage*.

At our entrance, heads rose, smiles formed.

"Hey, Genevieve," a couple of voices called out.

That was going to take some getting used to.

"Oh my God, girl. I can't believe you came down here." Clem, the older lady I'd seen at the strip club's bar, bustled over, her hands clutched together in mild panic. "I need to apologise. I had no idea who you were when we met before. None of us did. I would've been way more helpful. I should have been more helpful," she corrected herself. "I'm so sorry for being a dick."

I touched her shoulder, shocked. "Stop. You've nothing to apologise for, Clem. I didn't tell you who I was."

Back then, I hadn't even been the person they thought I was now. Their boss's woman.

Another woman crept over, her expression more sheepish. She was beautiful, obviously a dancer, made up in the style of an American country singer. "I need to fess up, too."

Lara wiggled her fingers. "This is Dixie," she introduced.

Dixie dropped my gaze. "Just last week, I made a pass at your man. In my defence, he didn't tell anyone he was taken. Even Alisha had to pretend he was hers. He never fucks around, so I figured he was lonely and needed someone on his dick." She slapped her hand over her mouth. "Shut me up, someone."

I couldn't help my grin. "You all need to stop apologising. No one's offended me in any way. I'm just glad to be here."

It was the right thing to say. Around us, people visibly relaxed, chatter starting once more. Dixie blew out a relieved breath.

Lara squeezed my arm then directed me to a free dressing table. "I'll do your hair. You tackle your makeup."

I sought out Dixie. "Could you come, too? Chat with me a minute. I've got something to ask."

She agreed, and I settled into the seat and regarded myself in the mirror. After a week locked away with Arran I looked different. The same fair hair to the middle of my back, in need of a cut but glossy and probably better for a week with no straighteners or curling tongs. The same blue eyes and heart-shaped face. I couldn't pinpoint the change, but it was real.

At least I was alive.

Dixie snuck up a hand, her reflection in the mirror. "Let me do your makeup? I've been taking a hair and beauty course at college, courtesy of the club. I'd love to try out my techniques on you."

The memory came back to me of Arran describing how the money the club made was spent. I kind of loved that. With my acceptance, the two women set about tackling my scruffy state.

"What did you want to ask?" Lara said.

"It's about a friend of mine." I took a deep breath. "She worked the streets and was killed recently."

Dixie, midway through blending contour on my cheekbones, froze. "Killed? Oh my God. You knew that hooker who worked in North Town?"

"Dix," a man drawled from across the room. "It's sex worker or street worker. Hooker is offensive."

She gave him an unimpressed eyeroll. "Honey, I fuck for money. I can call it what I like."

"Still don't need to demean yourself."

"It ain't delulu if it's trululu."

He sniffed, and she came back to me.

"We've all been talking about it this week. Sorry for your loss."

"Her name was Cherry." I frowned. "Her street name anyway."

Dixie leaned in conspiratorially. "Chelsea, that's her real name. I guess you knew that, as her friend, but I overheard gossip. One of Alisha's recruiters tried many times to get her to come here, but she wouldn't even consider it. She liked her independence. Gotta say it made us all appreciate the safety of these four walls if there's a killer on the loose."

"Dixie." Lara hissed and jabbed her heated tongs as if to indicate discretion for me.

"Oh, well, I'm sure she'll be missed." Dixie made

a wonky sign of the cross. "What did you want to talk about?"

"I intend to find out who murdered her."

The chatter around me ceased. Dixie and Lara swapped a glance, then Lara spoke.

"Does Arran know you're going to do that?"

"No, but I'll tell him."

"Okay, phew. What do you want from us?"

I swung a look around. "Did anyone here know her?"

Grim shakes of heads and flat denials returned.

"Like I said, she didn't mix with us. I can ask around, but I never once saw her come here, and in all the conversations about her, uh, end, no one said they knew her personally." Dixie finished blending and moved on to my eyes.

My shoulders slumped. "Well, that's a dead end. I was hoping she'd have acquaintances in the same job. Someone she could've confided in."

Dixie pulled a sad face. "Maybe she only had you."

God, surely not.

It made me think harder. I needed another approach. Dixie drew on cat eyes that suited me so far beyond anything I'd ever tried myself, and I started over.

"What about clients?" I said. Dixie worked on the sex side as well as dancing. "Cherry told me a few things—"

"Stop. Not here." Dixie shook her head, loose curls flying.

"You can't..." I dropped my voice, cluing in. "You can't mention clients?"

"Not in terms of whatever you're about to say. As murder

suspects? People are listening, hun," she whispered back. "And by people, I mean gossips. You and I can have that chat, but not here or now. I need to hit the stage, and we're about done with your face if you finish your lips yourself. Find me upstairs tomorrow evening, and we'll grab a private room. I'm working ten PM till seven AM. Grab me before."

"I'll find you. And thank you for this." I gestured to myself.

"It's no trouble. You're such a doll. No wonder he didn't even cop a squeeze of my fine ass. Gotta go."

With a grin at Lara's outraged huff, Dixie slipped away, and I sat back, relieved to have that conversation ahead of me.

A short while later, I was transformed.

My hair tumbled down my back in loose waves, and my eyes were smoky grey with my lips cool-pink. I was pretty certain I'd never been this hot and told Lara so.

She waggled her eyebrows. "Clothes, next. Whatcha got?"

I gave an embarrassed shrug. "Very little, and nothing that would suit the club. Everything with Arran happened so fast, and I haven't even been home since."

Lara stepped away. In a minute, she returned with a black tube dress, an underwear set with the label still on it, and even a pair of pink heels that matched my lipstick.

"Anything you need, we've got it. There's a whole store of clothes, new and pre-loved. Anyone here can help themself and add to their own rack." Proudly, she offered her findings then pointed out a screen to change behind.

The secondhand clothes from Arran's friends came off me and the new set went on. All except the bra. The tube dress was tight enough to support me, and I had a moment of utter joy at seeing myself in it. There wasn't anything that special about me. I was mid. Unexceptional. But that was the point of a makeover, and I'd been made up beyond my wildest dreams.

I stepped out, and Lara did an exaggerated jaw drop.

"Hot freaking stuff," she informed me.

I stepped forward on the pink kitten heels. "Are you sure? It's not too revealing?"

Passing me with her boobs completely out, one of the dancers burst out in a laugh then jiggled for effect. I laughed, too, loving the moment I'd found with them here.

Cherry would've loved it. The piece of my heart that had broken for her panged. I wished she'd have taken up their offer.

Lara took my arm and patted it. "Are you okay? Where did you go?"

I snapped my focus to her. "Nowhere. I mean, just to my friend. I miss her."

Lara tilted her head in sympathy. "Aw, I get it. I cry at the good news stories I read. Don't get me started on actual tragedies."

One of the men who'd left for the dance floor, then returned for a costume switch, gave a small smile. "My cousin died a month ago. I didn't really know her as an adult, but we were friends as kids. Every time I think of it, I get cut up."

An Asian woman fitting a luxurious wig gave him a one-armed hug. "I lost my dog last Christmas, and I know it isn't the same as a person—"

"Dogs are family, too," the man corrected.

Her eyes welled. "He was my baby, and I miss him all the time."

One by one, others gave up their own stories, their pockets of sorrow, and just like with the makeover, the shared grief bolstered me. I'd missed having friends so much.

A music change had a gaggle of dancers rushing to the stage exit, and Lara tugged my arm.

"Want to go back and show the boss what he's got? Or we could go dancing in Divide? Or even upstairs to the fun floor. I remember you were interested last time we met, and you'll need to know your way to meet Dixie tomorrow."

"All of the above, but I really want Arran to see me like this."

"Yeah, you do."

She snickered, and I peered again at myself, seeking out my flaws. There was something wrong with me because I needed Arran's approval for how I looked. I wanted him to want me.

He was only faking for the sake of his reputation. I got that. And the smart version of me had a plan to use the knowledge I had about the missing child to get him to help me find my dad.

The not-smart version of me wanted him to drop the act and kiss me again.

And worse? For him to mean it.

23

Arran

With her arms folded and spiked nails out, Alisha stared me down across the office, her anger undented even though we'd gone over each of her gripes in detail.

The fights between clubgoers in Divide wasn't unusual, and the perpetrators had been banned.

The cops who came here for me led to Detective Dickhead tracking me down. They often scoped the club, making the police chief appear like he was monitoring us for the good of the public. No big deal.

The only concern I shared was for the drug dealer spotted on Divide's floor. Then again, those guys were easy to pick out. Nearly always alone, wearing jackets despite the sweltering heat of packed bodies, and standing in plain sight of the crowd. The guy was undoubtedly one of the Four Milers, and I needed to handle them for multiple reasons.

Just another day in the office.

Yet my old friend paced the floor as if motorised. "The problem is, Arran, you're not taking me seriously. You weren't here for any of it, and with Convict out, you left me no backup. You don't seem to care."

"Shade was here for the most part. Manny has your back."

"Shade has his own priorities, and it wasn't the same without you here. I didn't feel safe. On top of that, you allowed me to tell my staff that you were mine."

I raised my hands. "And?"

"I look like a fool!"

"I don't care about gossip," I snapped. "Gen and I revealed our relationship today. Tell them you were covering for me as a kindness to protect my privacy. Or make something else up. What does it matter?"

"It's my reputation."

"Still don't understand the issue or why you're stressing." I glanced at Shade who leaned on the brick wall by the window.

He twisted his lips, but worry crinkled his brow. Alisha was the steadier one amongst us. She managed the strip club and the floor above with no sweat. Tackling suppliers, settling drama among the workers, all within her remit and never a problem.

I was trying to be understanding, but she was giving me nothing. "Is something else going on?"

"Don't blame this shit on me. You're the one who ran off after a woman."

"I didn't just run off. I took my woman away for a week."

She made a noise of disgust. "Explain to me what happened with Convict. Why did he disappear on the same night?"

I closed my mouth. I had plans to deal with him but no time yet.

Alisha homed in on the gaping maw of lacking information. "It's to do with that girl, isn't it?"

"Do you have a problem with Genevieve?"

"Do I?" Alisha spat. "Genevieve this, that, and everything. I see how it's going to be. Any club business and your mind is going to be between her legs."

I rose, my fingertips spread on my hardwood desk. After Genevieve left, I'd changed into the black suit I wore if I was to be seen around the club's interior and shifted back into boss mode like a glove. "Because of our history, I'm going to pretend you didn't disrespect us. This conversation is done. I'm sure the club needs your attention more than I need to hear your jealousy."

"You think I'm jealous? Know what? You're just like the chief with his addiction for little blonde things." Alisha gave me one last furious, incredulous look and swept away in a cloud of expensive perfume, slamming the door closed at her back.

The dust settled.

A bolt of unexpected anger crawled through me, starting slow but building. Just like the chief? She meant my dad who'd bought her for me and probably abused her himself. That's what she thought of me?

Shade whistled low. "Handled that well."

My reply was barely more than a snarl. "Don't."

"I told ye she was angry; ye somehow turned that into her being jealous. Trying to piss her off more?"

"What else am I supposed to think? Then she has the nerve to spit that shite at me? I'm not like him," I bit out.

Shade eyed me. "Your da? Pretty sure she doesnae think that. She spoke out of line, but fuck if I know why."

Yet that accusation hit and blew up a kernel of doubt I'd always had about myself. I'd watched my father's ways and vowed to be nothing like him. I'd set my world up to be the opposite to his. But the way I fucking yearned for Genevieve had me thinking different. At the flesh auctions, Dad would fight for the 'little blonde things', as Alisha put it. He'd forget everything else apart from winning the woman.

The way I felt right now, I'd probably throw myself off a cliff for Genevieve.

What if Alisha was right?

"While we have a quiet minute, there's a few things I need to update ye on." Shade crossed the room so he was in my eyeline rather than at my back. "The guy Genevieve named, Don, is nowhere to be found. People talked about him, but no one could give me a location."

"He's a member of the Four Milers, though?"

"Badge-wearing, flag-flying. Yet Convict's been watching them and couldn't find the guy. He's desperate to talk to ye, by the way."

"Did he give an update on Genevieve's father?"

"Yes, but—"

"I'll hear it from you."

Shade studied me for a moment, no doubt judging my worsening mood and deciding not to push me. "He checked out Sydney's address. Sydney's ma came and went, but he didn't see her. I took over so he could move on to the next target, but didn't find much more than the fact her room still looks lived-in."

I didn't want to know how he'd seen the inside of her bedroom. Sydney and her mother lived in a tower block. Shade had balls of fucking steel.

And my friend's darkening expression told me there was worse to come.

"Convict discovered that she and Genevieve's dad had been at the Four Milers' compound." His words landed like bombs. "They were seen by a friendly local. Not only that, but they then went on to meet with someone from the Zombies."

Fuck. Of course her dad was thick in it, buddying up to not one but both of the rival gangs to mine. What the fuck had I got myself into with her?

"When was this?"

"Convict said he'll tell you himself if ye call. He stopped sharing with me."

I dropped my head back on my seat. Dark emotion boiled under my skin. I needed to compartmentalise and handle my crew. I hadn't told Shade why I'd iced out Convict, but he was one of the few I could trust.

I dialled Convict on a video call, setting my phone on my desk.

"Arran, thank fuck," my disgraced crew member answered. He was in his car, darkness around him, no engine sound. A black bandanna covered his throat—a skeleton one but reversed.

"You were asked to track down Adam Walker," I named Genevieve's father. "Give me an update."

"Sure thing, boss. But can I ask something first? For a week, you haven't picked up my calls. What did I do?" Convict moved the camera so it gave a view of his arm and the snake tattoo that had given him away.

It took me back to the game. To his hands on Genevieve. In my head, I replayed what I'd seen when I ran in, and dangerous rage challenged my reason.

"You broke my rules," I said, cold.

His mouth opened. Then he shut it again, whatever he'd intended to say clearly stalling out. "What are you accusing me of?"

"Either confess it or I'll assume you've been fucking me over in multiple ways."

Convict's eyes widened. "I swear to fucking God I haven't. You mean the game night. When I went into the basement. That's all I've done, nothing else."

"Fuck," Shade drawled. "What were ye thinking, man? That's well out of bounds."

"I wanted what they'd all signed up for," he blurted. Desperation laced his tone. "Just to try it out. You did, too, Arran. You went in and claimed a woman. You wanted the same—"

"I should put you through the fucking wall," Shade snarled.

I held up a hand. Instantly, both men silenced.

"The fact I went in, too, Convict, is the only reason you're still breathing." I was a hypocrite and I wouldn't hide from that, though I was still the leader of this crew and needed to manage him in a way I hadn't myself.

Convict ducked his head but nodded. "You have every right. I didn't know who she was to you, and I heard after that she'd gone in there by accident. I recognised her from when she'd applied for a job, so I didn't understand why the two of you... I mean, congratulations on the claiming. When I see your woman, I'll apologise to her. It was all a misunderstanding."

"You'll keep your distance, and there was no misunderstanding. You went into that basement after agreeing to my rules. Therefore, you wilfully disobeyed them."

"I swear on my dead mother's grave, I've never broken your trust aside from that. Please don't cut me off. Without the club, I've got nothing."

Despite the history we shared and how he'd been a friend for a long while, the right thing to do was cut him loose from my crew. The human side, the part of me that had always wanted people to trust and take care of, was the only reason I didn't jump to that.

But also, there was a darker reason: Convict was an ally or an enemy. I didn't need more of the latter.

"You're operating under a strike against you," I concluded instead. "Do everything I ask without argument and you might have a chance to earn a place back in this building. Until then, you're on the streets. If I hear one more thing about your loyalty that makes me regret my faith, I'll handle you myself. And stay away from Genevieve. You scared her in what was already a terrifying situation. For that alone, I should fucking end you."

He gave a subdued nod of acceptance. "Understood. Thank you. I won't let you down."

I instructed him to proceed with his report, and he described how he'd traced Genevieve's father from hanging out with Sydney two weeks ago to a sighting in Four Milers' territory and then with the Zombies only four days back.

"Find out what he did there," I ordered.

Though in my mind, that answer was limited to a few options. The Four Milers ran drugs and the Zombies guns. A go-between would be taking one to the other and that was a risky, shitty job. It had me believing Genevieve's father was aiming for membership of the Four Milers, presumably after being introduced by Sydney who'd already been tempted away.

I needed better proof than my guesswork. It didn't explain the missing money, so there was a hole in my logic.

With Convict's assurance of finding out more and proving his value, I hung up the call.

Shade cursed him out. "I can't believe he did that."

"You were seen scoping a councillor," I snapped at him in turn, my mood still miserable.

"The hell I was."

"Kenney came to me to warn me off."

Shade's humour vanished. "I've been fucking with the mayor, but I wasn't seen. He knew I was there because I wanted him to. He ran to the cops for that? Fucking spineless dick. Unlike ye to pander to him."

I could hardly respond, mired in a murderous haze made of Convict's findings and Alisha's bullshit. Or maybe it was my own making, and she was just calling it as she saw it.

Little blonde things. Obsessed. Fuck that.

A tap came at the door, and I yelled for whoever to come in. My chief of security entered, Genevieve behind him.

My mouth fucking dried. With her hair done and a tight dress encasing every curve, she looked phenomenal. Glossy, and classy as fuck.

My blood heated and flooded my dick. The bomb could go off in my club and I wouldn't be able to take my eyes off her.

Obsessed didn't even start to describe it. Horror darkened the edge of my vision. Alisha was right. If this was how my dad had been, I was just like him.

Genevieve stepped forward, her happy excitement dimming as she took in my glower. "I thought we could go on the tour, but you're probably busy. I'll go dancing with Lara instead."

Denial slammed down like a cage around me. "No. I'll take you."

"You don't have to if you're deep in something." Her gaze touched a clock on the wall then lingered on my photo beside it. There was a pause, and she came back to me. "We still have an hour to be apart. I'll come back, or you can find me."

"Weren't you listening? I said I'll take you."

Genevieve blinked, then clenched her jaw. "Maybe I'd rather go on my own."

"Unluckily for both of us, we don't have a choice."

I rounded the desk and claimed her hand. She tried to free her fingers, but I clamped them in mine. I should tell her she was pretty, a fucking knockout, but feeding that obsession would only make things worse.

Instead, I stormed out of the office with Genevieve in tow, and a worried-looking group of three pursuing us. Through the corridors, I stomped until we came to the internal door that divided the two halves of the warehouse, then I paused to enter the passcode.

The door opened to Divide, the pulsing bass of dance music a shock wave in the air and the black walls wet with humidity. Ahead was a packed dance floor, close to a thousand strangers crammed together and the mixed scent of sweat and perfume hanging over them.

I rarely came in here unless it was to see staff or get my knuckles bloodied breaking up a fight. Never seeking entertainment.

Genevieve twisted to say something to Lara, who frowned and gestured that she couldn't hear. The song switched, and a small torrent of clubgoers descended on the bar, cups of water and plastic pints of beer changing hands.

Manny touched my arm then pointed up a flight of steps to the VIP lounge. With Genevieve's hand still held tightly in mine, I drew her along with me to the steps where one of the staff opened the red rope barrier and ushered us upstairs. At the top, the hostess directed us to a booth with a view down to the dance floor. Genevieve and I sat in the centre with Lara and Shade bracketing us and Manny standing guard at a discreet distance away.

It was slightly quieter up here, enough to make out a fast-appearing waiter's drink order request.

I put my mouth to Genevieve's ear. She smelled too fucking good. "What do you want?"

"Freedom from you and world peace." She smiled sweetly.

"Espresso martini," I decided, banking on her caffeine addiction. Then added one for myself. I never drank on duty, but my head was fucked. "Macallan, straight up." Our most expensive Scotch.

The rest of my crew requested water, and our waiter slipped away, leaning over the bar to speak in the ear of the bartender, whose skeleton-print t-shirt was the club's casual uniform. No doubt I was the subject of their gossip. Nothing about this was normal.

A beat hit, and Genevieve sat forward as if recognising

the song. She slid a glance my way. "Dance with me?"

I shook my head once.

"Then you don't mind if I dance with someone else?"

"If it's a man, be prepared to watch him bleed."

Her lips quirked, but then she shrugged and wriggled over me, her delectable ass right on my lap, and out of the booth, extending a hand to Lara. The two women crossed to the VIP area's exclusive dance floor where a small group of clubbers took up space. They made way for my woman, as they should.

Genevieve rolled her body to the music, arms raised, and falling into the beat. I could only stare, hooked on her lithe body in that tight black dress. The spill of golden hair down her back, and how the club's lights twirled playfully over her. She laughed then bent in to whisper something in Lara's ear. The two of them giggled, cheering as the DJ mixed in another tune.

Manny shadowed them, his gaze going between the booths and the other dancers, alert for any danger. Likewise, I managed to regain enough control to alternate watching her with any other people who dared to even be near her.

Even just dancing, she wasn't safe.

If Genevieve and I were a real couple, two people who'd met and fallen in love, this would be my reality. Constantly looking over my shoulder to make sure no one was coming for her. I bred danger. Invited it to follow me around. Never once had I considered how that would affect a partner, even a fake one.

Then my anger rose again, because fuck the idea that this was fake.

She belonged to me.

Even if I had no idea how I could have that and not risk her life every day. Just as harsh came the rejection that I was my father. That claiming ownership of her smacked of how he'd collected women in the past.

The waiter reappeared with our drinks, and I grasped my cold glass and slammed back the Scotch.

I had to distance myself from her. Get myself under fucking control. For the sake of everything I'd built, I had to prove to myself just how little Genevieve mattered.

24

Genevieve

The pulse of the music moved through me, my spirit rising, a natural high battling the sour mood I'd picked up from Arran. I'd made the mistake of nurturing the cosy feeling he'd given me, excited to show him how I'd looked after my makeover, then gutted when he didn't react.

Hadn't he told me he'd be faking?

I had no reason to be pissed off with him, and yet there it was, a tight ball in my belly. Returning to the city was making me remember who I was. The song thrilling me—'Cola' by CamelPhat and Elderbrook—one I'd play when I sped through the city on my scooter, was bringing me back to life. To Arran, I was nothing more than a combination of an asset and a liability. He liked fucking me but he hated having me around.

My hurt bled from all the little stab wounds I endured every time I thought we'd made a connection. None of it was real. Why was I pretending to myself?

After a while of losing myself in the DJs mix, I was gasping for breath, overheated. Lara grabbed my hand. To dance with me, she'd stripped her waistcoat, leaving her in a skintight hot-pink slip and the black-and-pink shorts of her uniform. Hot as fuck.

She indicated back to the table. Drinks? God, yes.

We returned, and I took the cocktail glass in front of my place and knocked it back. Arran had called it an espresso martini. All I tasted was the caffeine. Absolutely delicious.

Then I chanced a look at Arran. His gaze found mine, but still that coldness held.

It made even less sense how my body cried out for his, and I rejected the pull. As if he felt it, too, his focus slipped down my form. It delivered images of sex. Me flat on my back and him thrusting into me. Me on my knees. His hands all over my skin.

A rush of anger slid through me for all I wanted and that would never be mine.

"I want to go to Divine now," I called over the thumping music. "You don't have to come."

Arran barely reacted. "I'm taking you."

"Wouldn't want to cause you any trouble."

Those eyes of his were almost black. "I said I'd give you the tour, and I'll fucking do it."

Right. Because the show had to go on.

"Fine." I spun on my heel and stalked away.

Back down the steps from the VIP area, I stomped, Manny dashing past to take the lead. Then a hand grasped mine hard. Arran, demonstrating his possession to all.

We left the club for the quieter corridors, crossing the central office space for the strip club entrance on the other side. But I'd been here and had seen all of that. I needed something else. My buttons to be pushed. My knowledge of his world to be complete.

I stopped him. "Upstairs."

His eyes held a challenge, but he gave a shrug and changed our direction for the stairs. Another passcode opened the door. My heart was in my mouth. It felt like the longest time ago that I'd had the third part of his business in my sights. Since I'd snuck around and been on the other side of this world. Now, I was tits-deep in it.

Temporarily, my brain supplied.

Before we entered, Arran gestured to Manny and Lara, indicating for them to return to work. Lara squeezed my fingers quickly then trotted down the corridor, Manny going the opposite way.

Leaving Arran, Shade, and me to climb the steps.

At the top, the atmosphere shifted.

I'd wondered so much about this part of the warehouse. How it operated, who was up here, though not what they got up to. I had a good idea of that.

We entered a muted, darkened space. The private strip rooms Alisha had shown me downstairs had padded walls and low lights. This was like that on crack. Thick, plush velvet gave way under my heels, the corridor stretching in both directions. Low, hypnotic music played in the background like a heartbeat. Still gripping my hand, Arran took us left, and we passed several rooms, all closed to prying eyes.

At the end, the space opened out into a wide room with a bar. Women stood or sat on chairs, some in skimpy outfits, others almost naked, and on the bar were baskets of shiny packets and small bottles. Condoms and lube, I realised. Wow.

A lift opened, and a man exited. One of the women

stepped forward to greet him. He said something to her, and she led him to a group of younger women. With his hands shoved in his pockets, he nervously indicated to one who bounced on her heels then beckoned for him to follow with a coy smile.

Arran put his lips to my ear. "This is where the clients enter. Anyone who comes up here has been vetted by my team and permitted membership. They want to fuck, or watch others fucking."

"Vetted?" I asked.

"We make a file. Test results, headshots, background checks, and full payment upfront."

The doors to a stairwell opened beside the lift, two men emerging this time. A slender woman with huge boobs held in a tiny gold bikini beamed and moved to claim them. The first, a man in his thirties and in a sharp suit, cupped the back of her head and spoke in her ear. She pursed her lips then centred herself on the other man who was perhaps ten years younger.

Then she kissed him.

As they locked lips, the suited guy crowded her from behind, one hand grabbing her breasts, the other cupping her between the legs. He pushed her bikini bottoms aside and revealed her bare pussy, fingering her right there in the centre of the room. She smiled into her kiss with the first man then broke away to whisper something to them. The three disengaged, and she brought them by a hand each in our direction, passing us to enter the corridor.

I wondered how they chose who went first. She didn't mind them both touching her. Obviously I knew things like this happened, but I'd never seen it.

I stared after them then twisted back to Arran. "Did

they get a two-for-one deal?"

Not even a laugh. "Tammy specialises in double penetration. Her regulars come from all over the country. The older man is a regular and has brought several different men in with him. Business partners, he calls them."

I wrinkled my nose. "Weird way of deciding who to do business with."

He just watched me. "Seen enough?"

I hadn't, not really. Witnessing men buy sex wasn't all that hot, even if my body was responding and warming up, my dress too tight and my skin tingling.

At my headshake, he exhaled and turned us around. The whole time, Shade had waited by the far wall. The fact that neither man had reacted in any way to the bounty of semi-naked women or the smell of sex in the air spoke volumes.

They were immune to this. I wanted to be as well.

At the next door down the corridor, Arran showed me in, Shade remaining outside. It was a theatre, with pairs of loveseats arranged in front of an erotic movie, full sex playing in black and white on the screen. In the seats, couples kissed or groped each other in full view of each other, some copying what they were watching, one older guy getting blown by his lady.

Arran squeezed my hand in question, but I shook my head. This still wasn't enough.

We left, and he took me inside the next entrance. This was different again. A room ahead behind panelled glass, clear in front of us but blacked out the rest of the way around, and doors to the left and right. Behind the glass, two women were under a spotlight on a velvet plinth. Both were glamorous in full makeup and with gorgeous hair, their completely naked bodies gleaming. Arran opened the door to the right, revealing a private booth. He locked us in and sat on a leather sofa, waiting on me. I perched next to him.

An announcer spoke over the PA system. "Kissing with nipples pressed together."

Behind the darkened glass that separated our booth from the central area, the two women rose upon their knees and followed the instruction, slow caresses of each other's breasts until their nipples met, their tongues tangling at the same time.

A shot of lust burst through me. I wanted my nipples played with and hot kisses, though not by another woman but the hulking man at my side. Except he'd never do those things for my pleasure, just his own. It had only happened when I was unconscious.

After a while of their display, the announcer spoke again.

"Scissoring."

The women adjusted their positions. They brought their pussies together and started grinding, going slow, and both moaning.

My breathing turned shallow, and my lips parted.

Damn, they had skills.

"Blondie, lie back. The other woman should stick her tongue in her cunt."

They shifted again, one reclining so her hair draped off the end of the plinth and touched the floor, the other making a show of spreading her legs and dipping her tongue to her wet pussy.

Arran's voice made me jump.

"In the other booths around us, people are bidding on the next instruction for the couple onstage. The winning bid is what gets read out. A good money-spinner."

I imagined the single men behind each of the other panes of glass, all with their dicks in their hands. Or maybe buried in a bought partner.

"Want to place a bid?" He indicated to a small screen and keyboard just beyond the sofa.

Heat rushed to my cheeks, but I kept my focus on the sex show.

Arran reached and picked me up, setting me down on his lap. I took a shocked huff of breath but relaxed back. If he wanted to be an armchair again, fine.

At another instruction from the announcer, the woman on top turned to face the other way, kneeling over her co-worker in a sixty-nine position. She returned to tonguing duty, and the one below palmed her ass cheeks, grazing her fingertips over the other woman's pussy.

Damn, this was sexy as hell.

Arran slid his hands down my thighs then parted my knees, spreading my legs over his. Then he widened his knees so my dress rucked up high. My breathing came faster. The women couldn't see us, I was certain. I couldn't make out even an outline of any other person behind the darkened glass panels. That didn't mean this felt normal, exposing myself to two people having sex.

Under me, Arran was hard.

I wriggled, getting a bolt of pleasure at his soft exhale into my hair. His fingertips grazed the tops of my thighs.

"Bring in two men for them to suck on," the announcer said.

There was a short pause, then a door opened and

two naked men entered the space beyond the glass. The women both sat up, smiling. A buff guy with a shaven head circled the two, his dick rising from half-mast to fully erect, his colleague's already there. Buff-Guy stood in front of the blonde woman and rubbed the head of his dick over her lips. The second woman took the initiative, pulling her man in with a happy, obviously faked sigh and her tongue out to guide him deep in her mouth.

At the other side of the plinth, the second guy wasted no time in thrusting home.

My breath hitched, my pussy wet and my body wired for sex. Under me, Arran pulsed, and I sank heavier onto his body, picturing us doing more than the actors were demonstrating. Him jerking into me. Filling me. Stretching me so wide.

Arran rolled his hips.

"Remembering my lips around your dick?" I asked.

If he said no, I'd die.

He laid a slow kiss to the side of my face. "You blew my mind, so yes, I am picturing that. I want something from you."

"Sure you do." Except I wasn't here to serve him. He'd taken and taken from me. I didn't care if this was turning him on. In fact...

I leaned to grab the keyboard, tapping in my instruction.

"You'll need to add a pin. Two-seven-six-eight," he growled against my neck, then delivered an open-mouthed kiss to the juncture with my shoulder.

I entered the code at the prompt, a timer showing me how long I had to place my bid. It looked like two-minute intervals. In my mind's eye, I imagined all the other bidders hustling to advance the sex show into something more. The obvious next step was both women getting dicked down, but there were so many other ways this could go. Maybe both men fucking one woman. Or the women both servicing one guy. What to choose.

But I'd woken up today and chosen violence.

Hiding my smile, I tapped in my ridiculous amount then turned the screen away. If Arran wanted to give me twenty grand a week, good for him.

"What did you ask for?" Arran murmured.

"Something just for you."

He thrust against me. "Is it what you want from me?"

"Wait and see."

The timer counted down, the women sucking away, moans and groans and ecstasy on every face.

Then the announcer returned. "The women take five and the men kiss."

On the plinth, the four gave each other surprised glances but stopped. Dicks left mouths, and the women slipped out of the door. Now, only the men remained, the two dudes locking lips, their wet dicks standing to attention but untouched.

In every other booth, I pictured outrage. Furious men jumping up to leave, or maybe frantically putting in a counter bid.

I cracked up, cramming my hand to my mouth to keep in the sound though my shoulders shook. Then I risked a glance up at Arran. "Sorry to ruin your fun."

But there was no frustration in his expression. Only the same dark need that I hadn't ruined with my guy show. "Thanks for the bid on my behalf, but what made you think my fun involves what's out there?"

I pressed against his erection, grinding my ass into him. "This says otherwise."

Abruptly, he grabbed my hips and spun me around so my knees landed on the sofa either side of him, my core right above his lap. My dress was around my waist, only the thin material of my gauzy underwear covering me.

Arran slid one hand to my backside, the other cupping my face to make me look at him. "I want free use again."

"I guessed that," I breathed.

If I followed the demands of my body, I'd let him do anything he wanted right now. Lay me back, strip me, and fuck me right here. But I'd been there and done that. It wouldn't end well.

"Is that a yes?"

Slowly, painfully, I shook my head, my teeth gritted, and my body rebelling. "No."

He worked his jaw. "Why not?"

"No is a complete sentence. I don't have to give you a reason."

Jumping up, I climbed off him, unwilling to risk something stupid like changing my mind.

Arran lurched to the door, but I exited faster. Back in the corridor, I tugged my skirt hem to make sure I was covered. Down the way, Shade lifted his eyebrows, but I had no attention to spare for him. Instead, I moved further down into the club.

Arran's voice chased me. "That isn't your scene, Genevieve."

How would he know? I barely understood where my sexuality started and ended, and I'd be damned if he dictated it.

Busting through an exit at the end, I discovered a wide-open area, this one busy with people, two thirds women and the rest their male clientele, and a few couples in between. Some propped up the bar, drinks in hand, but most were involved in some kind of sex entertainment. Golden cages hung from the ceiling, naked women dancing inside to a seductive beat. A woman and three men were putting on a live show on a floor-level stage, the woman blowing one guy and getting fucked by the other. I squinted, wondering what the last guy was going to do. He got under her, one of the others tipped lube down her, then he thrust inside her ass.

Holy shit. My cheeks flamed.

A quick glance behind me showed me Arran and Shade had stuck close by, which despite everything, I needed. Unlike in the other spaces, this was full audience participation.

One of the nearby cage dancers beckoned forward a watcher, a younger man who had his hands behind his back as if not quite knowing what to do. The caged woman smiled and rolled her hips over the array of brightly coloured sex toys in her cage. Then she turned her back and spread her legs, moving to the beat that filled the room, the invitation she'd given plain. They were there for use in fucking her.

At the side of her cage, another man groped her tits, feeling up her pierced nipples. She craned her neck to kiss him.

The nervous man's nostrils flared, and he stepped up and put his hand through the bars to collect a large pink dildo, holding it for a moment, his gaze stuck on the juncture of the woman's legs. Yet he didn't move. Like me, he was caught up. Probably new to this. Then another sex worker came up behind him and pressed on her tiptoes to whisper in his ear. He sagged and closed his eyes then frantically nodded.

She put her arms around him. Together, fingers interlaced, they took the toy to the caged woman's core and rubbed it up and down. Then they pushed it into her, spreading her pussy lips wide. The woman moaned and broke her kiss, her twisted ecstasy so hot to witness I had to look away.

Around the room, couples pressed together on sofas, some of them clearly sex workers, some in fetish wear, but others apparently normal couples who'd just come here to play.

Wide-eyed, I wandered through, taking it all in. Around a corner, a wall with the sign *Glory Hole* above it had a series of holes at groin height, presumably to stick dicks in judging by the guy palms flat to the wall and his trousers around his ankles.

Further on, a man was chained to a table, his chiselled, dark-skinned body bucking under the attentions of the woman fucking him. Two guys stood watching them, then one reached out to touch the man's mouth, his other hand frantically moving inside his trousers.

A corner of cushions had an orgy going on, then there was a series of private rooms with peepholes, like I'd seen down in the strip club.

I tiptoed over and peered into one. A woman stood over a man on a covered mattress. She peed on his face, his tongue out for the yellow stream.

I recoiled. Okay, one of my limits had been found.

The room continued on, a sign on the wall giving me a clue as to what went on deeper down. *Breastfeeding room.*

Fantasy rooms. Swings. Torture rooms.

A sign on one hall read: *No clothes beyond this point. No refusal permitted.* I inched away.

An arm curled around me. Arran. "Want to head back downstairs now?"

"Not even a little bit."

"Come on. You've seen plenty," he said.

"Don't presume."

"All right, then I just want you alone."

"And I want anything but that."

Overheated and in increasingly desperate need, I broke free of him and stalked to an alcove with a strange kind of upright cross on it. "What's this?"

The X-shaped cross had padded corners at the extent of the arms, and restraints on each.

A woman drifted over, her gaze touching the men behind me then coming to me. "This is a Saint Andrew's cross. Would you like me to show you how it works?"

I nodded, and she backed up to the frame, demonstrating how the user would be tied onto it, arms out wide above her head and legs spread. "The occupant is restrained at her wrists, ankles, and around her waist."

"So she can't stop anyone from touching her?" I figured out.

She gave a pleased smile. "Exactly. She'd wear a mask to add to the sensory effect. She can't see whose hands, mouth, or other parts are on her, or in her, but she can feel everything. If you tie me up, the three of you can play. Or you can hop in and I'll show your guys the ropes."

She trailed a finger down my arm. I sensed Arran behind me.

"That won't be necessary," he stated.

The woman startled. "Oh my God. Mr Daniels, my apologies. I didn't recognise you in the shadows."

She climbed down at a scramble, ducking her head to back away.

But she'd piqued my interest, and I touched the edge of the frame.

"I want to do this," I said.

There were people nearby. Lurking men and so many working women. I was losing my mind with need and at the same moment wanting to piss off Arran more than I could say.

He made a sound that was a mixture of a growl and pain. "Letting anyone here grope you?"

"Why, what do you care so long as you're one of them? You don't give a damn about me." I dropped my voice so only he could hear. No need to let the room guess we were in a lover's spat.

His lip curled, his shoulder muscles rigid. Likewise, his response was just for me. "You're right, I don't."

Hurt curled inside me. Fuck him.

With a swish of my hair, I climbed onto the Saint Andrew's cross, beckoning to the helpful woman to tie me on. It was just about my size, and I adjusted my position as she tightened the wrist restraints, the sensation of having my legs so wide alarming.

My dress barely covered my ass.

My heart beat so fast, but I wasn't backing down.

"How about the mask, honey?" she asked.

I nodded, and she collected a black eye mask with skeleton print.

She tugged it over my head, but I paused her so I could lift my chin in challenge at Arran. "Well, what are you waiting for? You wanted your hands on me. Come and get me or let the rest of them have a go. I don't give a tiny fuck which you choose."

25

Shade

Genevieve indicated for the staff member to lower her mask and rested her head back, her lips open over fast breathing and the skirt of her dress rucked up high around her spread legs to the point of revealing her pink thong.

Not that I was fucking looking.

I'd burn out the eyes of any arsehole who tried.

Arran circled the freestanding cross then stood right in front of her. Red streaked her chest where the sex club had got her flustered.

I'd expected the place to freak her out, yet she'd explored. Had fun tormenting Arran. I liked this lass. She was running circles around my friend. Still, there was no way he was going to let strangers participate.

A man neared, his interest obvious.

I huffed a sarcastic breath. "Don't even consider it, pal. If he doesn't break your fucking neck, I will."

The punter about-turned and slipped away. Arran held his gaze on me, something strange in his expression.

He lifted his chin. "She's on this for a reason."

I watched him, my certainty slipping.

"My woman wants someone else's hands on her as well as mine," he said a little louder.

I gave an incredulous laugh. "Ye want me to round up some of these fuckers to come paw at her?"

An unbearable thought. Arran shook his head. He'd die before he'd let them near her. I would, too. They'd chosen each other which made her precious to the crew. Arran practically shook with need, and I was seconds away from yelling for every other arsehole to evacuate the club so they could have the space to themselves.

Yet he lifted a finger to pause me, then beckoned the woman who'd helped her up on the frame to come closer. Whispered something in her ear.

She dipped her head and traced a finger down Genevieve's arm, making the lass jump.

What the hell?

Then he tilted his head at me, a challenge there.

Oh, fuck my life. He wanted me to be part of some twisted game.

I shrugged and moved closer to stand behind her, my friend dead in my eyeline and his spreadeagled woman on the frame between us. This wouldn't last long.

"Holding up okay?" Arran asked in a Genevieve taunt. "You've got men here ready to touch you any way they please. Fingers ripping your clothes, feeling up your cunt."

Genevieve's muffled voice returned. "Why not? You can't satisfy me."

I could've laughed at her comeback, but I valued my

throat.

"Won't is different to can't, baby," the boss retorted.

She went quiet.

"Last chance to call this off," he said.

After a beat, Arran indicated for the staff member, Felicia, to proceed. She trailed her finger across the top of Genevieve's strapless dress then yanked it down, her full tits freed.

God-fucking-dammit.

I averted my gaze. Glared at a man staring on, his hand sneaking down to his crotch, even though I had the same rush of blood downwards.

Whatever they were trying to prove to each other, I was still a fucking man. If I even stood near the boss's woman and popped a chub, I risked losing it to his rage. From our city-cleansing activities, Arran was deadly good at slicing off dicks.

Yet, he'd given me an order.

And his woman was bare-chested on a goddamned sex frame.

"Touch her," Arran turned his taunts on me. "Don't hold back for her sake. She wants it."

Kill me now.

Felicia obeyed instead, taking one of Genevieve's nipples in her fingers. The spreadeagled woman gave a gasp of surprise then a hot-as-hell groan. Arran, with his jaw slack and gaze fixed on that action, still didn't touch her.

Across the room, a woman appeared then almost immediately slipped out of sight behind a golden cage.

Dark glossy hair, big tits, a curvy-as-fuck arse...

My heart stalled. I stared, angling my neck, but saw nothing more.

In a rush, I was back to dark bedrooms and midnight waking. To being teenaged and wanting the unthinkable. I worked an immoral career, enjoyed a life of sin, but none of it was a patch on what I'd desired as a teenager.

The girl in the bedroom beside mine.

Her appearing in my room at night and our silent communication. Her stripping her clothes and climbing into my bed. Everly was the most beautiful, fucking crazy-making soul to have ever existed. She drove me to the edge of insanity.

She was the reason I knew anything about the right amount of dope to use to knock someone out, and why I'd started keeping a list of men to fuck with, eviscerate, or disappear.

Fury filled me.

If she was here, *again*, I'd fucking riot.

There was no reason for her to be near me, and if I found her, I'd throw her over my shoulder and march her straight out, yet... A better idea came to mind.

There was every reason for her to watch me play with another woman and once and for all get the message to stay the fuck away.

26

Genevieve

$\mathcal{B}$etween my legs, strong fingers grazed up my thighs, the burning need in me soaring to greater heights. It was Arran, I was sure. Even if he hadn't spoken, I knew his touch.

But the hand on my breast wasn't him.

I flexed my fingers stretched high above and to either side of my head, my fingernails touching the padding of the frame. My skeleton mask kept me blinded, and a low running panic wouldn't quit, my fear of the dark present.

Another hand grazed my side from behind me.

My breathing hitched. That couldn't be Arran. Some other man was going to have his turn. To touch me however he wanted. I'd put myself up here and I was going to see it out.

Arran's deep voice returned, close to my ear. "You have an audience, baby."

The fingers at my breast were replaced by a hot and wet mouth. The owner sucking my nipple and curling their tongue around to tease me.

I groaned at the sensation, wary and aroused in equal parts. Everyone was here for sex, but that didn't ease my uneasiness.

"Is that good?" he taunted.

"Y-yes."

Another mouth landed on my other breast, the two people hardening my nipples with their sucking. God, that felt so good and so wrong. Confusion broke over me in a chill.

"Have you any idea how many men here want to fuck you?" Arran taunted. "How many are dying to take a piece? Should we let them see more of you?"

"I don't care," I gritted out.

"Really?"

His fingers met the hem of my dress where it stretched taut over the very tops of my thighs. The two people sucking me, women, I imagined for the sake of my sanity, moved aside but didn't let me go. I pictured them shifting out of his way, giving him space for whatever shadowy game he had in mind.

Arran grazed his knuckle over my core. I moaned, the tiny contact delicious.

"Hope you're not attached to this dress.

A rip of material sounded, the hem tearing. Or... slicing?

His knife. He was cutting it off me.

I whimpered, somehow even more turned on, my underwear soaked and fresh air ghosting over my belly.

Then I felt it. The cold touch of metal at my core. He'd cut upwards then returned down low, the point of his blade kissing my flesh right above my clit.

I froze.

Didn't even breathe.

A tiny move from him and my gauzy underwear split from contact with the blade, exposing my most secret place. I stayed perfectly still, terrified, and horribly, awfully excited.

Arran rumbled a dangerous sound.

That icy hint of the blade caused a throb inside. One flinch and I'd bleed.

Then the knife moved back to my dress, slicing upwards so it shredded through the centre and finished the job of parting the two sides. My chest heaved, my breasts heavy and my nipples so hard they had their own pulse.

I tried to imagine how I looked, spread out on the cross, the ruined black dress hanging either side of me and only held on by the constraining band at my waist. Then my exposed breasts, now left alone, the women, or whoever, stepping away. Finally between my legs, my split underwear hiding nothing.

"Easier for someone to fuck you, now."

I jumped again at Arran's voice.

My panic swarmed, my pulse skipping out of time. I wanted to taunt him back or thank him for clearing the way. But my throat had seized.

Abruptly, he palmed me, straight between my legs, splitting the underwear fully.

In shock, I jerked and bowed out my knees, but I had nowhere to go within my constraints. He gave a low laugh and eased his fingers over my wet centre, not entering me but skirting over my pussy and my ass.

A moan tore from me. My hips rocked by themselves.

"Tell me what you think of my woman," he ordered.

He wasn't talking to me.

"Beautiful," a female voice replied.

"So perfect." Another woman.

"Nice tits on the lass," a man commented. "Ye hear that, everyone? Perfect tits. Not too small and definitely not too big."

Oh fuck.

The accent gave him away. The second guy was Shade, Arran's man, still here and watching everything. Why had he let him? Why did I? Yet Arran didn't stop. He glided his fingers inside me then spread them. Pulled them out slowly with an indecent sound.

God, this was everything I'd wanted from him, except not with others involved. It wasn't right, even if I couldn't open my mouth to say. Lips took my nipples again, and Arran worked me in repeated actions, using my arousal to swirl over my clit. As he did, big hands took my waist from behind.

Shade, definitely.

"She's begging to be fucked," he teased.

Arran's grip on my pussy tightened. I cried out. Both men swore.

"We can swap places, if ye like." Shade again. "In case ye need an expert hand to get her there."

"Even think of her cunt and I'll kill you," my man retorted.

Shade drew his hands up my ribcage until he cupped my breasts, better offering them for the women to suck.

All I knew was the rising coil of heat winding inside me. How it lit fuses throughout my body, every limb infected, every inch of skin alight. I needed this so much. Everything. I wanted Arran to fuck me but not with his friend here, too. Not with the women witnessing our depravity.

In the same breath, fear crept in that he might stop. Deny me as punishment.

Again and again, he thrust his hands in a rhythm, hitting a spot inside me. Shade still held my sensitive breasts, the women tonguing and pinching my nipples.

An orgasm neared, a hot flame about to explode.

Bowing my back, I keened out, the impact of finally getting close after so long destroying my mind. The only touch I wanted to feel was Arran, but I'd take it. Anything to get there. My body tightened, so ready to be satisfied. So desperate for completion.

Then he stopped. All of them did.

Hands and mouths left my skin. I panted, swivelling my head to listen, but no one made a sound.

"What are you doing?" I begged. "What's happening?"

A presence moved closer. I couldn't be sure who.

Material rustled, and then something pressed against my core, spearing over me and getting wet. A dick. Oh God. Heat painted me, desperation clinging to my every breath.

But whose was it? Surely Arran's.

Except I wasn't sure. He didn't say.

Fear laced my thoughts.

The man slid his thick cockhead up and down my entrance, then punched his hips and entered me.

I groaned, throbbing around his thick intrusion. My blood pulsed in my ears, so loud it almost deafened me. I strained to hear anything from the person inside me but could pick up nothing. No one else touched me. No other finger ghosted over my flesh. Everything was concentrated on the dick that spread me wide.

It was almost everything I'd wanted. So close, except for the fact I couldn't be sure it was Arran taking me for the ride. I was ninety-nine percent sure he wouldn't let another man near, but that one percent...

The owner of the dick bucked upwards, ruining my thoughts. Unbidden, another moan flew from my lips. It felt too good. Blindfolded and constrained, I could only surrender now.

Over and over, the man's dick thrust in and out, so big it almost hurt, but hitting a deep pleasure zone that had me seeing stars in the darkness. I'd lost all control of my body. All I knew was the approaching bright pleasure. The rhythm and dark delight of being fucked so good.

Maybe I didn't care who the owner of the dick was so long as he kept doing this. A spasm took me, and I hitched my breath, trying to stifle any more sounds so he didn't stop. The risk of denial made everything a thousand times more dangerous.

I just needed a little more.

Just a few extra hits.

My pussy clenched tight around my unknown partner, and I couldn't hold in a cry. Then the wall between me and completion crumbled. A brilliant, dazzling climax slammed into me. It started at the point he'd been hitting then broke over me in a wave, drowning me in deep satisfaction.

It took a long while until it released me from its grip. Until I could remember my name and why I was here.

Holy hell. At last. At long, goddamned last. I whimpered in distress and happiness. Behind the mask, my closed eyes fluttered. The man kept hammering away, his dick thickening, too.

My indignation returned in a rush. I'd got mine, and I was done with this game. I said the only thing I knew would be certain to bring things to a halt.

"Arran Daniels, your permission to fuck me has been revoked."

The man stalled, his hips stopping their jack-hammer action. Still inside me, he crowded in, his mouth coming next to my ear.

God, it was him. Arran. I knew his scent, just like I knew every other element that made up the man I'd tied myself to. Relief sprang tears to my eyes.

Anger followed.

He hadn't let me know it was him. Not until now. But then again, I'd done this to myself. My anger was for us both.

Arran breathed. With my words, I'd stolen his chance to come.

Then sure fingers peeled back the mask where it had slipped down to cover my lips. Arran kissed me, rolling his hips to fuck into me again.

I couldn't stop kissing him back. Allowing his tongue into my mouth to own mine. He filled two of my holes, his ownership clear to everyone around us. Then just as his dick thickened again, he pulled out. Liquid spilled over my belly. Ran down my skin, cool and unexpected.

Just like that, my emotions crested, and I burst into tears.

27

Genevieve

My ankles and wrists were freed, my waist restraint undone, then I was released into Arran's arms. His angry curse came with his draping my ruined dress over me as best he could. Then he picked me up bride-style, and I curled in on myself, leaving the mask on and trusting him to manage me, like the night he'd claimed me and had taken me from this place.

All I wanted was to get out of there.

Arran carried me away, and I had no idea where we'd end up. Only caring that he had me. Cooler air danced over my limbs, the sounds changing to tell me we were in the corridor, then something dinged and a lift moved us.

"Want to keep the mask on?" Arran adjusted his grip on me. His tone was surprisingly tender.

"For now." My voice came out thick, though I'd got the tears under control.

"The room was cleared. No one was watching at the end," he said.

I made no reply, though thank God for that small mercy.

Arran walked me out of the lift. We were further up in the warehouse, probably at the top. I'd counted eight floors when I'd scoped the place, nine including the basement.

Another pause, a door opened, a click which told me Arran had turned on lights, then he was setting me down.

He lifted the mask, drawing it up over my hair. His gaze roamed my face. "You were crying."

I claimed the mask to wipe down my cheeks. "I'm not now."

He held my gaze for a moment then nodded, handing me something from the end of the sofa. A blanket? No, a hoodie. I dragged it on, not caring if it got messed up from the sticky cum on my body. It would be all over Arran's clothes, too, and not just his arousal but mine as well.

When I'd wrangled it over my head, discarding the torn dress, I gazed around me. He'd brought me to an apartment, an open-plan space with red-brick walls and a grey stone kitchen with shiny appliances. A lamp by the side of my sofa plus three glass pendant lights over the kitchen counter provided a warm glow, shadows holding the corners. Twisting around, I took in a darkened hall behind me, all the rooms off it unlit. Bedrooms, I presumed.

Arran flicked on a machine. "Coffee?"

"Thank you." I brought my attention to the other side of the room where a floor-to-ceiling arched window looked out on the city. My breath caught. "Is this your home?"

"It is. Half the penthouse floor. Shade has the other half. No one knows we live up here, so if that's suddenly discovered..."

He left the rest unsaid—that he'd know it was me who'd spilled. I rubbed my arms, suddenly cold despite the clothing he'd offered. Screw him for not trusting me still.

Climbing up, I stalked to the uncovered window. Below, people came and went from the club entrances, taxis and bikes zipping about. The river flowed in a steady, black stream to the right, and the bridges across it sparkled with reflected light. TVs flickered in apartment block windows, and against the dark river came the flare of someone smoking on the dockside. Beyond, the taller city buildings had minimal lights on, most of their windows shaded.

My pulse quickened.

The very best part of Dad's apartment, maybe the only good part, was the view it had down the hill. Maybe I could even see the Crescent from here, if I cared to look. But it couldn't beat Arran's view. Instantly, I was hooked on the vision of the city in the evening.

I'd always been a night owl, and this made one hell of a roost.

The coffee machine clanked, then seconds later, Arran walked up behind me. "What made you come?"

I parted my lips, confused.

"Was it having more than just me touch you?" He held my hips in his big hands.

"I blocked everyone else out," I whispered.

He made a gruff sound of approval then nudged my hair aside to kiss the back of my neck. Damn him for that sweet touch. I tilted my head to give him better access, something inside me going molten.

"Give me free use again." Another kiss.

"No."

Arran pushed me against the glass, his knee spreading

my legs. "Why not?"

"I don't have to give you a reason."

He rumbled, drawing another kiss higher. His fingers hitched up my hem. "It would be different."

"How?"

"I wouldn't deny you. I liked feeling you pulse around my dick. I need it again."

"For your sake then, not mine."

"Christ, woman. I liked feeling you come because it gave you pleasure. That did something to my brain."

I considered that, my focus skipping from car headlights on the nearest bridge then to a group of men fighting near the water's edge. I tried to stay in control of myself, not on how I rode his thigh.

What he offered was all I'd wanted. What my body craved. Except there was one huge missing element in that he didn't trust me still. Not in the way I deserved. I'd been honest from the moment of claiming, but equally, I'd lied to him, too. I didn't know if we could come back from that.

Wait, why did I want to? My heart throbbed, my odd tears making sense. I cared. For some strange and very wrong reason, I needed there to be a version of this where he and I came to understand each other.

I pushed off the glass and moved away from him, stumbling. Dizzy, I held my gaze on him for a moment then wheeled around and sought out the coffee he'd promised. A cup waited on the tray of the shiny machine, steam rising. An espresso. Perfect.

I knocked it back then wiped my mouth with my hand. "I have a different proposal."

Arran stalked me, rounding the kitchen counter, but he held back from pouncing. Under the kitchen's lanterns, I posed, his hoodie long on me but giving me the cover I needed to put forward my thoughts.

"Free use for me."

"That's what I want."

"No," I corrected. "For me. I'm the one taking."

His eyes darkened. "Don't torment me. I want you in all fucking ways, but there is no chance I'm letting you tie me up or blindfold me."

"Because you don't trust me, and that sucks," I snapped back, suddenly shrill. "I don't know anything about you that isn't available through gossip or public record. Every time I try to get closer, you slap me back. I hate it."

"Why do you want to get closer? Why do you want to know more about me?"

I swallowed, emotions too close to the surface again. "It isn't to sell you out, but because when you touch me, something happens."

That serious gaze claimed mine, nothing in his features giving up his thoughts. Then some of the tension eased from his shoulders. "Same, little maniac."

I could've laughed at the nickname. He'd used it in my flat when he'd come to visit, and that felt like a million years ago now. But my humour was buried under other feelings I didn't understand.

"Tell me how it is for you," I asked.

Slowly, Arran shook his head, not giving me what I'd asked for. Then he changed direction again. "The grave I took you to in the woods was my mother's."

"I know that—"

"She was killed in front of me."

My mouth opened and closed. He watched me as if for confirmation that I already knew this. All I felt was shock. Horror on his behalf.

Then his words from the car came back to me, and I exhaled dismay.

"Your dad did that."

He inclined his head again. "You wanted to know more about me, what's your list of questions?"

I gave a huff of breath. "Everything. Who are you? What do you like and dislike? How did you get this place? Where did the money come from if you're not taking it from the women? Your friends in Scotland, how are they connected? Those are the kinds of things that got stuck in my head, but none of it seems important now. God, Arran."

He held up a hand, stopping me. "I don't want this. I never wanted you. At the same point, I want you with every beat of my heart, and the thought of letting you go is a stab wound into my chest."

A thrill struck my heart just as swiftly as pain followed.

"Give me free use in exchange for answers. Or anything you want. I'll sell myself out just to have your body. Just to have you." He advanced on me. Touched his forehead to mine.

Fresh desperation flooded me.

I didn't know what I wanted anymore. Taking up his offer meant forcing him to compromise himself. It didn't feel right. As badly as I wanted him, my desperation was to be closer, not to extract information like I was pulling teeth.

I backed away from his touch. Took another step,

ignoring the insistent tug to stay with him.

"I need a shower," I mumbled.

A muscle ticked at Arran's jaw. "Bathroom's down the hall."

On my bare feet, my heels left beside the sex frame downstairs, I walked away. The first turning off the hall was a bedroom, so I kept going. The next contained a spacious, all-white bathroom. Switching on the light, I went through the motions to get the shower running and sourcing towels.

My movements were autopilot, so I followed them, shedding the hoodie to a laundry basket and my ruined underwear to the bin, then stepping under the hot water. It sluiced over my skin, and I took a minute to scrub off my makeup, washing away the traces of the night. The track marks from my strange crying session.

Then I curled my arms around myself, upset crinkling my lips. What was wrong with me? Arran was offering anything I wanted in exchange for sex. Sex which would be good for both of us. I should accept, lie back, then leave him.

I didn't want any of that now.

My unfortunate heart ached for him. I wanted to uncover the story of his mother. I wanted to hug him and tell him I was sorry he'd lost her. I wanted unity and shared conversations. Not the push and pull of anger and hatred barely masked by lust.

The shower door opened, and I sprang my eyes wide. Arran entered, shutting us in then taking me in his arms. Naked, he tipped my head back to receive his kiss, his dick hard and between us. I met his lips, expecting a rough claiming, but instead, he commenced a slow exploration, his lips taking mine as if mapping them.

As he did, he took up the bottle of shower gel, the snap of the lid opening cluing me in to his actions. Then his hands were on my flesh, gliding up to my breasts. He rubbed the lather into my skin, focusing on my nipples.

He broke the kiss to speak. "I need every trace of every other person removed from your body. Lift your hands."

I obeyed, and he cleaned me then sank to his knees in front of me. "Where else?"

I gazed down at him, how the shower darkened his hair. We were both completely naked probably for the first time. There was something intensely vulnerable about it. All of our antagonism suspended. It gave me a chance to look more closely at that which I'd only glimpsed previously. One of his tattoos was the logo of the club—a skull with a bandanna around its lower face. Another was a surfer on a wave with mountains behind.

He had scars on his skin, round marks like cigarette burns, lines and welts from unknown sources. I'd seen them in my flat but hadn't wanted to stare.

Now, I did. He watched me, his jaw tightening.

"Answer me, Genevieve."

"Two people sucked my nipples. Your man held my waist then my breasts, and the last person pushed his way between my legs, fucked me, then came over my belly."

Arran poured more shower gel onto his palms, and I lowered my fingers to his hair, stroking over the strands while he cleaned my breasts again, my arms, my torso, and then my thighs.

Raising his gaze, he touched me between the legs. I breathed out, desire so close to the surface. He rubbed the suds over me, sliding back between my buttocks and taking his time. Another squirt of the gel landed on my clit. It was cooler than the shower's heat, and Arran rubbed it in. This time I let the pleasure play out.

We were in some kind of no-man's land. An amnesty.

My single orgasm from earlier felt like a gateway drug. An appetiser before a feast. At the time, it had been everything I needed, but now I knew it was nowhere near enough. With his light but thorough handling of me, Arran was only priming me up more, my body responding in insistent pulses of need.

I'd never get enough of him.

The realisation was swift and harsh. Even when he was done with me, I could never get over this.

His fingers entered me, and I gasped. My inner walls fluttered around his digits.

Arran dropped his forehead to my body. "I need to feel that around my dick. Please, baby."

The endearment took me under. My reply came out breathy. "Okay."

In a flash, he was on his feet and the shower was off, a towel around his waist and one bundling me up. Then I was in his arms with his mouth on mine. Still kissing me, Arran carried me from the bathroom to his bedroom, a bed with dark-blue sheets and a huge wooden headboard against a red-brick wall, another arched window uncovered and giving a wide view of the city lights.

They cast enough of a glow that the fact there was no lamp lit bothered me less.

Besides, my attention was all on Arran. He placed me down at the end of the bed then knelt between my spread knees, wasting no time in taking his mouth to my pussy. I arched my back, my sound of pleasure loud in the quiet room. Arran sucked my clit then speared his tongue into me. The warmth and the simple fact he was touching me there had me driving my heels into the mattress, trying to get closer still.

He lifted my ass to thrust his tongue in deep, the sensation incredible.

"Can't get enough of the taste of you," he growled into my flesh. "But I need to feel you more. I want you to come on my dick so I feel every single pulse."

Lifting, he boosted me to the top of the bed; our towels dropped, nothing between us but the warm evening's air.

Arran stroked his dick once then drove it inside me. He groaned, and it broke something in my brain.

"I need you to make that sound more," I managed to utter.

He cupped my face and kissed me, then drew back, staring down at where my body was taking him, cursing with his lust.

"I need you to come," he said.

I writhed, already closer than I wanted to admit. "Then make me."

Again and again, he thrust in and out, each time taking me higher and nearer to bliss. One big hand splayed across my chest then drew down to my belly, lingering to feel my soft skin. Then he cupped my mound, still pistoning away. The heel of his hand ground a circle into my clit. I reached for him.

He batted me away. "Hands to yourself. I want this one to be all me."

Fine. I closed my eyes and just felt. The pressure of his hand on my sensitive bundle of nerves. The stretch of his dick. That rhythmic pounding against my G-spot. It built and built, the sensation so perfect I could live in that moment. Swim in the joy of how well we fitted.

My inner walls pulsed with the beginnings of my climax. I moaned and flexed, seeking it out. Wanting it all. Dying to reach the finish line at last without fear of never getting there. Arran uttered a masculine sound of deep need but kept delivering that exacting action on my body.

I was so close. So urgently almost there.

"Kiss me," I begged.

"No."

I could've cried in frustration, but then my desire crested and I was soaring. I sighed in happiness, dizzy with good feeling as my orgasm smacked me down. Around Arran's dick, I throbbed.

He went motionless, only his hand moving until I stopped it with mine.

"Holy shit," he said, once my hearing had returned.

I hid my smile, bubbling over with happiness for what we'd done. He was still so hard, lodged inside me, our sex session nowhere near complete. But like this? I could see us having so much fun together.

In a rush, I had to make him come inside me. We hadn't done that yet, and I needed it more than I needed air. Or to keep playing. God. All of it.

I slid my wet channel up and down his rigid length, gripping him tight.

Arran gave a dark laugh. "Turn over."

Lazily, I flipped so I was on my front. "You an ass man?"

"I'm an everything man when it comes to your body." He grazed his fingertips down my spine, keeping on going past my backside to plunge his fingers into me from behind. Then he grabbed my hips and lifted me, his tongue sliding in with his fingers. He licked me clean.

"I did this when you were asleep."

"Went down on me?"

"Told you your taste drives me insane. Now I know how you taste when you've come."

I remembered something else he'd told me about that night, too. I shivered at the memory. "You fucked me with your knife handle, too."

Arran stilled. "Did that scare you?"

"It should've, but no." All sense left me when it came to this man.

He pulled away, padding from the room without a word. I sat up and watched the door, but he returned, his holster in his hand.

Thick leather. The black handle of the weapon ridged.

My breath caught. Arran had sat over me and used that knife. Cut my clothes off then pushed it inside me, all while I slept. What if I'd twitched or jerked in my sleep?

Slashed him by accident with my pussy?

I slapped a hand to my mouth, hiding my strange hit of dark humour.

"Something funny?"

No way was I admitting that thought. "I'm just nervous."

"You should be. Lie back on the pillows." Arran grabbed my ankle and tugged it, repeating the action with the other side to widen my legs, then knelt in the gap.

With the holster still in place, he ran the tool between my breasts and down my body. The city lights from the arched window reflected on a tiny slice of the blade beneath the hilt.

My breathing hitched. "Have you ever killed anyone with that?"

He didn't stop, drawing a leisurely trail over my belly. "What do you want to hear from me?"

"The truth."

"Yes, baby, I've killed men with this knife. Also with my bare hands." He reached the entrance to my pussy and eased the holster tip into me, the sharp, murderous blade contained within the leather.

My chest rose and fell, and a spike of alarm woke every nerve ending. "How many?"

"Not nearly enough."

Another push and the leather stretched me, getting stuck. Arran drove it around in a circle then yanked it free and flipped it, easing the handle into me instead. My body gave around it, accepting the intrusion.

On my elbows, I watched, unnerved but irrationally turned on, too.

With a flick of his thumb, he unclipped the button and removed the holster, revealing the cruel, evil-edged knife.

"Fuck," he drawled.

I shuddered, the sight of it between my thighs alarmingly hot. He pushed the hilt until it was flush with my body. I held still, the cutting edge starting millimetres from my skin.

"When I next stab this into someone's throat or heart, ending their life, I'll have this image in my head. Your cunt powering it up to deliver the killer blow."

He loomed over me. Kissed me. Kept the knife in place with his hand.

I pulsed around it unexpectedly and whimpered into

the kiss.

Arran settled back on the bed and stared at the place his weapon speared me. "I want to do this with everything I own. If it's dick-shaped, I want to fuck you with it."

I threw my arm over my eyes, trying to control my racing heart and perverted brain. "Don't you own any regular sex toys?"

"I own a fucking brothel, Genevieve."

My lips curved. "Got any here?"

"No. I told you I didn't use women before you."

There was so much to unpack in that sentence, but not now. "Then what else do you have to try out besides the knife?"

He watched me for a moment then pulled the knife from me, dropping it to the mattress. Then he pressed a kiss to my belly and left the room. A short while later, after a search and the sound of running water, Arran came back with an armful of items, though it was too dark for me to see what. Most, he set on the bed behind him and out of my sight, but one he handed over.

A skeleton mask.

"Put it on."

So he could do this without me seeing? God. "Show me what you've got first."

"No. I won't hurt you. Purposefully."

It was a trust exercise, then. Or a challenge. Damn him.

"From now on, I want to have items around me that have all been in your cunt. I want to pick up each and remember. I want other people to use them and not know."

"You're perverted."

But so was I. I slid the mask on and stretched my arms back, settling them behind my head, wriggling my ass to get comfortable for what he wanted to do. It was oddly safer with darkness surrounding me. In this room, with the city lights.

"You can guess each, or I'll tell you."

Something cold touched me between the legs, and I jumped. It was thin and narrow and slid into me without much resistance.

"A candle," he said.

"Unlit, I hope," I joked.

A pause followed, then the bed dipped. Moments later, a click sounded.

My mouth dropped open. "Did you light it?"

"Your pussy is on fire for me."

I yanked up the bandanna, but Arran grabbed my hand, forcing me to lie back. He removed the candle. Hot wax dripped on my thighs, and I jerked, but he held me flat.

"It's only candlewax. A safe version bought for use in the club. It won't scar."

More fell on my belly then my chest, hot but not burning. In my darkness, I accepted the little kisses of pain.

"Going to drip it on your nipples."

My breathing stuttered, but I held still and waited. The liquid splashed me, solidifying fast, my nipples hardening with the interesting sensation.

He drew his thumb over both, rubbing the solidified candlewax away. "Now your clit."

"Arran," I warned.

He didn't wait, the wax falling in hot speckles directly onto my clit. I groaned, confused but aroused by the heat. The fleeting pain.

He peeled away the wax again then climbed off the bed. A couple more clicks sounded, but nothing touched me. Still, I was alert for every sensation. Every wisp of air moving past.

Something brushed my inner thigh.

It was metal, the cold piercing my entrance and pushing inside. No thicker than the candle but harder.

"A round-handled spatula," Arran said. "I don't cook, but it's going to be there in my kitchen."

"Unhygienic," I grouched.

He fucked me with it, then the item was removed and another slotted in place. Small and cylindrical, barely any feeling at all.

"A pen?" I asked.

"Exactly. Your pussy is good at guessing games."

He whipped it away, something thicker immediately replacing it.

"We started off easy, but you're going to be a good girl and take everything I've got."

I focused on the new object, trying to relax. For no good reason, I wanted to impress him with what I could do. Behave for him and get his praise.

Arran parted my flesh around the square-edged possession. It stretched me wider, but I took it, trying to guess from the small rubber edges that dragged.

Unlike the others, he kept going, not stopping at a couple of inches.

"My remote control. Only used by me and rarely. You

should know how hot you look."

He kept going, driving it up into me until his fingertips were at the end.

"Swallowed it whole," he commented, awe in his tone.

My throat bobbed, and sweat broke out on my brow. My strange sense of pride was growing along with an increasing need for more. Whatever he wanted to give me.

Arran teased out the remote, no doubt coated in my juices, and I exhaled hard.

"The next is big. I need you wetter."

Something flat and completely smooth landed on my mound. I squinted into my mask, trying to guess what it was. He tapped it, then it vibrated. Damn. His phone? My heart raced.

He drove it over my clit in several passes back and forth. I squirmed, unable to stop the rush of need from growing. Then he eased the wide edges down towards my opening.

I started. "You can't put your phone inside me."

"Don't ever tell me what to do. From the moment you walked in here, you belonged to me. Don't forget that."

Arousal seeped down my thighs. My body responding to his possessive words. Damn him.

With the vibrations steadily pulsing into me, Arran angled the phone back and forth until he got the corners of it in. I breathed, pinned down by his actions. Scared and excited.

There was no way it could go deeper. It was too wide, too rigid.

Too fucking electrical to be safe, though hopefully waterproof.

But those vibrations had me rocking my hips subtly, chasing the good feeling they were generating. And I'd taken his knife. God, I was messed up.

Arran rumbled a sound of approval. "If you're going to come, I need to feel it. Every time needs to be around my dick."

I gave a tiny nod, and the phone left my core and moved back to my clit, the delicious thickness of Arran's dick replacing it and plunging into me. I moaned, not hiding how wound up I was, how ready for him. Yet he didn't budge, just holding still while the vibrations did their work with his phone flat to my clit. I focused on that and the stretch of him. I loved it so much.

A fast climax neared. I sucked in air.

"Fuck me, please," I begged.

Nothing, then a slow thrust in and out that nearly broke my brain.

I needed more. I reached for him, but he stopped.

"Hands to yourself."

"I want you to come as well," I said in a rush. "You wanted me wet. Use both of us to do it."

He didn't answer, just holding the phone hard to my body, the effect delivered right into me. I squirmed. It was relentless, unstopping.

The orgasm hit, and I bucked up then dropped down on his soft sheets, the strength of it just as hard as the last and so good. Yet I wasn't satisfied. It still felt like part of a buildup to something much bigger.

Without coming, Arran withdrew, uttering a growl.

I hadn't even finished throbbing when a new item was thrust into me. So thick. Icy cold. Almost too big for me to take, yet I did, loosened by the aftershocks of my climax.

"What the fuck?" I moaned.

"Cucumber from the fridge. You're so wet you could take anything now."

I wanted to joke about how you can't eat in everyone's house, but my amusement had gone. Need had replaced it completely. I drove my heels into the bed, the iciness a strange sensation as it pulled in and out of me. Then Arran's tongue landed on my clit. The heat of his mouth battled the cold inside, and a wave of emotion drowned me.

"Enough. I just want you," I cried.

"One more."

The vegetable went away, and my poor pussy throbbed, empty, and chilled, but not for long. A round, blunt-ended item ground into my core. Far too broad. Bigger than the cucumber. I blinked my eyes open under the mask.

"Whatever that is, it won't fit."

"It's a cylindrical sample of iron I kept from the renovations of the warehouse. A reminder of all I achieved that lives in my living room and is engraved with the completion date. Smooth, otherwise. You'll take it. Your cunt will accept everything I give it."

I moaned, dark desire eking into my blood. "It won't. That's impossible."

He twisted it, winding the base against me. "You can and you will."

There was no way. From the feel, it wasn't quite as wide as his square-edged phone, but there was no give. Just a solid metal cylinder.

Arran pushed it then retreated, teasing my flesh, not

going so hard as to hurt me, but not giving up either. Suddenly, I got the image of him using all the things we'd played with. Catching sight of the cylinder. Answering the phone. Pressing buttons on his remote control.

Stabbing someone with the blade that started it all.

In a rush, I got it. Why he wanted it. I'd be everywhere. Part of his everyday actions, whether I was in his life or not. Our unconventional relationship had an expiry date, but I was marking my territory in ways no one else would guess. More—he was taking that from me. It gave me a strange and powerful surge of lust, so much that I wanted this final test to happen.

"You need to be wetter still," he commented, low, need heavy in his tone.

"Come in me. I'll be soaked."

A pause. The cold metal left me. His warm dick replaced it. Then Arran reached to snatch off my mask.

His expression nearly broke me, the awe and lust on his features, but the room danced at the edge of my vision. The candle he'd lit had been placed in a holder on his chest of drawers, two others beside it, the flames dancing.

Somehow, his bedroom had taken on a romantic aesthetic. All without me seeing.

"We've never had this conversation, but tell me you're on birth control."

"Of course I am."

Arran hauled me up. "Good. If I'm going to come in your cunt, I want to see your face as I do it."

"Kiss me," I begged.

His mouth met mine in hunger. His arms ran around me. Suddenly furious, Arran lifted me to his lap, fucking into me hard. I gripped him, holding him to me as close as I could. In and out, he thrust, his hips working overtime.

Sex with him had undertones. His first time had been public and forced. Every time since had been strained in some way, me unconscious, him letting me think it could be his friend between my thighs. This was just us. On his bed. Surrounded by candlelight and a strange selection of impromptu sex toys, an added purpose only he knew the extent of but that I deeply needed.

Our mouths fused. His skin met mine in repeated hits. Then Arran slowed. Pulling back, he jerked into me, holding my gaze.

My vision was hazy, but I held the eye contact, thrilled at the sensation it gave me, my lips parted and my body so, so his.

He kept up the action, his expression darkness, need, and with a flash of something intensely vulnerable.

"Betray me and you'll destroy me." His words were thick. Laced with meaning.

Then his lips took mine again, and he thrust once more and held still. Inside me, his dick pulsed.

My pussy throbbed, and I cried out a moan, clutching him so tight that I could hardly breathe. Nothing had ever felt like this. I'd never done it but had wanted it so much.

It felt like trust, even if that could never be.

He pulsed again, his face buried in my neck, then Arran rolled us down to the sheets, his hot body wrapped around mine.

Moments passed. I remembered how to breathe.

Then I pushed him off me. Arran released me, blinking his eyes open, his forehead furrowed. Reaching out, I collected his cylinder and fitted it between my thighs. With effort, I pushed it in where he'd just left, the path easier now, made of deep relaxation and the slick combination of us.

No more panic. No fear. Just showing him I could.

Arran watched, his jaw slack and his gaze glued to the apex of my thighs.

When I'd managed a couple of inches, he took over and slid it out of me, throwing it to the floor. Then he slid his half-hard dick back inside, settling down to hold me close.

"I want to fucking live inside you."

I wanted to agree, talk, work out all the things that needed to be fixed. My missing father, Cherry's death, the fact I knew the child Arran sought.

With the flickering candlelight and intense exhaustion, I passed out.

28

Arran

In my arms, Genevieve slept. I'd drifted but not fallen unconscious, my dick still inside her keeping me awake. It thickened all the more, and I slowly drew out of her then back in. No rush or hurry, just feeling.

She had my cum inside her. I only wanted to add more.

We rested on the pillows, almost face to face, her head a little lower than mine, and I shifted back so I had a view down her body, the dancing candlelight revealing the place we were joined. With my knuckle, I caressed her cheek, down her throat then palmed her breast. Genevieve was a knockout. Perfect. *Mine*.

It made me want to ruin her, or lock her away.

Keep her for certain.

Continuing on, I spread my fingers over her pussy, spearing them around my dick. The wetness we'd created earlier dampened my fingers, and I thrust again, keeping it slow so she didn't wake, though this time, it felt suspiciously like I wanted her to rest rather than not join in.

Genevieve sighed in her sleep. I kept up my roll in and out of her tight channel. Now I'd done this once, the whole deal, I was addicted. Far beyond where the past week had taken me.

Fucking her slowly, I focused on the feeling of being in her, connected to her, her pussy swallowing my dick just like she'd taken all the shit I'd gathered from around my apartment.

Every single dick-shaped thing I owned or bought was going in her cunt at some point. A permanent reminder of my obsession.

I hardened even more and bit back a groan. Then Genevieve bucked against me, a soft sound of pleasure leaving her lips.

Her eyes opened, and she reached for me. Kissed me.

I seated myself deep inside her then grabbed her ass and lifted, swinging us both from the bed. Carrying her to the window, I pushed her against the glass and fucked into her, then dropped her legs, spun her around, and drove back in, her naked body flush to the cool panes and me behind her. Beneath us, the streets were almost empty, the few remaining clubgoers staggering home in dribs and drabs, the faint line of silver in the sky announcing the approaching dawn.

"This city will know you're my woman." I fucked her harder.

She reached for my hip, her other arm bracing the window. I found her clit and caressed her, needing to feel her throbs because I was half awake and focused on coming in her without delay.

Working her with nothing hiding my actions from anyone looking up, I sped up until I was fucking her in a fury, mindless. She cursed and grabbed my wrist, clamping down on me in a way that had me seeing fucking stars. Feeling her orgasms destroyed me. I allowed my body to take over, gave a few more punishing thrusts, and came.

Slamming, damning, conviction.

Ragged breaths and desperation.

Pure, unbeatable pleasure.

Keeping her clamped to me, I returned us to the bed, not wanting to let go. On the sheets, I still didn't release her, curling around her back. I touched where we were joined because my dick never softened around this woman, and got my fingers wet again. Took them to her lips.

"Suck."

Genevieve held my gaze and opened her mouth. I drove my arousal-coated fingers over her tongue. She sucked them, her eyelids fluttering closed.

Then we stayed like that for minutes, her light sucking on my fingers and my dick buried deep the strangest form of relaxation.

Eventually, she bit the pad of my finger, and I drew my hand away.

"There's something I need to tell you," she said.

Of course, the other shoe had to drop. The truth of whatever she was would come out.

"I talked to your staff about Cherry last night. I want to find out who killed her, and assuming it's Don because he happened to be there isn't enough. My gut feel is I need more information."

I furrowed my brow, surprised. "I'm doing my own investigation."

She entwined our fingers. "Can we compare notes

when we're ready? Between us, we might work it out."

For a moment, I stayed quiet, the weird sense of *us* shifting to something new. "Fine. Don't do anything dangerous."

"I won't. There's something else. I need you to help me find my dad. It's not what you think," she added quickly. "I'm not planning anything or plotting against you. It's for both our purposes. One because I need to know he's okay, and two, I think he has information you'll want."

I scowled into the dark room. "What are you talking about?"

Genevieve turned to face me, my dick leaving her. I scowled more and pulled her leg over mine, but she paused me with a press to my chest, something meaningful in her eyes that I didn't like at all. As if what she was about to say was dangerous.

"Back in your friends' mansion, Cassie showed me a picture of a child. She said you were seeking them and had been for years. I recognised the photograph. Then when we returned, I realised where from."

My breathing ceased. Shock froze me. There was no way.

Genevieve winced. "I just heard how that sounded in my head. That I've taken something deeply personal to you and made it into an opportunity for me. I haven't. It's true."

My jaw worked, but I couldn't form words, the coincidence too unlikely.

"It isn't a trap," she tried again but weakly.

"What does this have to do with your dad?" I managed, my tone hard.

"First, tell me who the child is to you."

"My sister or brother. My mother had a second baby, a long time after me."

She nodded, as if this was her conclusion from the backstory I'd had no idea she'd heard. "Dad had a girlfriend named Flora for a while. She had a kid. The child in your picture."

Fuck. I lurched over her, imploring her with every cell in my body. "Don't. Fucking don't do this."

"Jesus, Arran." She grabbed my wrist. "Her toddler's name was Addie. A little girl. Adelia. She was the same child as in your picture. Honest to God."

A girl. My heart thundered, and I hunted for the lie in her eyes. If this was a trick, it was the cruellest she could ever have devised. The problem was in the name she'd given—I didn't think she was playing me. Or maybe I just didn't want to believe it.

Addie. Adelia.

She dug her nails into my skin. "In my dad's room in our flat, there's a picture of me with her. Dad took that photo. It's all the proof you need."

I released her. Sat back. "Kids all look the same. How can you be sure?"

"No, they don't. I recognised her, and her dungarees."

"Was he the father?"

"My dad? No. He can't keep a secret to save his life. If Addie was his, he would've said. He and Flora weren't together that long, but I know after they broke up, they kept hooking up for a few years. Then she moved away."

"Where?"

"I've no idea, but Dad would know. They stayed in touch, even after her marriage. He was a shit boyfriend

to Flora, to Mum, too, but loved them and stayed friends."
She watched me. "That's why you need to find him as
much as I do."

I dropped down on the bed, my brain fucked up over
this revelation. Hope was a terrible thing. It sidestepped
reason and beckoned in betrayal. Yet this was the first clue
I'd had since I'd found out the child existed.

The girl. My sister.

"Blackmail doesn't suit you," I forced out.

She sighed. "Ever since I made the connection, I knew
you'd think that. Believe me or don't. You've got nothing to
lose. I'll fetch the photo. You can send your friends to find
Dad. Protect yourself however you need to. I'm not trying
to hurt you."

I didn't answer, lost in memories, abandoned hunts,
and dead ends.

I'd no idea what a happy family was like, but I hoped
Addie had it. I tested the name. If she wasn't real, that
name was going to fucking kill me.

"Why don't you know where she is?" Genevieve broke
the silence.

Suddenly wiped out, I drowned in the lifetime of stories
I had, of shit never shared, and the rigid hold I maintained
on my image and how much people knew about me. I had
a choice to make. Trust her and risk everything, or ignore
her temptation and stick with life as I knew it.

No. It wasn't a choice. Not anymore.

This woman had come to me for reasons I didn't fully
know. She'd taken over my world, and my senses. My
ability to stop her died.

Turning my gaze back on her, I found myself talking.

"You had a list of questions for me. How I got my money, how my friends are connected to my business. What I'll tell you starts with public record, as you put it, then goes deeper. But we'll start with the easiest part. My father, and my friends' father, ran a trafficking ring. They established routes through Europe and kidnapped girls and women to be sold for sex. My father is in jail for life for his sins, theirs is dead."

Genevieve stared, her beautiful lips apart.

"My father was the chief of police and a lord of the realm. Lord Kendrick. A title that can't be taken from him and will one day pass to me. With it came the estate I took you to as well as a lot of money. Most of it was seized by the government as it was tainted by his trade, but my father was devious. His inheritance from his father stayed locked in vaults in other countries. Untouchable by the law. His empire fell when I was seventeen. I couldn't handle the fallout so spent months sleeping in my car and evading anyone I knew because of my age."

"You were sleeping in your car at seventeen?"

I uttered a hard laugh. "Because I'd burned the house down. My mother was dead, my father in jail. I had nothing. My friends found me and supported me, but I was reeling. On my eighteenth birthday, I drove to my father's lawyer's office and told them I wanted to claim whatever was left of my birthright."

Genevieve's lip trembled. "I don't even know where to start with that. What happened to you in those months?"

"I fought for money. My dad had made sure I was strong, resilient, and used to pain. I let people bet on me and took and delivered beatings for money. It's how I met Convict. Shade was via a different path, though equally bloody."

"You survived, then you took that inheritance and made your empire. God, Arran."

Not one person had heard or summarised my background in this way.

Her eyes lined with tears. "How did you grow up? What kind of things did you see? Did your dad expose you to what he was doing?"

My pulse thudded, images flashing in front of my eyes that I wished I'd never seen. His parties. The bored, naked women waiting to act for him. The pain they hid. The delight in him when he got a response he wanted.

"He didn't hide anything. Even in my earliest memories, he abused women in front of me. He hurt them for pleasure and made me watch. Punished me with his fists if I dared disobey him, real or imagined. Now, when I hunt down and kill men who I know hurt women, I do it wishing they were him."

She recoiled, shock evident. "You... No. I don't want to know about them. How did no one rescue you?"

"He fucking owned the police. Who would they call? The people who worked for him were scared of him. I never left his house."

Her eyes shuttered closed. Then she leaned in and pressed a kiss to my forehead. Hugged me.

Fucking hell.

"He gifted me Alisha when I wasn't even a teenager so I could learn his trade."

"But you didn't touch her."

"Never once."

Her embrace tightened. "That's why you stayed a virgin. Because of everything you'd seen."

"Or had done to me."

"By your father."

It wasn't a question, but I left that hanging, the additional answer not forming. "When I was older, after my father had been caught and the fire erased our house, I tried to be normal, or at least copy what I saw other people doing. I tried to have sex. Never a girlfriend, but I let a woman come on to me in a bar then take me outside."

Genevieve inched back, her lips pursed. She swiped at her eyes. "Why is it that I don't know the woman, and am fully aware that you never fucked her, yet I want to kill her?"

Despite everything, I allowed a savage grin. "There's my little maniac. Don't you dare talk to me about previous boyfriends or they'll probably end up in pieces and floating down Deadwater River."

She sucked in a breath. "God. Fine. Tell me the rest of what happened."

"She blew me on her knees on the wet ground. All I felt was panic and anger. I let her finish, then walked away like an asshole. I tried it again, and the same thing happened. No pleasure, but a fucked-up head."

"How...? I don't know if I want to ask this. How do you feel when we sleep together?"

I watched her. The lips I'd tasted while she slept and now needed more and more. The body that I'd never get enough of. There was more at the edges of my thought, but I couldn't let it in. "Different."

She flinched. "No girl wants to hear that."

"Why, you don't care about my opinion?" I sounded petulant but I was stating a fact. From the start, she'd wanted to leave. She'd stayed but not out of devotion to me.

Genevieve's cheeks flooded red. She fell back, dropping eye contact. "What happened to your mother? Tell me that part. She's a missing piece in all of this, and I can't work out how she connects in. Who was she? Where did she exist in all this?"

"Audrey was a sex worker my father bought. He got her pregnant then took her baby, not letting her tell anyone else including me what she was to me."

"He took you from her? That evil bastard. Did you see her when you were growing up? Why didn't she say?"

"My father's control was absolute, and I assume he didn't feel there was any danger from her. Audrey regularly came to Kendrick Manor with the other women bought in to entertain Dad from the brothels established from his trade. She was as much part of my growing up as any other of the familiar faces."

"If she wasn't able to tell you who she was, did she try to get close to you?"

My mouth dried. I couldn't stomach what Audrey had done. Nobody knew this, though Camden suspected it after what he'd seen one night at Kendrick Manor. He and Jamieson had once tried to talk to me about abuse and living through it, but as much as I cared about my friends, I couldn't go there with them. Didn't want it said.

"No. She suffered for years then provided evidence against him and posted it online. A full account of everything she'd experienced at his hands, including about me. But for the seventeen years before that, she did exactly what my father told her. Performed for him. Rarely spoke to me. The only part of her I had, beyond DNA, was my name. She gave that to me. It's why I believe you about Adelia. It fits."

"Audrey, Arran, Adelia. She named her babies with her initial."

"She tried to fuck me, too," I got out, putting the words ahead of any sympathy that tried to diminish what she'd done. "On one of his twisted evenings, Dad ordered her to take me, and she obeyed. She heard him, crossed the room, and stroked my chest. Ran her hand down my body."

My throat clogged. I coughed to clear it.

"I guess she thought I'd never know who she was. Divine, because that was her sex worker name, was so messed up by the world, and by me and my father, that she would've gone there just to be close to me. So don't ask about sex and how it makes me feel. It's right there in the name of my clubs. Divine and Divide, because that's all I am. A son divided."

Genevieve's soft sound of dismay didn't stop me.

"In Divine, I spend my life trying to protect women and girls, yet I failed the mother and daughter who were the ones who mattered most. But that mother failed me, too. And I hate myself for even thinking that. Now you know exactly how to destroy me, Genevieve. Use that as you will."

29

Genevieve

*A*rran turned his back and stopped talking. Fucking hell. Broken by his father and abused by his mother, by rights, he should be the worst kind of criminal. A wreck of a person. Maybe in parts he was. He was also incredible. Brave. Brutal but in a strangely admirable way.

He killed bad people. Confessed it with the rest of his awful story. The marks on him were evidence of his abuse.

And in a breathtaking, pulse-racing moment of time, I fell in love with him.

The image I'd painted when I first knew him was rooted in my hatred for gangs. Cruel people doing bad things for their own gain. Arran was the opposite of that in every way. Everything he did was to try to right the wrongs of a past he didn't create but had suffered through. To revere the memory of a mother who'd been so messed up she'd failed him.

Unseeing, I stared at the steel ceiling rafters.

He protected the women in the club. He set up a game to unite people in love, albeit with a vicious start. In all the time I'd been his captive, I'd barely thought about the meaning behind that. Had he designed that game because it was what he wanted, a method to break through his damage? Yet he'd operated it with no intention of being a participant, watching all those other couples pair up, giving him an outlet to handle his trauma.

Up until I walked in and gifted him a reason to enter.

I shivered, bringing myself back down to earth with a bump. Whatever I felt for him, and however real that might be, there was no guarantee he'd ever feel the same. I wasn't foolish, even if I'd been a fool for him over and over. I couldn't kid myself that a man with that much damage would miraculously heal because we'd slept together.

So why did that make me want to curl up in a ball and cry for him?

Outside the window, the faint streaks of dawn pierced the night, and I rolled away, facing Arran instead of the daylight.

Fuck it.

I curled around his back. Wriggled my leg between his. Wrapped an arm around his upper arm so I could hold him then kissed one of his round scars.

After a beat, Arran, the broken king of the sex workers, tucked my hand against his chest. My heart beat out of time, and I clung on to the feeling, letting it wash over me until I closed in on sleep.

One thing was certain—this moment of traumatic peace wouldn't last.

When next I woke, it was to a night-dark afternoon, a summer storm lashing the city. Rain spattered on the arched window in Arran's bedroom.

I stretched against him. Both of us were still naked

under his midnight-blue sheets. We smelled of sex and disaster.

"Morning."

I blinked up at him, conscious of his wary tone. Without giving a second of thought, I reached for him and pulled him onto me. Wrapped my legs around his hips, the ridge of his dick between us.

"Give me back my permission to fuck you whenever I want." Arran's voice came out low and deliciously rough.

"Granted."

He drove into me, my body welcoming him, that insistent need never far away.

I'd dreamed of this, having fun in a bed with him. But in my imagination, we'd been happy. Not dragged down by all the other factors in our lives.

Arran kissed me and thrust in lazy, half-awake slides. He found my clit, easily getting me to the edge of pleasure. When I was close, he stopped his strokes and just moved his hand, groaning with deep need when I hissed out, convulsing around him in the way he'd told me he loved. It only made the climax more devastating. The knowledge of what I did to him and our shared desire and need. Then his control broke, and he rammed over and over until he came, too, triggering all kinds of echoed explosions throughout me.

Fuck, I was in such trouble.

We cooled together. I risked a glance.

He swatted my backside. "Go shower. If I come in with you, we'll never get anything done today."

I rose and skittered away, naked, and with the sticky essence of him seeping from me. Weird that I liked that.

Loved it.

I wrinkled my nose, not looking back. I loved him. How had I let that happen? Frustration broke over my afterglow. This wouldn't end well, and losing him was going to hurt. Better not to think about it.

In the shower, I blushed to recall the last time I was in here, and took my time cleaning myself thoroughly. Arran had shampoo and conditioner that I hadn't noticed last time. Both were specifically for blonde hair. Surely not his. I laughed to myself then got out, dried off, and used a moisturiser and waiting toothpaste and brush.

Back in the bedroom, the man I loved was on the phone. He pointed to a hairdryer on the dresser and then the wardrobe, stalking out to the living area. I opened the door, finding shelves of women's clothing plus more hanging up.

All my size. Huh. Suspicious. He probably wasn't having women sleep over often. Holding my towel closer, I extracted a gorgeous dress and took it to the door and peered out. He noticed me. I held up the item in question.

His lips curved into a boyish smile that did things to my stupid heart.

"Lara," he mouthed.

I blew him a kiss then returned to pick out clothes for the day. Or evening, according to my phone which I found in my bag on the dresser, presumably Arran having ordered it fetched for me at some point. It was nearly dark again, and I was fully in my creature-of-the-night era.

I had multiple missed calls from my brother and a reminder popping up, followed by a text.

Jon at Deliverus: If you don't come in tonight, I will have no choice but to let you go.

Shit. I had work in thirty minutes.

It was a crap shift—four hours to cover the evening rush only—a punishment for missing a week of work, despite my claim I'd been ill.

Riordan's missed calls would have to wait. After tapping out a fast response to my boss, I dried my hair and brushed it into a high ponytail, then yanked on leather leggings with ridged knees like biker wear and a cropped top over a t-shirt bra. There was a nice jacket that would work for being on the road. Lara had good taste.

As I readied myself, I took in my surroundings in a way I hadn't fully done when we'd arrived. Arran's place was high-end, from the engineered oak floors to the heavy furniture and beautiful fixtures. The impromptu sex toys had all disappeared, thankfully, but the candles had guttered to wax puddles on the wooden chest of drawers. That was the only element out of place. The only personalisation to give an indication of who lived here.

Perhaps that was why Arran wanted my...presence everywhere.

When I was just about ready, he reappeared, stabbing his phone to end his call with a huff of annoyance. He eyed the light coat.

"I need to go out," I informed him.

"Where?"

"Work. I start in thirty."

He jerked his head back, his expression souring. "Why the fuck are you sticking with that crap delivery job?"

My shoulders rose. "It's crap but it's mine, and I need the money."

"You get money from me."

Oh, he didn't go there. "Do I!"

"Yes, because you're my woman. I don't want you out there doing something hazardous for little reward when I can and will provide for you. You promised you wouldn't do anything dangerous. Was that another lie?"

I glowered at him. "Something's obviously pissed you off, but I'm not in the mood to indulge a temper tantrum."

"Just stating the facts. You're mine."

"I'm not a possession."

"Yes, you are."

"Just because you say so?"

"Well, you never would." He breathed evenly, hands on his hips, his expression that same infuriating neutral he'd worn on the video calls he'd made to his clients.

If I couldn't read his body language, his tight muscles and panic rolling off him, I'd assume he'd want me to agree.

But something else was happening. I stopped my response, waiting on him.

"Do you want an out, Genevieve? Should I call someone else to step in? Maybe the woman whose place you took would be happy to be at my side and pretend she liked me. Tell me now if you want to go back to your old life and never see me again once the month is up."

Natasha Reid was the woman in question, but aside from a stab of jealousy, she was far from the forefront of my mind.

Arran had got badly shaken up by my mention of work.

He'd moved on from the mistrust. He was invested, and it scared him. My heart cracked.

Crossing the room, I stepped into his space. "Is that what you want, someone other than me?"

He didn't answer, folding his arms as a barrier between us. I lifted them and slipped underneath so he was holding me. Arran's lips remained in a pout, but he let me rearrange him.

Then I pushed up on my toes and kissed his cheek, speaking to his soul. "I want to keep my job because it's mine and I'm a human being with my own thoughts, feelings, and independence. Nothing to do with you supporting me. This is my second week of being with you, and in that time I haven't been home once or done anything I usually would. In another two, you could throw me out. If I don't have my job, I've got nothing to go back to. Understand? I'll lose the flat because of whatever the hell my dad's done. Mouldy walls, shitty small-minded neighbours and all—it's my only home. I've got four hours of delivering food lined up in exchange for some semblance of security, so yes, I can do it, and no, it doesn't mean I'm leaving you."

Those strong arms tightened around me. His grey eyes scrutinised mine. "Security," he repeated, almost to himself. Then, more assuredly, "Let me drive you."

I adapted my plan of being on a scooter in the pouring rain to being chauffeur driven around the city. Not a bad compromise. "Okay."

He kissed me, an almost desperate claiming that I had to break or I'd miss logging in on time.

Together, we left his apartment.

"I'm still giving you the money you're owed," he griped.

"Can't wait to see what you bid on with it this time."

On the way out, Arran thumped on the door opposite his in the hall. There was nothing else up here other than steel framing the brick exterior walls, the stairs entrance, and the lift.

In just his boxer shorts, Shade answered, his black hair messy and in his eyes. Dark-ink tattoos crawled from his muscular thigh and across his chest to climb up his throat.

Last night, he'd held my breasts while Arran toyed with me. Looked like we were just going to breeze right on past that.

I adjusted my gaze away.

"In future, put some fucking clothes on when you answer the door," Arran intoned.

"In my defence, it's never anyone but ye. You're lucky I had shorts on."

"Gen lives here now so adjust."

Gen, he'd called me. Only people I cared about used that.

"Aye, sorry, Genevieve. Hang on." Shade disappeared, reappearing with a black shirt shrugged over his body.

Arran lifted his chin. "We're going to be out in the city for the next few hours. Are you good to hold the fort?"

"Nae bother. It won't be busy until later, so I can come along for the ride if ye need backup?"

"It's nothing wild. Gen has her delivery job."

Shade jumped his gaze to me, wrinkling his nose in an expression of disbelief. "Really?"

I rolled my eyes. "Yes, I still have a job."

"In the rain. Going about on your scooter from restaurants to lazy people's houses."

"Don't you start, too."

A laugh returned. "All right. Are ye leaving now?" At my agreement, he stepped back. "Give me two and I'll come. Don't like the thought of the pair of ye roaming the streets unprotected." Then he called into the depths of his apartment. "Leesh? I'm going out."

He shut the door, and Arran called the lift.

"Is 'Leesh' Alisha?" I asked.

Arran inclined his head.

I frowned, a thought occurring that hadn't last night. "Another 'A' name. She isn't...?"

"Related to my mother? No. Alisha isn't her real name."

Of course not. No one around here used their real identity apart from Arran. "Are they a couple? Shade and Alisha?"

He shrugged. "Not that I know of. She was screwing Convict at one point, and Shade's taste runs in another direction."

"He's gay?"

"No. A forbidden pussy direction."

At my laugh, the lift arrived.

He gestured to the panel. "This and the stairs door are coded if you want to come up. It's the same as the pin I gave you to use in the bid room."

"Two-seven-six-eight. I remember."

He leaned against the door, propping it open. I guessed to wait for Shade. Then he regarded me with something new in his gaze.

"What do you remember of Addie?"

I smiled. "I was twelve so thought her the cutest thing

ever. Those dungarees in your picture? They were soft in real life. Velvet. Her favourites. She was so smart, too, and she'd chatter away like anything, more than most two-year-olds, according to Flora."

"Did you know her birthday?"

I squinted, trying to recall any kind of party. "No, sorry."

"What about Flora, can you give me a description?"

I rattled off what I remembered of the woman. She was tall and curvy with fair hair. Similar to my mother, I realised. Nothing of her address or surname had made it through to my pre-teen mind.

"Was Addie happy?"

"Very."

"I've wondered how Audrey's death affected her. I never knew her as a mother, but she did. At least I assume so." He rubbed his hand over his hair. "I've wondered all kinds of things. Was her foster mother kind to her?"

"Flora treated her like her own and never once said she was a foster mum. It was obvious she loved her."

He went quiet for a moment, his gaze distant. "Want to know the shittiest thing about it? The part that haunts me? Audrey never told me about her daughter, even at the end. She could've asked Flora to bring her to me, or at least let me know she existed, but no. The only thing I can assume is that she didn't want me to know because she couldn't trust that I wouldn't turn out like my dad."

My heart hurt. "You don't know that for sure."

"True, but I can't deny it."

I took the opportunity to say something else I'd dwelled on. "I need to apologise to you."

"For what?"

"I said a lot of bad things about how you treat women. If I think back on it, it makes me cringe. You're so different to what I thought. To that public image you present."

"You like me now?"

Heat warmed my cheeks. "I don't dislike you, I guess."

The corners of his mouth tipped up.

Shade's door opened along the corridor. Arran reached and grabbed me into the lift. Then he hit the button to close the door.

"Wait," Shade called.

"Sorry, bro. It's the stairs for you."

The lift doors met, and Arran closed in on me, a kiss the answer to my apology. We only had eight floors to descend, but that was plenty to get me flustered, his tongue the wickedest, cleverest tool in his toolbelt. At the *ding*, Arran pressed the button to keep the door closed and kissed me some more. Breathing hard, he finally pulled away then captured my hand, taking me with him out into the hall.

Shade emerged from the stairwell and gave him a shove. "Dick."

We passed the staff entrance to Divide, a glance in showing me all the lights on and a cleaning crew hard at work in their black skeleton shirts.

"Student night tonight," Shade informed me. "Cheap pints. Naw so hectic as the end of the week. The strip club and upstairs will have the usual crowd and be rammed from ten onwards."

"On a Monday?"

"Businessmen away from home. They start the week as they mean to go on." He raised his eyebrows.

More insight into the undertow of the city. This place was another world.

Someone called us, and we paused in the corridor and turned back. It took me a second to recognise Alisha, the operations manager, coming from the stairwell. In day clothes, her mousy brown hair in a messy bun, and no makeup accentuating her features, she was barely recognisable to the glossy creature I'd seen when she was working.

Arran's comment about why she never wore a mask made sense. Her street disguise was effective.

Her gaze flicked over me then to the man holding my hand. Hostility crawled off her. "Why do you all have to go out this evening?"

Arran shrugged. "We'll be back by the time it picks up."

Her lips flattened. "You can't keep doing this."

"I'm not having the same argument again. Four hours, then I promise I'll be here for the whole night." He took a breath. "There's something I need your help with. Does the name Flora sound familiar?"

Alisha wrinkled her nose. "Who is she?"

"That's not important. Do you know anyone of that name?" At her headshake in the negative, he sighed. "Can you ask around the OG crew?" He gave the description I had.

Alisha shrugged, noncommittal.

I watched their interaction with a sinking heart. Arran called her one of the most important people in his life, and yet they were barely speaking. I was the reason.

"Mr Daniels? There's a visitor here for you," someone else said from the other direction.

Manny, the head of security, approached, another man at his side. Jamieson, one of Arran's Scottish friends.

Arran embraced his friend. Jamieson nodded to me then fist bumped Shade. I wasn't sure how much Arran's worlds overlapped, but he'd clearly brought his friends here in the past.

"Walk with us," Arran told his friend. "Tell me what the fuck you're doing here?"

Jamieson fell into step, and the four of us moved on.

"Cassie," he said with a frustrated grumble. His hand flicked a lighter wheel, a spark flying. "She got upset over something then took off. My guess is she'll end up here."

I drew my eyebrows in. "Have you checked with her friends?"

"Doesnae have many. We're kind of an insular family."

My heart gave an unexpected pang of understanding. I didn't have many friends either, though for different reasons. Then a memory hit me. "She said something about coming here. I'd forgotten until now."

Cassie had said she wanted to dance, but in case that meant on the pole rather than the nightclub's floor, I kept the details to myself.

"Fuck, she mentioned that to me, too," Arran said. "I'd assumed it was a joke because she said she wanted to dance here. I warned her off."

Jamieson's lip curled. "Red rag to a bull, man. She'll be around somewhere. She's not called?"

Arran snorted. "Like she'd give me notice of showing up. None of you fuckers do."

There was no malice in his tone, only the tolerance extended to family. But worry was there, too. I shared it.

Cherry had been murdered by someone unknown. That killer was still walking the streets. Even if he'd killed Cherry for a specific reason, that didn't ease my concern for any other woman out on her own.

We exited the warehouse with a gust of wind and rain splattering us. At Arran's car, he hustled me inside. Shade went to the next one over, another chunky, matte-black beast of a vehicle.

"We're driving around the city for a few hours while Gen works." Arran enunciated the last word like it was poisonous. "Come with? We can keep an eye out for Cassie's car."

Shade banged his fist on his wet roof. "Ride with me. Tell us what's up with your sister."

"Fuck riding shotgun. We'll take my car," Jamieson decided.

Shade scowled, then raised his hand. "Rock, paper, scissors…"

Still at my open door, Arran chuckled under his breath as if there was some inside joke.

"Shoot," Jamieson said. He smacked his fist against Shade's scissors. "Shotgun for ye."

Shade swore a blue stream. "I need to find a better way to call shit. Anyway, fuck not being behind the wheel. I'm taking my car, too."

Jamieson shrugged and strolled to an expensive-looking, gunmetal-grey vehicle across the car park.

I stared between them. "We can't drive three cars on one delivery route. We'll clog up the town."

Arran only shrugged, uncaring.

We took off in convoy. Arran's phone connected to the

speakers, and from the car behind, Jamieson filled us in on Cassie.

"She's been stressing about not having a purpose in life so signed up to business classes at a college, but got into a row with a lass who told her how privileged she was, just because she drives a nice car. She worked out where Cass lived and decided she didnae need to work for a living because of Daddy's money. In front of the whole class, she told her to get off the course and make way for someone who needed it. Like the bullshit our father put us through and the fact she was in foster care for the first years of her life didn't mean anything. Cassie's been working hard to manage herself, and this set her back."

"That's horrible," I said. "What did she do? Either tell her darkest secrets or brazen it out? Fuck that girl for bullying her."

"She threatened her," he intoned. "Got herself kicked off the group by her own actions. Not one for mincing words, my little sister."

Arran's hand curled into mine, keeping me with him as we drove the dark streets. At the yard for Deliverus, I hopped out. Jon, the boss of the franchise, stared over my shoulder at the cars behind me. The three big men watching my every move.

"I don't need a scooter tonight," I chirped. "Just a bag to keep the food warm. Sorry for the past week, it couldn't be helped. We good?"

He gave a faint nod and let me go without another word. Back in the car, I logged in to the delivery system and cued up my first job, then swiped to my playlist.

"Mind if I play music as I work?" I asked.

Arran gave me an indulgent smile then tapped his car's

screen to disconnect his phone and add mine so I could use his speakers, putting in an earpiece to keep the line open with his friends.

"Midnight City" by M83 surrounded us. Old-school nostalgia for the win.

Then I was out in the city and back to work. Slick, wet roads reflected neon signs, and the big overhead streetlights picked out showering raindrops. Grey clouds scudded over the dark skies, backlit by a faint moon.

All so familiar from a year of me doing this job. At the same time, all was completely different.

Everything else in my world had changed, from where I was living to the clothes on my back. Clinging on to this job felt vital. But doing it, I battled back a strong urge to return to the warehouse. Deadwater had taken on a dangerous feel, as if only bad things could come from roaming its streets at night.

Yet I couldn't quit. Arran's life had absorbed mine, and if he spat me out again, this was what I'd come back to.

Whether I liked it or not, I had to see it through.

Two hours in, with a dozen deliveries complete and no Cassie sighted, I exited an Italian restaurant, Shade shadowing me because Arran had taken a call. A few metres away, my man was still on the phone, whatever he had to handle an obvious issue from his frown and pacing.

I went to get back into his car. He gestured at Shade's. Alrighty, then. His conversation wasn't for my ears, and it only cemented how his existence wasn't mine. Hiding my bubble of hurt, I got in with Shade.

"Address?" he asked.

I stuck my phone on the dash holder, the first of two delivery locations coming up. At Shade's agreement, I linked up my music, and Shade sped us out, Jamieson and Arran tailing close behind.

I lined up A Perfect Circle's 'Judith'. A track my rock-chick mum loved. The eclectic playlist had been hers, featuring bands like Korn and Metallica, and I'd added to it over the years. It kept me feeling close to her. Emotion filled me, something about the city and my strange new relationship messing up my feelings.

Mum had been my model for independence. For her, life had been tough. She'd made it her bitch.

Oblivious to me fighting becoming a hot mess, Shade smiled approval, ducking his head to the tune, streetlights flickering over us as we rocked out to a song featuring killing in its lyrics.

At the drop-off, I delivered to the street door, no dark corridors in a tower block to get spooked in, and Shade stuck close.

I eyed him. "If you ever want to give up the gangster life, I can put in a good word with you for food delivery. You're a natural."

He pursed his lips. "I appreciate that. Speaking of being good at things..." His gaze sought out anything but me beside him on the pavement. "I did and said shite I shouldn't have last night. Been playing on my mind."

I cast my mind back. Amusement bubbled up along with embarrassment. "Nice tits, wasn't it?"

He sucked in a breath, hands diving into his pockets. His shoulders up around his ears. "If ye could take that from your brain and throw it away, I'd appreciate it."

"Done, though it wasn't your fault. Do Arran and I need to fess up to your lady for including you in our...whatever we want to call that?"

"There's no lady. I'm permanently out on my ass."

I snorted, because there was no way this guy wasn't pulling interest. With his dark hair and eyes, the tattoos all over him, and his brazen air of danger and arrogance, women must love him, even if he wanted someone unattainable. Forbidden pussy, as Arran called it.

On my phone, I tapped the job completion button, the next address loading. I already had the meal for it, grabbed from the last Italian restaurant, but the delivery was way across town.

I held it up. Shade's mild amusement dropped.

He shot his focus up to the other cars where Arran and Jamieson waited by open doors. "We have a problem."

Arran stabbed to end his call. Both were on us in seconds. My pulse spiked. Whatever was in his expression, I didn't like at all.

30

Arran

"Genevieve's next address is in enemy territory." Shade named a gang-owned street.

My blood iced over. "Not happening."

Gen peered between us. "I'm only going there to deliver food. What's the problem?"

"On a street I can't go without causing an incident."

Her cheeks reddened. "The system won't let me bypass a delivery that I already accepted. If I don't go, my work is over. Jon will fire me."

I shrugged, not hating that plan.

She glowered then grabbed my arm, dragging me away a few steps from my boys. "This is important to me. I told you why, and I'm not quitting just because you have enemies."

I spread my arms out. "What am I supposed to do, let you walk down a road I know is dangerous?"

"You don't *let* me do anything, it's my choice. And the place is only dangerous to you, not me."

"You're my woman."

"Are we public in the city? Do all the gang members know my face? No, they don't, so there's no problem."

"You don't know that. You're part of me now," I bit out. "What don't you get about that?"

Her spine stiffened. I stood taller, too. Yet again, we were in a standoff, neither willing to give way. Even though I was right.

"I can take care of myself," she decided.

"I'm better at looking after you than you are."

Gen's lips parted. "Oh really."

"You walked out in front of my car after stepping into the road with headphones in. That was on the way to work, wasn't it? Then you ended up in my violent game like a lost little lamb."

"You're such an asshole."

"Never denied it. I'm not above throwing you over my shoulder and taking you home." My jaw was so tight it could crack.

Her gaze darkened to something menacing. Sexy as hell, even if that hadn't been her intention. "Try it. See what happens."

Cautiously, Jamieson approached. He held up his phone with a map on the screen. "Shade and I were just checking it out. The address is barely a hundred feet down the road. I'll take Genevieve, as no one will know my car, and the two of ye can wait at the end. No territory encroached, plus you'll have full visibility of her."

Gen turned on the heel of her brand-new All Stars. "Perfect. Then I don't have to sit in the car with this jerk either. Not that he's wanted to all evening anyway."

I was the jerk. Got that. But her tone told me my

distance had hurt her. Fucking hell. I hadn't wanted to sit a car apart. It was necessary so she didn't hear my conversation.

"Opinion?" I asked Shade.

He raised a shoulder. "So long as we can see her, it's lower risk, but if it ends up in a rumble, I'd be down. I could do with the exercise."

Gen growled annoyance. "I'm not asking permission from any of you. Drive me or don't. I can walk it by myself otherwise."

Fucking infuriating woman.

Shade and Jamieson waited on my reluctant nod of agreement, and Jamieson and Gen got into his car, leaving me and my enforcer to follow.

We crawled through the city traffic, and I gripped the steering wheel like I could wring its neck.

Shade spoke in my ear. "If she's this stubborn about ye keeping her safe, how is she going to react when she finds out what you've done this evening?"

Music on Jamieson's end of the line told me our comms line wasn't live over his car's speakers. Gen had commandeered those with her playlist.

I rolled my shoulders, not answering and keeping a watch on the outline of her chatting happily to Jamieson in a way she wouldn't with me right now. I'd been on the phone for the best part of two hours, making an unexpected purchase. Another would be delivered to the warehouse tonight, ordered while Gen slept.

The first purchase was in Genevieve's interest, the second in mine. In both cases, I couldn't predict her reaction, despite her love of security, as she'd termed it.

Entertaining himself, Shade continued. "For that

matter, she's going to lose her shit when ye tell her about tomorrow night's mission."

That surprise was fully my and Shade's wheelhouse. Removing a predator from the streets, even if it was in another city.

"Or, she'll be happy," I argued.

"Brother, you're dreaming. If she finds out after the fact, she'll be furious. The man killed her ma. She deserves to be the one holding the knife, metaphorically speaking."

He might be right, but I wasn't ready to concede. I needed blood. We hadn't yet found her old man, so this was a good alternative. "Fill me in on preparations."

Shade had already explained how Convict had found Jordan Peters from the basic details I knew. He was still living the same life as a wannabe gangster, dealing coke. He also had a fifteen-year-old girl living under his roof who no one believed was a relative. Convict had been working his ass off watching him, establishing his patterns so we could do what we did best.

Shade was an expert at catching people to order. Knocking them out with a dose of something illegal. Ending them if needed. I was ready with the motive, delivering justice for Genevieve's pain and her lost mother.

The problem was, I was utterly and completely fucked over the woman.

She could ask anything of me and I'd do it. Deliver it. Fucking kill it if it looked at her wrong. She'd challenged me on considering her a possession, and I wasn't about to deny it.

What she didn't know was exactly how badly she had taken possession of me in exchange.

Ahead, Jamieson signalled right, entering a wide

street with a graffitied shop on the corner marking the start of Four Miler territory. The drug runners. The very people Gen's father had gone to for reasons best known to himself. He wasn't here, but she intended to walk straight up to one of the residences.

I pulled over, fighting a war inside myself to take her out of there. But Shade was right. I'd torch our relationship if I forced her hand.

"I made her vulnerable," I said into the line. "I've made her a target."

Shade's voice returned. "Women are always targets. She'll take on your enemies but also your friends, too."

For this battle, I wasn't sure I could just sit back and watch.

31

Genevieve

From the warm bag, I extracted the food parcel. It was small, as most were in the early part of the week. Just a couple of inexpensive pasta dishes.

"That house there." Jamieson pointed across the path to a plain, concrete-block residence.

I swallowed and popped my door.

Off the main road, it was quiet here. Eerily so, with few lights on, the streetlamp overhead dark and buzzing with a fault. Whichever gang had claimed this area was hiding behind crumbling rows of cheap houses. Drug dealers, maybe. The other choice was guns. Not that I knew shit about the gangs beyond what Arran had told me.

Aside from Dad being seen with them.

A raindrop landed on my neck, and I jumped, hurrying across the pavement. The weather had eased, but I wasn't about to linger more than I needed to.

Being here felt wrong. The sense I'd got at the start of my shift of being a fish out of water intensified. Arran's point made sense—being connected to him made me a target. Once word got out and my face was associated with his, I wouldn't be able to do this anymore.

I touched the gate handle, a trickle of fear slowing me. The house ahead was completely dark, not even the flicker of the TV to indicate someone was home.

"I don't like it," Jamieson said softly. "This was a mistake."

A mistake borne of my stubbornness. I wanted to be like my mother, independent and strongminded, but she'd got tangled in gangs and ended up dead. I could have laughed if it wasn't so tragic. Why hadn't my mind supplied that extra detail when I was facing off with my very own personal gang leader?

"I don't think I should ring the doorbell," I replied. "I'll leave it outside then they'll get a notification that it's been delivered."

"Thank fuck for that. Give me the bag."

I handed it to him, and the Scotsman leaned over the gate, setting it on the path.

There, delivered. I could mark it off on the app and move on. There was only an hour left of the shift.

I wasn't sure I could do this anymore.

Footsteps sounded. Further down the street, a man appeared. He stopped in the shadows, watching us. Waiting. My stomach tightened.

"Who the fuck are you?" he called out.

Without hesitation, Jamieson stepped in front of me, facing the danger. "Get in the car," he said in that same soft but deadly tone. To the man, he lifted a hand. "Just delivering food."

"In a fucking Aston Martin?" he intoned.

"Borrowed because of the rain." Jamieson forced lightness into his tone, backing up.

"Very generous friends you've got to let that kind of car down this side of the tracks." The man strolled closer. "The state of that, brother. What, a hundred K? Two?"

I peered around Jamieson. The car enthusiast was older, maybe fifties. My father's generation.

"Do you know where you are?" the older man said, louder. "This is Four Miler territory. You need to make your colours clear."

"No colours. Just delivering food, like I said," Jamieson insisted.

Colours presumably meant gang affiliation. But I'd got stuck on what the man had said. *Four Milers.* That was who my dad had been associated with, according to Arran. My pulse skipped a beat. He was right there in front of me, and there was no reason not to ask.

I stepped to one side so I could see the man more clearly. "Hey, do you know Sydney?"

"Who's asking?" He squinted at me.

"Adam Walker's daughter."

"That so? Don's girl as well, ain't that right?"

I stared, horrified.

The man continued, "How's your old man getting on with his job?"

Across the road, a door opened in another seemingly abandoned house. A man stepped out. A second followed, his hand going into his jacket.

Both had balaclavas hiding their faces, and a spiderweb tattoo crawled over the first's arm.

"Four Milers, three, armed," Jamieson said low,

touching his ear.

Tyres squealed from the way we'd come.

I caught my breath. Earlier, Arran had kept an open line between our cars, but I assumed that was only to have the conversation about Cassie. Of course they'd connected up again before this last drop.

As he spoke, the three men flinched, their focus skipping up the road. Horror took over my bravery. Jamieson had kids. If he faced off against members of a drug-dealing gang and got hurt, it was my fault. What had I done?

"Move." He spun around and tucked me under his arm, body blocking me across the pavement to his grey car.

Once I was in, he jogged to the other side, right as Arran's then Shade's cars tore down the street and halted just ahead of ours, blocking the road. Jamieson gunned our engine and spoke into his phone.

"I'll get her out of here. Stay alive."

He reversed from the space into the street, keeping on going backwards, the road too narrow to turn.

I dragged my gaze from Arran's car to him. "Wait, what just happened?"

"Their suspicions changed into a threat. If we didn't run, they'd have questioned us."

"Where's Arran? Why isn't he following?"

Peering between the rearview and the side mirrors, Jamieson picked up speed. "Giving us space to leave safely."

Misery swarmed me. "I only wanted to ask about my dad. Fuck. Arran's going to be hurt."

In the dark interior of the car, his friend chuffed a

laugh. "I know things between ye are pretty new, but trust that he can handle shite like this. Gang warfare is his bag. He wrote the book on how it goes down in Deadwater."

I stared into the shadowy road, centred on Arran's red taillights. Anything could happen. Just because he'd fought for his place in this world didn't mean he'd walk away now.

What if the whole gang emerged with weapons and set upon him? I couldn't believe the drop-off had been a trap, surely not, but he'd told me exactly how big an issue it was for him to go down there. I'd left him amongst messed-up criminals with a liking for violence.

He could be killed.

"We have to go back," I spluttered, but even as I said the words, I knew how ridiculous they sounded.

Jamieson made an off noise. "He'll hang me by my balls. I'm taking ye to the warehouse. Arran will let us know when they're away."

I hunkered down, my thoughts spiralling in all directions and the city flashing by without my noticing. My phone dinged, and I snatched it up only to find a timeout message from my food delivery app. I logged out in dismay. Let Jon fire me. So long as I got Arran back in one piece, I didn't care.

Soon enough, we were through to the centre of town and on the west side, following the river. The warehouse sat on the banks, a queue of what looked like students on the walkway outside of Divide and the usual stream of men entering Divine, the black-and-pink signs a homecoming now.

The place loomed big, like it had the right to judge me for harming its master.

Jamieson parked, then there was nothing for it but to wait. He didn't suggest going inside, and I didn't budge. Time passed. I checked my phone over and over, tried and failed to play my alphabet game to make the minutes go by faster.

After God knew how long, Jamieson lifted his phone. Waggled it.

I grabbed it and put it to my ear. "Arran?"

"Maniac."

I slapped my hand over my mouth, his warm tones so familiar. So *loved*. "Are you okay? What happened?"

"Nothing a negotiation couldn't handle."

I slumped, my heart pounding. "I pictured you riddled with bullet holes."

"Wishful thinking?" At my lack of an answer, he continued, a dangerous edge to his voice. "We're on our way back."

"I'm waiting outside."

"I know. Be ready." He disconnected.

I handed the phone back to Jamieson, unable to speak until Arran's car appeared on the approach road then spun into his spot, Shade right behind. I leapt out to lurch for his door, but he was already out.

Blood stained his face, a spatter on his shirt. God.

"Are you hurt?" I gasped.

"Not my blood, baby. Now get inside so I can teach you a lesson about knowing your place."

My breathing hitched, fight or flight kicking in. He was *furious*. I stepped back but he was faster. Arran grabbed me, throwing me over his shoulder, then marched to the club.

I thumped his back. "Let me go."

"Not until I've fucked some sense into you."

A laugh came from nearby and I hid my face, humiliation rising with my temperature. Thank God I was in leggings and not flashing my ass to everyone watching. Then we were indoors and outside the lift. It arrived, and Arran strode in.

I caught a glimpse of his expression in the mirror, something powerful stamped across his features. Desperate, aggressive need. I knew because I felt it, too.

He put me down, and I centred myself while he stabbed the button for floor three. The brothel.

"Listen."

"No. It's better for both of us if you don't speak." With controlled moves, he pulled a piece of material from his pocket. A skeleton bandanna.

I'd barely taken a breath when it was tugged over my head and covering my eyes.

The lift doors opened again and I was back over his shoulder and being carried down the hall.

"Everyone out," Arran roared.

Faint sounds came, people presumably leaving, but my thrumming pulse in my ears and the darkness around my senses took over my thoughts.

I'd scared him tonight. I'd scared myself, too. He needed to work out those feelings for both of our sakes.

Somewhere deep in the brothel, Arran stopped and set me down, the soft carpet giving under my All Stars. With purposeful moves, he wrenched my shoes, socks, and leggings off me. My jacket and top followed, leaving me in just my underwear.

He spoke next to my ear, and I realised he'd sat down.

"This is for me. You're going to take it."

"What are you going to do?" I said with a whimper that was half barely contained need.

"Spank you. Three times for putting yourself in danger and three times for forcing my hand."

"You're... You're going to hit me?"

"It's a spanking. There's a difference."

He pulled me, and I dropped onto his lap with a rush of breath, his jeans soft against my bare skin. Instantly, his hand was on my backside, and I gritted my teeth, wary but frustratingly turned on. He'd never hurt me, I knew that, but getting spanked was something else.

"Start counting."

"What?"

Arran smacked my ass cheek with the flat of his hand. I jerked forward with a gasp of shock, the pain nothing but the impact commanding every nerve ending.

"I said count."

"One," I gritted out.

"You don't fucking talk to men like that. You don't go anywhere near that road or any like it ever again."

"I won't. I'm not Don's girl," I stammered. "I know you heard that over the phone but I'm not. It's a lie."

"Mouth closed unless I tell you to open it." Another smack landed into my flesh, the other side from the first. "Count it."

His palm soothed the spot. I squirmed.

"Two. Arran, please."

He spanked me a third time, harder now.

"You'll listen to me and fucking understand that in circumstances like that, I know better. Got it?"

I whimpered and nodded because he was right. I'd refused to accept that my life was different now and insisted on doing that stupid job. I wasn't to blame for his or the gang's actions, but I'd take responsibility for my own.

"Three," I said, a little more contrite.

"Good girl." His fingertips brushed over the crotch of my underwear, then slid inside.

I groaned and writhed against him. Then went utterly still when cold metal touched my skin.

His knife blade.

The material split then fell away, fresh air touching my wet core that was bared to his scrutiny. A clatter followed like he'd tossed the weapon, thank God because it would be covered in someone else's blood, then he was touching me again, driving over my arousal but not dipping inside.

"You're fucking soaked from this, and you should see how pretty your ass is with my handprints on it. Now count the final three."

He slapped me again, alternating my cheeks and groaning when I released another unbidden moan. I didn't want to give up anything more, the fact I was wet from this was embarrassing enough, but I'd lost control. My body craved his beyond measure, and my arousal soaked my thighs.

Arran stroked my backside. "I think you liked this too much, baby. I need another way to punish you."

He rose, taking me with him until I wobbled to my feet, then he pushed me backwards until my spine hit a padded surface.

The Saint Andrew's cross.

I'd half expected a cage, or some other device, and his choice made me shiver. The last time I'd been on this had been such a mixture of pleasure and darker emotions, yet automatically, I stepped up, guided by Arran and lifting my hands on his muttered instruction.

With my legs held wide apart and my arms outstretched, I breathed, exposed and dying for more. I listened hard, trying to pick up any movement.

Arran's voice was barely more than a growl. "This is for me, understand? Not you."

Abruptly, he crowded me and punched inside me with a growl of pure need. I cried out, the position making his thrust so deep.

"Mine to own. Mine to keep fucking safe."

His strokes got harder and more punishing with every word, his fingers bruising my hips.

"Yours," I agreed.

I'd taken so much from him. His vow and his virginity. His peace of mind. I could give him this.

I also couldn't stop myself from taking. He stretched me so good. Every hit inside boosted my already heightened state from the spanking. I was so ready, so close to the edge, so desperate to reach it and fall. I pulsed around his dick, the first warning of an impending climax that was going to blow my mind.

Arran stopped. Pulled out.

I exhaled disappointment, bereft without him filling me. The room quietened. I focused hard to pick up on his location.

Something touched my ankle and I jumped.

It was his knife, rising up my leg, drawing fire over my thigh. He skipped to my belly, digging the flat side of his blade into my soft flesh.

Then it hooked under my bra and sliced.

Another two cuts and my last remaining item of clothing was gone, pulled away and no doubt thrown.

"You're as beautiful as you are infuriating." Arran tweaked my nipple.

I jumped, the action softening as his mouth replaced his fingers. He tormented me, both nipples sucked hard and lightly bitten. Love bites delivered into my skin until he rumbled approval at whatever he could see. The line of bites on my breasts. My shredded underwear and red ass from earlier. Him marking me however he wanted.

His hands took my hips and he entered me again with a hard thrust.

"So fucking wet."

Desperation filled me with every surge of his body slamming into mine. Sweat broke out on my brow. I needed to come. He wasn't going to let me, just like when he'd had free use of me and I'd been nothing more than his fuck toy.

A traitorous telltale pang of lust struck me, echoed by every pleasure point, my pussy squeezing his dick.

Arran stopped, *of course*, repeating the act of teasing other parts of me then fucking me all over again. Start. Stop. Killing me by holding off my climax.

Just when I thought I'd lose my mind, his actions surprised me. One by one, he released my constraints. My wrists first then my ankles.

My surprise was short lived. Lifting me, he spun me around the other way, so I was face-on with the cross.

Methodically, he tied me back onto it. I gave him no complaint, as hooked on this as he seemed to be.

"I could edge you all night as the club fills and empties, driving you insane with need."

Some messed-up part of me thrilled at his words. He wasn't done.

"But I need to come and fucking fast."

Arran toyed with my ass cheeks. I stiffened, my wariness returning.

He knelt and kissed my backside, biting where he'd spanked me, and adding to the marks he was leaving on my skin. My nerves blazed where he touched me. Between my legs, I dripped for him.

Arran captured some of that arousal and drew it back to my puckered rear hole. He pressed a fingertip inside and I moaned loud in shock. His tongue followed, penetrating me right there. Then another finger drove in, up to the knuckle. He rotated his hand, opening me up.

I couldn't close my legs or touch him in any way. All I could do was feel.

He spat saliva onto my ass then stood. Fear brightened every sense. His dick pushed against my asshole where his fingers and tongue had been. A much thicker presence bringing discomfort.

My moan turned into a choked sound of confusion.

"You'll take whatever I give you and you'll love it," he commanded, pushing deeper.

Two inches inside, he pulsed, thickening.

Him spearing me lit up something unexpected. A flare of pleasure that I focused on, letting every other emotion, the humiliation of being carted inside, the confusing spanking, fall away.

It felt good.

Arran's mouth landed on the back of my neck. He kissed me, giving me the edge of his teeth as he thrust into my ass. Then he bit me and bottomed out at the same time, our bodies touching and his arms around me. His groan matched mine from sheer pleasure.

"Tell me how it feels," he begged.

"G-good."

"I should hate that I need that."

"But you don't," I finished for him.

He rocked against my ass. Each surge charged me up, and I surrendered to the feeling and the fire he stoked inside me. My chest heaved. He tugged my hair to bring my mouth around to meet his. Savage, delicious man.

Arran broke the kiss. "You need to come because I'm too fucking angry to do it but I need that feeling around my dick."

He worked in and out, only a few times needed to return me to the beginnings of a fast orgasm. Then I was coming, spasming around him, and Arran growled and stilled, pulsing into me, too.

At last. God, I'd needed that so much.

I was still shuddering when he released me. Tossed my clothes at me and commanded me to dress. I had love bites, spank marks, and the unexpected prints of some stranger's blood on my skin plus a thousand emotions in my heart. The one that came to the top? If Arran was okay, nothing else mattered.

32

Genevieve

A slow clap met our emergence from the lift, and I dropped my gaze, not meeting the eyes of Arran's friends.

"Fuck off," he said lightly. "Shade, call a lockdown of the crew. We're mobilising."

I peeked at him. "Are the Four Milers going to retaliate?"

"Maybe."

"Will you close down the clubs?"

"No, it's better to have the public here." He gave a wolfish, cold smile. "Human shield, witnesses, whatever you want to call it."

I shivered. Outside his office, Arran was immediately swamped by people needing things from him. He kept my hand clamped in his, but I tugged it to get his attention. I wanted to talk to him about what the gangster had said. That my dad was on some kind of job. I also knew now was not the time.

"I need a shower and to get changed. Then I'm going to see one of the dancers. Is that okay?"

"Who?"

"Dixie. She's helping me with the Cherry thing."

He watched me for a moment, then lifted his chin to someone behind us in the corridor. "I'm going to be busy for a while. Being upstairs will be safer, but Manny will stay close. Don't fucking argue. Once you're dressed, come to my office. I've got something for you."

I kissed him, earning a darkening of his eyes that suggested approval of my act. Then with the chief of security in tow, I took the lift up to the eighth floor and stepped into Arran's apartment. A quick shower later, and I blow-dried my hair then applied a fast layer of makeup, keeping track of the time. Dixie started work at ten, and by the time I'd slipped on a high-neck fuchsia-pink baby doll dress, I had thirty minutes.

Pink for Cherry, because tonight, I was getting answers.

Outside the apartment, Manny was waiting patiently, and the two of us travelled back down to Arran's office. He knocked for me, and Arran opened the door. Over his shoulder, I spotted four or five men clustered on the visitor's side of his desk. Brutal-looking thugs, skeleton crew bandannas around their necks, tattooed arms, and even a glimpse or two of a holstered weapon.

Arran joined me outside, a box in his hand. Manny stepped discreetly away.

I tilted my head at the office. "Did the other gang follow you? Are they here?"

"I brought in a few people. They'll monitor the entrances and provide backup if needed."

All because of me. Embarrassed, again, I hid my face in my hands. Arran pulled them away and made me look at him.

"Are you scared? Don't be. The man whose blood I'm

wearing was a minor upstart who picked a fight with the wrong person. I doubt anyone would go to war for him."

"You said *was*. As in past tense?"

His expression gave away nothing. "Figure of speech."

I chewed my lip. "That man asked how my dad was getting on in his job. If he knew, and he's a minor player, that means Dad's definitely in with them, isn't he?"

He brushed a thumb over my cheek. "Perhaps. Now hold still."

Opening the long box, he revealed an item of jewellery. A necklace, or more specifically a choker, with lines of glittering stones at the top and bottom edge of a wide band, maybe two inches deep. It stole a piece of my dismay, blinding me with its shimmer.

Arran brought it to my throat. "Lift that pretty hair."

Why was it every command, even innocent ones, did things to my body? I did as he asked, and the gang lord clipped the broad choker around my throat.

I touched it. The band was a fine metal weave, light but strong. "Thank you, it's beautiful."

"It's for me as much as you."

I didn't get a chance to ask what that meant as Arran kissed me with a sudden ferocity that stole my mind and my breath. Just like that, he was done and back to work with his gangster buddies, and I had an exotic dancer to find.

In the lift, Manny checked our destination and pressed floor three.

"What's on the other floors between three and eight?" I asked.

I wasn't convinced I'd get an answer. People were tight-lipped around here, and I was still an outsider.

To my surprise, he readily gave up the information. "Floor four is a suite of private bedrooms. Five is where the cam girls work. Six is storage, and seven's empty. On the other side, Divide's high ceiling takes up four floors. For over two hundred years, this place was a bonded warehouse used for shipping. Did you know?"

He regaled me with facts until the lift doors opened, and we entered the corridor on the brothel floor. Blushing to think what Arran and I had done here, I trotted left on the plush carpet to the receiving room with the bar, drawing the attention of the first woman I saw. "Is Dixie around?"

"You're Genevieve. Wow. It's a pleasure. Follow me."

The pretty woman with a London accent led me behind the bar, Manny keeping close at my back. Through a taproom, another corridor had a security room on one side and a dressing room to the other, several women readying themselves at brightly lit stations. Most wore very little, if anything. A degree beyond the strip club's dressing room downstairs.

A topless Dixie hopped up and waved. "Perfect timing. Ooh, I love that choker. Come with me."

She tucked her arm through mine, and together, we stepped into a side room with two sofas. Manny poked his head in then closed the door with him on the outside.

Dixie heaved a happy sigh. "Bitches be jealous that we're besties." She brushed her hand down her chest, then squinted down herself. "Oh, fuck. Titties are out. Sorry, hun. I didn't even notice."

I flapped a hand, unbothered. "Don't worry, we've all got them."

Her eyes brightened. "These are new. Do you like them? Cost me a bundle, but I made that back the first weekend I used them."

In the past, I'd never thought it polite to stare at another woman's body, particularly her nipples, but the opposite appeared to be required now. I took a good look at Dixie's rack, perfectly round and high on her chest. She stuck them out and jiggled, proud and gleeful.

"If I was a dude, I'd be all over those."

"Right?" She cackled. "These tits have fucked as many dicks as my vagina in the past couple of months. Makes a nice change and gives the old girl a break. Now let's talk business. You need my help with hunting down your friend's killer."

My amusement dialled back. "I really appreciate it."

"I've asked around, super subtly, of course. Our recruiter found out Cherry was a real lone wolf. She had a studio flat the other side of the main road from the churchyard where she worked."

"So close to me."

"Yeah? Well, she'd been there a couple of years, no family, only a pet cat. She paid her bills, minded her own business. Nothing more to tell."

"What happened to her cat?"

"Aren't you sweet? Her neighbour's been feeding it since she heard Cherry died, but said she'll catch it and take it to a rehoming centre."

At least my friend had had someone to love. Dixie's background information had given me nothing else, though. "The night before Cherry was killed, we were chatting, and she made a comment about her last client coming like an elephant. Quantity, she meant. She said he'd be coming back with a friend she didn't like, so in my mind, they're both suspects."

Dixie considered that. "There are a lot of guys who overproduce like that. Got anything else to narrow it down?"

"Shit, yes. He's a city councillor. She said that if he got her pregnant, he was well-off enough to foot the bill."

Dixie nodded. "Suggesting she let him ditch the condoms, probably charging more for the right. Most street girls would never do that with a casual fuck, and if he was on her two days in a row, he was a regular. We have men who come here like clockwork, every day, the same girl. Got a phone?"

I held mine up.

"If he's a councillor, that gives us a really good hit list. Bring up the council meeting schedule. See who was where that night."

"We can do that?"

Dixie rubbed her hands together. With her help, I navigated to Deadwater city council's website and into their meeting list.

"The city councillors are often in evening meetings or engagements," she explained. "We can check the agenda to see who was meant to be there, then read the minutes to see if they stayed until the end. It's all accounted for because it's public spending. For example, there's a full council meeting this evening which finishes at nine-thirty. Right about now. In half an hour, two or three of the members will be here, looking for their favourite girl."

My pulse skipped. That gave us about ten minutes to prepare.

Dixie pulled up the meeting list from the night Cherry

was killed. Two had gone on late.

I grabbed a pen and paper from the desk. "First, I need to write out a list of all the council members."

She rattled off the names of nine men and two women.

I goggled at her. "How do you know that?"

She shrugged a slender, bare shoulder. "I hear things. Sometimes they stick. Oh, don't forget Mayor Makepeace. Cherry might have used the term 'councillor' for him as well."

That gave a list of ten.

Cherry had been murdered between nine and ten PM, according to the brief news article I'd read. Next, we went through the two council engagements.

"Look, this environment one was a dinner with a live band. It went on until eleven." Dixie leaned over my phone and pressed a link which loaded a page of photos. "Ooh, party time. I remember this now, because a couple of them turned up here in tuxes. It says here that the band performed at ten, so all these people dancing, we can cross off the list."

I nodded, following her train of thought. "There's no way they could have killed someone then got to a dinner dance in time to be photographed."

She pointed at me. "Bingo."

A sort through the photos of a sparkling evening removed four names from the list, including the two female councillors who were there with their husbands.

I mused on the remainder. "I think we can cross the mayor off as well. He's there in the photos."

Dixie shook her head, her curls flying. "Not so hasty. He's at the dinner table, but we don't see him dancing. It doesn't say if he left early, but let's not jump the gun."

"Okay, let's check out the other meeting. This one's for traffic and transport."

"Ugh. Those old boys are the worst. Their meetings nearly always involve them getting drunk at the end. It takes forever to make them come after."

At least they had a good notetaker, though. It allowed another two names to be removed.

I read out what was left. "Mayor Makepeace, and councillors Tony Hatchett, Anton Blake, and Benjamin Slaughter. One of them must have been Cherry's client. Do all of them come here?"

Dixie nodded. "You bet your ass. Ninety percent of that category of businessmen in this city use our services in one way or another. Some have girls go to their office or homes. Some come here. They don't stroll in the front door, or arrive via the strip club, if that's what you're thinking. There's a coded entrance on the west side of the warehouse. It leads to a lift that brings them right on up. The discreet way in." She considered the list. "Actually, I think we can take one more off of that." Her glossy red nail tapped the second name.

"Councillor Tony Hatchett," I read.

"He has a deal with a couple of our girls to exchange sexual favours for accountancy help. He's a finance guy."

"Why does that mean we can cross him off?"

"Cherry told you that if her elephant cum guy got her pregnant, he could help her financially, right? Hatchett is the worst cheapskate. One of those who wears his poverty on his sleeve, something to do with his religion. He drives a clapped-out piece-of-junk car that often breaks down in the city, and lives by himself in a mobile home. There's no way Cherry would think he was loaded."

I struck through his name. "Dixie, you're amazing."

She preened and pretended to flip her hair. "Anything for a bit of fun."

"That leaves only three."

Dixie took a deep breath. "And only a few minutes until one or all of them arrive, with any luck."

"How do we, er, test them?"

She pulled a face. "As far as I can tell, there's only one way to narrow it down. Whichever girl they pick is going to have to somehow save their deposit. Scoop up that cum. At the end, we can compare notes."

Our game was in play.

Dixie directed me to follow her then left me in the security office, a two-way mirror giving a view of the receiving room and a guard at a CCTV station.

Through the mirror, I watched her skitter over and spread the word about what we were doing to the women she thought needed to know. It was risky. If word got back to the men involved by someone with a big mouth, the reputation of the club was at stake.

Then the councillors arrived, obvious because Dixie made a gesture for me to pay attention to the men on the end.

One was fifty-something, in a smart suit, with mid-brown hair and no sign of grey. The second was younger and had a neat wedge of pale-blond hair and round glasses.

The councillors took drinks and sex workers down the corridor. Then there was nothing for me to do but wait.

But by eleven, the women who'd serviced two of the

three on my list returned.

Dixie hustled the sexual partner of each into our little sitting room. They gawked at me, two identical women who'd handled councillor Blake, and a busty brunette who'd been councillor Slaughter's choice for the night.

Dixie regarded them with a stern glare. "Any talk of what I asked of you, and what you've done, will not leave this room. Alisha will fire you faster than a bullet. Now gimme the goods."

The first of the twins reached into her bra and extracted a filled and tied-off condom.

I hid my recoil. This was their livelihood, but the sight of some slimy guy's sperm did nasty things to my stomach.

"After he watched us, he wanted us both to blow him, but I begged him to fuck me," the first twin said. "He had his face all up in Minnie's business, otherwise I'm sure he would have questioned why I put this on him. Luckily, we all came away happy."

The brunette smiled in success and pulled out another condom. "Slaughter wanted to fuck my tits, so I let him, then scooped it all up into here. Took a bit of effort. You owe me. He's down in the voyeur rooms now and he wants me to join him."

Dixie took both and held them up, tapping and squeezing the latex to settle the contents. "Am I imagining it, or is the one on the right noticeably fuller?"

I angled my head. "You're right. That's councillor Slaughter. But we've only got two samples. If the other guy is underperforming, anyone would look like they had more against him."

Dixie took a rushed inhale. "We need more samples. Girls, you know the drill."

The three hustled out, returning again in what felt like no time with fresh samples, this time from regular guys.

Again, Dixie lined them all up.

We waited for the contents to settle.

There was no denying it. Of all the filled condoms, Councillor Slaughter's cum volume was noticeably greater than all the others.

My heart sped.

Dixie let the women go with thanks and a promise of secrecy. Then the two of us sat back. On my phone, I searched for a picture of the councillor in question, a more formal version of the man I'd seen through the mirror.

"Am I looking at a killer?" I asked. "It still could have been one of the other two, if they were the friend he was taking along. Either way, it's possible."

"I don't know, hun. What's your plan now you have the information?"

I didn't have much, only one small clue, a piece of evidence that wouldn't stand up in court. Then again, I didn't live in a world where the law mattered so much anymore. "What would a real-life detective do?"

Dixie clicked her fingers. "Establish a motive. If he murdered Cherry, it was for a reason."

She was right. I needed to talk to Arran.

Out in the dressing room, I waved goodbye to the assembled sex workers and exited to the receiving room, Manny with me and Dixie seeing me to the bar.

A collection of men arrived at the same time, exiting the lift together and all in expensive suits like they'd left the same meeting to come straight here. Women flocked to greet them.

From the back of the pack, a woman approached, not staff, I knew in an instant, despite her tight dress of black lace with a wide brown leather belt, her killer rack, and a tumble of brunette curls. She was gorgeous and definitely out of place.

Dixie stepped forward, toe pointed and straight into seduction mode. "Hey, there. Seems I'm not going to win the title for prettiest titties on the floor tonight. Looking for someone like me, baby girl? We could have a lot of fun."

The woman blinked and passed a nervous hand over her chest. "Um, thanks? Your breasts are lovely, too, but it's actually her I want."

She indicated to me.

Manny exhaled through his nose. "This woman isn't on offer tonight. My apologies, ma'am. Dixie can help you choose—"

"No! I didn't mean for...that." Her gaze roamed my face. "You're Genevieve, is that right?"

"I am."

"Oh good. I'd really love to talk to you. My name's Everly."

I gave her the once-over in return. Her clothes were well made and her styling impeccable. Nothing about her screamed weirdo. Even so, I was cautious. "Walk with me and Manny. Dixie, catch you later."

With Everly falling into step, we crossed the receiving room.

"How did you know my name?" I asked.

"People talk. I'm in a position where I hear a lot. I'm actually here to talk to you on behalf of my father, though. He's the mayor of Deadwater. Perhaps you've heard of him?"

I fought to stop my jaw from dropping. Not half an hour ago, I'd been considering him a murder suspect. "I've never had the pleasure," I managed. "What kind of man is he?"

She dropped her voice. "I can't really say. It's actually Connor I want to discuss."

"Who?"

"Tattooed, works for your boyfriend?"

I never had got to the bottom of the names of Arran's crew. My money was on Connor being Convict. The connection snapped into place in my head, pity swiftly following. "Did he hurt you?"

"No, he never would. He's the best." She gave a small huff of breath. "Not that he'll talk to me. I applied to go into the game, like you."

My heart thumped. "You actually wanted to do it?"

Her cheeks reddened. "I mean, no? Maybe. I just wanted to get his attention."

"Girl, same. I needed to talk to Arran and found myself in there."

"No!" She cupped my elbow. "Are you okay?"

At last, someone had asked. I liked Everly in a fast instant. "Not one other person wondered that, but yes. I am."

We'd made it to the lift that would take us down to the office corridor. Manny frowned and touched his finger to his ear, listening to something.

Instantly, my back was up. This floor felt safe. No gang member could get up here easily, and Manny had men posted discreetly here and there. Downstairs was another story. I should be there. Not hiding from any danger that might find those I'd started to care about.

"What is it?" I asked him.

His gaze came to me. "There's a disturbance in Divine. A distressed woman shouting your name."

"She's shouting for me?" I cast my mind over the women I knew who weren't members of this club. Or more specifically, those who were interested in me. I came up blank, then suddenly remembered Cassie. She was missing. Perhaps it was her. "Is it safe to go check it out?"

"I believe so. Arran's occupied right now, but I have a team in the room."

I came back to Everly. "I'm sorry but I need to go."

"Of course. I knew this was a bad idea. Never mind."

She appeared so dejected, I paused.

"Give me your phone number and we can talk another time."

A little brighter, Everly riffled through her clutch to hand me a small card. Fancy. I took it, then the lift arrived and Manny and I were descending fast.

On the office corridor, we fast-walked to the strip club. In the middle of the open floor, a woman about my age swung around, the contents of her glass slopping.

She had her blonde hair loose in a spill down her back, just like mine, and a black dress, similar to the one Arran had cut off me.

Not Cassie at all. It was Natasha Reid.

The woman who should've been in the game but whose place I stole. I'd only seen her once on the video call I'd made to apologise, but her physical likeness to me was undeniable.

"It should've been me," she howled, her New York accent thick. "I'd clean up this place. You're all fucking dirty, do you hear? All you disgusting men who come in here with your dirty thoughts need to find Jesus."

To one side of the room, Alisha looked on, arms folded and her expression pinched. Lara stood beside her with a collection of waitresses behind. On the stage, the dancers had stopped to watch Natasha's meltdown, and the packed tables of men grumbled about the interruption.

I crossed to Alisha. Manny might've filled me in, but this wasn't my territory. It was hers.

Alisha flicked her gaze to me. "More trouble with your name on it."

Lara tucked her tray under her arm. "She arrived ten minutes ago, already drunk. I refused her service because she was rolling, but she grabbed a glass off a tray then started yelling at everyone. And calling for you."

"She said my name?"

"A few times. Know her?"

"Not really. We spoke once, but that was it." I scrunched up my nose.

Natasha continued her rant, targeting a group at a table. She'd called me out for having another agenda with the game. Was this hers?

"Pipe down, girl," one man snarked back.

"Don't you dare talk to me, you whore user. Go find a real woman." She wheeled around to the stage. "As for all you sluts on the poles, I hope you slide down on your diseased juices and break your necks."

Outrage filled me. I snapped my focus to Alisha. It was on the tip of my tongue to challenge her on doing something about this, but her expression pulled me up short. The chief of operations appeared afraid.

"Where's Shade?" She wrung her hands. "He's second-in-command. He needs to be here."

I summoned a smile. "I'll handle it."

Alisha's shoulders crept up. "You want to play boss and be the woman in the manager's seat, go for it."

I stepped forward, sensing Manny moving with me. "Natasha? What the hell are you doing?"

She sought me out, her focus wide and her classy appearance a shambles. "Genevieve, there you are. Should've known your thief and liar self wouldn't be far from these parts."

"Wait up. What's going on?"

"What's going on is this place is a sickening hellhole filled with filth and needs to be shut down. All of you are sinners."

"Watch your mouth." I glowered at her, my blood hot. "Don't you dare come in here with that shitty attitude and abuse the people who work here."

"Me dare? How about you daring to take the place that should've been mine? You stole that from me. I would've been his, and I'd be the queen of this club, taking control and cleaning up shop. Hear me?"

"Unfortunately," I intoned. "But there's one problem with that. You didn't get him, and your thoughts on what happens in this business are irrelevant."

She made an angry sound and stamped her expensive heel. "You're the one who's going to be irrelevant."

I gave her a soft, deadly smile. "Is that a threat? Out loud in front of all these good people? Let me tell you something, Natasha. Every single one of the dancers and staff members in this club are worth a hundred of you. You lost out because you deserved that fate. I really believe that."

Lara whistled. "Right on, sister. You tell her."

I glanced over. Even Alisha cracked a smile.

Only a few weeks ago, I would've pitied the women who worked here and assumed they were oppressed or had no choice but to sell their bodies. Now, I knew they were businesswomen, working an asset. They had skills I could only dream of, thoughts and ambitions. Fuck her for judging them.

I swung back to the crazed woman. "And another thing—"

Behind her, a figure crossed the room, a woman holding a Divine drinks tray, the black-and-pink staff uniform nipping tight at her waist. Her hair was loose and forward over her face, but she lifted her head to throw me a meaningful glance.

Moniqua, my brother's girlfriend.

My words stalled. If she was here, then was Riordan? Or worse, her cousin, Don? My brother would be in danger, but it would be the reverse if Don had decided to pay a visit. He'd be part of a Four Milers revenge act, undoubtedly.

Moniqua gave a single shake of her head and cut her gaze at the side exit of the club. Then she slipped out of sight behind a row of tables.

At the end of the room, the doors to Divine burst open.

Men stormed in.

33

Arran – *five minutes earlier*

*E*ntering my office, Shade and Jamieson carted in a bloodied, unconscious man between them. They dumped him on the floor, the door kicked closed behind them and only the three of us present.

The fewer witnesses the better.

Adrenaline swirled inside me, clamping hold of my gut and boosting my anger. I opened my mouth to demand they wake him, but my phone rang.

The name on my screen stalled me.

"The fucking mayor himself," I snapped.

Shade curled his lip and stepped back from the slumped body. "Answer the arsehole, then."

I tapped my screen. "Mayor Makepeace. To what do I owe the pleasure?"

A cold, calm voice answered. I pictured the man in his office, his thatch of brown hair with a reassuring speckle of grey at the temples, his awards and political pictures on his desk. A woman underneath, sucking him off.

"Mr Daniels, I'll make this brief. Your presence in the

city this evening was witnessed by too many."

He meant our tussle with the Four Milers. For fuck's sake.

"Unexpected and not to be repeated," I replied.

"Be that as it may, it compels me to act for the sake of maintaining peace. I have to be seen to be in control, as you're aware."

I watched Shade, with his tight jaw and bloodied hands. He knew well enough about the mayor's love of control.

"Understood," I gritted out. "Do what you need to do."

There was silence for a moment, then, "Is our arrangement...well?"

In disgust, I hung up the call, and in an even sourer mood, circled my desk to the prisoner. "Wake him up."

Shade lifted the man's drooped head with two fingers under his chin.

Then drove his fist into his jaw.

Convict dribbled blood. "Stop. Please."

"Shut your damn mouth," I ordered.

He jerked, peering at me through a swollen eye. "Arran? God, brother, I'm begging you."

"Save your breath. I gave you one chance to redeem yourself, and I'm a fucking fool for my leniency."

"I've done nothing wrong, I swear it."

"Don't bother. We found you in Four Miler territory, fronting up for them. I knew the second I saw you outside that house who you were, you dumb fuck."

After Genevieve had mentioned the way Convict stood, the tilt to his head, I'd seen it in the gangster in a balaclava by the side of the road. He'd hidden his face and his snake tattoo this time, but I'd seen through it.

It was his blood I'd spilled, along with the idiot at his side who'd tried to defend him. It was the main reason I was almost certain Red, the leader of the Four Milers, wouldn't go to war over this. He'd taken my man and lost.

Fuck both of them.

"You've switched allegiance. Screwed me over without the decency to call in your side change."

I nodded to Shade who kicked out again, landing his boot in Convict's gut. Our traitor choked up vomit and blood, pink drool sliding from his mouth. My enforcer righted himself and turned away, white-faced and shaking. For all our love of violence, neither of us could enjoy this. Convict had been a friend. Loyal from the start. Until he'd chosen not to be.

Convict took a shuddering breath. He might not feel pain, but the man was suffering. "I'm not double-crossing you. You gave me a job and I did it by any means necessary."

"Which was to be in Manchester watching Jordan Peters."

"And to watch the Four Milers to find your woman's old man. Peters went on the road, so I drove home today. I was going to come in but—"

"Someone offered cash for my head? What was it, Convict? The money or a personal beef? You wanted a better position here, well, congratulations, I'll bury you under the fucking foundations."

"I did it for Genevieve. You have to believe—"

I rammed my knuckles into the side of his face. "Take her name out of your fucking traitorous mouth."

He moaned. I freed my knife from the holster, fucking

gutted with how this had gone down. My own crew member, one of the closest people to me.

A hasty knock rattled the door.

Without waiting for an answer, Tyler burst in, one of the crew I'd called in as extra security this evening. Whatever this was, it had to be fucking good. None of them would dare interrupt otherwise.

The tough-as-nails crew member didn't even blink at the scene. "Sorry to interrupt, but drop everything. We're being raided."

Holy fucking hell. I was back at my desk and snapping open a hidden drawer in a flash, Shade rounding to my side to pull a hidden weapon of his own.

"How many Four Milers?"

"No, boss. It's the cops. They're in Divine, throwing their weight about."

I stalled, swore, then dropped the gun I'd picked up. Shade did the same, his jaw clenched. We continued, stashing our knives away. Shade took another blade from his boot. A third came from somewhere else on his person.

Lastly, I pulled my wallet and keys, leaving it all.

"What fucking timing," I snarled.

"Prime time for someone else to slip in," Shade returned quietly.

He was right. "Tyler, get back outside. Make sure your people stay far back but keep watch. No one else comes close."

He acknowledged me with a dipped head. "We locking this place down?"

"Only Divine. The nightclub stays open but only for those already inside. People can leave but no one else can come in. All internal doors are locked."

Tyler left us. Through the open door, pandemonium had broken out. People running. Fear high. I knew exactly how this was going to go down. Why the cops were here and who they wanted to see.

Frustration consumed me, and I came back to Shade. "You know the drill. Take Convict away. Get the staff organised and whatever damage has been done to Divine cleaned up. Get the crew in line." Then I gestured to Jamieson to include him in my commands. "While I'm gone, guard her with your life." They couldn't doubt who I meant. "Whatever else happens, don't let her out of your sight."

34

Genevieve

Divine had been trashed, bottles spilled and cracked plastic glasses underfoot. Tables had been tipped over and chairs broken in the stampede to leave. Half-naked dancers clustered at the back of the stage, uniformed police blocking their exits and corralling them into a huddle. At the main entryway, customers filed out, a flood of red-faced men hurrying away with their heads down.

Natasha slipped out with them, the cowardly bitch.

In the centre of the floor, Alisha held her own against two cops, a manicured finger swinging from one to the other and her lips running loose with a torrent of venom.

We'd flipped roles. Now, I was frozen up, fright holding me to the spot.

Never once had I been in trouble with the police. The only times I'd encountered them was when I'd come home from school and found one at my door, there to tell me Mum was in hospital. Actually dead, but they didn't say that. Then the last was the beat cop who'd given up the scant details of Cherry's murder. I didn't blame them—they were only doing their job—but I had no idea what my role was now.

If I was so inclined, I could probably walk straight out the door, like Natasha had done, and undoubtedly Moniqua. There was no way that gang-affiliated woman would've hung around for my sake once the police had raided.

But I didn't want to go. I'd done nothing wrong. They could arrest me if they wanted.

I'd switched sides.

Against the tide, Arran stalked through the room. Fear stabbed my heart. He shouldn't have come in, but I knew in the same breath that he'd never leave his staff to handle this alone.

Staring at him, I took a step. With the smallest glance my way, he flattened his lips. At his side, his fingers made a slicing gesture.

A hand took my wrist. "Don't let them know who ye are," a man said in my ear.

Jamieson. I glanced up to be sure.

He muttered something to Manny, and both men moved casually to bracket me.

Arran didn't stop until he was face to face with a huge policeman. A brutish older man with an unpleasant, self-confident smile. At a word from Arran, the man produced a piece of paper, a warrant of some kind, I guessed. Arran read it then folded it and slid it into his back pocket, all while the big cop watched.

On previous nights, Arran had donned a suit to be seen out in the club, but today, he was still in his jeans, his blood-stained clothes unchanged from earlier. Yet his expression was neutral, no visible sign of the anger I knew he had to be feeling.

He looked like a gang member caught in the act. This couldn't have been worse.

To my right, the cops surrounding Alisha suddenly rotated her, yanking up her hands to be cuffed. Horror joined my fear. At the same moment, up on the stage, five or six of the dancers were also clamped in handcuffs.

"Suck my ass, fucking pig," Alisha snarled at the one holding her. Her wig of long, dark curls had come askew. "If you don't think we can all see your dick is hard from touching us up, think again."

"Alisha," Arran's voice cut through the hubbub. She fell silent, and he snapped at the guy who had to be the lead officer, "Is any of this necessary?"

"You tell me, Mr Daniels," the officer replied.

What he said next was too quiet for my ears, but I saw the result in gut-wrenching slow motion.

Arran offered up his wrists. The police officer snatched them behind his back and handcuffed him, yanking hard to test them.

A shout reared in my throat. I cut it off, finally learning my lesson about being impulsive. Instead, I pressed my fingers to my lips, waiting for the second where his gaze sought me out again. Arran cut me a look, right as he was being marched outside.

There was not a single thing I could do to help him.

Along with Arran, they took a red-faced Alisha and six of the dancers, fearful expressions on all of the Divine staff members' faces. A number of police officers were still in the room, questioning others one by one.

"Genevieve?"

I turned to find an ashen-faced Lara approaching.

"What do we do?" she asked.

For a second, I had no idea why she was asking me, but then it clicked in. Arran had gone, Alisha, too, and Shade was nowhere to be seen. She hadn't asked Manny. For now, I was in charge.

The remaining police officers moved together and spoke in low voices. I marched over.

"If you've finished doing damage, the staff need to lock up and get this place back in order."

One with a tidy moustache regarded me. "And you are?"

"Unless you're arresting me, that's none of your business."

His lip curled under the hairy caterpillar decoration. "Do you work here?"

"Nope. Just trying to help these good people out."

They swapped glances then shrugged, two peeling away to the exits. Moustache Cop stayed with me. He leaned in, a glance spared for Jamieson and Manny who'd remained at my back.

"Say the word and I'll take you out of here. In handcuffs, if you need it to be believable."

I recoiled. "Why would you think I want that?"

A week ago, I would have taken that rescue and walked right out. Everything in my life had changed.

"Didn't think you belonged here, but my mistake." Moustache Cop gave me a final look then turned and followed his colleagues.

Lara hurried after him, bolting the doors. She came to me. They all did, a distressed group of dancers and staff.

"Everything's going to be okay," I told them.

I wasn't sure if that was true—Arran was gone and Alisha with him—but I'd do everything I could to safeguard the business while they couldn't.

"What do we do now?" one of the women said.

"We clear up so tomorrow we can carry on."

Relief flowed over the group, and we got into the task of undoing the damage. Shade appeared with a quiet word about how Arran instructed him to hold back—it made sense that both couldn't get arrested—and got stuck in cleaning. Tables and chairs were righted or switched out. Bottles and plastic went into recycling bins. A carpet cleaner handled the worst of the spills. A cleaning crew would be here in the morning, according to Lara, but even they would've baulked at the level of mess, and the act of resetting the space had calmed all who'd stayed.

"Good job, everyone," I called. "Let's call it a night."

A few of the dancers remained while the others left.

Hayden, I thought his name was, approached me. "Genevieve? I have a shift that starts at midnight." As if he was worried about being watched, he pointed upstairs with his other hand cupped to block his finger.

"I'll take you through," I said with a smile.

At some point after the raid had started, the interior doors between the strip club and the office corridor had been locked. Interestingly enough, the code Arran had given me for the lift and his apartment opened those, too.

Out in the hall, the thankful dancers continued on for their next shift.

Shade, Jamieson, and Manny stood in a line, watching me. They had done so for the past hour as if taking their eyes off me was tantamount to a death sentence. Maybe Arran had threatened that.

"Any news on our fugitives?" I leaned against the wall, suddenly weary.

I hadn't eaten today, I realised. Nor was I all that hungry, not with Arran gone.

"Nothing yet," Shade admitted.

"Manny, go ahead and return to normal duties," I said. "Assuming these two are going to stare at me all night, I don't need three of you."

Manny nodded reluctantly. "I just got a message about a fight in Divide. Some crazy young woman was up dancing on the podium and four guys decided to brawl over who was taking her home. My team are handling it, but tonight's made me jumpy. I'd feel better if I checked it out."

I released him, and he stepped through the door to the nightclub side, the pulsing music becoming almost deafening for a moment then fading.

"Student night ends at one, doesn't it?" I asked.

Shade inclined his head. "In an hour, that place will be empty, and the only customers will be upstairs."

"Does that make things more dangerous for us or less? Arran called the public a human shield."

His enforcer snorted. "Sounds like something he'd say. Don't worry, we'll keep you safe. This building is bombproof, fireproof, you name it."

I recalled Manny saying it had been a goods warehouse, so fireproof made sense.

I focused in on Jamieson who stared at the doorway Manny had gone into. Something about the sharpness of his focus bothered me.

"What's wrong?" I asked.

He took a breath. "What's the odds that the girl your head of security has gone in to tame is my sister?"

I groaned. "God, she said she wanted to dance and the strip club is closed. Shade, can you ask Manny for a description?"

Shade rattled off an instruction to Manny then spoke the answer he was being fed in his earpiece. "Black hair in tight curls. Short. Tiny dress, attitude, won't come down. Fuck."

A fraught Jamieson paced to the door. "We need to pull her out."

"Manny and his team are handling the fight," Shade reported, continuing to listen. "It's getting worse in there, but we can't leave Genevieve either."

The worry in their voices infected me with the need to do something. Despite her anger at me, I'd liked Cassie. She had spoken sense and stood up for herself and what she believed in. A world *I* now believed in. She was also only nineteen and in a crisis. If she left or was thrown out, anything could happen.

"We can't leave her. We're all going in," I decided.

"No fucking way," both men stated.

"What if someone grabs her? What if she's hurt?"

Shade pointed at me. "What if someone recognises and takes you? I vote we lock ye in Arran's apartment,"

"But then you'd still have to leave me to get Cassie. It won't work."

Turning on my heel, I strode in the other direction to the changing rooms for Divine. Inside, I snatched up a baseball cap from a coat hook and bundled my hair under it.

"That's a weak-as-fuck disguise," Jamieson commented.

"Manny's allocating two people to wait the other side," Shade supplied. "Shite, if this goes badly, Arran's going to fucking murder us. Genevieve Jones, ye don't stray more than two feet from our sides. No eye contact with anyone. If anyone even breathes on ye—"

"You sound just like Arran. But this is probably a good time to mention I saw my brother's girlfriend here earlier. She left with the cops, but quick, let's go. Cassie needs our help." I launched myself through the door.

As Manny promised, two security officers in skeleton t-shirts met us the other side of Divide's staff entrance. Instantly, I scanned the crowd. Near the main entrance, Manny was pushing his way through a throng of clubgoers, one scrawny student guy under one arm, and his meaty hand around the scruff of another. Both swung out punches but had no effect on the chief of security.

To think, he'd been babysitting me when this was clearly his element. Behind them, three or four of Manny's team were deep in the middle of a boiling mass of bodies, some of them still involved in their scrap, others trying to get out of the way. Some sweaty-faced individuals danced on, oblivious.

Above it all, on a plinth at head height to the crowd, though clearly not meant for dancing, Cassie stood, her teeny silver dress matching her heels, and her wild, black curls loose in a thick wedge around her pretty head. She wound her body to the thumping beat from the DJ. A man broke loose from the fight and grabbed her ankle. At my side, Jamieson lurched, thrusting his way into the crowd.

Stalled in her movements, Cassie scowled down at the grabber, then with impeccable balance, stabbed her other heel into his hand. The man howled, though the sound didn't make it over the music, and he fell away, clutching his injury.

I grinned at her, and at the same second, her gaze fell on us.

Cassie's eyes brightened, and she mouthed my name, clasping her hands together, a little chaos goblin above her kingdom of admirers, as vicious as any of them.

We reached the edge of the brawling group, ten feet from the plinth, and thick within the crowd of sweaty clubgoers. My dress stuck to me with the humidity and the press of so many people, though Shade and Jamieson fought to make enough space so we could breathe.

Jamieson pointed at his sister then to the floor, an indication for her to come down. The cocky woman cupped her hand behind her ear in a pretence that she couldn't hear, and Jamieson glowered.

Across from us, someone reared back an arm and tossed a missile at Cassie. It struck her shoulder, and the grin left her face. She clutched her arm and glared, going from fun-loving pretty girl to ice queen in an instant. I'd seen it before, and my hackles rose. I didn't want her hurt.

Jamieson turned back to me and tilted his head at Shade, rage in his dark-blue eyes, then he turned and dove into the crowd, flattening people in his path to reach the person who'd hurt his sister. Or maybe to help her down, because she moved to the edge of the plinth.

Shade waved across the room to Manny then pointed at the DJ. To cut the music? At the far edge of the fight, Manny's people pulled two more men out, leaving a gap for a second.

Through it, I caught a glimpse of a familiar face.

I stared open-mouthed into the crowd. I was seeing

things, surely.

Then a surge followed, people shoved aside, and that same person drove right through until he was in front of me.

I took in every feature. His hair brown with dark-blond highlights, his eyes green unlike mine. It had been weeks since I'd last seen my brother.

"Riordan," I uttered.

That's why Moniqua had been here, and what her glance across the room had meant. He'd come looking for me.

Just as I was taking him in, he reached for me. The heavy music cut out. Riordan captured me in a rugby tackle and threw me over his shoulder.

In the same instant, Shade wrestled me back then threw a punch at my brother. Riordan returned the act, laying his fist into Shade's gut. The two men tussled.

"Get your fucking hands off my sister," Rio yelled. "Gen, run for it."

In shock, I staggered back on my heels, Manny's skeleton t-shirt men right behind me. Overhead, bright lights sprang on, dousing everything in sudden, sobering white. At the club entrance, the big doors were thrown open, the team working to get everyone out.

"Time, everyone. Divide is now closed," the DJ announced. "Blame your friends for the early finish and get the fuck out."

Amid dismayed groans, the room began to empty.

"Go, now," my brother repeated in desperation.

"No, Rio." I rubbed my forehead.

"She doesn't want to be here," he yelled for whoever

was listening, dislodging Shade from his vice-like grip before being captured again. "She's been kidnapped. Fucking held hostage."

My heart throbbed. "You came here to save me?"

"Of course I did. You're my sister. It's my job to protect you."

Space appeared around us. With his arm around my brother's neck in a chokehold, Shade forced him to his knees. Behind, a furious Jamieson had Cassie's attacker on the filthy floor with a knee in his spine. Reluctantly, he stepped away to hand over the arsehole to the security team.

On the plinth, Cassie sat on the edge, her ankles crossed and her head tilted to one side. Her gaze was fixed on my brother, curiosity and fascination in her stare.

"That one," she said, audible at last now the fuss had died. "I'll take that one."

35

Arran

Detective Dickhead, Chief Constable Kenney, gifted me a crocodile smile from across the brightly lit interview room. I'd drive that fucking expression down his throat.

In the same breath, I was relieved that it was him heading up the joke of an interrogation, because it only meant one thing.

The flash-and-bang raid on Divine.

The handcuffs on me and my staff, and the slow walking of us to the police transport vans with the cage inside.

The asshole needed a public takedown with as much fanfare as possible, no doubt courtesy of the mayor.

I'd not given him the satisfaction of putting on a show and had barely bothered reading the warrant he'd produced. Last time, it was Divide he'd raided, claims of drug dealing being the excuse. This time, the file read *organised prostitution*. Neither were worth the paper they were written on.

It was bullshit—they'd find no evidence of sex work in Divine, and the warrant didn't permit them to search anywhere else in the warehouse, and the access routes to the floors upstairs would be blocked off. The brothel wasn't a single organised business. It had no name, and the sex workers were all self-employed, contracting the different services they needed to share such as client vetting, security, room rental, and cleaning. Each individual paid her, his, or their own way. I knew the law and skated it with expert precision.

Hence why I knew this was a mockery of real police activity. It pissed me off that he'd taken in Alisha and some of the dancers, though.

"Let the others go," I said, low and deadly.

He gave an easy shrug. "In time, they'll all be sent on their way."

"With nothing on their record?"

"That depends on you."

Something in his eyes made my skin crawl. I'd been cuffed any number of times in the past but despised it. My father had done it to me as a boy ahead of beating me bloody.

This asshole, his puppet, knew it.

This was a power play. There was no way I was letting this motherfucker see it through. I leaned forward, putting every ounce of menace in my stare. "Let me make this clear. You're going to release everyone else you took or I'll pull a tooth for each of them. I'll do it publicly, just like your little raid."

His smile dropped. "I told you I would."

"Now, Kenney."

The chief constable worked his jaw then strode to

the door. He disappeared for a moment then returned. "They'll be home in an hour."

"Safe travel, too, not in a fucking police car."

He glared but tapped out the order on his phone.

Somewhat mollified, I sat back. Lifted my cuffed hands. "Going to remove these?"

Kenney snorted. "I will when I'm ready. I've got a reputation to uphold."

"Coward." I sneered, enjoying him being on the spot. There was a balance in Deadwater, and it wasn't made by law and order. Same as any other city, money and secrets paved the way for business activity, and I had those in spades.

"I'm just trying to do my job," the chief constable bit out. "If you want me to leave your warehouse alone, you can't be out in the city visibly causing problems. People fear gang warfare. Two people ordered dinner this evening and ended up with a fight on their doorstep, their footage looking a lot like you. They called the police and the local authority. I had the councillors in my ear making complaints. You know I have to uphold those. Or at least be seen to."

I already knew the reason behind the raid—an act that would make the local gossip columns and appease the conservative element of the town. It was why I'd been displayed in full view in the back of the police van with my half-naked dancers around me. I'd had them all hide their faces, but the pictures had been taken.

Yet he had a point. The minor scuffle with the Four Milers had been unfortunate.

"It couldn't be helped," I said.

Kenney dropped into the opposite seat. Set a meaty

hand on the folder of papers in front of him. "Do me a favour and take it out of town next time, or I'll be forced to press charges."

"They won't stick. The mayor will see to that. You can drop it with the explanation—he already told me he'd be doing this."

He recoiled, then his gaze searched mine, hunger within. "What have you got on the mayor?"

Wouldn't he like to know? I spread my cuffed hands as wide as they could go but didn't answer.

"What else have you got for me?" I asked.

He didn't have that folder for no reason. Typically, Kenney would drop off his cases at the home of a neutral party then tip me off that I had work to do. Looked like tonight he was killing two birds with one stone.

"Names for you to have fun with." He opened the folder, revealing a prison docket. Rapid-fire, Kenney gave me the details of three men on probation. All sex offenders in one way or another, and all considered a danger to the public, even if the prison service had no choice but to release them.

We all knew the patterns, the paths that people like Bradley followed on their release from jail. We'd be on these men like white on rice.

Shade would be delighted.

Then the chief constable turned the page. I squinted at the thicker pack underneath, the title *Post-mortem* across the top.

Kenney tapped the first sheet. "The official report into the death of Miss Chelsea Gains. Cherry, as she was known. You wanted to see this, and this is the version that will go out to the public."

Suggesting there was another that wouldn't be widely shared.

"What's being hidden?"

"The hooker was pregnant. Three months."

I lifted my gaze. "DNA results?"

He gave a single shake of his head, his lips flattened. "Won't be done. She'll be cremated as soon as possible."

"On whose orders was that information restricted?"

He flew a hand over his head. "Above my pay grade."

"Bullshit. You're top brass now."

My mind sprinted over the possibilities. Genevieve's friend had been killed in such a specific way that I'd taken it as a message to me, but this new evidence was a smoking gun. A motive for someone to take action then hide the evidence at the very highest level. I couldn't make the link back to my world. That was the infuriating part.

The chief constable only shrugged. "Like I said, above my pay grade. If you're smart, you'll leave this alone. She was a nobody, and no one gives a fuck about dead hookers. Give me a couple of hours and a recorded interview, and you'll be released without charge, and I can get to bed. Everyone's happy."

That was where he was wrong. I cared, and so did Genevieve and my crew.

This was yet another body to add to our count.

36

Genevieve

The five of us took over Arran's office, Riordan and me at the big desk, and Jamieson leading Cassie to a sofa that had miraculously appeared at the back of the room, a new lamp lighting the corner.

My heart melted. I'd mentioned to Arran how austere his office was, and now this.

From the doorway, Shade pointed a finger between us. "Stay. Here. None of ye move while I secure the building. There will be a guard on the door, and cameras are watching. If ye, brother dearest, make one wrong move then Jamieson will escort your arse outside and set ye on fire. Got me?"

To mark the point, Jamieson flicked his lighter wheel. Riordan swivelled his cuffed hands behind his back to stick a middle finger up to Shade.

"Can you at least remove the handcuffs?" I asked him.

"Your brother is a member of a rival gang. So no."

Riordan snorted. "Fuck that."

"Yeah, well, Arran will want to meet you all the same.

You broke into his club and tried to take his woman."

"She's my sister and is owed my protection. Plus I walked straight in the front door. If you really thought I was a gang member, your security is shit."

Cassie gave a happy sigh, her head on her hands, her gaze never leaving him.

"Whatever. My word stands. Cuffs on and under watch until Arran returns. He can decide what to do with his new brother-in-law." The enforcer left us.

Jamieson turned back to his sister. "Cass, help me out here. Start with what the fuck you were doing with that attention-seeking bullshit. You've scared us all shitless."

Riordan tapped my foot with his. "Are you okay?"

"Of course. Are you?"

"You're the one in this place. What happened?"

"I'm here because I want to be. I wasn't kidnapped."

He studied me, looking so much like our mother, it almost hurt. The fact he was over six foot and she had been my height made no difference when he shared her green eyes. They crinkled around the edges in concern.

"What was I supposed to think? You were seen with these people, and you told me you were staying with friends, which was an obvious lie. We needed the money so we didn't lose the flat, and there was only one conclusion I could reach."

"That I'd sold myself?"

His worried gaze soaked me in. "Did you?"

"No. I am staying here, though, but because I'm dating the man who runs it."

Riordan's concern shifted to outrage. "Arran Daniels? Are you insane?"

"I'm not going to get your blessing, then."

"Don't even joke. That man's reputation—"

"Is well earned," Jamieson quipped from the sofa. "Don't mess with his woman, whatever her relationship to you."

My brother cut him a glare then came back to me, dropping his voice even further. "We'll return to that later. I found a way to get the money we need to save the flat."

My heart sank. There was only one route to that amount of cash, and it wasn't working long hours on a building site. "Please, Rio, don't do anything stupid."

He poked his tongue into his cheek. "Like you haven't?"

I'd done so many idiotic things and missteps I'd lost count. That wasn't a debate for now.

I took a deep breath, centring my thoughts. "I'll use the university fund. I know you're going to argue, but it's my choice."

Riordan's expression faded from concerned to bleak. "If only you'd answered my calls. The money is gone."

I stared at him. "What?"

"I went back yesterday to check the mail. All the landlord would say over the phone was that the debt wasn't theirs anymore, which made no sense, so I assumed something else had happened. I found the door open and the place turned over. The cubby in your bedroom was emptied. The prospectus gone, including the envelope with the bank card."

The university prospectus had contained my savings account details. The only people in the world who knew about it were my little family. Three of us including me.

"That doesn't mean the money's gone." But as I said the

words, I found my phone from the pocket of my hot-pink dress and logged in to the bank account I rarely checked but had added to for years.

The balance was nil.

"What was your PIN?" Riordan asked.

I breathed the answer. "Mum's birthday."

"Dad took it. I can't think of another answer."

I sank in Arran's leather seat, heartsick. Of all the things Dad could've done, the disappearing, the lack of contact, this was a low blow.

"Was much else taken?" I whispered.

"No. He did a sloppy job of staging it."

We shared a look of horror, and of absolute defeat.

My brother exhaled hard. "This whole time, I feared the worst. I thought he'd crossed the wrong person or got himself into something he couldn't undo. I pictured him dead."

I pressed both hands to my lips. "I had, too. We'd be orphans."

"Exactly. I was more worried about the effect on you than me, but now I think he's up to something else, but I have absolutely no idea what."

Heaving a sigh, I told him what I knew about Dad's interactions with the Four Milers, including how yesterday one of the members had implied he was on a job.

I gazed at my brother. "Are you a member?"

That same outraged expression returned. "How can you even ask?"

"Because of Moniqua. Her family are deep in it."

"Her cousin is. They don't have any other family. She's

not a member, and anyway, I wouldn't join a gang just because I'm fucking some woman."

"You were paying her rent, and she came here tonight wearing a stolen uniform so she could sneak in."

"Because she needed help and owed me a favour, not because we're that tight. I needed someone else to walk into the strip club because if I'd seen you on the stage, I don't know how I could've handled that."

He cringed. I hid my relief. Riordan didn't lie to me. As kids, he'd always spoken the truth even if it got him in trouble. If he loved Moniqua, he'd wear it proudly.

"Did her cousin come with her?" I asked.

"No. She told me she hasn't seen that piece of shit in over a week, thank fuck. Something happened with him, and he's been off Moniqua's back."

Good for her.

"Dad talked a lot recently about missing Mum," my brother suddenly said. "I keep coming back to that, but I don't know why. How does that link him to a gang? What does it mean?"

The door clicked open, Shade returning. "Alisha and the dancers have been released. They're home and safe."

I exhaled in relief. "What about Arran?"

"No news yet. The warehouse is locked up tight. It could be a long night, so I suggest we go upstairs to wait it out."

Cassie bounced to her feet. "I'm starving. Is there food?"

Together, we took the lift up to the eighth floor. I'd insisted on my brother accompanying us, and Shade had blindfolded him as a precautionary measure. In Arran's apartment, I opened the fridge, making myself at home. It was surprisingly well-stocked, perhaps for my benefit considering how he'd populated a wardrobe for me already. Cassie and Jamieson had obviously been here before, because both settled straight in, Jamieson making a call, watching the city out of the arched window. Cassie grabbed a blanket from a spare bedroom and made a nest in a corner of the sofa, her heels kicked off by the door.

She pointed to the big TV on the brick wall. "Can anyone see the remote control? There's an ice hockey match I want to watch. The Colorado Titans versus the New York Guardians."

Shit. The remote.

Without lowering the phone, Jamieson remarked, "Since when are ye into sports?"

She poked out her tongue. "Since I saw how hot the men are. Church, my favourite player, had a lower body injury, but he's back. Boy is fine." She cocked her head. "Do you think lower body means his dick? I hope not."

Riordan chuckled then coughed to hide it.

Hurrying over with a bowl of chicken wings and dip, I sought out the remote and found the channel for her. Arran's perverted game had taken that device out of action for anyone else. I hid it in the breadbin then did a circuit of the room, collecting up anything else we'd abused.

With the violent sport giving us something to focus on, we snacked and waited, the big arched window stealing my attention from the hockey boys fighting. Somewhere out there, Arran was in a police station.

My brother, still blindfolded, refused food and sat on the rug, resting back against the sofa, only the lower half of his face visible. Cassie alternated her watch of the screen with tracing her gaze along his unshaven jawline. When his breathing slowed, I knew my tough older brother had fallen asleep. It was four in the morning, and he started work every day at dawn.

I gestured to Shade. "I'm going to offer him one of the spare beds here."

He'd taken calls, pacing the hallway for much of our wait. "Not here, ye won't. I'll take him over to my place. I have a bedroom with an external lock."

A locked room? I wasn't going to touch that thought with a bargepole.

Gently, I shook my brother awake, and Shade led him out of the door and across to his place.

Then I, too, claimed a blanket and curled up in a seat.

Finally, darkness stole over me. I shouldn't have been as tired as I was, but a power nap took me under, the stress making unconsciousness seem like the better option.

Until the door softly snicked open.

A tiny sound that barely pierced my sleepy state. The opposite was true for Shade and Jamieson. Both men leapt up with sudden alertness, ghosting across the dark room in silent speed to intercept the incomer.

I snapped on the lamp.

Shade's knife flashed in the light.

Arran was home.

37

Arran

The blade slashed towards me, stopping an inch from my throat, the knife owner's arm around my neck. At the same moment, a second man reeled away, pulling his punch.

"Fucking hell. Ye couldn't knock?" Jamieson said.

At my back, Shade uttered a laugh and loosened his grip.

I was quicker than him.

Grabbing his arm, I yanked him off balance, then bent forward, squatted, and hauled him over my back in one fluid motion. He flew across my shoulder and crashed to the floor with a startled laugh, his weapon miraculously holstered again.

Then he climbed to his feet and embraced me, smacking my back hard. "Good to see ye back, arsehole."

Jamieson joined him. "I taught him that move."

"Then you're an arsehole too," Shade grumbled in return.

From the sofa, Cassie sat up and blinked owlishly.

You're back. Cool beans. I'm going to bed." She picked up the blanket around her and trotted off down my hallway like she owned the fucking place.

I didn't care. My focus was fully on Genevieve, relief slamming into me that she was safe. In soft leggings and a sweatshirt, all her makeup removed, and her hair in a messy bun, she was the picture of everything I'd needed to come home to, and the emotion in her eyes told me exactly how she'd felt about my arrest.

Closing in, I collected her into my arms, throwing an instruction to the rest of the room. "Give us a minute."

"Just a minute?" Jamieson queried.

Shade answered with a laugh, "Give him a break, he's new to it. Stamina takes time to develop."

In my bedroom, I kicked the door closed then dropped down against my pillows so Gen could huddle against me. She whimpered, and I just fucking held her. Then I found her mouth with mine and kissed her hello.

"You broke the four-hour rule," she said against my lips.

"I know, baby. I'm so sorry. It couldn't be helped."

"Does it mean our game is over?"

My chest tightened. "No. Not at all. I just have to make it up to you."

She inched back, examining my face, her fingers brushing over my brow. "Are you okay?"

"Perfectly fine. Were you worried?"

"Of course I was. How would you feel if you saw me taken away like that?"

Savage anger flashed through me. "I'd tear apart the world until I got you back."

Her throat bobbed under her choker. "That's how I felt, and I couldn't do a thing about it other than pretend I wasn't yours. So much happened after you were just gone. Cassie appeared. My brother came here and Shade locked him in his apartment. I just... I needed you so badly."

She held my gaze, some weird, messed-up shit surging in me. I wanted to hurt something as recompense for the pain she'd suffered. Remove Kenney's head from his body. Maim myself for being the cause.

Realisation hit me like a brick. Our bond was stronger than I'd even started to comprehend. I was connecting to her, embedding deep hooks. I fought with her, lost myself in fucking her, and unequivocally intended to keep her.

"At the end of the four weeks, you're not leaving me," I said.

Genevieve's breath stuttered. "Okay."

"What do you mean okay?"

She gestured between us, her legs either side of my hips, her free hand over my heart. "Things are changing between us. It's moving so fast I can't keep up, but even the thought of not being with you for a day is unbearable."

"Entirely," I agreed.

For a beat, she just watched me, her lips parted as if ready to say words she couldn't quite manage. "I need to ask you something." She took a shuddering inhale. "Do you love me? I mean, could you?"

"No." The refusal came easy. "That isn't a word I understand, and I have no place for it."

Her shocked expression had me sitting up.

"It doesn't matter. I'm obsessed with you. I intend to possess you for all time. You're mine, do you understand? Love has no use for us, and we don't need it."

I kissed her again, stealing her warmth and finally feeling something was right.

Gen made an angry sound and broke away, shoving me back. She climbed off me. "Then we have a problem, because I'm falling in love with you."

I stared back. "No you aren't. Or if you are, you need to stop. It's just the game."

"God, Arran. The game? This is a real relationship."

"Call it whatever you want, just leave love out of the equation." I threw my hands out, hot under the collar. "I'll give you everything. My protection, a home with me, the degree you want—I'll drive you there and back every fucking day, every part of my life. It's yours."

"But not your love."

"I'm not withholding it from you. I don't have the capacity. I never received it, and any sentiment like that was beaten out of me. Don't ask for something I can't give."

Her chest rose and fell, her scrutiny intense. "That is the most tragic thing I've ever heard. Not that it happened, though that's bad enough, but that you won't even try."

She left the room without a backwards glance.

In the living room, I found her on the sofa. She wouldn't meet my gaze.

After an awkward beat, Shade spoke. "Catch us up with what happened after your arrest."

"Chief Constable Kenney needed me for show and tell," I said.

Methodically, I filled them in on the reason for my arrest and the information he'd given me on the sex offenders he hoped we'd hunt. Shade made a note of the names.

Genevieve curled in on herself.

I took her hand, clamping down when she tried to pull away. "He shared something about Cherry. She was pregnant."

Fresh shock filled Genevieve's eyes. "That's awful."

Completing the explanation, I told them how the man responsible would never be known.

Genevieve excused herself for a moment to use the bathroom, then returned, her cheeks damp. She took a deep inhale. "That's made me so fucking angry. What right have they got to cover it up like that? I've got some information to share. I think I've identified who Cherry's wealthy customer was. The one she expected the night she died and was bringing a friend she was scared of."

Everyone watched her.

"Don't ask me how I found out, but I'm reasonably certain that councillor Slaughter was that client. I've no idea who the friend was, but the counsellor's a suspect."

"Slaughter." I drew my eyebrows in and tracked back to the few previous conversations I'd had with the man. Nothing stood out.

Gen gave an unfunny laugh. "Aptly named, isn't he?"

"He's a customer of the brothel. I've met him. Can't say he left an impression, but it's good to know." I took up my phone that I'd collected from my office and tapped out a message. "I'm passing a warning on to Alisha so security can stop him coming here."

She curled her lip. "He was in tonight. What if cutting him off from the brothel means he looks for other street workers?"

"You want me to keep him close?"

"It might be better. Just make sure he's monitored."

I considered the choice. "We have a protocol for men like that. Weapons checks and safeguards for the women."

My gaze lingered on Gen's choker.

"Originally, I couldn't work out a motive for him." She brushed back her blonde hair which was escaping the bun. "If you were going to kill someone, you'd need a really good reason, wouldn't you?"

"Yes. Random murders are extremely rare. People kill for all kinds of reasons, but they're always specific."

"Like what?" she asked.

"Revenge. To hide secrets. To send a message."

"Is it safe to assume Cherry could've been killed because she was pregnant and that was a secret that needed hiding?"

Shade nodded. "It isn't a smoking gun, but it's a motive. A counsellor wouldn't want it to be known that he'd had a baby outside of a relationship, let alone with a sex worker. What doesn't make sense is how that tracks back to you, Arran."

Genevieve looked between us. "Why would it?"

Jamieson lifted his eyebrows at me. "You're shite at sharing information."

From the depths of my flat, Cassie called, "I told him that already. Did you clock the choker? Pretty, indestructible, kinda wide."

My woman squeezed her eyes tight shut for a moment then trained them on me. "Would you please fill me in to what everyone else obviously knows but I don't?"

I reached for her. She moved away.

"Before the information you discovered about

councillor Slaughter, I'd believed that Cherry was killed as a message to me."

Jamieson rolled his hands. "Because...?"

I kept my gaze on Genevieve. "Because the murder method was exactly the same as how my father killed my mother."

She stilled, then her fingers crept to the jewellery at her neck.

To save her the trouble, I continued. "He slit her throat with a knife. She was naked and restrained. Then he left her to bleed out on the floor where she fell. I already told you she was a sex worker. The parallels are there."

Shade spoke. "I had a feeling the Four Milers were behind it. They enticed away Sydney then Convict. They're taking potshots."

Genevieve's gaze shot to him. "What happened with Convict?"

"He betrayed me," I admitted. "He was there at the Four Milers standoff."

She stared at me. "My brother came to find me this evening, his girlfriend, too. He said Don, her cousin, had something happen to him and he's not around anymore. That man was my first suspect because he was on the scene, but that's another tie-in."

Shade nodded. "Unless Red is the orchestrator. He leads the gang, and if he's smart, he has a route into the police where he could have discovered what happened to your ma."

He and Jamieson started a conversation, Shade recalling all the minor gang interactions we'd had over the past year. Mostly, they were territorial scuffles. Nothing major. I sensed the weight of Gen's stare on me.

She groaned in annoyance. "I hate what happened to Cherry. Why would someone do that? Why do men have such a problem with caring about others?"

I worked my jaw, but she wasn't done.

"You, for example. You claim that you'll never love. What's up with that? Why would anyone not want something so perfect?"

The two men stopped talking. At the hall entrance, Cassie peeked around.

I lowered my gaze on Gen. She was upset, hurting for her lost friend, but that was no reason to spill shit. "This isn't the time or place."

"Isn't it? When would be? What if I had been the one killed? Would you look back with regret or just move on because love was never on the table? You could walk away and get on with life as normal."

"Like the good councillor?" I snarled. "Are you comparing me to him?"

She gave a sarcastic laugh. "To a psychopath? No. What could you possibly have in common?"

Deep emotion rose in a wave. This conversation needed to stop, but I needed her happy again, too. I had no fucking clue how to get back to what we had.

In tandem, my and Shade's phones blared with alerts.

He snatched his up faster than me. "Something's activated the security system."

I clicked into our network. On one of the camera feeds, a person scaled the wall of the building, keeping to the shadows but not evading our system as they climbed the bars of a window. They got so far then scrambled and fell, our measures keeping them from getting any higher.

Leaping up, I paced to the window and dialled Tyler whose team were here for a couple of days.

He picked up. "We're on it."

"Who?"

"Unknown. One person, I believe. They were around the front then circled. My team converged, but the guy's gone. Fucking spray paint left on the wall."

Paint? For fuck's sake. The camera triggered was on the west end of the warehouse. Whoever did it must have been lurking for a while ahead of making their attempt. Another message to me, undoubtedly.

"On my way down," I told him.

Shade was already at the door.

I went to Gen. Kissed her. "Keep this door locked." I switched my gaze to Jamieson.

He held it, no words needed. He'd protect both the women under our care.

Then it was time to hunt down a graffiti artist.

38

Shade

Out of the lift, Arran went right to go to the back of the warehouse. I took the opposite direction. He didn't ask, and I gave no explanation. I didn't need to.

I'd heard his call. Whoever had sprayed paint on the exterior walls was either a moronic kid with no idea who he was messing with or a person who wanted to make a point with a cheap shot.

My money was on the latter.

If I was that individual, I'd be out there still, watching for the reaction I craved.

In the darkest corner of the warehouse's grounds, the south side by the river, I exited and slipped straight into the shadows, an expert in using them like my crew name suggested.

Voices and radio static came from Tyler's team. One strolled the perimeter, coming my way. I held still until he passed. This was exactly why I needed to be out here and doing this. No gun for hire could know the place as well as me, and while I respected Tyler, he didn't usually work the warehouse. He was Arran's intercept guy, heading out to ports and transit locations to take on new trafficking routes that popped up.

The trade that never died.

Alone again, I haunted the night-drenched surroundings. Instinct tugged my senses. I swung my gaze to the front of the building. Well lit and on a pretty brick-lined promenade at the end of the river walkway, it was the least likely place for trouble. Aside from fights between clubgoers at kicking-out time. Yet I followed the intuition, making it to the corner to give myself a view of the entrances to Divide and Divine.

From the street, a car accelerated.

My focus sharpened.

Tyres squealed, then in a rush, a vehicle bore down fast on the warehouse. It had the boot open and the windows blacked out in a way that couldn't be legal. Meaning this wasn't a car used often, or the blackout film had just been added.

I dialled Arran.

The driver performed a tight turn then reversed in hard, aiming straight at the club entrances. The car smashed into a low bollard, jerking the front wheels up. With the engine still on and fumes billowing, the driver crawled through the centre, only their shape visible through the dark glass.

I stuck my phone in my pocket and sprinted.

A naked body was shoved out the back of the car by gloved hands. The person dropped heavily to the ground in a tumble of limbs, and the driver whipped back to his seat, too fast for me to see anything but the skeleton mask he and the body both wore.

I couldn't miss the blood, though. A slash of it gleaming under the yellow streetlights.

Driving my feet into the ground, I was almost on them.

"We've been rammed. I think someone's hurt," I yelled for the benefit of Arran if he'd answered my goddamned call.

The black car's engine sound changed, then the vehicle lurched forward, a cloud billowing after it. The driver floored it.

Grey smoke swirled around the body dumped outside of the strip club. A blonde woman, nude, a red gaping slice across her throat, the bandanna only covering her upper face.

I stared at her in horror, then croaked out the words, "She's been killed and dumped."

Halfway up the hill, the car choked, stalling. They'd fucked it up in the crash. The driver scrambled out on the wrong side for me to see anything but their movement.

Furious, I took off, running hard to chase them down.

39

Arran

Sprinting around the building, I saw nothing for a long moment. Then my peace was shattered. A body left naked on the ground, her face covered by one of my own crew's masks, and her neck glistening with blood.

Genevieve.

Gen with no choker protecting her throat. Gen with no chance of survival from the depth of the cut.

Anguish clamped hold of my stomach, and I stopped, unable to take another step. Subconsciously, I knew it couldn't be her, but it gripped me all the same.

All the life she'd given me iced over and died, like she had. Tyler jogged past, two of his team with him and the rest monitoring the other side of the building.

He squatted next to the body and peered closer. "Fucking hell," he bit out, then raised his focus. "This a police job? Lot of cameras around here. There'll be eyes on us from the flats down the way."

He was right.

I couldn't move my lips.

"Shit. Did you know her?" He tugged the mask from her face.

The terror released me. It wasn't Gen. Not her beautiful eyes in these unseeing duplicates, not her lips.

My heart restarted, beating too fast. Packing away my horrified, gut-wrenching thoughts, I managed to speak.

"Her name's Natasha Reid. I'll make the call."

A short while later, Natasha's body was being scrutinised with photographs taken from every obscene angle, an ambulance arriving with lights swirling. Cops swarmed the place, Detective Dickhead lauding it up.

I handled him, getting Manny to pull the CCTV footage. Not that there was any concern over the facts: There was no blood on the ground where the body had been dumped. Nothing like the scene where Cherry had been killed, despite the reused method.

Natasha hadn't been murdered here.

She'd visited earlier and made a scene, though. Alicia had told me. The mask use made me think it referenced that. Perhaps that had been the intent.

Whoever had laid a dead body on my doorstep did so to tell me something, yet I had no fucking clue what that message could be. The graffiti around the other side was a single red line, mimicking a slit throat.

The fact they'd picked someone who looked like Genevieve drove fear through me like nothing else.

From across the wide harbour promenade, Shade reappeared and gave a single headshake in the negative. "Lost them. I tried every which way. They were a street ahead and I was faster, but it's like they were a ghost. They just vanished."

"And they wore one of our masks?"

He glanced over at the body which was quickly being concealed by a forensics unit, hours of work ahead for them. A van zoomed up, a TV crew hopping out, the female reporter instantly talking into a camera.

Shade and I strode inside without pause.

Kenney was in the operations office, one only used for CCTV monitoring. Alisha didn't even come in here to do the rotas.

He set his gaze on Shade. "Mr Michaels. I just watched your actions on the cameras. Any specific reason why you were hanging around outside at the moment the body was left?"

"He came down with me to investigate the graffiti," I snapped.

The chief constable huffed. "Both of you will need to come in to give a statement."

"Later." I turned my back and walked away.

Shade followed.

In my office, and well out of the earshot of Kenney, I dropped into my seat. "For three days, we're on complete lockdown. All events cancelled. Staff can come here if they want to stay safe. If they were scheduled to work, they'll be paid. I'll make a public statement about doing it out of respect to the dead woman."

Shade sent messages. "You're expecting trouble."

I exhaled hard. "I don't know. It was a warning, but to what end? How many people saw Natasha? A couple of hundred when the strip club was raided. A lot more if she was still around when the club kicked out."

My phone buzzed. I scowled at the incoming message.

Red: Not us.

I held it up for Shade.

His eyebrows rose. "The Four Milers are denying it. Would they lie?"

We both stared, baffled. They'd been on my suspects list, and in the past, Red had happily lauded his victories over me.

My phone buzzed again, Gen calling.

I let it ring out.

"Does she know what happened?" my friend asked.

"No. Go ahead and tell her, then stay up there and make sure Jamieson does, too. There's something I need to do."

He watched me for a beat then stood. "Stay alive."

"Always do."

My best friend left, and I changed into a pair of dark jeans and a long-sleeved shirt. An inverted bandanna over my hair made up the rest of my disguise, and I slipped out of the back of the warehouse unseen even by the dozens of prying eyes.

The scare I'd had at seeing Natasha and thinking her Genevieve had loosened something inside me. Gen was in love with me, she'd said the words, the first person to ever have done so. I was holding on to the mistrust that had been there since the night she came to my warehouse.

It was time to get to the truth.

From the car park, I took on the hill that rose steeply beyond, passing rows of terraced houses and blocks of flats. I didn't stop until I was outside the church where Cherry had been murdered, but I passed that, too, continuing on until I reached the Crescent. On the steps outside Gen's flat, I barged the street door. It popped easily, and I was inside.

Up the stairs, I revisited the route I'd taken on my first and only other visit, then I was outside Gen's flat. The lock was busted, tape keeping it closed as if someone had broken in and a proper repair job hadn't yet been carried out.

I prowled through the shadowed rooms until I found the master bedroom. Entered and sought out the pictures on the wall. Enough light came through the uncovered window to fall on two girls in a family photo in the middle of many. A twelve-year-old Genevieve and a toddler.

I unhooked it and slid to the floor.

After all these years, I was finally getting to see another picture of my sibling. Gen was right—all kids didn't look the same. Addie was so recognisable, grinning and in a padded snowsuit, not the rainbow dungarees. They were outdoors, and from the warm clothes, it was autumn or winter. Months after our mother's death.

Addie must've known Flora well to have been so content so soon. Was Flora in a relationship with Audrey? Were they neighbours or co-workers? One thing was clear. Audrey had a contingency plan for her baby after she died. She'd supplied evidence on my dad then expected the worst from it, and he'd delivered.

Another point hit me. Genevieve had told the truth. Her story was real, and Addie existed in her past. Her dad would be able to help me fill in the gaps.

In a decade of creating my own world, and bringing people closer to me, this route in through my past tripped me up. Connected up parts of my life that in the same moment felt out of control and utterly needed.

Another photo caught my attention—a family portrait. A very young Gen and her brother, and their parents with their arms around each other. Even after they'd separated, and the mother died, her dad kept the picture up. Not out in the living room for the sake of his kids, but in here, right in his eyeline when he was at rest.

"Hello? Who's in there?" an elderly female's voice came.

With a sigh, I stood, taking the picture of Addie with me. Out in the hall, a woman poked her head in the door. She spied me and reared back, her stick raised.

"I've called the police already. Don't you move."

I did move. My time here was done, and I had a home to go to. I exited to the hall, the woman cringing away. Then recognition dawned, and she narrowed her eyes.

"I know who you are. Your face was on the late-night news. I have an alert set up and I saw everything about you and those... those naked women! You should be in prison."

"And yet here I am," I drawled, dropping down a couple of steps. Wait until she copped the news about the second murder. She'd probably be fainting away and calling me the Devil.

"What are you doing breaking into people's homes?

Even the lowlifes who live here don't deserve that."

With annoyance, I turned around. "I didn't break into anywhere. I own the place."

Her mouth opened. "Excuse me?"

"You heard me."

The woman set her stick down, her stance wobbly. "I had a message from my landlord saying he'd sold the Crescent. Surely not to you?"

I gave her a winning smile. "Correct, Arran Daniels, strip club owner and your new landlord. Actually, to be more specific, it's in Genevieve Jones' name, so she'll now be collecting your rent, and that of everyone else who lives here. I was looking for property to invest in, somewhere to renovate and offer as a home to my staff. This is close to work and will do nicely, if Gen agrees."

Bullying old ladies wasn't in my nature, but the neighbour was pissing me off.

I tapped the wall to mark my point. "Be nice to your new neighbours, or it'll be you with the eviction notice on your door."

At the warehouse, the front was even busier with two new reporters doing pieces to camera about the murder. I stole in through the back and took the stairs up to my apartment, knocking on my own goddamned door so I didn't end up almost dead like earlier.

Returning here had never felt like this in the past. The desire to stay in, rather than always be out. I had someone to come home to now.

From the sofa, Gen watched me enter, Jamieson and Cassie with her and Shade on the phone. I held her gaze, recognising fear and worry, and my fucking heart hurt.

"Everyone out," I ordered.

Cassie's jaw dropped in outrage. In her hands, she brandished a notepad and pen. "Hell, no. A dead woman was dumped on your doorstep. We've been continuing the detective work. Give us five minutes then you can have the room, m'kay?"

Gen's gaze held mine, the space shrinking to just the two of us. "Where did you go?"

"Your flat."

She sniffed. "Not for much longer."

I crossed the room. Set the photo down then collected her to my lap and just fucking held her. "I bought the Crescent in your name. Is that security enough?"

Her focus lifted from the picture frame to me. Strong emotion clogged my throat.

"A choker to protect my neck that I can't get off. A property purchase based on a single word from me. Arran. Do you know what this is?"

"Taking care of what's mine, that's all."

She huffed in disbelief.

Cassie made a cooing sound. "Ye guys are so cute. But can we focus, please? Genevieve said that Natasha woman had been here earlier in the evening, kicking up a fuss and making a spectacle of herself. She pissed off a lot of people, but who'd kill her for that?"

Shade ended his call. "Councillor Slaughter has an alibi for the murder. He was in the brothel all evening and only left half an hour ago."

"We're assuming whoever killed Natasha also killed Cherry," Cassie explained. "That could be a duo, though. Slaughter is meant to have had a friend, so the second person could've been tonight's murder culprit."

"The mayor is close to Slaughter," Shade took up. "He was here earlier, too, but left about an hour before Natasha was killed."

I brushed my fingers down Gen's cheek, wallowing in the need to clamp her to me, and to get her to understand that I was hers, even if she didn't get the exact words she wanted.

Jamieson spoke. "Does anyone know the mayor? Why would he kill a random woman? I can see a motive with Cherry if he was protecting the reputation of his council member, but that's still a stretch and fucking risky. Plus Natasha would be a complete stranger."

Shade snorted. "Don't think he doesn't enjoy risk. He's ruthless."

Cassie tilted her head. "Ye know him?"

Something dark swirled in Shade's eyes. He gave a short nod.

Gen adjusted her position. "I have his daughter's phone number. I can call her and ask a few subtle questions to help us work it out."

With a recoil, Shade stared at Gen. "Why do you have Everly's phone number?"

"She was here this evening. We spoke."

He wheeled away, hiding whatever was in his expression. "Lose it. She has no business being here or speaking to anyone."

"Shade," I said, low and clear. "Order Genevieve around like that again and see what happens."

He heaved in a breath, annoyance simmering.

Cassie gazed between us, her head swivelling as if she were at a tennis match. "So by my count, we have

Councillor Slaughter for Cherry, the mayor of Deadwater for Natasha, but without any real evidence, Red from that other gang—"

"Who's already rejected the claim," I added. I told them about the message Red had sent.

"Do ye believe him?" Cassie asked.

"Actually, yes, in the case of Natasha. That execution style fits a gang MO, but he'd be the first to claim it. With Cherry, there's no motive."

"Huh. Well, maybe there's honour amongst thieves. Who else, oh yeah, Don the scary gangster, some alternative friend to the councillor who allegedly knocked Cherry up, and another unknown copycat, perhaps. That's a lot of dudes. Let's not forget ladies. Don't leave us girls out."

Gen gave a short laugh. "Do you want your name added to the list, Cassie?"

"Not me, silly. I'm just trying to be thorough."

Gen pondered that. "If we're looking for women, how about my elderly neighbour? She hated Cherry. Or Moniqua? She was here tonight. And even perhaps Alisha. If we find a link between any of them and Natasha, that'll narrow it down."

I pulled back. "Alisha? Why the hell would you suspect her?"

"I don't, really. Except she would've been pissed off at the scene in the club, oh, and she's in love with you."

"No, she isn't." I rejected that out of hand.

Gen shrugged. "What if she followed when you visited my flat on the night Cherry was killed? Jealousy is a motive."

Shade answered. "She wasn't there. I trailed Arran as backup. I even saw Cherry in the churchyard."

I stared at him. "You followed me? I didn't know," I added quickly to Gen. On that evening, Gen had asked me if I'd come alone. I hadn't lied. It also didn't surprise me that Shade had fucking stalked me.

Gen paled. "Did you talk to her?"

"No, I watched her, but she didn't even know I was there. She was alone the whole while."

"Did you see Don's car?" I asked.

"It passed me. I saw Genevieve react but couldn't make out the occupants. It didn't return. I gave the plate to Convict, but he couldn't trace it, and Don still hasn't been found." Shade paced the room, his gaze distancing.

I sat back. We were no closer to working this problem out.

"Add Chief Constable Kenney to your list," I instructed Cassie. "He drove out to find me to warn me off messing with the councillors. He could've been acting on their behalf with Cherry. I'm less sure about Natasha. He was at the station with me then came straight from there to respond to our call."

Cassie jotted his name. "Was there technically enough time for him to do it?"

My brief consideration of the timeline worked. "Possibly."

"Then he's on the list. Does anyone have anything else to add? Because this is a hot mess full of assumptions and maybes."

"Then ye know what we do? We pick a fucking direction," Shade suddenly said. "Technically, everyone on our list could be guilty, but that's going to get us nowhere. Occam's razor says the more assumptions you make, the less likely it is. Ergo, the most obvious answer is the truth. Everyone, simplest solution, now."

He pointed at Jamieson who stretched. "The gangster. He was right there at the church when Cherry died."

Cassie peered at her sheet and ticked a name. "Two votes for knifey Don."

Shade swung to Gen, and she slowly gave the same name.

"From the start, I thought it was him," she said.

I shrugged.

"Choose a fucking side," Shade ordered.

"Then I'll go with Don," I agreed. "Cherry feared the councillor's friend, but all those men use my brothel, and none have ever hurt or scared a woman here. Who's to say she told anyone about her pregnancy? Or even knew herself."

Shade rubbed his hands together, doing what he did best. Deciding on a death sentence. "All roads lead to Don. Gang affiliated, known to be violent, wanted Gen and saw her with another man so had a trigger to go into a murderous rage. Think about it, he tracked ye down, Gen. That shows purpose. Killing Cherry was an outlet."

Gen shivered, curling in on herself.

I hugged her. "Plausible, but how about the murder method and the link to Audrey's death?"

"Either he heard about that from elsewhere and emulated it, or it was a coincidence. One of the main factors we considered was the fact Cherry and Audrey were both sex workers. If we put Cherry at wrong place, wrong time, that reduces it down to a typical for-show killing method."

Cassie made more notes. "And tonight's murder?"

Shade continued pacing, working out his thoughts. "The timing is interesting as the two of ye are public now. Fuck, that's it. His gang now knows—they had confirmation tonight. He followed Genevieve's brother and his girlfriend here and picked another target to show Arran his anger. It fits that he'd use the same method and the woman he grabbed resembled Genevieve. It has to be him. All we need to know is if it's possible." He turned to Gen. "The one person who'll know more is your brother. Good for me to question him?"

Gen climbed up. "If I'm in the room, sure."

The three of us left my place and entered Shade's across the hall. His apartment mirrored mine with the oak floors and exposed metal beams, but there was more of his personality on display including knives on a wall, not all of them decorative.

He stopped outside a bedroom and unlocked it. The light sprang on, and a disorientated, still masked and bound Riordan stumbled to his feet.

Gen gasped. "You left him tied up?"

"Of course I did. He could've jumped me when I released him," Shade replied, miffed.

I stepped into the plain room. "Riordan, my name's Arran. I'm going to remove your mask so we can see each other."

He held still, and I peeled the skeleton bandanna over his head. Pillow marks lined his flushed face, and his brown hair was flattened. In his features, I could track the connection from the boy I'd seen in the family photo to the man who shared a strong resemblance to my woman.

He blinked in the light, taking me in with a dirty scowl

then seeking his sister. "You okay?"

"I'm good. Sorry you've been tied up for hours."

Riordan rolled his shoulders. "Yeah, maybe I had that coming from barging in like I did. What time is it?"

"Six," Gen replied.

He brought his focus back to me. "I have to get to work. You letting me go?"

"I will once we've had a little chat. What can you tell us about Don?"

Riordan frowned. "Not much. What do you want to know?"

"Is he a known killer for his gang?"

A slow nod followed. "He boasts about it. Each time his boss gave him a job like that, he'd brag how he's one step closer to a top spot. I had no time for his bullshit so didn't pay him any attention."

"When was the last time you saw him?"

"Couple of weeks ago. He was at Moniqua's when I stopped in for a quick... I mean, I went to see her."

From the doorway, someone snorted a laugh. I twisted to spot Cassie listening in. My narrowed gaze did nothing to deter her.

"Where does he usually sleep?" Shade pressed.

Riordan named a block of flats in the no-go area, but a flat-lipped expression from Shade told me he'd already checked it out.

"Anywhere else he's likely to be?" I continued.

Riordan gave an exasperated huff of breath, like we were taking up his time. "Why do you want to know? I'm not his fucking keeper."

I let a cold mask descend over my expression, allowing the man to see who he was talking to. "Because you let a man into your sister's life who intended to do her harm. If it wasn't for you, Gen would never have met that piece of shit and he'd never have followed her home. Now tell us what we need to know so we can stop him from hurting anyone else."

Riordan stared at me, then his shoulders dropped. "Fuck. You think he killed the woman on our street?"

Gen confirmed his guess with a nod. "He was there that night. I didn't want to tell you in case you worried."

"Of course I'd fucking worry, and rightly so." Riordan gazed incredulously at his sister. "I would've slept at home rather than on the work site. All I heard was a rumour from Moniqua that he was interested in you. I warned him off over text because he wouldn't answer my call and said that we'd have a problem if he went near you. He never replied. That's why, when you and I spoke on the phone, I asked if you were seeing him. Just to be sure he hadn't somehow sweet talked you into his bed. Having you anywhere near the gangs is fucking killing me. I blame myself." He glared my way.

"Another woman was killed tonight," Shade added. "She was brought here and left outside. Could Don have followed ye and your girlfriend this evening?"

Riordan stared then swore. "To grab Genevieve from us once I got her back? Then killed someone else when he couldn't? Fucking hell." He hung his head. "Not that I knew of, obviously, but you're thinking Moniqua is in touch with him."

We all went quiet. After he'd tried to take Gen from me, I wasn't about to throw Riordan a welcome party into my life, but I liked his quick mind, and more, I pitied him.

It was the very thing I feared—that my lifestyle would hurt her. From his point of view, it already had.

Riordan took a heavy breath. "I'll see her tonight. She claims she's worried about him, so we can do a drive around. I'll let you know what happens. If she tells me not to bother, that's also a message."

I swapped a glance with Shade, and he slid a hand around Riordan's throat.

"Double-cross us and you're a dead man walking. We don't tolerate men who hurt women, understand? I'll see ye out. Need a ride home?"

Riordan blinked at the two sides of my friend. The hard line and the helpful. "I brought my bike. It's parked in your fucking car park because I wasn't hiding."

Shade reinstated his blindfold, and we left the apartment, Gen hugging her brother goodbye then coming back to me. She drooped with exhaustion.

The lift took the two men away. Jamieson stood in my doorway.

"What now?" he said.

"The five minutes is up. I'm kicking you all out and taking my woman to bed." I curled an arm around Genevieve. "If Don is the culprit, which sounds likely considering he was escalating in violence and Riordan accepted the accusation easily, we need to find him. Until then, he might act again. We'll stay locked down until Friday night, and my crew will be out looking for him in force."

"If ye don't find him?" he asked.

"Then we open the doors again. Once a club night has passed, we'll see what's arisen. By then, Riordan should've shaken something out of his girlfriend, and Kenney should have results back from Natasha's post-mortem."

Cassie snorted. "Doesn't take a genius to tell how she died."

I eyed her. "Cherry's gave us a motive we believed for a while, so don't dismiss it."

Jamieson palmed his sister's shoulder. "On that note, we'll head home. My family is missing me. Cass, let's go."

Cassie hovered, her eyes rounding and a small plea coming my way. "Okay, but can I come back? I like it here, and this has been more fun than I've had in forever."

I sighed but agreed, once the heat was off. Having Cassie under my roof meant I could keep an eye on her, and fuck knew she needed something to do.

One by one, they all left. Jamieson and Cassie hitting the road, an angry but resigned Riordan escorted off the premises, and Shade to his own bed.

At last, I closed the door on the world and took Gen to our room.

She let me hug her. "I can't help but feel my brother's in danger."

"The acts have all been against women, plus he's a big guy. He can handle a world he chose to go into."

"Just like I wandered into yours and am due whatever comes my way? Great. Will you take the choker off now?"

"No."

"Fine."

In my arms yet so distant, Gen curled up and slept.

I couldn't. All I could think about was how in this lull of the storm, I was going to prove to her we had everything we needed, exactly how things were.

40

Arran

*T*hroughout the week, we kept to the warehouse, holed up and with the stories about Natasha settling. News articles screamed about there being a serial killer on the loose, but the police downplayed it, pointing out the differences between the two women and how the lack of any connection made it highly unlikely.

We didn't share our theory, nor did we need to.

Natasha had put up a series of increasingly angry posts on her social media in the days leading up to her death, stating how she had found religion and was going to dedicate her life to helping others turn their back on sin. This made her a target, according to the cops, and someone coming at her for that made a much more likely outcome than any random link to a street worker.

An arrest was made. An online troll had posted comments about her being hypocritical and a fake which made the keyboard warriors connect him to how she'd been dumped outside a strip club. He was released soon after, but the blame game took the public's attention from Deadwater and off my front door.

The police action on Cherry's case dwindled, implying she wasn't as valuable as Natasha, but they were wrong on all counts.

Meanwhile, Gen's brother had gone on the drive about with his girlfriend and found no sign of Don. He reported that she was distraught. That even another gang member they spoke to was worried. All of which gave us nothing to go on.

I put all my energy into winning Gen over by being the world's best fucking boyfriend. I brought her coffee when she woke, cooked meals, and played us movie marathons on a TV I'd rarely watched in the past. I also took the time to give Gen further pieces of myself, letting her in as much as I could. I explained how Chief Constable Kenney had previously worked for my father, and how I had evidence hidden away of how Kenney had once provided a service disposing of bodies. She listened about my deal with the mayor, too, and how I paid bribes to a number of people to keep them sweet so my business could operate unhindered. All the dark corners of my world exposed.

We fucked. A lot. Even angry at me, Gen couldn't stop herself from wanting me.

She got fired from her food courier job, and though I had no regrets about her never going back to that shit, it bothered me how blue she had become.

On the fourth day of lockdown, I accepted a delivery at the warehouse and took it to her. A pet carrier which I opened in the apartment's living room, releasing a fluffy brown cat. It padded forward, posing for a beat, whiskers out.

"Cherry's," I told her. "Dixie informed me you discovered she'd had a pet. The neighbour had taken it to a centre, but I had people track it down. Believe it or not, getting approval to take home that animal took longer than buying the Crescent."

With an expression of sadness mixing into a softer emotion, Gen settled on her knees and held out a hand, letting the cat go to her, its huge yellow eyes curious.

"Her name's Rosie," I offered.

Gen picked Rosie up. She hugged her, and the cat instantly sheathed its claws and kneaded her leg.

"Her collar is the exact shade of Cherry's hair. At last, I can do something in my friend's name," she murmured into the thick fur which would be all over my fucking place. "I'll look after her baby. Thank you for finding her."

My gaze burned into hers. "Is this enough? I want our lives to be like this always. Next week sees the end of our month, and I can't handle the thought that you might leave."

She held Rosie closer. "No, it isn't enough."

"What will be?"

"I hurt, Arran. I didn't ask for this, just the same as you didn't, but now I have you, I can't go back to not loving you. If you can't love me back, I'll always be in pain."

I remained tight-jawed. "I'm going to propose to you on the very last day. It's the final stage, usually a public engagement announcement or a blood bond, but we can register to marry instead."

That ache inside her was right there in her eyes. She shook her head, sorrow plain. "You have to say the word 'love' in marriage vows. You'd be a liar. Sorry, Arran. But lying in that oath is a dealbreaker for me."

Then she locked herself away with Rosie and the box of cat things I'd had brought up, and left me to plan for the clubs' reopening this evening. I had no choice but to keep going. With the warehouse not taking in money, my staff were missing out on tips. I preferred keeping them close, too.

Plus nothing else had happened. No further act of violence or threat, no graffiti and no more bodies. Shade, who had taken Kenney's list of new jail releases and already handled one of the men, took the night off and stayed at the club, adding to the boosted security.

We watched the crowds and skirted the rooms.

The night passed with barely even a skirmish on Divide's packed dance floor.

On Saturday, I met with the team, and we made the decision to stay open. That night and Sunday went by without a hitch. Still nothing on Don, still no retaliation.

On Monday evening, after we closed from the student night, I sought out Shade. "Free to help me handle some business?"

There was something I needed to do, and that hadn't gone away, only been suspended. Gen's father was still missing without a trace, but her mother's killer was top of my list to manage. An almost desperate need to prove myself to her reigned over me, and having Jordan Peters dead and her mother avenged would go a long way towards that.

Shade slid a knife from his jacket and tested the blade. "I'm down."

"I don't want to leave Gen unprotected," I said, though my mind was already out the door and driving south. We'd need to be quick—I was still under a four-hour restriction from being away from Gen's side—but it was possible.

"We'll leave a full crew here until we return. Are ye tracking her?" Shade asked.

"Tracking her?"

He gave me an eyeroll like I was an amateur then gestured for me to follow. Upstairs, in his apartment, he opened a kitchen drawer and brought out a device.

"Point that end at her skin, the upper arm or padded part of the arse is best, then squeeze the trigger. If she's asleep, she might not even feel it."

I turned the tool over in my hands. "How does it work?"

On his phone, Shade demonstrated a map with an icon over it. "If she moves, the map will show you where. I'll set it up for you."

"Who are you monitoring?" I gazed at the icon. It was in a nice part of town with big houses behind a gated entrance. I squinted, trying to see the street name. "It isn't one of our marked men, not in that part of the city."

He dropped his hand, and the screen blackened. "One I don't look at often."

"Whatever you tell yourself, brother."

Shade lowered his gaze. "Ask again and I'll tell Gen what you've done."

Fine. In a minute, he had the software ready for me. Then I was leaving his apartment for mine.

A little squeak of greeting came from Rosie, and I trod out of my shoes and stooped to stroke her fuzzy head, then entered the bedroom, closing the door to keep the cat out.

Lying on her front, Gen slept. She'd been keeping busy finding ways to help out in the club. An early start meant she'd crashed before the sun was up.

I approached on soft feet.

We were heading into autumn, but the evening was

still warm enough for her to be only covered by a sheet, her outline fucking mouthwatering. I set down the gun and peeled the cover back, already hard for her.

In the dark, her breathing stayed easy, no sign of awareness that I was present. I cut away her sleep shorts. Carefully shifted her knee to expose her to me. The last time I'd done this, it had wrecked me. I'd used her as a plaything. I also knew she hadn't minded.

Her pussy lips were soft under my tongue. I licked and teased until she was slick with gleaming arousal, that taste of her fucking incredible.

With one hand, I freed my dick and stroked myself. I'd do anything for her. Anything.

Also anything *to* her.

Kneeling over her, I ran the head of my dick over her slick centre, then pushed inside, just a fraction at a time, perfectly slowly until I was all the way in. She constricted around me, and sweat broke out on my brow.

My breathing came hard. My body fucking shook.

I picked up the gun. Set it against her perfect, round ass cheek, then with zero hesitation pulled the trigger. It jerked against her, and I tossed it behind me, fucking into her with a hard stroke, a distraction from any pain.

She groaned, her hand coming out to find me.

"Going to fuck you then I'll be gone for a few hours," I told her.

"Gone?"

She tried to rise, but I held her down, delivering my promise with repeated hard thrusts until we both groaned in need and bliss. When she came, I stopped for a second to feel her then emptied my balls into her, always needing her pleasure.

I pulled out and licked a tiny spot of blood from her ass cheek, then reinstated my clothes, concealing the gun in my back pocket.

Sleepily, Gen flexed her limbs and peered at me. "I'm worried. Where are you going?"

"To kill Jordan Peters."

With a shocked breath, she jumped up.

"I won't lie to you," I said into a kiss, my fingers spreading over the choker that I wouldn't let her remove. "He's been a dead man walking since you told me his name. I'll call you when it's done, then I'll be back before our time is up."

"You do all this but you won't tell me you love me." Gen stepped back, then said louder, "Four hours or less."

"Don't leave the warehouse," I ordered.

At least if she tried, I'd know.

41

Genevieve

The lift descended the warehouse's interior, and I subtly rubbed my backside. One of my cheeks throbbed like an insect had stung me. Probably something to do with Arran removing my clothes in my sleep again, though it wasn't like him to be clumsy with his knife.

Once he left, I couldn't sleep for worry. I'd played with Rosie for a while, but even she'd curled up to rest. Divide and Divine were closed, but the brothel would be open a while longer, so maybe I could find someone to chat with.

At my side, a member of the security crew silently marked me. Unsurprisingly, one had been waiting outside the apartment door, a man I distantly recognised from being in the office with Arran when he'd brought in another team after the encounter with the Four Milers.

I didn't know his name, nor had he offered it, and it was a little strange that the security chief himself wasn't the person waiting for me.

"Isn't Manny around this evening?" I asked.

The lift passed the sixth floor.

The guard glanced my way then gave a single nod, the bright lift making his features all the more severe. "Mr Manford is monitoring the third floor, miss."

The brothel. Where I wanted to hang out. My lingering unease was slightly mollified. I trusted Manny. He was friendly and shared random facts.

The light illuminated the floor-five sign. At four, the lift stopped, the doors opening.

I squinted out into the corridor. It resembled a hotel with single doors spaced at intervals. What had Manny said, that it was made up of bedroom suites? "Why did we stop?"

My guard drew his dark eyebrows in and pressed the button for three. It did nothing, the doors remaining open. "I'm not sure."

He touched a button at his lapel. "Penthouse lift has failed." At whatever he heard in his ear, he nodded and exited into the corridor. "We'll take the stairs while someone looks into the lift. It's only a single flight."

"Okay." I stepped out, my hackles up.

He gestured for me to go ahead.

I hadn't minded exploring the warehouse with Arran, or with Alisha for the short tour she'd given me. But this man was a stranger, and creeping along a softly lit and apparently deserted corridor with him behind me felt off.

A door opened ahead, and a woman slipped from a room, heading the other way from us. I breathed and started walking. Then a man appeared from the same room. In a split second of seeing his side profile, I recognised him.

The mayor of Deadwater.

My lips parted in a degree of unwarranted shock—

he used this place, I knew that—and my fingers went automatically to the choker at my throat. But then my breath was knocked from me as, in a rush, my guard turned on me.

I gave an *oof* that was cut off by his arm muffling my mouth. Abruptly, he threw me into a dark bedroom. Floor lights sprang on.

The guard released me, and I spun around.

I wanted to challenge him and ask what the hell he was doing, but fear held my tongue. Instead, with my heart racing, I backed into the suite. A huge bed with black-and-pink linen took up a big portion of the room, and a wet room lay beyond, with a spa bath and tiled walls and floor.

Perfect for clearing up spilled body fluids. Such as blood.

The man spoke into his comms system, still peering out the door. "Roger that," he said then snicked it closed.

Shutting us in.

An icy chill slid down my spine. There was no way I could rush the man, and even if I could, what if they were all in on it? All working for one of Arran's enemies?

What if he'd been biding his time until the one evening Arran was away? It all made sense, and I cursed myself for ever leaving the apartment.

The guard shifted, revealing a holster under his smart jacket. Oh God, this was where it all ended for me. Right in the place I'd started to feel safest.

But the man wasn't advancing on me.

In fact, he appeared to be doing his job and guarding me. Warily, I peered around, making a second assessment of the room. If someone else was here, that was his role.

Bringing me to them.

Yet there was no other person in sight.

"Copy," the guard said to whoever was on his line, then his gaze cleared and he bobbed his head at me. "The corridor is safe, miss. We can proceed."

"Pro—? Why did you throw me in here?"

"Mr Daniels explicitly said to protect you from being seen by a list of names. This was the first available solution for concealment."

I set my hand on my hips, trying hard to contain my emotions. He had been hiding me, not trying to hurt me. "The mayor is on that list?"

An inclined head gave me my answer, then the guard held the door, ushering me out.

I fast-walked past him then straight down the hall to the stairwell, running down the single flight. The brothel floor had never looked so good, and I sought out any familiar face.

In the receiving room, empty of any clientele, Alisha was at the bar, a glass of some peachy cocktail in hand, and a blonde wig and full makeup deployed.

Throughout the week, I'd tried to talk to her but got nowhere. She was pissed off with Arran, still, and unwilling to be friends with me. It was time we had it out. Not only for the sake of calming my nerves, but for Arran, too.

At my arrival next to her, she cast a glance over me, rolled her eyes, then turned away.

"Gen! What can I get you?" asked Sunny, one of the brothel workers who sometimes worked the bar, too.

I jerked my head at Alisha. "I'll have what she's having."

"That's fruit juice, honey." At my shrug, Sunny grinned and trotted away to mix up my drink.

"Alisha," I said.

She ignored me.

"Alisha, please. Can we talk?"

"I'm working."

"Are you? Because it's dead in here, and I have never once seen you up on this floor. Got five minutes to spare for me?"

She took me in, hostility in her eyes. "Watching me in order to take over, I see."

"What? I have no desire to run this place. Why would you think that?"

That hadn't been where my mind had gone with her at all. Nor did I truly suspect her of murder, even though I'd added her to the list. I did think she cared about Arran more than she said, and that, at least, we had in common.

Alisha clutched her drink. "Because... I don't know. You're here, aren't you?"

"Which means I want your role? No, you do a better job than I ever could. I love it here but I don't want to take over. I actually plan to get a degree in nursing."

Sunny handed over my drink, and I accepted it with thanks. When I came back to Alisha, her hostility had only grown.

"Well, aren't you just a virtuous girly," she snarked.

Biting my tongue, I tried again, still unsettled from my earlier scare. "Why do I get the impression that concern for me running the warehouse isn't the reason you don't like me? What is it? You might as well spit it out."

With a heavy breath, she stood from the bar stool.

"Follow me. There's no need for this to be a public debate."

In the dressing room behind the bar, she took a seat at an unlit station. I eased into the next chair, ignoring that annoying sting of pain from my ass. My guard, who'd stood sentinel across the room while we'd talked, stayed outside.

Alisha pursed her lips, not making eye contact. "You want honesty?"

I swallowed. "Sure."

"It's nothing personal. My concerns are for Arran. You won't like the reason." At my head tilt for her to continue, she took a short inhale. "His father is the worst person to have ever breathed air in this world. I mean evil to the core. You have no idea how bad his reign of terror was, and his son lived right in the centre of that."

I frowned, trying to follow. "Arran hates his father. He does everything he can to avoid being like him. He actively works to fix the damage the man caused."

Alisha finally met my gaze, some depth of despair in her eyes. "Then you came along. A pretty blonde girl who's just his dad's type. After years of him finding out who he is and establishing this place, protecting us all, one arrow into his sexuality and the tide starts to turn."

"I don't understand. How is our relationship a threat to anyone else?"

A staff member strolled into the room, her posture changing from perky to exhausted the moment she was out of sight of any customers. She spied us and grabbed a bag, disappearing into a shower room.

Alisha dropped her voice. "Why would you understand? You know shit about him. Listen to me, and I'll tell you what the implications of this relationship are. I was given to Arran when he was a skinny boy of about twelve and I was an experienced fifteen-year-old. That's sixteen years of knowledge and of watching out for him. He surprised me right from the start by rejecting my advances, and I was devastated because I assumed I'd be punished for not doing my job."

"He told me this from his point of view. I can't imagine what your life was like."

"Don't try, a person like you can't even comprehend it. Arran told me to leave his rooms, but I burst into tears, and he stopped dead like he'd never seen real emotion in his life. After that, we talked, and between us, we agreed that we'd lie to his dad and to the rest of the women. He swore to me he would never share his father's obsession or treat women like that man did. I believed him. I trusted him. Don't you see? He wasn't ready for what his dad wanted, which was to follow in his footsteps."

I listened, trying to work out her meaning. Slowly, a horrible picture materialised in my mind. "You think from dating me, he's ready now?"

She held herself so taut she could fracture. "You tell me."

Outrage filled me. I was ready to yell that from someone who was meant to care about him, to be fiercely loyal after their shared traumatic experiences, she was betraying him in the worst way.

Except another thought sprang up in its place.

Alisha was scared. So afraid that her glass shook in her hand. Her life was this place, she'd told me so on the tour. Arran managed everything, so any difference in him was terrifying to her. She took no part in a leadership role because that would affect what worked, what kept her alive. My coming along upset a carefully balanced apple cart, and the impact for her would be life-changing.

For all that I thought I was fitting in here, I'd missed this major issue.

I calmed myself and placed my words carefully. "I will never know how bad things were for you or for Arran, but I know in my heart he'll never be like his father. He and I are in a relationship. He didn't buy me, and I'm here because I want to be. We're unconventional, sure, but we're real."

Alisha leaned in, clinging to every word. "He hunted you down. He's controlling you."

"Yet at one word from me, he'd drop to his knees. I don't fear him."

Slowly, she sat back, deep concern still etched on her brow, but something else there, too. A shifting of opinion, maybe. A reduction of her terror. "He looks so much like his father, but maybe inside he's got more of his mother."

"Did you know her? What was she like?"

"She's the only person who knew about our deal. Audrey was kind and sexy as hell, but scared, all the time. Did Arran show you her video? The one she made exposing his dad?"

I stared, my brain making the connection. Arran said his mother had provided evidence on his father. My breathing caught. "That's still available?"

"It's been online for a decade. A series of women made them, but she was the only soul who lost her life because of it. Hand me your phone."

I did, and Alisha searched until she found a video. Then she pressed play and handed it back.

She left me alone to watch.

An ordinary, pretty woman in her mid-thirties appeared on my screen, a medical mask the only attempt at concealing her identity. She spoke clearly and started her story of being sold into prostitution by a family member. I curled in the chair, hearing Arran in her tones. Seeing him in her hand gestures. Audrey spent most of her life as a sex worker but never had the protection of a place like Arran had established.

The more I watched, the more tears fell. The staff member left the shower and silently handed me a tissue. I swiped at my cheeks and thanked her but couldn't take my eyes off the story.

"Women should have the right to choose if they want to sell their bodies. I don't want that taken away from me," Audrey said, wrapping up her tell-all. *"What I hate is seeing girls pushed into it in the way I was. Or women having kids taken away from them when instead they should be given support. My son was raised by his father—the man who bought my time and who considered my baby as his property."*

Her expressive eyes crinkled at the edges.

"I had no hope. No one to turn to. I never got to take care of my little boy, was never permitted to tell him I was his mum for fear that I'd never see him again, and that cut me up. If anything should change, women need to have a voice. That's why I made this video today. I never had one, and at last, I got the words out."

When it finished, I started it over again. How must Audrey have felt each time she saw Arran on visits to service his dad at Kendrick Manor? She'd cared about him. Missed him. No wonder she tried to do anything to spend time with him, in her own traumatised way.

It was such a contrast to my upbringing where Mum would tell us she loved us multiple times a day. We were showered in hugs and affection.

Audrey and Arran had nothing but pain dividing them.

Arran would've seen this video for sure. His mother's tell-all led to her death, and he would've watched it knowing that this vibrant woman was doomed to die. It made me want to find him and hug him. It made me want to forgive him anything.

"Genevieve?" Alisha appeared at the door.

I dried my eyes. "Alisha."

"Actually, it's Rachel." She gestured to herself.

Oh, her real name. I gave a watery smile, happy to know it.

She beckoned. "I wasn't planning on doing this, but he asked and now I see the point."

"Who asked?"

"Roscoe." At my blank stare, she grumbled. "There was me thinking you were paying attention. Arran's man?"

Stumbling to my feet, I followed her, faking recognition. Roscoe was Shade's real name, then, because Convict was Connor, I'd already discovered, and the only other man who Arran kept close was Manny, who I'd spotted in the security room. Weird thing was, I'd assumed Shade had gone with Arran on their outing, but more, my mind was stuck on Audrey. On her bravery in making a video that called out the chief of police for abusing her for so long.

The lift descended. It was only when Alisha and I were exiting it that I realised it was working again. And where we were.

The basement.

I hadn't been down here since the night I'd wandered into the game, though it had featured in one or two of my dreams. Alisha guided me along the corridor and unlocked a door. Then we were out into the wide-open concrete expanse, most of the lights off with shadows deep, and the air several degrees colder than upstairs.

I crept through, hugging myself and suddenly chilled. "Why is he down here?"

"Arran didn't tell you, then. Figures." Tapping the key on her palm, she paused. "I'd like to think I was wrong about you, but I learned a long time ago to trust my instincts."

"What do your instincts say about me?"

"That you need what's about to happen."

Something was wrong. I backed up a step, twisting to eye the way back to the lift. There was no way I was staying down here. Especially in my shaky-as-fuck state when my senses were working overtime and screaming danger. It was only the fact I'd made a mistake in panicking earlier without need that held me in my place.

Leaving it too late to help myself.

Alisha opened the door once more, stepped through, and locked it again. Alone in the space, I spun around.

A tapping came from the metal gantry above.

I raised my gaze, and a man appeared. Bloodied and bruised, he was barely recognisable, black eyes swollen almost shut and a limp in his slow walk. Not Shade, though. I was certain of that.

"Genevieve," the beaten man said in greeting.

Handcuffs clinked, loose on one arm, and obviously partially unlocked by someone. They swung over the tattoo of a snake.

With slamming, awful realisation, I knew who he was.

I'd been locked in the basement with Convict.

42

Arran

*E*mpty, rain-slick roads directed us into an industrial district on the outskirts of Newcastle, our hunting ground tonight. This city had a problem with cocaine dealers targeting the student population, so tracking down drug supplier, Jordan Peters, had been easy. Lots of people to bribe and more who happily gave up information for free. At least Convict had handled that right. I couldn't think about his betrayal and how he had probably been working more for the Four Milers' benefit than mine.

My sole focus was on getting this guy.

Though I'd driven with due care and attention, my mind was fixed on providing this vengeance for Gen. Shade tried to chat, but all I could manage was the mantra that we couldn't fuck up this job.

Not a problem I anticipated.

This would be an easy capture, then we'd drive Peters back to the boathouse, tell him his crime, and dispose of him. Maybe Gen would like to be the one to do it. I'd at least offer.

On the other side of the nondescript but fast car, in his Shade held the small leather pouch where he kept his drugs and needles. He'd come prepared, also with trusty knives hidden about his person. We both had plain black bandannas ready to go.

A car cruised by, the driver not noticing us parked alongside a line of utility vehicles. After a beat, I switched on the engine then drove in pursuit, keeping the headlights off and only taking a corner after I was sure the other car had turned. The driver cruised into a yard. I halted way down the road and watched two men step from the shadows. Then the man himself, Peters, with his arrogantly identifiable bird tattoo by his eye, exited the vehicle and rounded to open the boot with a short greeting to the men.

A drugs drop, but one that wasn't going to go his way. Our plan was to let this play out, then interrupt at the end. The other men would disappear at the first hint of a shakedown, and we had a practised routine in disabling a getaway car then taking down its owner.

I breathed steadily, my muscles tight and adrenaline in my veins. I needed to get out there. I'd filled Shade in on how this arrogant fuck had terrorised Genevieve's mother to the point the woman crashed her car and died. He had a track record of causing harm. The streets would be better with him gone.

Movement at the far side of the darkened warehouse caught my eye. Shade tracked it, too. A figure crept along the line of the building, not all that stealthily.

"Who the fuck is that?" my enforcer asked.

I didn't answer, scowling into the night. A third party, particularly an unknown one, was a problem.

"Call it," Shade said.

"No." Going back empty-handed, and not being able to give Gen something else emotionally loaded in place of what she'd asked, was out of the question.

Shade exhaled. "I don't like it. He's about to launch at them, and we've no clue who he is or why he's sneaking in. It shouldn't be us copping the surprise. It puts us in a position of weakness."

He was right.

Then the clouds shifted, and the black shadow lifted to give me a fast view of the man. My mouth dried. I leaned forward, but the night reclaimed him.

That face...

I'd never seen him in real life, but I was ninety-five percent certain I was looking at an aged Adam Walker.

Gen's father.

Shock struck me. Why was he here? I knew from the background check that he was familiar with the area, but... The answer came to me. Peters had killed Adam Walker's ex-wife. If he cared about her, like the bedside photo suggested, or even just for the sake of his kids, it gave him a good reason to want the man dead.

If I could take him, the mission had gone from revenge to giving Genevieve back a family member she missed. The stakes had radically changed.

"Let's go—" Shade started.

I was already popping my door and climbing out, silent in the night and ready to stalk a stalker.

A muffled swear from behind told me Shade was hot on my heels, but I kept my gaze forward, crossing the dark path and heading down the warehouse's border of dense trees and hedgerow.

Gen's father neared the men who were examining whatever Peters had in the boot. Occupied at the car, they hadn't noticed yet.

Everything that happened next seemed to move in slow motion.

My pulse, thudding. I was so close. Close enough to see the glint of metal as Gen's dad raised his hand. A gun? What the fuck?

A siren wailed, and blue lights swirled, coming in fast.

The weapon fired, the flash and bang a bright explosion in the night.

But as I lurched forward to intercept, something caught me. Confused, I twisted back to Shade. The needle in his hand jabbed into my neck.

My closest friend muttered a quiet, "Sorry, bro," and down I slid to darkness.

43

Genevieve

In a desperate scrabble, I ran to the door Alisha had left by, yanking at the handle. It wouldn't budge. I bit back a scream.

Convict descended the metal steps, his handcuffs rattling. "Stop. Don't be scared. I know I look like shit but I'm not going to hurt you."

"Stay away from me."

"I swear on my life, just hear me out. Alisha gave me five minutes to say my piece, then she'll be back."

"I don't believe you."

He reached the bottom. I gave up on the door and backed away, keeping space between us. The man had a wicked limp, yet still he moved.

Convict stopped and held up his hands. "I need to apologise. Arran told me to stay the fuck away from you—"

"Then why didn't you?" I breathed. My hands shook with my fear.

"Because I hate the thought of what happened. Please,

Genevieve. He told me that, and in the same breath, said how much I'd scared you. I'm so fucking sorry. I shouldn't have been in here during the game, but all the women who signed up for it were supposed to want the hunt and the chase. I thought you were playing."

"I wasn't. I told you to stop."

The broken crew member hung his head. "I know. I've replayed that over and over. I got caught up in the fever of it all and thought I was a player. I should never have been in the game. My life is over because I fucked that up."

I wasn't about to feel sorry for him, but some of my panic lifted. "I need Alisha back right now. How do I get her to unlock the door?"

Convict sniffed. "When the five minutes is up. There's something else I need to tell you. I found your dad."

My jaw dropped. "You...? Arran didn't say."

Hurt welled up in a fast wave.

"He doesn't know. He wouldn't listen to me. Alisha didn't believe me either."

"Tell me everything."

Convict halted to lean heavily on a metal support pillar. "I tracked him down to the Four Milers. He had a girlfriend there, Sydney. She used to work here. Then, alone, he went to see the Zombies. They're the gun runners, so my guess was he picked up a weapon. I confirmed it later when I saw it with my own eyes."

I rotated the explanation in my mind, frantically trying to work out what on earth my father was doing. "Why would he want a gun? He wasn't doing gang work, surely."

"Think he might have been. He had a target in a different city. I followed him all the way there and watched him stake out this man." He curled his bloodied lip and gave me a sympathetic half-smile. "I'm so sorry, darlin', but he was a dead man walking the minute he took that job. Fronting up against a big-time supplier? Badass, but a suicide mission."

I spun around and walked away a couple of steps.

None of this made sense.

Not the lack of contact, or the affiliation with people Dad despised. Something must have happened to make him do this. "Did you actually see him take on this other man?"

Meaning was he dead. Meaning was my father's body in a morgue somewhere.

Convict shrugged, and guilt took over his expression. "No. I watched him practice loading his gun. Poor guy's hands shook. Then I did something stupid. While there, I met up with some old boys I'd served time with who asked me to deliver something to the Four Milers. I was coming back to see Arran anyway so took the money and did the drop. It was harmless. Nothing to do with women or our territory. You and Arran happened to be on the same road on the same night. That's why I'm in here. Like this."

I closed my eyes for a moment. I couldn't pity Convict the decisions he'd made, but I deeply pitied my dad. The description of his shaking hands was so familiar. Dad's problem with alcohol meant he often trembled, and my heart was sick at the thought of him in whatever desperate state he'd got into. If only he'd spoken to me or Riordan.

Reality crashed in. He wouldn't have survived the dangerous job he'd taken. Dad didn't know how to operate a gun, and he'd make easy pickings for some psycho drug dealer.

He was dead.

All this time of him being missing, I hadn't lost hope. I'd believed this just another drunken escapade, and my soft-hearted father would reappear, recuperate for a few weeks, then get back into life as normal. But it wasn't to be.

The clink of handcuffs pulled my focus back to Convict. Belatedly, I realised I'd got his name wrong. He was Roscoe. Shade was Connor. What a night for getting a full understanding of Arran's crew.

"Sorry for both things," Convict finished. "Arran will see that your dad is avenged. He'll clean up Peters and right the wrong."

I squinted at him, several things becoming clear at the same time. Arran had gone after *Peters*. Peters was no longer the small-time dealer who'd scared my mum into crashing her car, but a major supplier who Convict feared.

I spluttered the words. "Jordan Peters is who my dad went after?"

Convict nodded, but my heart had sunk all the way to the cold stone floor of the basement. I'd lost my father, but maybe I'd lose Arran, too.

44

Arran

The low drone of an engine pierced my consciousness, the fast-moving vehicle I was in bumping on a road. Darkness surrounded me, a thick blindfold over my face. I raised my hands—goddamn it—cuffed to my seat belt.

Furious, I wrenched in my seat with a growl of rage, but it was like I was in a hole, the drug I'd been injected with clouding my senses and muffling sound.

"Fucking hell, hold still," Shade's voice came from nearby.

Another needle stabbed me, the small prick of pain enraging me further, though I was defenceless to avoid what I couldn't see. I waited for the horrible ebb of unconsciousness, but it didn't come.

Instead, my brain fog cleared. My breathing evened out.

"I'm going to remove your bandanna now."

A hand touched my face, the material pulled away. Instantly, I took in my ex-best friend at the wheel of the car we'd arrived in.

He scowled at me. "Don't fucking panic, and stop looking at me like that. Everything is fine."

Fury darkened my vision. "You fucking stabbed me, Connor."

Shade rolled his eyes then returned his focus to the road. Around us, dark countryside sped by. "A necessary evil. And don't forget ye gave me permission to do exactly that if ye were about to do something stupid."

I recoiled. "Permission?"

"Don't ye remember?" He put on an English accent. "If I ever do something stupid for a woman, stab me."

I stared at him in absolute outrage, unable to connect the dots of what had just gone down. I had said that, back when I'd taken Gen to the Great House for our week's hideaway. "I didn't mean it literally."

"Bit late to tell me that."

I lifted the handcuffs. "Am I a prisoner?"

"Don't be ridiculous. That was just to stop ye from lashing out and making me crash. Here."

He tossed a set of keys to my lap. I grabbed them up and undid the cuffs.

Confusion filled me. If it was anyone else in the driver's seat, I'd strangle them with my bare hands, but Shade was the last person I'd ever thought would betray me. Nothing made sense. "I'll give you thirty seconds to explain what the hell you did and why."

Shade sighed. "What do ye remember?"

His drug was messing with my head, but the scene returned. The dark car park after a downpour. Our target ahead. Another man creeping in from the shadows.

"Gen's father," I spat.

"Good. It's useful for me to know that particular drug doesnae fuck up memory too much. Okay, we were poised to take down Peters, but then Genevieve's father appeared out of nowhere, and instead of stopping and waiting, ye were moving on him."

"Because she's been looking for him for weeks."

The streetlights flashed over him. "I'm well aware. Ye weren't listening to me. Ye were about to blow our cover, then her old man raised the gun and fired. Remember what happened next?"

Blue flashing lights. "Cops?"

"A patrol passed by, right at the wrong second. Instead of beating a retreat, ye lurched forward, right as shite went down. In a heartbeat, I saw exactly how it was going to unfold. Peters dropped, the two men he was supplying jumping into their car, the cop calling in for hasty backup, us trapped. I had no choice but to take control and save ye from yourself. I took ye down, knocked ye out, and hid your arse in the tree line. I did everything necessary to keep ye safe, using that permission you'd given me. I knew you'd be pissed off, but it's better that than arrested outside the safety of Deadwater or dead."

I scrubbed my face, dirt on my hands from that fucking hedgerow. "How the hell did we get away?"

"Because I'm damn good at my job. As the two in the car rammed the cops, disabling both their vehicles, I scooped up the old man and spirited him away. Then I returned for your heavy arse and got ye to safety, too. We stole away along the next warehouse's rear exit right as a fuckton of cops swarmed."

My mouth opened. "Her dad...?"

Shade ticked his head towards the rear of the car. "In

the back."

I spun around. There, in the back seat, was Adam Walker, Genevieve's father. Out cold but breathing.

When I came back to Shade, he wasn't smiling.

"Revoke the right, and I'll never do it again, but don't blame me for saving ye in the best way I could in a split second of thought. You're my best friend, and you've put your neck on the line for me on more occasions than I can count. I love ye, man. So shut the fuck up about it and think about how you're going to make your girl happy when we're home."

He stopped talking. I did, too.

A snore from the rear seats pierced the silence, and Shade's lips twitched like he wanted to laugh, but concern was constraining him. Perhaps that he'd overstepped so far he couldn't come back. But Shade was my boy. For him, I'd take a bullet, and in his way, this was him taking mine.

Begrudgingly, I gave him what he needed. "Permission revoked, asshole. And thanks."

At last, my friend smiled.

45

Genevieve

*A*lisha wrung her hands, her mascara obviously waterproof because her cheeks were wet but streak-free. She'd released me from the warehouse's basement, escorting Convict back up to the captain's office where he was supposed to be a prisoner. Until she'd let him go the minute Arran's back was turned.

Convict had been the one to tell her of my scare at his hands. I'd been too shaken up to speak.

In Arran's office, she paced in front of me.

"I didn't know he was in the game," she repeated. "He only said he needed to apologise and tell you about your dad. I knew he'd never hurt you."

"I thought you were handing me to him," I replied quietly.

"Shit. And you were terrified. I thought I was doing something right." She rubbed her arms, shaking all the more.

Already once this evening, I'd forgiven her on account of her fear. Looked like I needed to do it again.

"It's all right. At least it's ended well," I said.

Alisha darted her gaze to me. "Arran might not think the same."

"I'm not keeping it a secret so don't ask."

She managed a subdued nod. "That's fair."

For a moment, I sat with my worries, the pile teetering high. Yet at least Arran's safety wasn't one of them. I'd messaged him, getting a reply that said he'd return in minutes and for me to wait downstairs. Thank God for that.

"I don't know what he'll do with Convict, but I'll explain everything that happened," I said. "In both your cases, I'll make sure he understands the intent was good. I'd like us to be friends."

I didn't know what the future could be for me and Arran, but I knew I couldn't lose him.

Alisha watched me. A small smile broached her perfect lips. "I'd like that, too. You know, while you were in the basement, I had a long think about Arran and I realised how wrong I was. I've lived in fear most of my life, but he has, too. Except we're scared of different things. When I thought it through, it all makes sense to how he's been behaving."

"What are you talking about?"

"Arran's greatest fear is losing a woman he loves. He never had a mother, but he fiercely loved Audrey from the second he knew until the second her heartbeat gave out. I thought his ability to fall in love was broken, now I see I was wrong."

I jerked my gaze away, suddenly hot. She thought he loved me. If only I knew that for sure.

Sounds in the hall reached us, then Arran appeared in

the office doorway, Shade behind him and a man carried between them. Their prisoner's head was down and his limbs dragging, but a snore said that he was asleep and not dead.

It took me a horribly long moment to register what I was looking at.

Then I leapt to my feet and clasped my hands to my mouth. "Dad?"

Arran deposited my heavy father on a chair and gifted me a smile. "Alive and well."

I whirled around and hugged the man I loved, fresh tears welling. Arran banded his arms around me and held me close.

"You found my dad," I squeaked, shocked and my voice breaking over a sob.

"Leesh, come with me." Shade said.

Alisha clucked her tongue. "Fine, but I'm not gambling with you again. I don't want to lose my tips."

"This isnae a night for poker." His voice grew quieter.

I wondered if he was upset with her too, until her comment came.

"Cribbage?"

It was followed by his laugh.

Their footsteps disappeared down the hall. Cards. That's why he'd been undressed while she was in his apartment. They were a proper family here. I loved so much about this place.

Pulling back from Arran, I peered up at his face, checking him over for any new injury. Then I dropped my gaze to Dad. Slumped in the seat, he snored on, his hair and beard the same scruffy salt and pepper as always.

His pot belly just as round. In the time he'd been gone, it didn't appear he'd suffered much. I was glad. Even if I wanted to strangle him for the mess he'd got me into, I couldn't regret any of it.

"I want to know everything," I ordered.

He brushed his thumb over my cheek. "Anything."

And that was that. He filled me in on the night's events. I exchanged my own story, asking him to temper his anger at both Alisha and Convict for my sake. Then he carried my dad upstairs to Shade's lockable spare bedroom so he could sleep off the drug the enforcer had doped him with.

Tomorrow, my father and I would have a chat. But tonight, I just wanted my man to hold me.

In Arran's apartment, we showered, our lips meeting in a kiss with no end. In his bed, we rolled together, him fitting inside me like he was meant to be there. Then we slept, so close, and I knew without doubt I never wanted to let go.

The following day, late afternoon, Dad woke with complaints and an appetite. Arran gave me the time alone I needed with my old man.

Dad paused Arran at the door. "Wait up there a second, young un. Did I get him?"

Arran smiled. "Peters? Right between the eyes."

Dad sat back on the sofa with an exhausted but happy smile. It reduced when he came back to me. "I expect you wondered where I went."

"Both me and Riordan searched the city. We panicked."

Dad raised his grey eyebrows. "Your brother, too? I figured you'd both think I was off on a bender."

"We were far off the mark. A revenge mission, Dad?

Really?"

I heaved a sigh, and he continued.

"It was the anniversary of your ma's death, the day I left. I had this idea, see. Nothing was right since she was taken from the world, and it burned inside me." He tapped his chest. "I'm getting on now, and my hands shake. If I didn't take the time to do it, I might not have had another chance, and believe me, it needed to be done. That bastard, Peters, had to die. I owed it to your mother and to you kids. Sorry about the money, though, I needed it to buy a gun, then I ran out of cash and had to take more to follow that bastard around. I'll pay it back. There's reward money to be had for his death. I'll be able to claim it."

"Don't. Please. I'm just happy you're alive." I took his hand. Held it. Forgiveness was my word of the day, and happily I'd take him alive over any other result. "By the way, I've moved out of home now. And I have a cat."

Brushing past his legs, Rosie chirped a greeting.

Dad reached to scratch her head with a thick finger. "Seems to me a lot has changed. On the phone earlier, Riordan yelled at me for how worried you'd been, but I wasn't so concerned. Thought you'd got yourself a boyfriend when I saw him visit you at the flat."

I stared at him. "When did you see that?"

"I was popping home and saw you both from along the road. Then this car sped past down the hill and hit a lamppost. It burst into flames, and I stopped to watch. Cops and fire engines were there fast, but it made a real sight. I was trying not to bump into you. You know I can't keep secrets, I would've given up the whole plan and you'd have tried to stop me."

Vaguely, I remembered hearing about a car fire a

couple of streets away from ours, but it hadn't registered as important. Not until right now when I knew Don's car was still missing.

"What kind of car?" I said, my throat tight.

"Dark green, a man driving, far as I remember."

"Did he get out?"

Dad shrugged, his interested gaze taking in Arran's apartment.

God. Quickly, I took up my phone and texted Arran, asking him to check with his police contact. If that was Don's car, and he'd perished in that fire, that would explain why we couldn't find him.

With one mystery potentially solved, at least in part, Arran and I took Dad home. Later, I'd let him know that I owned the place, but he'd had enough surprises for now.

46

Arran

For a decade, I'd pictured the house I was looking at now, and I'd been oddly close to the mark. A sweet three-bed semi, a garden to the front and back, in a quiet suburban location. Trees and trampolines. Normal family life.

My little sister's home.

Parked across the road, a good distance away so we wouldn't be noticed, we watched the house, Gen finishing her ice coffee and me just fucking frozen. In the background, one of her soundtracks played. Something soft and sweet marking the comeuppance of my life.

"There, that's Flora. It's them," she suddenly said.

A small group of people ambled up the road. A mother with three girls, the older two in school uniform, and the youngest toddling along. I stared at the tallest of the children. *Addie*. Even at twelve, she was the image of our mother, from the shade of her hair to the way she moved.

The toddler stumbled, and Addie stooped to pick her up, holding the smallest one's hand while the second girl grasped her other and they swung her between them.

Flora, the mother, smiled at her children.

Gen took a short inhale. "She's happy."

I held my breath, waiting for the pain, but none materialised. The family entered their Edinburgh house, shoes kicked off and school bags discarded.

All these years, and she'd only been one city away. Every time I went north to see my friends, I passed within minutes of her.

"I used to daydream about providing a family for that child," I said into the minutes of silence that followed. "But she has one."

"It doesn't mean there's no place for you in her life."

Unmoving, I stared at the now-closed front door.

"The more I think about it, the more I believe that the reason Audrey kept her secret was so your father never found her," Genevieve said.

I swung my gaze to her. "You think he's Addie's dad as well?"

She interlaced her fingers into mine. "I watched your mum's video again yesterday. Think about it. She had a baby that she loved so much but couldn't keep. She didn't get pregnant again for a long time, which considering her profession, suggests she got wise with contraception. Where did the second baby come from? Had to be purposeful, right? I think she was trying to recreate the one she'd lost. But even if I'm wrong, Audrey had already suffered her worst nightmare in having a baby removed, so complete secrecy was her only safeguard."

My chest panged. "Implying it was nothing to do with me."

Something inside me unravelled. Something tight and cutting that had sliced into me for years.

"I'm sure you can get Shade to organise a secret DNA test if you need to be sure. Either way, are we doing this thing?" She touched her door handle.

"Wait." I clenched my jaw, trying to catch up with my spiralling thoughts. "What if she doesn't want anything to do with me?"

"What if she does? She has a right to know."

Had Flora told her, or was I just as big a secret as Addie had been to me? Flora had those answers, and more I wanted to know about our mother. Yet I couldn't make myself climb out of the car. "I thought I needed to make sure Audrey's child didn't suffer in the same way I had. I wanted to give her what I'd missed, but she's happy, isn't she? Addie doesn't need me. Not like I need you."

Gen reddened, her emotions close to the surface. "You missed out on love. Don't tell me that today, the final day of our month together, you're ready to understand that?"

I choked, making a noise halfway between laughter and shock. "I can't love. I never learned how."

"People learn either by example or by trying. You never heard the words until you met me. Yet all your friends love you and have been showing you that for years. In return, you provide them with care, respect, and safety. Every single person who works for you gets that. For those closest, you'd step in front of a blade for them. That's all a form of love."

Her eyes darkened. She pressed her hand to my chest, facing me.

"Then there's this breathtaking, unstoppable need between us. You want to possess me, use me, but also be there for me and support me. That dark ownership, that die-for-you desire, your crazy proposal, that's love, just broken down into its component parts. You're not calling it what it is. So when you're ready, say the words. They're already true."

"That's being in love?"

"Ever felt it for anyone else?"

"Never."

"But you feel it now?"

I tested the word in my head. Couldn't make it reach my lips. "Say it to me."

"I love you, Arran."

"Again." Since she'd started, I couldn't hear it enough.

"I'm so in love with you I want to strangle you sometimes."

I tried to laugh. It came out cracked. "I don't know if what you're saying about parts is true, but that list is just the start of what I feel about you. So whatever it is, you have my broken pieces. They'll always be yours. I hope that's enough."

"Can I take this off yet?"

She tugged at the choker around her neck. I'd taken it off her in our apartment using the tool that opened the clasp but put it right back on when she slept. And hidden the tool again.

"Fuck no. The threat to us isn't over."

"Then try out the words, because I know they're there."

"I...might...want to fuck you."

She glared daggers. "Try again."

"I...might...have a lineup of shit I'm going to put inside you later."

"Fucking hell. Again."

I stared right back at her, my heart pounding. "I might just be in love with you."

"Then one day, I'll marry you."

I kissed her. Fever rose in me.

Gen started and grabbed my wrist. "Duck down."

I curled my lip. "Happy to, but probably better to drive away from these family homes first."

She jabbed at the house. "No. Adelia is coming."

Addie and the other older girl were leaving, the two in shorts and t-shirts. Both carried a tennis racket. They walked straight past us, not paying any attention to the car.

I watched them go and considered the point that Flora was now home alone. Fuck. I could do this. I waited for them to be out of sight then popped my door. At their house, I knocked on the door, Gen scampering to keep up.

It swung open, Flora in the frame with her youngest on her hip and her smile broad. "What did ye forget?"

Agog, she stopped with her lips moving, but no further words came out.

"I'm Arran," I said. "This is my fiancée, Genevieve. I think you've met before. Can we come in? I swear I mean you no harm."

I had no idea what her knowledge of me was, or what Audrey had told her, but it felt best to lay the groundwork. Clearly, somehow, she recognised me.

Flora held still for so long I expected a door slam, but then she opened it wider and stepped aside. "You'd better come in."

In her comfortable living room with toys and kid artwork everywhere, she settled in a chair, her face pale and her toddler at her feet. We took the sofa.

"Why are ye here? I think I know but I want ye to confirm it," she said.

"You knew my mother, Audrey."

She gave a small but quick nod. "You're right, I did."

"And the girl that just left is my sister."

Flora took a shuddering inhale. "Oh God. Aye, she is. Do ye know her name?"

"Adelia. Gen told me."

"It's good to see you again," Gen said quietly.

Flora flicked her gaze to Gen. Her fingers trembled. I didn't want her to be afraid. I'd known nothing but a broken home, and I wasn't about to change hers.

I gentled my tone as best I could, though inside I fucking shook too. "I've only just found out Adelia's name. For half my life, I've been searching for her. I can see she's happy, but I want to know more and whatever you know about Audrey. Is that okay?"

Flora took a deep breath and rubbed the space between her eyes. "You're due that. Your mother would've wanted it."

She commenced a story of how she'd worked at the same brothel as Audrey and how they'd been friends. When Audrey had gotten pregnant the second time, they were sharing a flat.

"She took me under her wing when I had no one else, and after she'd given birth, she signed me up to have joint parental responsibility for your sister. It meant I could help out with taking her to the doctor and that kind of thing. Or that was my assumption. I didn't question it, I loved being an aunt, and I was only young so it felt like an honour. Then one day, she called me and said she'd done something dangerous. She made a video."

"About my father. She helped put him in jail."

Flora held my gaze. "I knew then why she'd signed me up to co-parent. After your father did what he did, Addie had no one left. She became mine."

"You adopted her?"

"I didn't need to. The paperwork your mother arranged covered everything, and it wasn't like your father was going to intervene this time around."

This time. "He's her father, too?"

"Aye. Ye really didn't know anything."

Holy shit. Another blank page filled. "Does Addie know? About any of it?"

"I told her that both her parents died. She doesn't know she has a brother. I'm sorry for that. She's a gentle soul, just like Audrey. She would've wanted to find ye, and I'd already done that on her behalf. I heard ye ran a brothel and it scared me. I left the game a long time ago. I'm married now. I don't want my girls to go anywhere near that life."

I sat back, my head spinning.

Memories swarmed me. Of the mother I'd never truly known, of the father who I'd done everything to avoid being like. Whose sins I'd tried to atone for. Would Audrey have judged me even though everything I'd done had been in her name?

Flora had, and I'd been found lacking.

Gen took my hand, her touch an anchor to my torment. "You're mistaken. Arran provides a safe place for women to work. He set up the warehouse to help everyone his father abused. People just like Audrey. He isn't what you think."

Flora watched her. "I remember you as a little girl. You were the age Addie is now. You wouldn't agree to marry someone like the man who killed your mother."

There was a challenge in her voice. Gen flushed red.

"Arran's wonderful. He's all Audrey and nothing of his father. And the man you speak of is dead."

Flora sucked in a breath. "Your father did it, then." She slid a look at me. "Regardless, you're still a brothel owner, aren't ye?"

I bristled but tamped down my ire. It was time to set aside the control freak in me. I could be more than a single-minded person commanded by the forces of my past. I'd learned along the way to be a little more reasonable.

"I've never encouraged a woman to sell herself but I will always protect those who choose to do it. Most of them were forced at some point, and I have never judged them, only offered them the respect and safety they're due. I am a child of that life, and I'm not ashamed of what I am, at least not my mother's part. It's up to you when Adelia finds out about her past, but I would like to meet her. One day. When you're ready."

Flora gazed at me for a long moment. "Then yes. Give me some time to work up to telling her."

Gen thanked her for me, grabbing a pen and paper from the coffee table to write out our phone numbers.

Flora gave hers in return. "There's more I can tell ye about your mother. Like your fiancée here, she loved ye. She'd come home from working at your da's house full of stories about her son. She wanted ye to know who she was, and once tried to take ye aside to spill the secret, but your da..."

"Threatened her?" I kept my tone light for the sake of her child.

"No. He threatened you. That was the point she decided enough was enough and he had to be brought down. Then the video happened, and ye know the rest."

Her life for mine. Audrey had given her life for mine. When I'd believed her messed up enough to overstep any line just to be close to me, it was an act to get me alone before her life ended. If only she'd taken the risk earlier. Then again, I understood why she couldn't.

Flora checked a clock on the wall. "I'll try to remember the things she told me. I think you'd like to know. But the girls' tennis lesson is only thirty minutes at the park down the road."

Gen took the hint. "We'll go now so Addie doesn't see us."

I stood with her, needing the guidance. At the door, Flora apologised again for not telling Addie about me, this time, with more feeling. Maybe I'd convinced her I wasn't like my father.

I drove us back to Deadwater with my numbness turning to something else.

"Are you okay?" Gen asked when we were outside the warehouse. "Your sister is going to love you when she meets you. And that stuff about Audrey, it was sad but also good, wasn't it?"

"I think so. I'm just..." I made shotgun fingers at my head and pretended to shoot.

"Everything looks different now," she guessed.

I kissed her. My fiancée—because she hadn't protested it—melted onto me. Need streaked through my body, and

I reached over to unclip her seat belt.

"Inside," I muttered.

Upstairs, locked away, I undressed her, kissing her until we were both breathless. She tumbled onto the sheets on the big bed and I went with her, parting her knees then lowering myself into the gap.

I sucked and licked her until she moaned my name. Then I went back for more, committing myself to a lifetime of this. Her. I was in fucking love, and somehow happy about it.

The game that I'd devised, along with Shade, where couples came together in violence and found deep, unbreakable love had caught me too. I'd watched it play out over and over, and imagined being in it, though never with the intention of competing. Then Gen came along and I was so fucking glad she had. She'd changed me for the better. I was never letting her go.

After orgasm three, felt on my tongue and branded on my mind, I eased up her body and entered her. I was so hard I could hammer nails with my dick.

Gen took a short breath. "What, no random household items first?"

"Are you asking?"

She blushed an even deeper red. "I mean, maybe later?"

"Which did you like?" I took a guess, remembering how wet she'd been. "The wax."

"That, and maybe the cucumber."

"Hot and cold. Like your man."

"No, you're all warmth and softness. It was hidden under ice, but you melted for me. Now come inside me before I go insane."

I laughed and ran my hand under her ass to lift her to meet my thrusts. Fucking heaven. Then my finger glanced over a tiny bump, and I remembered something else I needed to say.

"By the way, I shot a tracker into you, right here."

Outrage filled her expression. "You did what? I thought I'd been bitten. You wait until I get you back for that."

I cracked up then fucked her like a piston, turning her complaints into moans.

"I won't apologise for protecting you."

"Because you love me."

"Because I love you, little maniac."

She came again, throbbing around my dick and pulling me into a drugging kiss.

Gone for her, I might've been, but now she was mine, I was keeping her, no matter what it took.

47

Shade

Exiting the boathouse, I wiped the blood from my blade on my shirt. At my car, I stripped, disinfected my knife, and went through the motions of cleaning myself up and disposing of my bloodied clothes in a fire I'd stoked for the purpose.

Tonight, I'd been busy.

Kenney the cop had supplied details of three perverts who needed to be taken off the streets. Two were now dead. The third I'd pick up later in the week.

Yet even with the ability to take out my moods on the men's bodies, disposing of them in happy little slices, I was still unsettled. Uncomfortable in my skin. Summer had turned to autumn, and changing seasons affected me. A whole lot affected me.

I threw myself into the driving seat and stared into the dark. I should've felt calm or maybe even fulfilled, not infected with energy.

A message appeared on my phone.

> **Arran:** Come back to the
> warehouse. Need to talk to you.

I passed a hand over my face. The last thing I wanted
was to go home.

> **Shade:** Going to need to give me
> more than that.

> **Arran:** Natasha Reid's post-
> mortem has an interesting
> inclusion.

Huh. That report had been a long time coming, either
because the coroner had dragged their heels over making
it public, or the detective just hadn't given it to us.

Putting the car in gear, I set out.

As usual, the front side of the warehouse was busy with
clubgoers. Also as usual, I slipped in a private entrance,
staying in the shadows. Arran wasn't in his office, so I
jogged upstairs, finally locating him in his apartment.

He let me in, his phone at his ear and one foot out to
stop Gen's cat from escaping. I picked up the animal and
stroked its head, a loud purring commencing.

I was all about the pussy...of the other variety.

That was probably what I needed tonight. To fuck.

Arran continued his phone call but pointed at the
kitchen counter, and I found the report and sat on a stool
to read it.

"So they'll DNA test his charred remains," Arran said
down the line. "Why wouldn't that work? Right, so he and

Moniqua are cousins but not blood relations. Then that's a dead end."

He caught my eye. I got the implication. He was talking about Don who the police now believed had died in the car fire. With the vehicle not registered, and the driver having no form of identification, they'd sat on it as an unsolved case. Not uncommon in a busy city with a seedy underside, but it didn't feel right to me.

We knew from Riordan that his ex-girlfriend was devastated over Don's demise, though she was probably the only person who gave a shit. She hadn't heard from him, and had believed the car to be his, as Genevieve had done. So far, so cut and dried. If he had murdered Cherry, then somehow crashed and died, that still left Natasha's murder unsolved.

Arran wrapped up his call and joined me. He turned the page of the post-mortem results and underlined a section with his finger.

The toxicology readings.

I blinked, the recognition unexpected. In my line of work, I'd tried a number of different drugs, utilising a few favourites, depending on what I needed.

Natasha had been drugged before she was killed, knocked out by a toxin I'd recently started using. My mind raced over the connection.

Arran tapped the page. "That familiar?"

"Aye, it is."

"Who else knows the drugs you use?"

I shook my head, searching for a connection but coming up blank. "Only the guy who supplies it, the pharmaceutical rep."

"Who else does he sell to?"

I made a lips zipped motion. "I pay for his silence, and he gives nothing in reverse."

"The Four Milers peddle more than just party drugs. If he's dealing to them, that's a link."

He continued on, but my mind had taken a sharp turn. Natasha had been knocked out with the specific drug that I used. In analysing both of the murders, we looked for signs of Arran being targeted, or perhaps Genevieve.

What if we'd been wrong?

I'd followed Arran to the Crescent to make sure he was safe when visiting his woman. There, Cherry had died after I'd stood watching her as much as anything else around me. Then we'd had the police raid, with Arran arrested, and me, the second-in-command, left at the helm. Natasha had been dumped on the doorstep with my drug in her veins.

My heart seized up then restarted, and I pushed away from the counter, the kitchen stool falling.

"What?" Arran demanded.

I backed to the door. "What if we entirely mistook who the killer was targeting? Or what if they changed target? Or had more than one?"

He stared. Then his eyes narrowed. "You?"

"If one or both deaths are in any way a message to me, then she's in danger."

He didn't ask who, didn't need to.

There was only one person outside this warehouse who I gave a damn about. One person I'd sworn to stay well away from but who I never stopped thinking about. Would never stop protecting.

Even if that meant me standing over her fucking bed in

the middle of the night while she slept.

As I ran for the lift, I loaded the tracking app which detailed Everly's movements. I hadn't lied when I said I tried not to check it, but trying and succeeding were two different things. She kept daytime hours, unlike me, and right now should be in her bed in that fancy-arse house.

But the tracker was blinking.

My stepsister was on the move, and I had the worst feeling that it wasn't of her own free will.

Epilogue

Everly

Something had woken me. A noise, or a sensation on my body, I wasn't sure which, but it had drawn me from sleep and out of my room. Noiselessly, on bare feet and wrapping a silk dressing gown over my skimpy sleep clothes, I padded to the stairs then sat at the top, eyes open for danger and my stomach a tight ball of worry.

Minutes passed. Cold air crept around my thighs.

My father's mayoral house was designed to impress, and the entranceway had high ceilings so sound echoed. But tonight, it was as silent as the grave. No one else was supposed to be here but me. Father was away for the night, and any help he employed was daytime only. Perhaps that was it—the reason behind my jumpiness. When he was here, he brought others with him, and the house would be busy.

Not empty, with sinister, hollow rooms staring back at me.

Moving on down the steps, I peeked into the receiving room. Nothing. The front door was firmly closed, too, which I checked with a quick test of the lock. Turning,

I faced the shadowy interior with trepidation. Between checking the rest of the house and hiding away in my room, I knew the more appealing option, but the house contained valuable antiques and other items of importance. If someone had broken in and my father discovered I'd done nothing, he'd...

I couldn't finish the thought.

Swallowing fear, I forced my feet to move and stole on down the hallway. All the rooms to the right were public spaces, and all those to the left were private, the kitchens, the pantry, Father's office. I prowled into the space nicknamed the council chamber for its wood-panelled walls and the oval, highly polished table in the centre with heavy chairs surrounding. More business got done here than in Deadwater Council's actual seat of power.

Thankfully, it was empty, and the French doors that led to our gardens shut. No smashed glass. No wrecked ironwork. I checked the bathroom, the sun room, then a small side room where I'd had the misfortune of catching more than one man in the middle of an exposing act with a lady.

All tranquil, nothing to give me any pause.

Yet for me to have been pulled from sleep, it had to have been *something*. Ever since childhood, I'd slept hard, usually with my door barricaded and unconsciousness a welcome release from my tense existence. Managing Father was like walking a tightrope—one wrong move and I'd cause one of his moods. Sleep was a comparative place of safety, like a form of self-defence or hibernation. Then as a teenager, when hormones kicked in and left me sleepless, I struggled for a while until my body regulated and solved the problem.

Oftentimes, it was almost like being drugged.

I'd be out cold until daylight returned, and grateful for it. If only I had that now, rather than playing security in a big and empty house.

Back in the hall, I crossed to the kitchen entrance, one hand out to push the swinging door.

Something creaked.

My heart thumped. I whipped around, trying to locate the source of the sound. In my position in the centre of the corridor, the noise could've come from multiple directions, stone floors and hardwood surfaces bouncing it to me.

Another creak, closer.

My pulse picked up, and my breathing turned jagged. I backed away until my shoulders touched the pillar of the council chamber's entrance, the door open behind me but at least that space cleared and checked.

My bravery shook. My hands did, too.

Nothing moved in the slice of the house in my vision, but I hadn't made up what I'd heard.

My phone was upstairs, foolishly left behind. We had a patrolling security team on our gated community, and I would've called them right away except the man who was working tonight creeped me out. His gaze roamed my body whenever he saw me. My father dismissed my concerns, stating how no man would put his job on the line for a girl like me, meaning either my position as his daughter or the fact that in his eyes, I was overweight. But still, he'd come here if I called the emergency number. Or the police would, but that would set hares running and Father would be notified.

Plan better, Everly.

Okay. I breathed through my nose. Get upstairs, grab

my phone, call the security creep, get dressed to meet him. I could do that.

I shifted my weight to set out. A material-covered hand slammed down on my mouth, covering it and my nose, blocking my ability to draw breath.

It muffled my shriek, too.

The intruder ran his other arm around my body and under my breasts then lifted me like I weighed nothing, carrying me into the pitch-black council chamber.

He adjusted his hold, and darkness threatened the edges of my vision, just like I'd wanted. Except for the fact I was in some stranger's possession, and my worst fears had come true.

"Connor," was my final strangled, silent word.

Right as a second man launched out of the shadows and I knew my life was over.

The End. For now.

More drama, steam, and clues to solve this murder mystery in book 2!

https://mybook.to/ConnorsClaim

Want to read how Arran pushes Genevieve's buttons in a return trip to the basement? Download a (smutty) bonus scene here https://dl.bookfunnel.com/2etou4lvk8. (*This adds you to my reader list. Unsubscribe with no hard feelings if this isn't your jam.*)

ACKNOWLEDMENTS

Dear reader,

Hello, sex and murder lovers. How are you holding in there? Arran's book was always going to be a wild ride, but phew. That got intense.

I have a question for you - who's the killer? I want your guesses. Luckily, the series is rapid releasing so you don't have long to wait to find out. Hop into my Facebook reader group and tell me who your money is on. I wonder if that will change as events unfold.

Regarding Arran, after the Dark Island Scots series concluded, I had a slew of emails come in asking, no, begging me to write his story. The broken boy. The one left behind. What happened to him in those dark years before and the rudderless ones after? His mother dead, his father behind bars, his home ashes. Our boy could've gone anywhere.

Did you imagine this would be his fate?

Did you get his obsession? Protecting the women he couldn't when he was younger. Defending their lives in the only way he could. He gave them a home, set up a world around them where they could operate in safety, and never, ever touched them.

Then Genevieve walked right into his game, the one he set up to create love matches in a way he desperately needed himself. She never saw him coming, and he definitely didn't expect her. Still...fireworks.

We still have so much more to come, too. I'm cackling to see what you make of the next in series.

Now for the thanks. First, to you, my reader, for taking the plunge with me into a new series. I love you for your constant support and cheerleading. To Liz, my PA and friend, you're the best, always! To my beta readers Elle, Sara, Shellie, and Lori, your input helped so much to bash Arran's rough corners into place. (Blame Sara for slipping a little more into darkness to one scene.)

To narrators Shane East, Allie Rose, Ella Lynch, and Theodore Zephyr, and Kathleen and Troy with their production team at Dark Star – thanks for an incredible audiobook performance. Also to Erika for proofing things my end. Hugs!

To Amanda on Instagram for the artwork - wow, it's perfect. To my editor Emmy Ellis, you rock, and proofreaders Lori and Patricia - thank you for hunting down the most tenacious typos. To graphic designer and formatter Cleo Moran, I love everything you've created for this book and thank you for putting up with my process of refine, refine, refine. To cover designer Natasha Snow, the cover is just gorgeous. Also to Najla Qamber for the discreet paperbacks. I'm in love. Thanks to Jo Adams who won my reader group competition to name a character.

To my ARC and Street team, you really are awesome. Every single one of you. Your enthusiasm and posts made my heart sing and calmed my nerves in the build up to this launch. I should never have worried about setting out on a dark little jaunt. You're always there with me.

Lastly, to N&M, who indulged my pacing and plotting as the story fell into place, I love you both to the moon and back.

Love, Jolie

ALSO BY JOLIE VINES

Marry the Scot series
1) Storm the Castle
2) Love Most, Say Least
3) Hero
4) Picture This
5) Oh Baby

Wild Scots series
1) Hard Nox
2) Perfect Storm
3) Lion Heart
4) Fallen Snow
5) Stubborn Spark

Wild Mountain Scots series
1) Obsessed
2) Hunted
3) Stolen
4) Betrayed
5) Tormented

Dark Island Scots series
1) Ruin
2) Sin
3) Scar
4) Burn

McRae Bodyguards
1) Touch Her and Die
2) Save Her from Me
3) Take Her from You
4) Protect Her from Them

Body Count
1) Arran's Obsession
2) Connor's Claim
3) Riordan's Revenge

Standalones
Cocky Kilt:
a Cocky Hero Club Novel
Race You:
An Office-Based Enemies-to-Lovers Romance
Fight For Us:
a Second-Chance Military Romantic Suspense

ABOUT THE AUTHOR

JOLIE VINES is a romance author who lives in the UK with her husband and son.

Jolie loves her heroes to be one-woman guys.

Whether they are a brooding pilot (Gordain in Hero), a wrongfully imprisoned rich boy (Sebastian in Lion Heart), or a tormented twin (Max in Betrayed), they will adore their heroine until the end of time.

Her favourite pastime is wrecking emotions, then making up for it by giving her imaginary friends deep and meaningful happily ever afters.

Have you found all of Jolie's Scots?

Visit her page on Amazon

http://amazon.com/Jolie-Vines/e/B07MKS5JSC

and join her ever active Fall Hard Facebook group.

https://www.facebook.com/groups/JoliesFallHardFans

9 781738 572335